TriQuarterly

TriQuarterly is

an international

journal of

writing, art and

cultural inquiry

published at

Northwestern

University

TriQuarterly

issue 124

Women beside a large cistern at the Illinois State Penitentiary, Joliet. (Chicago History Museum.)

The essays in this volume are grouped under the title "The Violence" both because several of these authors have contributed to the Chicago Historical Homicide Project and because a preoccupation with violence and murder, pain and suffering, is shared by law and literature. Real and imaginary tales of murder and rage are the staples of moral discourse in both realms. The law and literature each attempt to impose their own crafted formality, a structure, a limit upon that human behavior which destroys, does harm and causes suffering. The sexual aspect of violence, of killing, is obvious, compelling, undeniable, and confounding. So love and sex and rape are in the stories, as are birth and death. Literature introduces laughter and irony and celebration in the face of them, and is our survival.

The first thing any society does when it begins to organize itself and write it down is prohibit killing, except under certain circumstances allowed to those with the power to act in the name of the law. Both literature and the law are dumbfounded when faced with the possibility that the fable of Plato's Cave may be based on an incorrect premise: Some people in some circumstances don't want "The Good," even when the shadows on the wall are shown to be shadows.

The law and literature attempt to corral violence, literature by imaginatively recreating it, and then allowing us to live through it and still live, the law by rounding up and then jailing, and sometimes killing, those who defy the law and commit violent acts.

These essays address these relationships, each in its own way. Literature is the forgiving art, and the law, with its obsessive multi-numbered definitions and insulting, obfuscating language offers only punishments. Both literature and law will continue to have no answers, but to brood upon the incomprehensible harms, as do our authors.

Thanks are many: to the Northwestern University School of Law and the Faculty Research Funds; Dean David van Zandt for his continued support of my investigations; Dennis Glenn and the staff and students at the

Distributed Learning Center of the School of Communications; Marcia Lehr and Pegeen Bassett and the wonderful staff of the Northwestern University Libraries and many others at Northwestern University.

Thanks also to Susan Firestone Hahn, Ian Morris, and the staff of *TriQuarterly* and Northwestern University Press. Special thanks also to the Chicago History Museum.

Finally, I want to acknowledge Juana Haskin, Faculty Assistant at Northwestern University School of Law. Her unflagging dedication to this project means that it all gets done.

Leigh Buchanan Bienen

CONTENTS

Editor of this issue:
Leigh Buchanan Bienen

Cover collage by Mark Swindle
(Images courtesy of the Chicago History Museum.)

Leigh Buchanan Bienen

The Record Keepers

I would not be here, now, sweating in the August humidity of 2005 writing this, with an ink pen on a yellow legal pad, had I not read on an otherwise ordinary sunny Wednesday morning in August of 1998, an account in the *Chicago Tribune* describing the restoration of an extraordinary set of books, a systematic record of homicide cases kept by the Chicago police, uniformly and without interruption over a period of sixty years, from 1870-1930.

It was unusual to be in Chicago in August, and I might just as well have missed that story. The article by Charles Madigan in the *Tempo* section on August 19, 1998 immediately captured my attention. Its headline—"Crime—Chicago Style"—and the black and white pictures made clear this was a story about murder, and I had been doing research on homicide since beginning my first criminology project in Ibadan, Nigeria, more than twenty-five years earlier.

The pictures—newspaper photographs from murder cases of the 1920s—linked the set of historical police files to images of men and women who, as I read the article in the summer of 1998, were shockingly modern. These were city people. The men wore black three button suits and hats, the women demure dresses with precisely embroidered white collars. The men were pictured smoking cigars, grinning, ducking beneath their hats on the way to lockup, or staring straight and boldfaced at the camera.

Madigan's article told a story about the conservation of a set of large, leather-trimmed volumes containing case descriptions of homicides that

9

read like movie scripts, thousands of stories: "fresh from the street, summarized by some clerk with perfect handwriting and an educational background that obviously emphasized sentence structure, punctuation and complete thoughts, however dark they might have been, the books amount to unfiltered news." [Charles M. Madigan, "Crime-Chicago Style," *Chicago Tribune, Tempo*, August 19, 1998, p. 1,7.]

More than 11,000 stories, in fact. Three years later when duplicates were removed, after coding and seemingly endless data cleaning, there were individual records for 11,439 victims, including names and addresses, and more than 9,000 individual defendants, most of them named. The 11,439 homicides were typically identified by an address for the place where the crime occurred, a date, and included information about the criminal prosecution.

The Homicide Books began soon after the great Chicago fire in 1871, and the records continued without interruption through periods of civil strife, economic prosperity and depression, through the building up and tearing down in a great city as its population doubled—twice. They kept on going through waves of expansion and contraction of economic and industrial activity, through the great migration of Blacks from the American South and alongside the continuing immigration from overseas of Germans, Swedes, Poles, Russians, Jews, and Irish.

By the turn of the century this was a city of big money, retail stores, manufacturing and shipping, railroads and streetcars, home to the meat packing industry, lumber mills, and 750 newspapers and journals, including the *Chicago Tribune* and the *Inter-Ocean*, and several other daily papers each with a circulation of over 300,000. Among its other civic agencies was a suicide bureau. In 1904 more than 77,000 horses lived within the city limits, which were constantly changing throughout this period, as were the streets, as the city settled and re-leveled itself, redrew its boundaries, and redefined itself once again among its teeming neighborhoods.

There were public libraries, public schools, parents and teachers communicating in dozens of languages, thousands of churches and shops, huge mansions for the rich, and for the poor: tenements, defined by law simply as any house or building let out to more than three families. The phrase "tenement dwellers" came to stand for the privations of the working poor, often employed doing piecework in the garment trades, especially the newly arrived immigrants from Prussia, Russia, and Bohemia. National investigators from the United States Department of Labor came to the Chicago slums—their term—in the deep depression of 1893 and counted how many lived where and in what conditions, and exactly how little money they earned. Our own homegrown Chicago reformers, then later the Progressives, defined and then took on their social problems: juvenile vagrancy and delinquency, prostitution, alcoholism, the spread of diseases, especially the often fatal venereal diseases, literacy, the improvement of the status of women, children, immigrants and blacks, and the establishment of the rule of law.

During all of these times, in all of these places and among all of these people, homicides occurred, and were recorded by the police in the tall, staid, leather-trimmed record books, according to a simple, systematic index based upon the name of the victim and the date of the killing. The Homicide Books catalogued violence in an orderly and predictable manner, even if the killings were senseless, and the police and judges were unpredictable.

Homicides happened on the busy thoroughfares, in living rooms and kitchens, in expensive bedrooms in the mansions and on the factory floors, in armed confrontations with the police and the National Guard, at labor meetings by the lake and on picket lines. Homicides occurred on Sundays and Wednesdays, in December and in July, spiked dramatically after 1918, and a rotation of anonymous record keepers kept writing down the names and addresses, and the facts in the systematic order prescribed.

The handwritten records marched through sixty years, different ink when a different transcriber noted whether the weapon was a knife or a gun, changes in the style of lettering as the pedagogy of penmanship changed. The names and addresses of victims and defendants told a story of economic migrations and ethnic neighborhoods, and the recorded names of the arresting police officers gradually changed from being Irish. The first Negro police officer was appointed in 1872. Throughout all this time there was a person writing it down, doing his job, making the record, and keeping track of cases using a chronological alphabetical system, which was easy for later generations to figure out. Then the record keeping suddenly stops. In 1930. Without anyone offering a bureaucratic explanation or saying why.

Perhaps the keeping of these Homicide Books was discontinued in response to Washington asking for the keeping of crime records using a new national system. The United States government, the Federal Bureau of Investigation, the FBI Crime Reports—still an important source of records on homicides in the United States—began in, and continued from, the 1930s. But neither the present FBI homicide reports, nor the disaggregated, detailed version, the Supplemental Homicide Reports, have the immediacy of these succinct case summaries in the five volumes of The Homicide Books, 1870-1930, from one hundred years ago.

Is it the identification with a particularly vital place? The historical distance—so far, yet so near. The street names, and the names of the people, formal, yet familiar. The period was rich, and the set of records spans much that is important in the contradictory history of Chicago and the nation: the World Columbian Exposition in 1893 and the severe economic depression that followed; race riots in 1919 and the continuing pressure of race and ethnicity in the politics of the city; the Spanish Flu in 1918 and the struggle to establish public health institutions; temperance, prohibition, and epidemic alcoholism; the fight for suffrage and against sex slavery for women; the periodic attempts to clean out the Augean stables of the corrupt Chicago City Council and ward politics; and the palpable presence of the law and legal institutions on every page, sometimes in conditions of embarrassing undress.

Today, visible reminders of this period are everywhere: in the grand, massive granite structures on the lake and river; in the city's glorious parks and fountains; in the many photographs and written accounts and academic studies of how people lived and what they saw around them; in the political tracts and ambitious plans for reform; in the tumultuous history of the organized labor movement before and after Haymarket; and in the city's art and literature, still strongly and defensively identified with this place. Novels, newspapers, paintings, grand staircases and balconies, and hundreds of thousands of photographs remain.

These photographs raise more questions than they answer, images of elaborately dressed men and women engaged in provocative, undocumented activities; a young boy about ten, grinning, carrying a younger child on his back; another smoking and standing in a garbage strewn alley; a band playing in the rain next to an unidentified body of water on a forgotten holiday; a group of women in white shirtwaists and long black skirts and a man in black with a book—perhaps a Bible—walking up to the edge of an enormous cistern at Joliet Prison; another group of women in prison, all wearing identical white cotton pinafores and skull caps, holding lesson books upright in front of them. They all seem as if they are waiting for us to take account of them.

This city proudly recorded that it used up fifty-two million barrels of cement in 1907. Then there are the parades long gone, thousands of men and sometimes just women, marching down La Salle Street or Michigan Avenue, often in uniform, sometimes carrying banners and flags, in the rain, in the snow—in Chicago the weather is always part of the story—the gray stone buildings draped in red, white, and blue bunting, and horse carriages waiting at the curb. Troops being sent to the Philippines? The Armistice in 1918? Temperance? Suffrage?

So much evidence, including from the Homicide Books, of how people lived and worked, rich and poor, on the streets, in the tenements, in their elaborately furnished, dark mansions. People documented what they saw and how they wanted that changed. Injustice, unfairness, there was a passion for making things better, for making Chicago the greatest city in the world. The commentators gave themselves license to say what they thought was wrong with what they saw, and what should be done about it, in a fierce, forthright manner which seems more foreign than their high boots or ruffled collars. When they saw something they thought was wrong they had a passion to do something to make it right, or so it seems from the written records they left behind.

In the late fall 1998, I finally got to the archives of the Chicago Police Department. The gloom had set in and the heat and humidity of August was hard to remember. It had taken many entreaties over the phone to set up an appointment to look at the actual Homicide Books, in the flesh, so to speak. The police archives were then on State Street—they have since been moved again—and being taken back into the office required being announced and admitted through a series of locked gates and steel doors, with police officers on walkie-talkies approving my progression at every barrier.

The office of the archivists themselves, two no longer young police officers who were once again the caretakers of the Homicide Books, was a small, windowless room with a government issue desk and the floor completely covered with papers and folders stacked to the ceiling. The two friendly officers in charge of the archives retrieved the big heavy Homicide Books from a locked safe, and cleared off a place on a chair, placing the first volume in my hands. I asked about the photographs. No one knew anything about official police photographs, although there might have been some once. Seeing page after page of handwritten case summaries, I asked if these Homicide Books could possibly include all the homicides in Chicago during the period. I knew an affirmative answer was a sentence to years of work. And it was.

I had spent much of the previous two decades studying patterns in homicide and capital punishment, nationally and in New Jersey, since the reinstatement of the death penalty in New Jersey in 1982. As soon as I saw that the Chicago records had been kept systematically and chronologically, I knew this was an important new source of data on homicide for scholars and legal historians.

My first obligation, a self imposed one, was to make available the factual information about these thousands of homicides during a period of importance in a place of historical significance. My own research on homicide and capital punishment had begun when I was a law student in the early seventies in Ibadan, Nigeria, where the heat and unremitting humidity destroyed both paper records and the will to record. In 1998 after decades of working with criminologists and criminal lawyers on issues of homicide and capital punishment, and witnessing historic legal developments unfold, I knew this set of homicide records must not only be preserved, but made accessible to scholars and others. The records were a mirror and a window.

The first and most immediate goal of preserving the contents of the Homicide Books had already been accomplished in Springfield by the Illinois State Archives copying the Homicide Books onto microfilm, and making copies of the microfilm available for a small fee. I got the microfilm. The microfilm of the handwritten records now had to be copied again: a word for word, sentence by sentence, the transcription including periods, commas, dashes, misspellings, inaccuracies, duplications, and any and all other bits of data, exactly as originally recorded. That laborious task was the first to be accomplished; it took more than one year.

There was one single important addition with this third copying: a new sequential record number for each case, beginning with the first entry in the first Homicide Book for 1870–1911, the first entry being under the letter A. Case No. 1 wasn't the first homicide recorded, but it was the first case in the Homicide Books and the first case in what was to become our newly created data set. The addition of a new, independent record number for every case anticipated the needs of future quantitative researchers, including myself. This number, our new number for each entry became the case tracking number, or locator, for all the cases as they traveled from one information management system to another, and eventually to the outside world and to other researchers.

After the cases were turned into typed versions of the handwritten case entries, they became coded numbers and words on a spreadsheet. Then the data were aggregated and summarized and transformed into charts and graphs and tables. Each case kept the same case number through all the data transformations: in the sequential text file, in the displays of the data in the various programs used for the management of the quantitative variables; in later sorts and manipulations of the data, and finally on the interactive platform for the cases on the Web site.

Each permutation introduced its own way of looking at the homicide cases and at the history they called forth. I searched for and found outside funding, and the Northwestern Law School provided consistent, important support. After the second summer of coding, at the end of another sunny August, twenty part-time student employees—some in saris, some in shorts and sandals—sat in an air-conditioned room full of computers and entered into computers all of the data from the twelve pages of data collection for each of the more than 11,000 cases. That part took only a couple of weeks, including double entry for accuracy. Each case was translated into a series of codes for more than 300 variables, to be eventually reduced to 125 working variables. With each successive version the data and the cases became more systematic and more abstract.

Independent homicide researchers were recruited for an academic Conference on Homicide in Chicago and to write research papers for publication in Northwestern's *Journal of Criminal Law and Criminology*, itself founded at the School of Law in 1911. Everyone now wrestled with issues of conceptualization, program compatibility, and comparability across data sets. Researchers took the cases and the data and related the information to their particular interests and areas of expertise, sometimes reformatting and recopying our version, and together they provided a kaleidoscopic view of the cases and the period. The Conference was held at the Northwestern University School of Law in November of 2000, and the weather cooperated. None of the researchers from around the country was prevented from coming by snow, sleet, or inclement conditions for flying, not even those coming from Boston.

Another crisp, russet fall came around, and with the pumpkins and chrysanthemums came some basic quantitative results. Tables, graphs, and charts could now be made. Time series, percentages, cross tabulations emerged from the computer like ghosts from a closet. Regressions were not far behind. Questions which could not have been asked before quantification now hung in the air, unanswered: Why was the increase in homicides so large after 1918 and through the 1920s? Automobile accidents, organized crime and prohibition, a phenomenon of reporting, demographics?

The variables of interest to criminologists, urban historians, sociologists, and legal scholars included: age, race, gender of victim and defendant, weapon, location and address of the homicide; relationship of victim and defendant (captured, in order to preserve the richness of the data set, on five differently defined variables); outcome at trial, sentence

Gender of Defendant by Gender of Victim,
Percentages and Frequencies, All Cases, 1870-1930
(N=8864)

	Male Victim	Female Victim	Total
	%	%	%
	(N)	(N)	(N)
Male Defendant	92%	85%	90%
	6421	1570	7991
Female Defendant	8%	15%	10%
	586	287	873
Total	100%	100%	100%
	7007	1857	8864

Note: The total is 8,864 because only cases where gender of victim and gender of defendant were both know were included.

imposed; a number of important and precise dates for legal adjudications and events; as well as names, addresses, and other miscellaneous information. The data set, as we were now calling it, made newly accessible information for genealogists, and anyone with an interest in crime, such as mystery writers, novelists, and playwrights.

I was still enough of a humanist to create, within the quantitative data set, files which were simple verbatim descriptions, or shorthand entries for circumstances of the homicide, relationship of the parties, or location. These descriptions then could be retrieved, with the names, addresses and dates, alongside the quantitative codes on a spreadsheet. In the slang of quantitative researchers, the data from the 11,439 historical homicide cases could now be sliced and diced, analyzed in hundreds of ways.

The dates, names, and addresses in the records were always important; and they remained so in the new database. Dates tracked other events—trials, the decisions of grand juries and coroner's juries—and led to other sources. Addresses were keys to neighborhood and ethnicity. With the coded data files, it was possible to do entirely new kinds of sorts and searches, e.g.: to pull up all 288 cases which occurred on Halsted Street between 1870 and 1930, ranked by date.

This list is a micro-history of the city. Halsted Street was one of the great spokes leading into the city. People walked, rode, and drove into the center along Halsted Street for sixty years. As routes and neighborhoods and demographics changed, those changes are reflected in the homicides on that street. When the streetcar came in, it brought one kind of change. When the saloons moved farther away from the center, the residential pattern changed. Here is a sample of life on Halsted Street, as seen through the progression of its homicides:

September 24, 1876
> Smith, James, 28 years old, fatally injured in drunken brawl in saloon . . . [case no. 2123]

August 14, 1877
> Polz, Henry, died, home, 709 S. May St., from pistol wound in left breast received during labor riot at Halsted St. viaduct, July 26, '77 . . . [case no. 1856]

May 8, 1880
> Tobin, Minnie, 17 years old, knocked down with hammer and trampled to death, 129 N. Halsted St., by her drunken father . . . [case no. 2405]

November 19, 1880
> Mong, Ye, Chinese laundry man, shot dead in front of his laundry, 187 N. Halsted St., by Edward Powers, who was arrested and confined, claiming the shooting was in self defense, the Chinaman having followed him with a knife . . . [case no. 1416]

July 20, 1884
> Harvey, Ada, alias Daisy Clifford, prostitute, 18 yrs., shot dead in room, 48 S. Halsted St., by Clem Sudkemp, 27 yrs., who committed suicide by shooting . . . [case no. 871]

May 23, 1897
> Dawson, Mrs. Nellie, shot dead, 80 1/2 S. Halsted St., by her husband John Dawson, who escaped . . . [case no. 549]

June 22, 1903
> Dettimer, Williams, 38 years old, died in County Hospital. Shot in fight with negroes . . . [case no. 586]

June 5, 1904
> Fussey, Louis, 30 years old, shot dead, 61st and Halsted Sts., by Officer Axel Burglind, whom he assaulted. Off. Burglind discharged by Coroner's Jury June 6, 1904, but censured for being too hasty in shooting . . . [case no. 755]

November 13, 1910
> Braasch, Mrs. Pauline, 32 years, died at home, 3342 N. Halsted St., from abortion . . . [case no. 317]

October 11, 1915
> Boerema, Henry—Age 5—Struck down and killed by auto in front of 7346 So. Halsted St . . . [case no. 3017]

October 26, 1915
> Kapper, Sam,—Age 28—shot to death at Harrison and Halsted Sts., in shooting affray between union and non-union garment workers . . . [case no. 4113]

June 5, 1923
> Ritter, Rudolph—Age 30—Fatally assaulted 2/18/23 in vicinity of Van Buren and Halsted St., supposedly a disorderly house . . . [case no. 6917]

November 7, 1924
> Barbas, Angelo—Age 35—Shot to death at 2:15 A.M. just as he emerged from a restaurant at 735 So. Halsted St., by two or more unidentified men who used shot guns. Barbas, who was convicted for murder he committed about a year ago, was out on a writ . . . [case no. 5837]

June 27, 1928
> Manos, Nick, alias Mavronatis—Age 35—shot to death in front of 401 So. Halsted St. at 4:10 AM, 7/27/28 by Jerry Matura, for no apparent reason. Matura, who was heavily intoxicated, went into a nearby restaurant, boasted he had 'just got a Greek' and went to sleep . . . [case no. 10508]

August 16, 1930
> Rodriguez, Maria—Age 28—Found dead in a clothes closet on 8/16/30, in her home, 2nd fl., 17 So. Halsted St., with her throat cut. She had apparently been hidden there for the past two or three days. Murdered by an unknown Mexican, alleged to be her husband, whose arrest was recommended by the coroner . . . [case no. 10934]

Just as easily it was now possible to retrieve all abortion cases—that is, all cases in which women died after an illegal abortion—all murder/suicides, all homicides with a gun in 1900, and other categories, including miscellaneous and random categories, such as all homicides involving a victim or defendant named Reilly or Smith. This was one of the great gifts of the coded, database: it could show you the unexpected. It was like browsing in the open stacks of a great library.

Data creation followed a disciplined protocol: deciding what could and should be preserved in a quantitative file and how to define the variables. The work involved part-time independent research assistants over the summer and consultations with graduate students, data management experts, and quantitative social scientists along the way. This was not an approach that lawyers typically took to homicide cases. Certain data were critically important: names and addresses of specific victims and defendants, the dates of the homicide and subsequent legal events; descriptions of the scene or comments by the arresting officer; dates of coroner's inquests, trials, and hangings—events which might be reported in the local newspapers, if you could find those newspapers, if they still existed.

And were there newspapers during this period! Our appetite for constant news is not new, just the way we receive it. Newspapers published several editions a day, as well as "extras" or special editions to report an event of importance: the declaration of war, a strike, the death of a public figure. In addition, there was news from ticker tapes, the wireless telegraph, later the phone. In novels of the period people send love notes across town several times a day. News was everywhere—in saloons and salons. And people wanted the latest all the time. Being able to get the news was one reason people chose to live in cities. When the pony express riders went to the frontier, their saddlebags were filled with newspapers, eagerly awaited, read, and passed on, even though their content was no longer news in the cities.

More than 750 newspapers and periodicals were printed and distributed in Chicago around 1910, in tens of languages and dialects. Several of them, including the estimable *Chicago Tribune*, had a circulation exceeding 300,000. The *Chicago American*, the *Chicago Inter-Ocean*, the *Chicago Record-Herald*, the *Chicago Evening Post*, and for this project, the all important *Chicago Tribune* published without interruption during the entire period and is now available—for a fee—online with the capability of being searched for names and by date.

Now, the circulation of the *Chicago Tribune* is over 600,000, and it is eighth in the country in circulation. Readership has been sadly declining and the circulation of the *Chicago Tribune* is surpassed by the ahistorical *USA Today* (2.3 million); the grammatically correct, wan *Wall Street Journal* (2.1 million); the standard bearer and still the preeminent natural newspaper for news, the *New York Times* (1.1 million); the *Chicago Tribune's* own wholly owned *Los Angeles Times* (900,000); the *Washington Post* (707,690), which at least analyzes and reports on Washington news and gossip; and two other undistinguished dailies.

All the major newspapers today are busy trying to make money with the new technology. All now have Web sites, and deliver their news and pictures as email subscriptions, in addition to functioning as old-fashioned newspapers with a print edition. Only the *Wall Street Journal* makes money on their Web version because from the outset they have charged a fee for the Web subscription, and they offer certain proprietary financial data online. All Web news outlets report breaking news and post color photographs of disasters, the latest murder, all to the accompaniment of bouncing, brightly colored advertisements, which fish for your attention with lines and words on rhythm. The Web versions of the newspapers update their breaking news in real time, scooping their own print editions.

Not that 1890s *Chicago Tribune* wasn't filled with sensationalism and advertisements. Murders, adulteries, the peculations of politicians, and their underlings then, as now, sold papers and were the staple of the front page and breakfast table conversations, over coffee at the clubs and at home. Crime was always front page, and one good murder could be counted on to sell papers for weeks, and months, then and now. And selling papers makes advertisers happy. The advertisements are time capsules, messages intended to sell tickets to theatrical performances and baby carriages—and now, a record of what people wore, how they looked, how they imagined themselves, and what they aspired to be and own.

The online scans available for a fee from the historical *Chicago Tribune* clip a story and its continuation and present it surrounded by a blank white field, leaving the reader without the special experience of reading a newspaper page by page with several stories on each page. The layout of the page, the last minute additions, the commercial banners that sneak into the margins, the breaking news headlines—all these items have large cultural value. The lotteries, the baseball scores, the weather—always connected to how we experience time—the political gossip as refracted through the headlines and placement on the page, and the space given to stories, all these tell who thought what was important on that day, at that time and that place.

The research was becoming more about the times, and about sea changes in the way people lived, over the decades, changes brought by electricity, the arrival of the automobile on the streets, and the disappearance of the horse.

The date of the coroner's jury is usually included in the case summary, and those coroner's jurors may have given interviews to reporters. Coroner's inquests were lively proceedings. There was no requirement of secrecy surrounding testimony before the coroner's jury, unlike the grand jury. The police officers, not the state's attorneys, offered the state's case at the coroner's Jury. One reason for the keeping of the Homicide Books in the form they were kept may have been so that the police officer would have the basic facts about the murder and the scene when testifying before the coroner's jury. The coroner's historical archives might even have a transcript of the proceedings, including the verbatim testimony of witnesses. If the case had generated sufficient interest, the witnesses' testimony before the coroner's jury would be transcribed and reported in the daily newspapers. And those reported accounts were vivid, immediate. Suddenly, people dead for more than a century were speaking, and seemed very present and alive.

Two years into the research, I found myself driving a rental car through snow and sleet, and the construction of the Big Dig at the Boston airport, to visit Nicholson Baker and the American Newspaper Repository in New Hampshire, to look at copies of the actual *Chicago Tribune* for what I was now referring to as my period. The distinguished novelist Nicholson Baker and his wife had rescued the last surviving print copy of many nineteenth- and early twentieth-century newspapers and found a home for them in an abandoned millhouse in Vermont. I was traveling hundreds of miles to read the print editions of the *Chicago Tribune* from 1880 forward, which included the World Columbian Exposition, and the important day, June 26, 1896, on which Governor John Peter Altgeld pardoned the three Haymarket defendants who had not been hanged on that clear, cold November day in 1887.

The centerpiece of the front page of the *Chicago Tribune* on June 26, 1896, was a large rectangle featuring ink drawings of the heads and shoulders of the twelve jurors in the Haymarket trial of 1886—not the four anarchists who were hanged (always a visual guaranteed to sell newspapers, a hanging); not the police officers who died during the incident (the ostensible reason for the hysteria surrounding the Haymarket trial); not the flamboyant judge (who sat on the bench flirting with the well-dressed young women at his side), but the twelve men who decided the fate of the 1880s terrorists, head and shoulder portraits showing elaborate neckwear and large amounts of fashionably trimmed beards and moustaches. It took my breath away.

The governor's pardon message was only ostensibly the news on June 26, 1896—the 18,000 words which he composed himself over a period of days, excoriating the jurors and the judge, the bailiffs, the prosecutors for the standards of law at that trial. There were drawings of some of the other principals, and of the Haymarket monument to those who had been hanged, but it was the twelve male jurors who were front and center. They were still the news. The layout of the front page showed the art of studied visual composition, and conveyed a substantive message. And here it was in front of me, on a cold snowy morning, when I was days from home, reading the front page with the noise of the river behind.

Altgeld's political career was destroyed by this act of clemency. Not a single local newspaper, nor the international press, nor the leading citizens of Chicago, not even Jane Addams, supported the clemency decision. William Dean Howells was alone as a literary figure in praising Altgeld. Many commentators focused on the fact that the pardon overturned a jury verdict, not that the verdict and the trial were characterized by juror bias, outright bribery, lies on the stand, and other corruptions of the legal process. Yet the *Chicago Tribune* story wasn't about Altgeld, his political career, the injustices, or even the fact of the commutations. The story in 1896 was still about the trial, a retelling of the collective drama of the Haymarket trial in the fall of 1886. As if anyone had forgotten it. And that was the message conveyed.

When I ask myself now, four years later still, what was thrilling about seeing that 1896 front page live, so to speak, I have no simple answer. Partly it was the hunt: for copies of the papers from the period, spurred on by the startling discovery that the originals of nineteenth- and early twentieth-century newspapers have been systematically destroyed by libraries and archives, those in charge of preserving our heritage. Partly there was something appropriate about the fact that the only uninterrupted run of the print copy of the *Chicago Tribune* was in a warehouse in an abandoned mill town in New England, and getting to it required a plane trip and hours of driving through the snow. The online edition of the *Chicago Tribune*, not available in 2000 when I made the trip to the warehouse on the river in New Hampshire, might have revealed later that the portraits of the jurors were at the center of the front page, but that would have deprived me of the thrill of finding it for myself, at the end of a long emotional journey. If every fact is accessible at a keystroke, then everything retrieved has the same cost, or no cost, or no value, because it was never lost, and thus can never be found.

Then there were the items I wouldn't have known to ask for: in the original newspapers the front-page reports of the arrivals and departures of minor European royalty (Princess Diana's predecessors), with breathless descriptions of their haberdashery and jewelry, as well as their solemnly reported comments upon the weather—always the weather—and their surprise at the beauty of Chicago. Nor would I have seen the advertisements for the rattan baby carriages with the enormous hoods and wheels or the suede shoes with tassels. All these were worth the trip to the deserted mill town where the American Newspaper Repository then kept its treasures, worth the driving through snow on unfamiliar country roads, worth the maze of the Big Dig, the incompetence of MapQuest, and even the aching back.

Thanks to the British Museum, which had saved and bound a strange collection of nineteenth- and twentieth-century American and European newspapers, and the resourcefulness of Nicholson Baker and Margaret Brentano, founders of the American Newspaper Repository, and their determination to save those remaining copies, I was able to look at the same newspaper and read the same story which John Peter Altgeld himself and an outraged public read on June 26, 1896. It was a defining moment.

The 1896 print edition wasn't even very fragile. Because the newspapers had been bound and kept flat inside a heavy book—like the Homicide Books—the paper was well preserved, just a little brown around the edges, as if it had been slightly singed by the passage of a century. These were rather thin pages of an otherwise recognizable newspaper, without photographs, capable of being turned without gloves and read. "Remember," Nicholson Baker gently reminded me, "this is the sole surviving copy in the world."

The technology for reproducing photographs in newspapers was not perfected until around 1911, so that these copies of the *Chicago Tribune* from the 1880s and 1890s, and even into the early twentieth century, featured sketches and line drawings as visuals. For the duration of the World Columbian Exposition the Sunday edition of the *Chicago Tribune* included a tinted drawing, capable of being framed, of a scene from the Fair, the Liberal Arts buildings or the Japanese Island. Later, the *Chicago Tribune* published a literary supplement every Sunday with some sixty pages of original fiction, including serialized fiction, by the best and most famous writers of the day, Dreiser, Sinclair Lewis, and many, many women. An online search would have found none of this.

* * *

When I first was reading the law in New Jersey some thirty-five years ago, before going to Nigeria and turning myself into a homicide researcher, in those days, not long ago in real, historical time, courts, the official receivers and keepers of the records, would not accept any kind of copies, of briefs or complaints, or affidavits, for filing or any other purpose. In Nigeria when I did research on homicide cases before the state supreme court, the records I finally got my hands on after a great deal of searching were original handwritten case reports by judges. There were no copies. The judges' handwritten summaries of the facts and the law was all that remained of the case, and this is just how the British Assizes were recorded. Occasionally an exceptional writer, a master of narrative would appear, and there would be more than just the facts and the result.

Sitting at a small wooden desk in Ibadan on the top floor of the courthouse, in a small tidy room with a few moldering books on its shelves, watched over by a single silent clerk, there, dripping in the Nigerian humidity—no air conditioning there, then—I copied out the information I needed from these handwritten reports of state supreme court cases. They were the only records of the judgments of this court— a perfectly respectable court, where the able Nigerian lawyers and judges argued in white wigs and black robes—and they had been keeping those for only a few years. Written in the succinct formal British tradition, there was enough there to get started. Besides, I had only completed one year of law school, and I was teaching myself criminal law.

I transferred the basic information onto coded sheets, then onto rectangular punch cards, and got back the quantitative summaries on green bar paper. The conscientious American academic setting up the computer center at the Nigerian university—the computer itself took up all of the space in a house-sized, air-conditioned building—persuaded me to be the first to archive my data at the new computer center for the use of future researchers. I did, and as of a few years ago, no one else had since archived their research or made use of my data. Those files are unreadable now, and all of the computational power of that house-sized machine can be held in the palm of my hand.

When I was a law student the copying machine and the computer had not yet revolutionized the practice of law. Generations of lawyers and judges relied on real, live clerks and legal secretaries to copy the law by hand, and later to pound it out on manual typewriters with twelve carbon sheets behind the original. Typewritten copies had been accepted by courts in the United States since the turn of the century. Even a mere thirty years ago American courts, ever punctilious, would not accept erasures, corrections, or smudges. The Law archived its collective wisdom in shelf after shelf of identically bound books whose very titles—*Tenth Decennial Digest*—not to say their contents could not be challenged. Error did not exist there. Law students were trained in the art of editing and writing by being the publishers of law reviews, because this was preparation for the specialized publications and briefs for the federal courts. The miraculous Wite-Out had not yet come and gone. Strong-armed secretaries—their biceps developed from wrestling with piles of documents and hoisting tied brown case files—knew how to spell and understood the grammar of an English sentence. These women might also have been in charge of keeping track of a lawyer's court appearances, travel schedule, his wedding anniversaries, family birthdays, and other markers of the lawyer's life. They are replaced now by an army of much higher paid legal assistants, time management programs, electronic calendars, paralegals, word processors, personal desk assistants, spreadsheets, and computer filing systems.

The very term itself—word processing—tells us that what we are doing when we highlight phrases and paragraphs and move them around the document on the screen is not writing. Writing is sitting down with a pen, or a brush, and paper, or something like it, to record in a sequential way our thinking, the conversation inside our heads. So we compose sentences, and do what writers have thought of as writing, in Europe at least since the Middle Ages, and in China and Egypt and elsewhere for thousands of years.

There is writing that is indentations on clay tablets, and writing that is stylized figures on the side of a sarcophagus. All communicate between the absent writer and the present reader. Part of the message is: this is how we lived, what we thought and felt, at this time and this place. This is what we looked like, what we ate and drank, where we put our heads at night, this is how we reproduced, loved, and buried our dead. And now we will be telling future generations about ourselves on the Internet, using the word processing programs, although still saving and printing perhaps for a few decades more. What goes out on the brand new Internet is also the record of the past for the future.

Before the paperless world actually arrives, as historians and writers, as humanists in the broadest sense, we need to ask how our records will be kept, and retrieved. Going to the courthouse or the police files or the coroner's archives, or to the newspapers and looking for the records of our lives and deaths, the tracks of our contemporaries and our children, is not going to be an option one hundred years from now. Is our society going to leave behind nothing but the rubbish of forgotten code and unusable machines, and have no readable record of this present, unique, time and space bound experience of the human condition?

If the prior system of record keeping was faulty and haphazard, at least something was preserved. And courts, especially courts, and other legal bodies, considered it their duty to organize and keep, to write down, and to count and copy, for the record, trivial or important, what happened to people before the law once a case was a case and was stamped with an official number and seal of judgment. In civil matters it was reports of feuds among the living over money and property; in criminal cases it was about murder and mayhem, and physical harm. Courts may have thought they were filing these cases away for their orderly selves, but they were keeping them for us.

After the basic information on the 11,439 cases of homicide from 1870–1930 had been transformed into quantitative data and tracking codes, and the qualitative information—names, addresses, dates of significant legal markers in the case, circumstances and relationships among the parties—were included and made available in summary form, after the academic conference in 2000, after the publication of the first set of research papers in the *Journal of Criminal Law and Criminology*, then the question became: How to make all this data and the 11,439 case summaries available to other researchers and potential researchers, to educators and the public, for genealogists, for high school and college students and their teachers, murder mystery fans, for anyone, in short, and for free? Another bronze and russet fall had turned into a silver, cold winter. I was wearing sweaters and thick socks as I sat surrounded by out of print books and pamphlets from the 1890s.

By this time I had fallen in love with the history of Chicago and had come to see the homicides as 11,000 historical tableaus. Each case report froze, as if on a windowpane, a sequence of fragmentary interactions, or scenes between victims and defendants, bystanders and the police. Then defendants and the families of victims came before the law's minions—bailiffs, court officials, jailors. Each case was a series of vignettes, very thin slices of the law in one of its many reincarnations.

There were so many actors—judges, jurors, victims, their bereaved loved ones, police, prosecutors and defense attorneys—hangmen. These tableaus of time-stopped lethal interactions were set out on the changing map of Chicago streets and to the tempo of the ongoing pulse of everything else that was happening in the city—explosive economic development, the Progressives' passionate attempts to clean up the city and the poor, the rise and fall of Yerkes' street car empire, the parade of mayors and aldermen and police chiefs, the risible excesses of wealth.

Sometimes a celebrated case captured the collective imagination of a generation, or a century, and those legal interactions came to stand for everything else from that time and place: Haymarket, Leopold and Loeb, McSwiggin. Then the records and commentary bloomed into thousands of pages and pictures. Everyone had an opinion, and the principals basked in the footlights. Just as intriguing were the dramas involving people whose names were never known and thus could never be forgotten. The accounts of their deaths were the only records of their lives one hundred years later, or so it seemed. I took it upon myself to fill in as many details and connections as possible, to make it easy for others to find their subjects, using the police records as a way to find photographs, obituaries.

By 2003, five years into the project, another winter had turned to another muddy spring, and another sleepy summer. A new class of students in bright pants and dull sweatshirts, all with laptops, was on campus. It was now self-evident that the Web was where all these cases, in their old and new frames, needed to be placed, or stored, or repositioned. From the beginning the goal had been to make the 11,000 cases accessible. Now that was made specific as a goal: to put all the cases up on the Web in their original—now transcribed—format, the sequentially numbered case summaries, and simultaneously to link the text transcription of cases to the 125 coded variables of criminological and historical interest. Initially I simply planned to park the coded data set at a university research data archive, for the use of social scientists, professional criminologists, and legal scholars. The development of the Web created the potential for far wider distribution. I was fortunate for having proceeded slowly.

The technical people first said it couldn't be done, that the sequentially numbered cases in their original narrative form could not be linked to the quantitative data so that the two could be viewed together. A Northwestern undergraduate solved what turned out to be not a trivial conundrum, demonstrating again that those for whom computers are a first language, a primal vocabulary, are most likely to find the solutions to the puzzles.

Fall turned into another glassy January, and after months of work by others, all the cases and the coded variables were there and ready to go up on the Web. The 11,439 cases had been liberated from my computer, from the designer's computers, from the microfilm, from the printed page, from the twelve pages of paper for the coding for each case, and from their original incarnations, as handwriting in the tall heavy Homicide Books in the vault in the Chicago Police Archives. I was still clinging to my Xeroxed copies of the microfilm, and to my printouts of the data, for security. But something significant had happened. The cases had entered the new world.

We were now in the dark, short days of the final development stage for the site, equivalent to the tenth or twelfth or twentieth draft for a writer. We knew where we were going, the shape was there, but the form and surface could both be altered. Things could be added and taken out, just as they could before going to print. Whole configurations could be reorganized and moved around. A core of people were involved in the creative process. The designer found archives of photographs, and they added new dimensions. The technical people had their areas of expertise. I had mine.

Everything was sitting on a single server, and could be brought up and displayed on a large screen in an instant. The Web seemed to be an infinitely expandable space, a notebook without any spirals or covers. Why ever stop adding or revising? All the paper remnants of the world of 1870–1930 could go up there. Thanks to the strength of its design, the Web site now could incorporate photographs and drawings, as well as whole books, newspaper articles, reproductions of historic documents, legal filings, in addition to all versions of the 11,439 cases. Now the challenge was: how would all this historical information be structured and managed?

The original organizing scheme of the police Homicide Books was based upon the chronology of the murders, each entry alphabetized by name of victim and ordered by date of the homicide. When cases entered the legal system, the legal procedures and categories were the organizing system. What order governed the Web?

A homicide is designated by the police as a suspected murder, the people involved are now characterized as defendants and victims: more transformations into legal categories. Other legal events continue the procedural progression: the coroner's jury refers to the state's attorney; the state's attorney, the prosecutor, takes the case to the grand jury, which either does or does not produce an indictment. Later the case may go to trial and judgment with a verdict handed down. One legal event follows another in an orderly sequence, ending with a hanging. The existence of a formal case after the homicide leads to the possibility that other records exist elsewhere in another archive.

The legal categories had been coded and carried over into the quantitative database, but once the cases were coded, the legal categories no longer controlled the organization of the information, as they had in the court records. For example, prior to the quantification, if a researcher wanted to find every homicide that resulted in the death penalty in the Homicide Books in the period 1880–1890, the only way to do that was to go through every case as they appeared and make a note, or copy out, each capital case. A researcher would have to do exactly what I did when I was sweating over the records of criminal trials in Nigeria in the early 1970s. Every researcher had to invent and impose a new order, tailored to an individual goal. Now, the interactive database allowed anyone to look for any category or identifier: women, police, children, Russians, guns, or suicides.

A variable had been created for whether a case was a capital case and whether a death sentence had been imposed. It was now possible to pull out by code all of the capital cases, or all of the death sentences, in the database. The first round of coding and quantification had greatly facilitated legal analysis, but it was laborious and required familiarity with spreadsheets and programs for quantitative analysis. The new interactive database brought the ease of information retrieval to a new level. To access the details of a crime, it was no longer necessary to be trained in quantitative analysis. A variable could identify all capital cases, or all gun cases, or all female defendants, and the interactive design allowed all cases in that category to be pulled up instantly, and to be listed chronologically.

The initial entry into the database, what was put into the police records, was controlled by the police for their own institutional purposes. The records of subsequent legal events were controlled by a host of anonymous actors: county clerks, prosecutors, coroner's juries, grand juries, judges, lawyers, petit jurors. A researcher going to the Cook County Clerk's office would look for cases by indictment number or day of judgment, then by name of the defendant. The coroner's archives would keep their records by date of death and name of the victim. The police records were ordered by chronology of the homicide and the alphabetical ordering of names of victims. The interactive database was not hemmed in by any of these imposed orders. What then was to be the new logic for the data on the Web, and how was it to be apprehended? New text needed to be written, introducing the cases and background materials to a new audience. The Web site was not just for lawyers and homicide researchers who came knowing what they were looking for.

What was to inform, to illuminate all of this information? The character of the explanatory writing changed. As a writer I no longer had control over how what I wrote would be read. There was no check or editorial guidance, or verification, as to what text would be put on the Web site to accompany the cases and the large new quantities of other material. Little paragraphs, or a few sentences, were dropped into slots on the Web site. There was no opportunity to build a narrative or develop an argument. Thumbnail descriptions were tied to cases, to documents, and to publications on the site. Bits of text were linked to cases, to photographs, to commentary. I created new large amorphous topic areas, such as "civil unrest" and "the rule of law" and plopped large chunks of variegated text under those headings. I didn't know in what sequence or how the material would be viewed.

Others worried about the capabilities of servers and programs, and of navigation systems. Ski season came and went, and I slogged across the snowy parking lot on days when it seemed the sun was only shining elsewhere, to work in the windowless den of the computer design team—professional staff, faculty, graduate students, undergraduates. We complained about the weather and snacked on high carbohydrate hibernation foods. Programs with names like Sequel or Flash were the subject of heated arguments. It reminded me of when I was on the board of a Chinese language school many years ago, and listened to incomprehensible, passionate debates about the relative merits of various Mandarin character transcription systems. The titles were intriguing, but I didn't understand any of the discussion. Periodically someone would jump on a nearby computer as if it were a horse standing at the hitching post, and they would be off typing at a gallop. I took to just asking as simply as possible if I could do what I thought I wanted to do. The technical wizards showed me I could do things I never would have thought to ask for. This was truly a new world, and to first encounter it in this setting—a windowless room filled with computers, screens and cameras—was somehow appropriate. No one worked with pen or paper. To reach the small, utilitarian table and chairs in the center of the room, it was first necessary to climb over cables and tripods and heavy metal suitcases of equipment. The real work places, ergonomic wonders of comfort and lightness, faced the computer screens.

The English language, and its structure, our Roman system of dates to cut into time, the street names to identify place, names of individuals, our categories for legal events, and the new case tracking numbers were important for labeling and sorting, but they were only identifying tags in this world. They were the nametags on the luggage. They had no meaning for the people designing the system that was going to stitch all of this information together. How would this material be ordered now that it had escaped its physical boundaries in the Homicide Books? The old physical books were confined, limited, and inaccessible, but at least you knew what was in there and where they were.

For the system to have any coherence, the names and dates of the cases had to remain prominent in the new organizing system. They were our alphabet and calendar rolled into one. We had to retain some of the traditional ordering of information, while breaking apart the old legal categories. No matter what the new technical issues were, or what else was up there, these were still cases of law, and our audience was people interested in these homicide cases, not just other computers. The Web site had to be able to communicate not only with other servers and Web sites, but real, live people were going to be looking at the screen at the other end, just as there had been real live people writing in the Homicide Books a hundred years ago. Some of the structure imposed by the legal system had to be retained. That was the first imprimatur of order. Treating each case as a distinct unit would be another fundamental organizing principle. That was how the police treated the cases, how the courts treated the cases, how people generally thought of them, and that was not going to be changed. We would retain that logic, and that dictated much of the structure of the Web design. The procedural spine of the legal system survived the transportation to outer space, at least for this project.

Meanwhile, what was this writing? It wasn't an essay, or a scholarly discussion in which you could count on the reader knowing the difference between manslaughter and murder. It wasn't a forum in which someone was going to correct your mistakes, or point out that your argument was unsupported. You could make any sort of foolish statement and not be contradicted. Yet, it wasn't fiction, and certainly not poetry. It was just prose, the great residual category for bad and good writing.

I privately decided I wasn't going to knowingly make any false or untrue statements, and that I would only make assertions I would be comfortable defending if an intelligent, educated interlocutor were looking at the computer screen over my shoulder. I was going to hold my own writing to a professional standard of precision and factual accuracy. If I expressed an opinion, it was identified as such. Everyone counseled that the pieces had to be short. Pieces? They were paragraphs or sentences that popped up at a click, like those cartoon advertisements on the newspaper Web sites. Still, I would try to make my sentences educational, without being too serious. And I kept my dedication to grammatically correct sentences, and my diction was what I came to think of as quasi-academic. I aimed for a fact specific, consistently neutral, and informative tone, like that of a well written, reliable background piece in a respected newspaper or magazine. I called up a critical and intelligent editor to read over my shoulder.

As I began to write the text, or *content*, as it was called, for an imagined new reader online, I was writing into the blizzard of my ignorance as to who was out there and what their interests or level of education might be. We promised ourselves in the future to survey the visitors to the site. In the meantime I knew nothing about who was going to be reading this, or if anyone would. And someone else was deciding where these nuggets of text would go.

Notice that now everything is a group effort. At the early stages of the project I was sitting with a pen and yellow pad and writing in my usual manner, and what I was writing was sentences and paragraphs for an article, for a book, either fiction or nonfiction. Now I switched to composing on the computer. I would write the sentences, define a topic, explicate it a bit, and then give the development group the text, and they would place it in some drawer or cupboard on the Web site. The content under the large subject matter categories—the *Rule of Law*, *Capital Punishment*—took the form of short introductory essays aimed at the literate college undergraduate, or the perceptive gentle reader, the imagined, welcoming intelligence believed in by all writers.

The writing was very different from writing an essay for a journal or a newspaper, a publication with an established style, where the publication dictates the form and style, and the writer has some sense of who the readers are. The formalities and the subject boundaries here were uncertain, or nonexistent. There were no student law journal editors to ask whether every statement needed a footnote, no grammarians to question the placement of a semicolon. The sequence of the text would be controlled by the reader, now called the visitor. The term properly implied a transitory, flimsy relationship between writer and reader.

Giving up control of the sequence in which a writing is to be read means giving up control of mood, narrative voice, identification with character or author, the building of an imaginary world, forming and anticipating a sequence of responses through rhythm and repetition of metaphor and image, giving up the art of composition. Can writing for the Web ever be a literary art, or even a craft, absent these constraints,

I ask myself, typing madly. The freedom and mobility of text on the Web site are exhilarating. And all those trees to be saved! But, still . . .

When the Web design was finally revealed, I was mesmerized by its spectacular, full-color beauty. It was so much more than text. Sequences of evocative photographs and images, text and image linked to dates and a time line, imposed coherence to the huge variety of material. The cases, those same 11,439 cases, are still the spine of the Web site, anchoring the subject and its trajectories. Without the cases the site is a rich but random collection of historical texts and images. The written text, the commentary, the words, the word created images, the sentences I write provide context, but are not by themselves the most expressive part of the site. The beauty of the design is what takes your breath away, along with the realization that there is such a long historical record there. The words, the text, the photographs are descriptive accompaniment to the archive of 11,439 cases, the still beating heart of the project.

The Web site included the entire symposium issue of the *Journal of Criminal Law and Criminology* devoted to the first academic research on the homicide cases, all three-hundred-plus pages of academic discourse, graphs, tables, charts, was "up there," as I was thinking of it. Also on the site were contemporaneous works such as the 1500 pages of the *1929 Illinois Crime Survey*, a monumental work of criminology and urban history, difficult to obtain in print and essentially unavailable to those without access to a first rate university library. Once I discovered how easy it was to put up whole books, those rich contemporaneous studies of the social and legal system, as well as original documents, such as transcripts of the confessions of Leopold and Loeb, there seemed to be no walls to the expansion of this virtual library of contemporaneous materials and commentary. The cases had led me through libraries and archives to other Web sites, and to photographs and documents whose expressive richness raised more questions and whetted my appetite.

Almost everything from this period was in the public domain and currently not easily accessible to the general public in print. I was intoxicated with the prospect of resuscitating worthy and forgotten works, such as the *1929 Illinois Crime Survey* and the *Report of the 1919 Commission on Race Relations*, another tome, filled with interesting commentary and narrative, with page after page of statistics. The commentary in *If Christ Came to Chicago* by William Stead, called the most famous journalist of his day, is as brilliant and insightful today as when it was published. And there were special reports and civic documents by committees and commissions, spurred on by the passionate and literate Progressives who loved to count and categorize. Everyone wrote, it seemed, and wrote so well. And they loved to describe people and circumstances, and collect statistics. Portraits of homelessness, vagrancy, prostitution, drunkenness, juvenile delinquency—the poor, the rich, their income and no taxes—it was all there documented, and forgotten.

As the winter dwindled down, I sat bundled in my magnificent, draughty work place, next to the leaky leaded windows—another reminder of the early twentieth century—deciding what should be added, put in or out, what could or should be scanned, and how to characterize these forgotten publications and tracts. Who could now be believed? Where was the check on accuracy for these passionate outcries for reform, for justice, for the rule of law? Why had so little of it all come about when so many, including the rich and the powerful, wanted it?

Every day as I walked into the Northwestern University School of Law building I encountered the large, sober, reverential portrait of Levy Mayer, the man who was the principal opponent of the Progressives' wages and hours legislation in the courts and in the state legislature at the time of Florence Kelley and John Peter Altgeld. He was not forgotten, the building bore his name, but his adversaries were. Did that mean he won the ideological battle? Most of the commission reports were self explanatory; but some—the Reports on Sin and Vice and the many Evils—required linkage to the present, an introduction. They were what we would now call self published, and in a city where 750 journals and magazines flourished, they came and went and somehow people figured out what they wanted to read and who was reliable.

The first person accounts and life stories needed no explanation. I had a new appreciation for the knowledge and skill of librarians, indefatigable friends of the project whom I talked to almost every day. Together we looked forward to the day when all this text would be off our shelves, off my floor and out of their offices, delivered to the Web to be read by others. We were co-conspirators in the plot to make available books and documents about this period of Chicago history, and we were helped by the fact that most of our material was government documents or written prior to 1924. But I still couldn't get away from thinking of the Web as a physical place, capable of being destroyed or brought down.

We now called ourselves the Chicago Historical Homicide Project, and cheerfully linked to other Web sites, archives, and special collections. Events and people from the period—crusading judges, women from Hull House, flamboyant defense attorneys who may have had little or no connection to the homicide cases, child prostitutes, women sewing in tenement houses, homeless and disabled veterans, truant boys and girls about to be shipped out of the unhealthy city to work as indentured servants on farms—walked onto the virtual stage, our Web platform. The city committees issued weighty reports; the newspapers published their own investigations. So many ideas about so many issues that are still issues today—crime, education, social disintegration, violence, poverty, abysmal working conditions. Only the nationalities—for Bohemia read Guatemala, for Russia, read Mexico—had changed. The commentators were literate and optimistic, interested in getting people to do something about the social wrongs visible all around them.

As we put up more and more historical material, the words of the dead and the photographs were creating the narrative tone of the Web site. The voices from the period were as expressive as the pictures. The reports on special topics were self-contained, published as books or pamphlets, and meant to be read autonomously. And each had its own individuality. These texts, whether it was an account of life in a brothel, or detailed drawings describing how to make a bomb, added context and richness, but didn't create a structure for the whole. And if my new text wasn't leading the reader to turn the page, to click from one topic to another, to go from one idea to another, then what was providing the organizational framework? Images, certainly. The contemporaneous voices. The timeline, still. Although their prim order in the Homicide Books had been broken apart as the controlling narrative sequence, the 11,439 individual homicides were still the backbone, the continuing track through the six decades. The sequence of murders, the quintessential criminal act, was providing the structure, the form.

If a visitor was interested in women, or guns, or gang murders, strikes, or the killing of children, or the death penalty, the cases with those characteristics could be easily retrieved. A gray and rainy spring came around, and I stared at photographs of large women dressed in black standing under black umbrellas, some horse-drawn carriages waiting beside them, a march to demand the closing of the Levee, Chicago's notorious district of gambling and prostitution. I knew in those low sky, glowering Chicago days when it seemed as if the gray would be there forever, that the Web site would never be finished; and prostitution, lawlessness, and gambling, still solidly dug in, would never be eliminated.

Topics such as *Labor Unrest* and *Legal Corruption* incorporated huge, wet bundles of text about events and people, and were hung out like sheets and shirts and on the temporal clothesline. The pictures of the women were haunting. There they were, standing next to a stove, surrounded by wheezing children, sleeping on the piles of unfinished sewing on the bed, when the sky was black with soot, and there was no indoor plumbing. The entire text of *Hull House Maps and Papers* had to be up there, especially the ethnicity and wage maps. The slightly blurred image of the 1894 text describing the "sweating system," and the astonishing colored maps of the weekly income and ethnic identity of the households in the worst slum in Chicago, had to be accessible, to everyone—teachers, students, the inquisitive housebound, anyone who cared. The subject remained relevant, as art the maps easily survived one hundred years—beautiful, precise, factual, timeless in their scope and challenge.

The home page provided the initial organizational framework. It had text, pictures, and directions for navigation to other parts of the site—a book jacket and a table of contents merged into one—but more flexible and interactive, and of course governed by a click, not the turn of the page. I was now conducting live, filmed interviews with researchers on the project, recording how the researchers today thought about the historical cases, and how their present work had been influenced by research on the historical cases.

Then, why not interview some judges in their eighties who grew up in the twenties and were trained by lawyers who actually knew the Cook County court system of the 1920s? Spring came. We shed our winter layers of wet wool and down, and all of us vowed to be more diligent about going to exercise at the gym right next door. It rained and rained, making the black pavements shining and slippery. I thought of the women with their black umbrellas standing at the end of the temperance parade. The technicalities of publishing photographs in newspapers was just developing, and the umbrellas, the puddles, and the carriages were a blurred, inky black—atmospheric, if imprecise.

The days were getting longer, and the optimistic students who worked on the site biked to work in sandals and cardigans, arriving shivering in our cave walled with computer screens. They were thinking about their coming graduation and hoping they would be in more clement climates in graduate school next year. The young, in time differently and focused on the future—tomorrow, next year, next week, hoping for better weather then, helping to transport the past into the present.

Launch day for the Web site was set for June 7, 2004, and it dawned bright and fair. The now several dozen faculty, students, and others involved in the project eagerly awaited the countdown. There was a university press release. This was like a publication date, but different. The *Chicago Sun Times* ran a half page story on the Web site and the availability of information on 11,000 cases of homicide in Chicago from 1870–1930, with some pictures. We waited.

The site received 77,000 hits in the first three days, seriously threatening to shut down the Northwestern University development server at the School of Communication where it was housed. We were ecstatic and in a state of shock. The technical people scurried to keep the server running. After that initial rush, traffic settled down to about 30,000 visitors per month, and leveled off there. A year later it is at the level of approximately unique 16,000 visitors per month. Dozens of people are still downloading all 11,439 cases, in coded and in text format, with the count now at close to a thousand for people who have downloaded all the cases. We still don't know who they are, or who the 77,000 were who cruised by on opening day.

What does this mean for me, the writer, the person who started out to tell a story and to release 11,000 case narratives from their imprisonment in microfilm so they could become data and fly away to other researchers and writers? Nothing I had ever written—except possibly an Op-Ed in the *New York Times*—had ever reached 77,000 people. But was this publishing? Who knew whether or not these 77,000 visitors, perhaps from another planet, and certainly from another era, actually read a word. Certainly only a very tiny percentage visited most of the Web site or read most of the content.

Still, the fact that a thousand people would download the entire data set of 11,439 cases implies that the goal of making the data set easily available to a large number of people for free accomplished. The interactive format of the Web site made the data set assessable to far more people than would have been willing to read all of the handwritten cases on a microfilm reader. People may not have cared to read what I and my colleagues said about them or the period, but they wanted the cases. The cases, coded and in their original text form, continue to be downloaded in their entirety every day. I now look at them from a different, disaggregated perspective, not as 11,000 individual dramas, but as thousands and thousands of data points which have now been shared with hundreds of thousands of others, like bits of dust thrown up into the sky.

Thanks to the ease of operation of the interactive design, anyone with a minimal familiarity with a computer and standard programs, anyone who can click, can bring up all gun cases, or all homicides involving husbands and wives, abortion, all homicides in a saloon, or which occurred on December 25th or July 4th. It is not necessary to be familiar with quantitative data processing techniques in order to do such a customized search. Anyone who has ever purchased something over the Internet with a credit card can now review all 11,000 cases of homicide as recorded by the police from 1870–1930. This opportunity for the instantaneous reordering of cases is something that would never have been imagined by a police scribe in 1880 carefully writing the names, dates, and circumstances of the arrest and conviction in homicide cases. And the way the information will be used in the future cannot now be anticipated by those of us reading this page.

So, why the hesitancy, why not just plunge into the sparkling and amorphous world of the Web? Why not just replace all the paper, documents and books with on line access to text? After all, the telephone, the telegraph, the printing press, all other technologies which were to have revolutionary impact, were first resisted, then adopted piecemeal, then finally became part of the landscape. Educational institutions are beginning to think about developing archives and libraries of Web sites. It may take a while, but we are headed towards a world where information is not stored or found in physical books. No more big stone libraries filled with bound books and writing, no more reliance upon physical text. Once text is up there, it is up there forever, indestructible, permanent, interactive, there for everyone to edit or copy. Every day thousands of new sites go up on the Web, and every day thousands come down without leaving a trace that they had ever been there. Not even a pile of ashes.

The practice of law has already been revolutionized by this transformation in text management. Law firms have been quicker to adopt the new technology than academic institutions. Most courts now function on the assumption that everyone involved in a case will have access to all relevant papers simultaneously and online. Depositions are taken live with long distance video hook ups. Evidence, motions, affidavits, judgments, precedential case law, statutes, briefs—what was once handed around as printed paper to be copied—is now accessed through the Web and sent electronically, all participants downloading it in their own places at the same time. If the new technology is good enough for the law, why not for literature, why not for the rest of our writings?

What is the downside, in the slang of the day? For courts there are huge problems with verifying factual accuracy. Anything and everything goes up on the Web, and who knows its provenance. Documents can be altered without leaving a trace of intervention. But courts and adversarial attorneys have always and will continue to wrestle with issues of forgery and authenticity. Lawyers, librarians, and the rest of us will find new ways of verifying text. After all, figuring out who is telling the truth, exposing confidence men and imposters, has been the business of courts of law since their inception. Whether it is detecting a phoney signature, sniffing out a scam, finding a faked filing, decoding unauthorized textual changes in a security filing, the enterprise—finding out who is lying, and who is truthful—is the same. The old-fashioned trappings of the law, the swearing on the Bible, the sealing of documents with stamps, colored wax or gold, the dressing up in robes and wigs, the tying of ribbons around official documents were always meant to distance, to intimidate, and they can still serve that purpose. The paper trail leading to trials can be replaced by electronic documents, while the live drama of a trial is preserved.

My aesthetic hesitations come in part from a sense that presentation on the computer flattens and makes undistinguishable all writing, all text, all ideas, all information. Everything looks the same when it comes off the Web and onto the computer screen. The computer and the Web are great equalizers, and that is to be applauded. Opportunities for education and self-instruction are now available in remote mountain villages and in the poorest city, if there is Web access. Schools need not have walls or classrooms, nor museums or libraries. Great texts, and our humble police records, no longer need to be locked away within their physical prison, accessible only to those with the keys to the vault. Who could not be in favor of that? Books, maps, records, works of art, music, financial information, history, previously only available to a tiny, literate wealthy elite in a few places where there were libraries, can now be made available to everyone. The Web is the largest document known to any civilization, already holding more information than all of the books in the Library of Congress.

Perhaps the Internet will do what television has failed to do: create and make affordable high-quality mass education on a worldwide scale. So much of traditional, legal, book-bound education was directed to keeping the undesirables out, and that part of the game has changed. Still, the new world of the Web is technically challenging, and elites will always find ways to erect gates to shut. The Web should not just be for the global distribution of advertising and pornography, racial hatred and calls to violence. Literacy at the very least, and then beyond that, education. On the Web you have to be able to read, even if computer literacy is not the same as the old-fashioned reading of books. The economic, technical, political, and legal barriers to achieving the goal of providing education on the Web are a serious challenge to the West, the richest society in recorded history, and literacy alone is not enough.

Mine is not a hesitation, then, about the astonishing possibilities for education on the Web, but rather a wistfulness, a longing for some parts of the old: the special feeling of holding an original hundred year old document in your hand, the conspiratorial crackle of old paper, the soft feel of newspaper from 1896. The computer has leveled the playing field in the great global game, but now all texts are presented as equals. The poem, the novel, pornography, advertisements, cartoons, fake reality, sensationalized news, the hysterical and unthoughtful, the accounts of mass murders and rapes—all get the same treatment, the same representation in high contrast. The way we used to live didn't allow the whole world to come in every minute, all day and all night.

I am grateful that 77,000 people cruising the Internet stopped off at our site at launch date, even though they threatened to crash the host server. How many stayed long enough to notice that the 1929 *Illinois Crime Survey* among its 1500 pages included an unsurpassed essay on "Homicide in Chicago," as well as John Landesco's meticulously researched and elegantly written chapters on the history of organized crime in Chicago? There is more truth about violence to be found in those pages than in a thousand reality based cop shows.

The floury feel of old documents, their spicy smell, the rustle they make in their boxes, as if they are waiting for you, their surprising silken sheen, the sense of awe that comes from reading handwriting from a hundred years ago—these can be preserved. The occasional ink blot in the Homicide Books, when the pen is put down, the less than perfect rectilinear formation of the letters as the record keeper, perhaps an unpracticed new recruit, more comfortable holding a gun than a pen, looked up, hearing a clatter as something dropped on the concrete floor of the Harrison Street police station. Perhaps in answer to a shout for help, the pen is put down for a moment, leaving a blot to protest the interruption on the page of the Homicide Book. The telling comments—"unknown female white baby found dead in hallway by tennents [sic]"; "motive was jealousy"—showing that a live, sentient person apprehended the information as it was being recorded. These comments are worth a hundred data points. The contemporaneous diction, the expressive phrase are lost when the information in the sentences is recoded into analytic variables.

The computer will have to find its own expressive language, a new grammar, a new diction, perhaps one that melts together words and pictures in a new way, something as revolutionary as the moving picture or animation. Control over the manner and timing of the apprehension and comprehension of images will be part of this new art on the Web. It was so when the Buddhist monks took their paintings and sculpture into the caves of Dunhuang in the ninth century, and it remains so today.

I am wondering, who will be the record keepers of our lives, and deaths, for the next generation? If the law contains so much of our history, our politics, our documents, our pictures of ourselves, how are we going to archive the information from today's cases? So much goes through the daily feed of print and photographs, that nothing is saved, or archived. It all becomes technologically inaccessible very quickly. Courts, hospitals, police, universities do not maintain records to be accessible fifty years from now, or even five years from now. Because of the law we know Martin Guerre's wife, Mary Queen of Scots, and Mrs. Palsgraf. In the future, who will come to know us?

Cook County Criminal Court Building and Jail.
(Chicago History Museum.)

The papers say there have only been a few times since 1871 when the temperature has risen above one hundred in the summer in Chicago, and today it is well over 104. I am remembering the heat wave of a decade ago when hundreds died in stifling rooms because they were poor or disabled or abandoned. The Progressives would have made sure it wouldn't happen again. I am thinking of how many Augusts I have spent here. Today there is no one outside walking on the sidewalk, a few hardy souls stand knee deep, silent in the lake, still cool in August. Air conditioning is no longer considered an innovation, but a necessity.

Keeping a record of how we live, of who we are, is a fundamental human obligation, requiring a pause, then dreaming, followed by the writing of words and sentences, the consideration of images. It requires thinking about what is important. Sometimes this record keeping, the sorting out, doesn't go quickly, and sometimes written words shouldn't be skimmed, but read slowly. This is why I am back with my pen and yellow pad, once again dripping in sweat in another Chicago August, intoxicated by the scope of the Web, but writing an old fashioned essay which will appear in print with other old-fashioned essays, to be read slowly.

Contemplation is required in the face of contradiction, human cruelty and injustice; before the joy and sweetness of love; the ironies of history. The recognition of the chance intersection of circumstances, individuals, and opportunity, at a particular time and place, demands a pause, an intake of breath. The conundrums of Haymarket, the tissue of fabrications wrapped around the murder of McSwiggen. Reading history, we know how events came out—everyone is dead at the end—but the echoes and ramifications, the "what-ifs," remain mysterious. We know how laughably wrong prognosticators were in the past, people such as the secretary of transportation whose policies were based upon the firm conviction that commercial air travel had no future. Ordinary people would never get in a plane, or tolerate having airports near to the cities where they lived. How to decide who to believe today?

Many said that photography would make painting obsolete, and that the motion picture would destroy the theater, but certain utilitarian functions of theatre and painting, telling the facts of history, preserving the actual look of the present, were only shifted. Painting and theater are flourishing, perhaps because they have shed their limited utilitarian traditions. Art on the Internet is being born. It will be interactive, use words but perhaps not have words as its central form of communication. The artists will find a way not to be restricted to the small scale of the common computer screen. Because it will be people finding new ways to communicate with people on the other end, even though there is much technology in between, there will be art.

Is there a new logic for getting from the beginning to the end of a story? We recognize what a story is, although we may not be able to precisely define it. When the record keepers wrote down these cases they weren't a collection of stories. The log was a list of independent, autonomous acts of violence. Hints of a story appear in the collection of cases when circumstances are described, or actual speech is quoted. One of the great attractions of murders is that they are stories where we know one part of the ending, the end of the victim's life. Our curiosity is simultaneously piqued and satisfied. The story can then travel in either direction, forward with the story of the defendant before and after the murder, or backwards to the life of the victim and what precipitated the murder. Then the structure of the legal system is superimposed, adding counterpoint, irony, and the opportunity to bring in other characters, other scenes: the arrest, a grand jury, an indictment, a trial, an appeal, perhaps an execution. The controlled order of who can speak, to whom, and about what topic, in what order, all that formality of the trial regarding the release of words provides structure, adds drama, makes a story. The interest in murder, murder mysteries, and crime will not go away.

Without law the human need for stories remains, the need for art, for craft, for beauty, to make sense of the world is essential to the human condition. Those police officers, our scribes, were sometimes fourteen-year-old boys with a rudimentary knowledge of reading and grammar, yet they served this then future generation well and responsibly. Doing their procedural duty, they wrote it down, honestly, simply, including the dates and details and the names, and a comment or two, so that we coming later could look for more. And because this city spoke out, wrote it down, we found their records.

Will subsequent generations be able to say the same thing about us: that we preserved and left for them the accounts of how we lived and died, of the quality of our lives, the feel of what it was to be on the streets and in the houses and public buildings in this city, at this time. Law and literature have that function, separately and together.

Soon it will be fall again, this summer's drought will have come to an end. The students will put on their wind breakers, their Chinese-made sneakers, everyone with a new, lightweight laptop, and another generation of freshmen will complain about the weather and the wind as September goes to October. And some of them will learn to become record keepers. Some of them will be looking into the past. Some will be readers, all will be familiar with computers. Some will be artists on the Web. Some will be writers. Some will take on the obligation to keep the accounts of how life was lived by their generation, and to find what we left behind. And we will watch and help them, while we are still here, in another August.

A Note on Sources

The Chicago Historical Homicide Project Web site can be found at homicide.northwestern.edu. The interactive database gives access to all 11,439 cases from 1870–1930. *Hull House Maps and Papers, The 1929 Illinois Crime Survey, If Christ Came to Chicago*, the "Symposium Issue" of *The Journal of Criminal Law and Criminology* can all be found there in their entirety under *Publications*.

The author would like to thank the Northwestern University School of Law Faculty Research Funds, the McCormick Tribune Foundation, the Joyce Foundation, and the John D. and Catherine T. MacArthur Foundation for their continuing support, and acknowledge the work of the Northwestern University School of Communications, Distributed Learning Center (Dennis Glenn, Director), and the many many others who contributed to the Project and the creation of the Web site over the past several years.

Catharine R. Stimpson

Do These Deaths Surpass Understanding?: The Literary Figure of the Mother Who Murders

Once, when I was a student of English at Cambridge University, I casually bought a textbook about criminal law, thinking that this might be interesting. Standing on the street, in a chilly mist, I opened the book at random. The case that I stumbled upon transfixed me. It was dated 1560, had been decided in the Chester Assizes, subsequently printed in a textbook to illustrate the mental element of "malice aforethought," and read:

> "A harlot woman was delivered of a child. She laid it away, alive, in an orchard, and covered it with leaves. A kite struck at it with its claws. In consequence of being thus stricken, the child died very soon afterwards. She was arraigned of murder, and was executed . . . For she had intended the child's death; and *voluntas reputatur pro facto*." (Turner, p. 109)

Ever since, I have hovered over these words—as if I were a bird, at once protective and of prey. I have often asked myself about the harlot, who she might have been, what she might have looked like, what she might have felt and said throughout her ordeal.

Now I am team-teaching a course in law and literature with Stephen Gillers at New York University Law School and distribute the case to illustrate how law cases can be thought of as stories, as narratives. Thinking of law cases as stories is but one of the relations between law and literature. These two immense activities so frequently overlap that they form a series of Venn circles. Each is textual, concerned not only with narratives and narrative voices but with figurative language and metaphor. Each, as my harlot's case shows, examines subjectivity, mental states, motives, passions, drives, urges. Each confronts the most elemental of questions about humanity and its moral and social systems. What is justice? Who are the just? What is crime? What is punishment? Not surprisingly, given law's scope, writers great and small steal plots, characters, and themes from it all the time.

Yet Venn diagrams have blank spaces where the circles do not overlap. Law and literature have their obvious generic differences. Literature is freer and, despite its many rules, has fewer boundaries and limits. One might bitterly remark that tyrants, in their contempt for law, aspire to the condition of writers. The condition of literariness has a cascade of consequences. For writers, literary language is richer, wilder, more varied. For readers, incessant, even compulsive, re-readings are not only necessary but desirable. A significant test of a literary work, indeed of any artistic work, is how well it bears up under the pressure of new readings, interpretations, and performances. In part because of these capacities, literature can go where the law cannot. Shoshana Felman has written brilliantly about a new relation created in the twentieth-century between trials and historical trauma. Justice takes on a social and psychological obligation. It is "not simply punishment but . . . a marked symbolic exit from the injuries of a traumatic history . . . liberation from violence itself." (p. 1) Yet, literature can provide literary justice, exploring trauma in a way that the law neither can nor does. Felman states:

> Literature is a dimension of concrete embodiment and a language of infinitude that, in contrast to the language of the law, encapsulates not closure but precisely what in a given legal case refuses to be closed and cannot be closed. It is to this refusal of the trauma to be closed that literature does justice. The literary writers in this book thus stand beyond or in the margin of the legal closure, on the brink of the abyss that underlies the law, on whose profundity they fix their vision and through whose bottomlessness they reopen the closed legal case. (p. 8)

Infanticide and child murder are such resisting traumas. In 1976, the great poet Adrienne Rich published her significant texts about motherhood. In *Of Woman Born: Motherhood As Experience and Institu-*

tion, she distinguishes between infanticide as "deliberate social policy" and mothers who murder their infants and children. Radically mapping the linked chambers of motherhood and violence in "the heart of maternal darkness," she writes of the power a mother has over the life of a child, one of women's few sources of power. She then asks us to consider the acts of "numberless women (who) have killed children they knew they could not rear, whether economically or emotionally, children forced upon them by rape, ignorance, poverty, marriage, or, by the absence of, sanctions against, birth control and abortion." (p. 258) "My" harlot is such a woman.

Rich's compassion reflects two inseparable historical developments. The first is a modern shift, observable between 1770 and 1800, in the representation of mothers who kill their children. The "woman who murdered her infant was no callous criminal, but a desperate person." (p. 260) Queen Victoria supported the abolition of capital punishment for the crime of infanticide, cruelly punished earlier in English and Scottish law. The second is the rise of feminism. Rich looks back at the heroic figure of Elizabeth Cady Stanton, the first feminist to defend women charged with infanticide. Culture and society have forced such women to betray their best selves, binding them with "'the triple cord of a political, religious, and social serfdom—that have made (woman) a pliant, pitiable victim to the utter perversion of the highest and holiest sentiments of her nature.'" (p. 262)

Despite these changes, the mother who kills—"my" harlot—signifies the bad woman. Few human figures are more horrifying—and fascinating because horrifying—than the mother who kills her children. She may seem even more uncontrollably awful in monotheistic cultures that lack a powerful female goddess—for example, the Hindi goddess Kali—who must be worshipped, adored, and feared. Such goddesses channel and legitimate female violence. The shudder that the murdering mother provokes has sources deep within us. Not only has she killed the most vulnerable among us, the weakest, the most frail. She is meant to sustain these most vulnerable of creatures among us—literally with her own nutrients in the womb and then with her breast milk. Lacerating these creatures, pulverizing them, she apparently violates the most fundamental of moral and natural laws. Because she has given birth to her victims, when she murders them she is also destroying part of herself. The act of murder and the act of suicide are inseparable.

And we, the spectators and judges of her acts, go through a complicated process. We are at the end of a chain of trauma that begins with a trauma the mother might have suffered, which links to the extreme trauma of the child, which in turn links to our far milder trauma of identification with the murdered child. We, too, were once so vulnerable. Simultaneously, we feel relief. We may have been damaged by our mothers, but we were not killed. So distanced, we can sympathize with the innocent. This combination of fear-inducing identification and fearless sympathy is what Aristotle may have meant when he spoke (or so Aristotelian texts testify) of the pity and terror that tragedy inspires.

Of course, infanticide and the figure of the mother who commits infanticide or child murder must be placed within a specific historical context. Yet, as I have thought about the harlot's case, I have wondered about two great patterns of representation of such women. Like law and literature, these patterns are at once overlapping and distinct. They can exist together in a single work, even if one is foregrounded while the other is not. In the first, the work pushes and pulls us towards understanding the deed. To be sure, the woman has done a sad and awful thing. Often no court of law could condemn her more strongly than she condemns herself, find her guiltier than she finds herself. Yet, her act is explicable. It makes a terrible sense, given her circumstances. Reading literature leads to comprehension.

In the second pattern, the work takes us beyond the comprehensible and asks us to apprehend a passage from the human to the suprahuman. The human is at once natural and social, though the natural is partly socially constructed. The suprahuman is beyond both the natural and the social. The murdering mother—and this is another reason why she is so frightening—has traveled beyond the human boundaries within which we normally dwell. We do so for good reasons. Boundaries are necessary for individual and group survival. We need limits, structures. And the murdering mother is also of our world. She has not wholly broken free from the gravity of boundaries. She has wrapped her children in blankets, fed them, kissed them, dispatched them to primary school. She signifies the possibility of being us and not-us simultaneously. As she is at once us and not-us, she is within and beyond our capacities for comprehending and judging, be the judgment one of blame or exoneration. Reading literature leads to liminality, being on a threshold, one eye seeing the human, the other the suprahuman, an expanding universe that can include the "abyss," the "bottomless" of which Felman speaks.

Some literary scholars and critics who have stared into the literature of infanticide have concluded that the ghastly inverted Pieta of the

Portrait of Anna Smith sitting with her two children, Frank and Catherine in a room in Chicago, Illinois. (December 10, 1919)
Smith, Baby Boy—age one week—pushed off a window ledge by its mother, Anna, at 1036 E. 43 St. Coroner released the woman as being of unsound mind.
(*Chicago Daily News* negatives collection, DN-0073597. Chicago History Museum.)

mother who slays and the slain child represents a trauma so vast and appalling that cannot be represented, cannot be communicated. These events, believes Aimee Lynn Pozorski, are "unspeakable." Many narratives about trauma—for example, William Styron's novel *Sophie's Choice*—show tangled paths that the traumatized person follows in order to be able to speak. In *The Feminine Sublime: Gender and Excess in*

49

Women's Fiction, Barbara Claire Freeman brilliantly analyzes *Beloved*, Toni Morrison's novel about slavery and the infanticide it coerces, as one of several sites of the "feminine sublime." Revising the fascinating historical theory of the sublime by crossing it with gender, she postulates a feminine sublime, "neither a rhetorical mode nor an aesthetic category but a domain of experience that resists categorization, in which the subject enters into relation with an otherness—social, aesthetic, political, ethnic, erotic—that is excessive and unrepresentable . . . a crisis in relation to language and representation that a certain subject undergoes . . ." (p.2) At the heart of *Beloved* "lies a project . . . the process of translating and figuring events that exceed our frame of reference, and the need to attest to emotions that can be experienced only after the fact of their occurrence." (p. 122) All this is persuasive. The suprahuman can begin where speech must stop, but the suprahuman is not limited to the unrepresentable. It is all that is beyond the human, our powers and capacities, for good and evil. The superhuman is us writ large. The suprahuman is alien to us, and because alien to us, subject to different configurations and projections, tinctured with both exaltation and dread.

In many cultures, the figure of Medea is the archetypal, prototypical, and stereotypical murdering mother. The writer who stamps her identity is Euripides, his play about her, now about 2500 years old, animating both of these patterns of representation. To be sure, the figure and the play have been incessantly interpreted and reinterpreted. As the classicist Marianne McDonald writes, "Who or what is Medea? Is she a living being? A goddess? A character performed by an actress? A symbol? A text? The ancient text? A modern recreation? Many texts? . . . How do we translate her for ourselves? . . . Has she only transcendental significance? Or is she only significant because she resonates internally for each of us?" (p. 116) Despite the resilience and malleability of Medea as a figure and the play as a cultural phenomenon, the basic narrative is compelling enough to retain its stability. Medea is a barbarian princess, the daughter of the King of Colchis, on the Black Sea. In the Greek symbolic geography of the play, she already dwells beyond the boundaries of civilization. She is in a wild zone. Jason, a Greek, the leader of the Argonauts, comes to Colchis seeking the Golden Fleece. Medea helps him, falls in love with him, and sails off with him. They return to Greece where, married, they have two sons. He then leaves her for the daughter of the King of Corinth. In despair, jealous, vengeful, and yes passionate, she kills their two sons.

Boldly, Euripides uses Medea to dramatize the social and legal diffi-culties of women, their widely enforced subordination to men. This in-sight, in addition to the play's understanding of why Medea might be angry, helps to make all of her actions psychologically comprehensible. She creates tremendous havoc other than killing her sons. She betrays her father and homeland; murders her brother; tricks the daughters of King Pelias, Jason's uncle, into killing their own father; and fatally poi-sons a robe and diadem that her sons present to Jason's new wife and that kills both this woman and her royal father. The sheer number of vi-olent acts is astonishing, but all of them are justified in the name of love, a supreme human value, or in the name of love betrayed, a blasphemy against the human heart and marriage. Moreover, Medea does not want to kill her sons; she hesitates before she does so. She does so in order to act on her self-defined sense of justice. Her speeches—which are a test for the greatest of our actresses—move with lightening speed between statements that express her hatred of what she must do and her resolve to do what she hates to do. This is the "us" vector of the play.

The "not-us" vector of the play is as strong. For Medea is more than a murdering mother. She is a witch. For the Greek audience, this is, like her birthplace, a mark of her non-Greekness. For all audiences, this is a mark of her suprahuman quality. Near the end of Euripides's play, Jason returns to his old home to see the blood of his sons trickling down the steps. Then Medea appears, in a chariot drawn by dragons, with the corpses of her sons. She is literally above and beyond us. She and Jason have one last, vituperative exchange. She vows to bury her sons, and to exorcise their murder, and then leaves the stage to Jason and the cho-rus, the voice of the human community. By then, given the horror and violence of the murder of the boys, we may have forgotten one of Jason's speeches, in which he himself has had a fantasy of being himself suprahuman. The context of the fantasy is that men might have chil-dren without women, that men might reproduce themselves by them-selves, a fantasy that, of course, murders women. However, Jason can only try to imagine the suprahuman, a subjective exercise that is but a crude re-arrangement of conventional gender roles. Medea, if aban-doned, is the more soaring figure. She drives beyond the threshold of the human.

Infanticide and child killing—whether committed by public au-thority or private agency—are arguably historical constants. Like incest, it occurs across groups and classes, although the poorer women of lesser status seem to be more often prosecuted. Given the wildly uneven presence of records and documents about infanticide, we will never know its extent. The literary representations of infanticide and child murder are available, and since the late eighteenth century, a loosely defined canon of imaginative works about them in English has emerged. I now want to read and test some of these texts to see how strongly my two patterns appear in them.

In 1798, William Wordsworth wrote and published "The Thorn" as public attitudes about infanticide were evolving. He was aware of other poems about it. Comparatively short, his consists of twenty-two stanzas of eleven lines each. Apparently limpid, it bristles with complexity. For example, those twenty-two stanzas of eleven lines each. Twenty-two is two times eleven, and "The Thorn" is an interlocution, a dialogue between two speakers. The first describes a desolate, mysterious scene on a mountain-top: an aged thorn bush, "Not higher than a two years' child," overgrown with lichens and hung with moss; a little muddy pond three yards away; a beautiful, multi-colored heap of moss, the size of an infant's grave. Often a woman in a scarlet cloak sits between pond and this heap, crying "Oh misery! oh misery! / Oh woe is me! oh misery!"

When the first speaker seeks an explanation of her actions, the second professes ignorance. "I cannot tell; I wish I could; / For the true reason no one knows." Nevertheless, he tells a story both about the woman and the reactions of the community to her. In a later note, Wordsworth imagines him as a sea captain who has retired to "some village or country town of which he was not a native." Without sufficient occupation, he becomes "credulous . . . talkative from indolence . . . prone to superstition." The woman, Martha Ray, is a familiar victim in the narratives of infanticide, the once lively virgin who has been seduced and abandoned. Over twenty years before the time of the dialogue, she had fallen in love with a Stephen Hill. They had planned to marry. He is a cad, engaged to another woman whom he does marry. She is left pregnant in "pitiless dismay."

This much of her story seems to be trustworthy, but the second speaker, that sea captain, then spins out a series of unanswered questions and local lore that commingle the natural, the human, and the supernatural. In part, superstitions reflect an irrational belief in the supernatural, which may make us more amenable to imagining the suprahuman. Before Martha's child was born, was she crazy, or had the impending birth restored her to her senses? Was a child ever born? If it was, was it born dead or alive? Are voices coming from the mountain those of the dead? If the baby was born alive, did Martha hang it from the tree, as some say, or did she drown the baby in the pond, as others say? They also say that you can trace a baby's face in the pond looking up at the spectators. Eager to bring Martha to justice, some community members try to dig up the baby's bones, but the moss and the grass all around begin to shake and warn them away. Though deprived of physical proof that the baby is buried beneath the moss, "all do still aver" that this is its grave. The second speaker ends by establishing some cognitive solidity in what his senses tell him: he has seen heavy tufts of moss try to drag the thorn to the ground; in both night and day, he has heard the woman cry "Oh misery! oh misery! / Oh woe is me! oh misery!"

Poor, dwelling alone in a hut, Martha might suffer intensely whether the baby was stillborn or a victim of infanticide. Nature seems indifferent to the exact cause. What matters is that a baby died and that a woman could bear but never rear it. The stunted thorn and muddy pond are symbols of their blocked lives. If Martha did kill the baby, the poem implicitly gives us the materials for understanding why and for sympathizing with her consequent, life-long melancholy. Because of Stephen's deception, she has passed from the passions of love and sexuality to those of lamentation.

However, a possible infanticide is less the focus of the poem than the instability and contradictions of the interpretations of it. Only Martha's constant, all-season refrain consistently conveys a single interpretation: this is woe, this is misery. In the same note in which Wordsworth asks his readers to cast one of his speakers as a retired sea captain, he writes, ". . . Poetry is passion; it is the history or science of feelings. Now every man must know that an attempt is rarely made to communicate impassioned feelings without something of an accompanying consciousness of the inadequacies of our own powers, or the deficiencies of language." (p. 701) Through the creation of Martha, the poet points to a suprahuman domain of linguistic omnipotence and resonant adequacy.

Scholars have documented George Eliot's debts to William Wordsworth. Indeed, the epigraph for the first of her astonishing novels, *Adam Bede*, is from his poem *The Excursion* (with a minor misquotation). Published in 1859, but set at the turn of the nineteenth century, *Adam Bede* has as one of its sources a story that the young Mary Ann Evans had heard twenty years earlier from the wife of her uncle Samuel Evans. The aunt had visited a condemned criminal in jail, a young girl who had murdered her child, refused to confess, and was hanged. Revising and amplifying her source, Eliot creates a pretty but naïve and vain seventeen-year-old girl, Hetty Sorrel, who lives with relatives, the Poysers, a farming family with vitality and integrity, proud of their reputation. Another relative, Dinah Morris, a Methodist preacher of intense spiritual qualities, stays at the Poysers from time to time. In a prophetic moment, she fears for Hetty, her imagination (in an echo of Wordsworth) seeing "a thorny thicket of sin and sorrow, in which she saw the poor thing struggling torn and bleeding, looking with tears for rescue and finding none." (p. 160) Adam Bede, a carpenter, is in love with Hetty, but she has an affair with Arthur Donnithorne, an army officer who is destined to become the local squire. Arthur is no cad, ruthlessly grabbing sex across well-marked class lines. Indeed, Mr. Irvine, the Anglican reverend, calls him "weak, but . . . not callous, not coldly selfish." (p. 432) However, it is Hetty, not Arthur, who becomes pregnant.

Unable to tell anyone, Hetty's responses, her increasing isolation and confusion and desperation, are a paradigmatic narrative of the mother who commits infanticide. She contemplates suicide, drowning herself, but fears that when her corpse is found, people will read her secret on her body. She is consumed with shame, a pervasive emotion in the representation of women who commit infanticide. As a protective mechanism, she accepts Adam's offer of marriage, but then flees, seeking out Arthur in his army camp. His unit has left. Her money running out, she resumes her wandering journey. Its conclusion emerges in court, after her arrest for a "great crime—the murder of her child" (p. 417). The testimony of witnesses builds her new identity, that of criminal. The responses of most of her friends, family and the community to the trial reinforce it. A shopkeeper has taken her in. A baby was born in the night. The next day, a laborer finds the baby buried under a nut bush. The day after that, the laborer and a constable find Hetty there. After a jury finds her guilty, she is sentenced to die by hanging, but Arthur, in a redemptive act, rides to the gallows with a pardon. She is instead transported overseas, England expelling its refuse to the colonies, where, in a few years, she dies. Arthur, too, goes abroad, as a soldier. When he returns, he is a shattered veteran.

Eliot exonerates neither Hetty nor Arthur, especially not Arthur, who has had the advantages of class and gender. Some wrongs can never be righted. Self-centered, the two have violated the highest, most unselfish love, that of a mother for a child, "that completest type of the life in another life, which is the essence of real human love." (p. 441) They have brought great suffering to others as well as to themselves. An innocent child is dead. Yet Eliot, with the psychological genius that her moralism never flattens, makes Hetty knowable, representable, capable of eliciting a reader's understanding and compassion. She is of the human world.

Hetty's agony on the night before her execution is the vehicle through which a reader can also apprehend the suprahuman. Throughout her trial, she has obstinately both refused to tell her story and to show remorse. She has rejected the language of autobiography ("This is what happened to me"), of the law ("This is my crime"), and of a religiously-charged morality ("I am sorry. I repent."). Dinah then visits her prison cell to share what both women believe will be Hetty's last hours on earth and to try to bring Hetty to God's love and mercy. For Dinah, Hetty is less criminal, a violator of man's law, than sinner, a violator of God's. Finally, after Dinah's prayers and appeals to the Savior, Hetty breaks, sobs, and embraces Dinah, "I will speak . . . I will tell . . . I won't hide it any more." (Her account of the burial of the baby gives feeling and detail to the actions of "my" harlot.) After her confession, she can pray for mercy. Hetty has been her conduit to the suprahuman, God's grace and forgiveness. Perhaps the defining feature of God's grace and forgiveness is that we need not be alienated from it, that it will like Christ Himself and because of Christ Himself enter the human world.

Like "The Thorn" and *Adam Bede*, "Old Woman Magoun," published in 1909, takes place in a rural village society. Barry's Ford is no pastoral idyll, but a place that seems at once static, frozen in time, and in the kinesis of decay. Once prominent families, among them, the Barrys, have degenerated over time. A gender-marked village, the men tend to be far lazier than the women, especially the tough, hard-working matriarch Old Woman Magoun. She is protectively raising her beautiful granddaughter, Lily, whose mother died in pregnancy when she was sixteen, having been seduced by Nelson Barry, another literary representation of the dangerous and caddish scion of a leading family.

Broke, Nelson plans to sell his daughter, whom he has previously neglected, in order to pay his gambling debts. Unable to protect Lily legally, Old Woman Magoun watches quietly as the child eats some deadly nightshade berries because they look pretty and taste sweet. She is silent, not because her act is unrepresentable, but because she would stop the chain of action she is forging if she were to speak. She can represent her act to herself privately only too clearly. Lily becomes violently ill, her distress blamed on eating sour apples and milk. When Nelson arrives to claim her, he finds a dying child and a weeping grandmother. After Lily's funeral, village life goes on, although Old Woman

Magoun carries the child's rag doll, a emblem of the girl whom she has treasured above all else, when she takes eggs or produce to the market. Letting Lily die, in order to save the child from the sexual and social perils of the adult life that awaits her, Mother Magoun dramatizes and makes intelligible a child murder that, as Sandra Gilbert and Susan Gubar write, is a way of battling a "male enemy indirectly." A heart and life-breaking weapon, infanticide simultaneously reveals a woman's power and powerlessness. "The act of infanticide . . . is a woman's most potent form of revenge against men because it destroys the patrilineage, but at the same time it is a telling sign of female vulnerability because it reveals that one of the few kinds of power a woman has is destructive power over her child." (p. 73)

Tersely, Freeman twists Western myths and symbols to deepen the agonizing conflict between a protective, stubborn maternal figure and a corrupt paternal figure and the unworthy suitor whom he encourages. The ungilded Lily, a name redolent with religious and heraldic connotations, must die. Lily also takes on the role of Persephone in a partial re-enactment of the deep ancient narrative of Persephone, the daughter seized by Pluto, the god of the underworld, for whom Demeter, her mother, searches. Only this Demeter destroys Persephone before Pluto can carry her away. Crucially, these allusions, well within the realms of Western culture, do not evoke the suprahuman. It is Mother Magoun who does. As this angel of death tenderly nurtures her delirious grandchild, she promises her that she is traveling towards a beautiful place with unfading blue flowers, singing birds, golden roads and walls, and a mother waiting for her. What could be more alien from a Barry's Ford than paradise?

Despite the degeneracy of Barry's Ford, it is at least a free town, and as a result, the distance between it and the world of American slavery is almost as great as the distance between Barry's Ford and paradise. Toni Morrison's *Beloved* is a supremely important act of the moral and historical imagination, using fiction so courageously and craftily that the traumatic memories of slavery cannot be repressed, forgotten, or gussied up—despite our every wish to do so. Like George Eliot, Morrison transforms a historical case, that of Margaret Garner, a slave who ran away in 1856 and escaped to Cincinnati. The novel begins in a haunted house in Cincinnati in 1873. The Civil War has been over for eight years, but Reconstruction has already begun.

The dominant complementary figures in Morrison's narrative are Paul D, the man struggling to survive slavery, and Sethe, the woman who does so. She is only one of the slave women, in history and literature, who kill their children. Her mother has thrown away the babies that were the result of rapes. However, as Ashraf H.A. Rushdy writes accurately, "Morrison insists on the impossibility of judging an action without reference to the terms of its enactment." (p. 47) Infanticide is a socially and emotionally logical response under a system of slavery that makes every vicious effort to destroy black families, the capacity of black men to father their own children, and the capacity for black women to mother theirs. Baby Suggs, Sethe's mother-in-law, has had eight children with six fathers. Only one, Halle, stays with her. "What she called the nastiness of life was the shock she received upon learning that nobody stopped playing checkers just because the pieces included her children." (p. 23)

With Halle, Sethe has been able to send three of her children to freedom in Ohio. Then, in 1855, raped by having the milk sucked from her breasts by the nephews of her owner and horribly scarred by being beaten, she gives birth to a fourth child, a girl named Denver, in a boat on the river she must cross to Ohio. She arrives at the home of her mother-in-law, Baby Suggs, on the outskirts of Cincinnati. No one knows why her husband has not been able to keep the rendezvous for the escape from slavery. The central scene of the novel, an American hell, takes place in Baby's woodshed twenty-eight days later. Men come to take Sethe and her children back to slavery. She tries to kill them in order to save them. Two boys and baby Denver survive. She succeeds in cutting the throat of a little girl with a hacksaw. This murdering mother is no Medea. She is neither vengeful nor jealous. Far more exalted, she wants her children to be free. "I took and put my babies where they'd be safe," she later says. (p. 164) Sethe is imprisoned. Later released, through community pressure, she buys a tombstone, after prostituting herself, and has the word "Beloved" carved on it. A ghost, "full of a baby's venom," begins to haunt 124 Bluestone Road.

Eighteen years later, Sethe's life, which she keeps going by keeping time (past and future) at bay, is torn apart. Paul D, who has been owned by the same people as she has been, arrives at her home. He temporarily banishes the ghost. He is as traumatized as she, but they might together discover the possibilities of love, and a semblance of normalcy. However, a mysterious young woman, Beloved, also enters the house. She is the ghost not only of the murdered child but of all the dead of the Middle Passage. She may also be a young woman who has escaped from a white man who has imprisoned her as a sexual slave.

After being seduced by her, Paul leaves the house. Only with great strength does Denver escape. Psychologically, Sethe and Beloved merge. Sethe is possessed. Her release comes because the women of the community decide to help her. They debate, briefly but pungently, about the meaning of Sethe's murder and possession. Finally, they decide, led by a woman named Ella, that she ought to be exorcised and freed. Ella is another woman who has refused to nurture one of her babies, the consequence of a rape, "a hairy white thing, fathered by 'the lowest yet.'" (p. 258–9) In such circumstances, infanticide may be a wholly comprehensible refusal to feed a bastard line, and an act of self-survival. The community's exorcism is an exercise of forgiveness of Sethe. Afterwards, Sethe and Paul D can meet again, battered though they have been, in a time present in which some memory has been restored.

The ghosts in *Beloved* represent the shadows of traumatic memories and the possibility of the flow between past and present, the dead and the living, the human and the supernatural. Ella respects ghosts, within limits. If a ghost is like Beloved, "if it took flesh and came in her world, well, the shoe was on the other foot. She didn't mind a little communication between the two worlds, but this was an invasion." (p. 257) It is not Beloved's ghostliness that places her on the threshold between human and suprahuman, but visions of her as an animated spirit, at once nymph and demon. After the exorcism, a child sees "a naked woman with fish for hair." (p. 267) *Beloved* cannot permit its readers to linger too long or too happily with wispy imaginings of the suprahuman. For our task is to remember the historical torture, torments, and murders of slavery, which white people, white humans, created and maintained and from which they profited. Even the kindest of slave-owners, Mr. and Mrs. Garner, were still slave-owners. Only if we remember can we begin to answer Paul D's question. Talking to Stamp Paid, a core of goodness in the African-American community, Paul D asks, "'Tell me this one thing. How much is a nigger supposed to take? Tell me. How much?'" "'All he can,'" Stamp Paid answers, "'All he can.'" To this, Paul D can only utter, in words as blunt and rhythmic as a whip, "'Why? Why? Why? Why? Why?'" (p. 235)

Beloved is a slain child who speaks. However, the murdered child in literature rarely speaks, except through its last cries. But some children manage to survive, and they can speak. This is the story of Jane Eyre. Jane is an orphan, whose parents die when she is a baby. She is left in the custody of her maternal uncle, Mr. Reed, but he, too, dies, leaving her in the custody of his widow, the physically vigorous but cruel and spiritually barren Mrs. Reed who hates Jane and permits her three ghastly children to torment and bully her. When Jane is ten, Mrs. Reed sends her away to a brutal school and pretends, when a relative inquires after Jane, that she has died.

Jane survives and eventually leaves her school and becomes a governess in the house of that modern, tormented hero, Mr. Rochester. She is summoned back to her childhood residence (one cannot call it a home except with bitter irony) as her aunt is dying. In a series of sinis-

Portrait of Antonia Jacobs, sitting next to Mrs. Mary Brendecke, who is holding five infants on her lap, on the porch of the Brendecke Hospital. Mrs. Brendecke was accused of burning in a stove some infants born at the maternity home, which was located in the Near West Side community area of Chicago, Illinois.
(*Chicago Daily News* negatives collection, DN-0005100. Chicago History Museum.)

ter, surreal scenes, Jane sits with her aunt, who does not always recognize her. In them, her aunt confesses that she hated Jane, that she was jealous of Jane, that she betrayed Jane, that she said Jane was dead. Jane, however, forgives her. She shows suprahuman spiritual grace, even as she realizes that the surrogate mother who would murder her has no doubt died without extirpating those desires. Jane broods, "Poor, suffering woman! it was too late for her to make now the effort to change her habitual frame of mind: living, she had ever hated me—dying, she must hate me still." (p. 211)

Given the hatred with which she has been raised, Jane's tasks of self-invention must also include those of discovering, accepting, and giving love. She begins to do so in school. She continues to do so with (Edward Fairfax) Rochester. Having survived the murdering mother, Jane begins to love Rochester, but then runs away from him after she learns about the existence of Bertha Mason. She is about to marry another man, St. John, when she again enters into the domain of the suprahuman. She dismisses St. John, goes to her room, and prays, but, significantly, "in my way—a different way to St. John's but effective in its own fashion." (p. 370) Her reward is to seem "to penetrate very near a Mighty Spirit; and my soul rushed out in gratitude at His feet." She then can act. She tells her readers, "I rose from the thanksgiving—took a resolve—and lay down, unscared, enlightened, eager but for the daylight." The next day she embarks upon a journey that will take her back to Rochester.

These narratives all give us the materials of understanding of my harlot and others. They do more as well. The word "blame" is related etymologically to "blasphemy." Are we to blame murdering mothers? Accuse them of blasphemy against the laws of nature and morality? Perhaps, but these narratives of my second pattern also warn us against locking ourselves into easy judgments, self-righteous blamings. For we ourselves might then be guilty on two counts: first, of blaspheming against suprahuman domains that we have barely begun to comprehend; and second, without diminishing the crimes of the murdering mothers, of lacking a suprahuman capacity for spiritual grace.

Notes

Below are the works from which I have quoted or to which I have alluded. Each of the literary works that I treat has inspired a mass of critical commentary that people might wish to explore for themselves. Of the very recent work on infanticide and literature, I found three of particular interest. Two are dissertations: 1) Aimee Lynn Pozorski, "Figures of Infanticide: Traumatic Modernity and the Inaudible Cry," *DAIA*. 2003 Aug. 64 (2), 503, Emory U, 2003, a study of eighteenth- and nineteenth-century British culture; and 2) Ann Wierke Rowland, "Unnatural Crimes." *DAIA*. 2002 Nov. 61 (5), 1855, Yale U, 2000. which focuses on twentieth-century culture and modernity. The third is Josephine Gattuso Hendin, *Heart Breakers: Women and Violence in Contemporary Culture and Literature*, New York: Palgrave MacMillan, 2004, which argues that "Child murder comes to the fore as a subject of interest when cultural attitude about motherhood are in crisis." (p. 106) The work on law and literature is burgeoning, but Deborah W. Denno, "Who Is Andrea Yates? A Short Story About Insanity," *Duke Journal of Gender Law and Policy* 10 (Summer 2003): 1–139, is an impressive review of connections between law and literature and analysis of Andrea Yates as a convicted mother as murderer.

Because I do not consider abortion infanticide, I have not written about it.

The absence of *Sophie's Choice* (1979) by William Styron is one that I regret. This massive, searing novel explores traumatizing evil, especially the Holocaust, but also slavery, the sadism of the deranged mind, and the interlocking masochism of the traumatized one. In Auschwitz, Sophie must choose which of her two children will be sent to a certain, immediate death. However, the Nazis kill that child. To say that Sophie does, is at best a callous reading.

Ashraf, H. A. Rushdy. "Daughters of Signifyin(g) History: The Example of Toni Morrison's *Beloved, Toni Morrison's Beloved: A Casebook*, ed. William L. Andrews, Nellie Y. McKay. New York: Oxford University Press, 1999. pp. 37–66.

Bronte, Charlotte. *Jane Eyre*, ed. Richard J. Dunn. New York : W.W. Norton and Co., Inc., 1971.

Eliot, George. *Adam Bede*, intro. by Gordon S. Haight. New York and Toronto: Rinehart and Co., Inc., 1956, 2nd reprinting of 1948 ed.

Freeman, Barbara Claire. *The Feminine Sublime: Gender and Excess in Women's Fiction*. Berkeley: University California Press, 1995.

Freeman, Mary E. Wilkins. "Old Woman Magoun," *A New England Nun and Other Stories*, ed. Sandra A. Zagarell. New York: Penguin Books, 2000.

Gilbert, Sandra and Susan Gubar. *No Man's Land*, Vol. I, *The War of the Words*. New Haven and London: Yale University Press, 1988.

McDonald, Marianne. *Ancient Sun: Modern Light: Greek Drama on the Modern Stage*. New York: Columbia University Press, 1992.

Morrison, Toni. *Beloved*. New York: Alfred A. Knopf, 1987.

Carolyn Frazier and Dorothy Roberts

Victims and Villains in Murder by Abortion Cases from Turn-of-the-Twentieth-Century Chicago

In *The Jungle*, published in 1906, Upton Sinclair renders one of literature's most disturbing portrayals of urban poverty by recounting the experiences of Jurgis Rudkus, a Lithuanian immigrant who labors in the foul Chicago stockyards. Jurgis beats up the boss of the factory where his young wife, Ona, works when he discovers the boss has compelled Ona to have sex with him by threatening to fire her. Upon his release from jail, Jurgis finds a malnourished Ona screaming in pain from the throes of premature childbirth. He has no money to pay a doctor, so Jurgis desperately seeks out a midwife in a flat over a saloon at the top of a dingy flight of stairs.

Sinclair's description of the midwife reflects the stereotypical image prevalent at the turn of the twentieth century. Madame Haupt "was a Dutch woman, enormously fat—when she walked she rolled like a small boat on the ocean, and the dishes in the cupboard jostled each other. She wore a filthy blue wrapper, and her teeth were black." (Sinclair 181) She cruelly haggles over the price for her services, finally accepting the meager amount Jurgis brought with him on the promise that he will pay more within a month. When Madame Haupt approaches Jurgis after tending to Ona, "Jurgis gave one glance at her, and then turned white and reeled. She had her jacket off, like one of the workers in the killing beds. Her hands and arms were smeared with blood, and blood was

63

splashed upon her clothing and her face." (Sinclair 187) The midwife callously disclaims any responsibility for Ona's fate and asks for some brandy for herself. Jurgis rushes to Ona's bedside in time to see her take her last breath: "Her life had hardly begun—and here she lay murdered—mangled, tortured to death!" (Sinclair 189)

In turn-of-the-twentieth-century Chicago, the leading professional organization of physicians skillfully deployed this image of the midwife—as greedy, incompetent, and unscrupulous—to pursue a campaign against midwives who performed abortions that ended in the pregnant woman's death. By investigating midwife abortionists and providing evidence against them at trial, members of the Chicago Medical Society significantly contributed to the enforcement of the criminal abortion law against midwives. More importantly, Chicago doctors performed a remarkable rhetorical feat to condemn midwives and save themselves. The medical establishment portrayed midwives who performed illegal abortions as villains and pregnant women as their victims, but cast doctors charged with the same crime as victims of villainous women who pressured them into performing the operation. The Society made effective use of female stereotypes, depicting women as at once vulnerable and domineering, irrational and scheming, to accomplish this rhetorical magic act. By both enforcing the law against abortion and driving midwives out of business, the medical profession eventually succeeded in securing its dominance over women's reproductive health. (See Reagan; Schoen; Siegel)

Murder by Abortion in Turn-of-the-Century Chicago

As a result of a national effort by the American Medical Association, most states had passed statutes criminalizing abortion at all stages of pregnancy by the turn of the twentieth century. (Reagan; Schoen; Siegel) Abortion was outlawed in Illinois in 1867. Under the Illinois law criminalizing abortion, anyone who "produced" an abortion unnecessary to preserve the pregnant woman's life was guilty of a high misdemeanor and could be imprisoned in the penitentiary for one to ten years. A woman seeking an abortion was not guilty of a crime. "Despite women's participation in abortion, however, the law did not allow for the indictment of the woman who received an abortion," notes historian Johanna Schoen. "By definition, her role was that of the object upon which others acted." (Schoen, 148) If the abortion caused the woman's death, the abortionist could be charged with murder. The defendant need not have intended to kill the pregnant woman; the mere intent to produce the abortion was sufficient to sustain a murder conviction. (Will)

Despite the formal legal ban on abortion, it is well documented that women in Chicago continued to seek and receive abortions throughout the entire 108-year period that abortion was illegal. (Reagan) According to historian Leslie Reagan, abortion was widely accepted until the 1930s and frequently performed by both physicians and midwives. (Ibid.) Estimates of induced abortions in Chicago at the turn of the twentieth century range from 6,000 to 10,000 per year. (Bacon) One obstetrician speculated that of all women in Chicago who bore children during the period, nearly half of them aborted at least one pregnancy before reaching age 35. (Reed) Both physicians and midwives performed abortions for women who requested them. As a general rule, immigrants and low-income Chicagoans called upon midwives to perform abortions, while more affluent residents visited physicians for this service. Even physicians within the mainstream medical community routinely performed abortions for women who could afford their fees. As one Chicago doctor noted in 1908, wealthy women "have no difficulty in securing professional services to help them out of their difficulty." (Yarros, 961) Given how financially lucrative this relatively simple procedure could be, many mainstream physicians who were in principle opposed to the practice nevertheless agreed to oblige their wealthy patients.

It is impossible to document precisely the number of deaths resulting from this underground operation. The estimates, however, were large enough to cause concern. John Traeger, Cook County Coroner from 1899 to 1904, expressed amazement at the "alarming frequency" these cases entered his office. (Traeger, 35) Evidence available in medical journals and newspapers suggests that physicians and midwives shared responsibility for performing abortions that ended in death. In her exhaustive history of criminal abortion, Leslie Reagan concludes that these practitioners likely had "comparable safety records for abortions." (Reagan, 77)

The Medical Society's Campaign Against Midwife Abortionists

Although the crime of murder by abortion had been on the books for decades, prosecutions for this crime were "extremely rare" before 1900.

(Minutes of Chicago Medical Society Meeting, April 12, 1904) In the early 1900s, however, Chicago physicians were instrumental in the dramatic increase in enforcement of the abortion law. In 1904, the Chicago Medical Society resolved to improve Chicago's poor track record for prosecuting abortionist-murderers. (Minutes of Chicago Medical Society Meeting, May 8, 1904) Prominent obstetricians Dr. Charles Sumner Bacon, Dr. Rudolph Holmes, and Dr. Charles Reed were granted permission by the Society's governing council to form a special committee to investigate the problem of criminal abortions in Chicago. By 1906, the group was established as one of five standing committees of the Chicago Medical Society, officially titled the Criminal Abortion Committee; theirs was the only one dealing with a substantive issue rather than an administrative aspect of the Society.

When the Chicago Medical Society's Criminal Abortion Committee decided to wage war on those committing the crime of murder by abortion, it understood that its strategy needed to be more comprehensive than the "ephemeral campaigns" of the past had been. While Chicago physicians and newspapers had launched prior anti-abortion campaigns, these efforts had yielded few prosecutions of abortionists. Its overarching social goal may have been to reduce the incidence of abortions among married women in Chicago; but its practical aim was to increase prosecutions for the crime of murder by abortion. During its first decade of operation, the committee focused its energies on assisting the state in prosecuting those who committed this crime.

The Criminal Abortion Committee's investigation of midwives' involvement in criminal abortion was particularly intense. In 1907, the committee created a spin-off investigatory group called the Committee on Midwives, chaired by Dr. Holmes, who held the same position on the Criminal Abortion Committee. At no time during its first ten years did the Criminal Abortion Committee carry out a similarly organized investigation of its own physicians. Indeed, one of the benefits of membership in the Chicago Medical Society was its pledge of support and protection should its physicians encounter legal difficulties. (Frazier) The committee was probably largely responsible for both the increase in successful prosecutions that occurred between 1904 and 1913 and in the disproportionate representation of midwives among the defendants.

The Criminal Abortion Committee's reports and activities throughout its first ten years displayed a distinct bias against midwives as a class. Committee members referred to midwives variously as "nefarious," "foolish," "insidious," "lax," "careless," uneducated," "untrained," and "vicious." (Bacon; Bacon et al; Holmes 1904) This bias may have sprung from physicians' competition with midwives for obstetrical patients created by the overcrowding of the medical profession in Chicago. In contrast to the ample earnings of the average physician today, the income of many Chicago doctors at the turn of the century was meager. One physician noted in 1906 that his Chicago colleagues "frequently find much difficulty in making more than a bare living and often cannot do that." (Keyes, 498)

Moreover, organized medicine was seeking to elevate itself during this period, to convince the public of the nobility of physicians and the preeminence of conventional medicine for treating illness. (Reagan) Whereas medical practice embodied modern progress, the Society argued, midwifery was "a remnant of medieval times." (Holmes 1920, 27) In the language of social Darwinism, physicians predicted that midwives would eventually die out, to be "survived by the fittest." (Ibid., 29) By vilifying midwives, the society polished the image of its own members.

The Committee furthered this comparison by highlighting midwives' primitiveness. It described midwives as "illiterate, ignorant women," who were "deficient in learning and ability." Inadequately restrained by legal regulation, midwives were compared to the "proverbial bull in the china closet." (Ibid., 28) According to physicians, midwives' "crude minds" were incapable of comprehending the complexities of medical care. "The old saw that a little learning is a dangerous thing was never so true as in the case of the midwife," Dr. Holmes wrote. "Badly taught, inadequately experienced, she can never grasp the broad fact that the delivery of a woman is a serious problem." (Ibid., 29)

More fundamentally, the medical profession had a huge stake in maintaining control over the practice of reproductive medicine. Because families universally needed reproductive health services, they might begin to rely on midwives as their primary health care providers. Taking over midwives' business enabled physicians to oversee this "gateway" to the entire practice of medicine. (Petchesky, 81) Moreover, controlling reproductive medicine gave the predominantly male medical profession power to help determine women's proper role in society. The American Medical Association's anti-abortion campaign described the regulation of abortion as essential to enforcing feminine morality and women's duty to bear children. (Reagan; Siegel) By recreating childbirth as a "serious problem" that could only be treated by highly trained professionals, doctors ensured their dominance over women's reproductive health.

Suppressing midwifery resulted from and reinforced the prevailing gender, race, and class hierarchies. As working women, midwives violated the lingering Victorian norm that placed white women strictly in the domestic sphere. The law and culture of the early 1900s reflected the view that these women were naturally unsuited for the work place. (Olsen, 1498–1501) Only three decades earlier, the United States Supreme Court held in *Bradwell v. Illinois* (1873) that the Illinois Supreme Court did not violate Myra Bradwell's constitutional rights when it denied her application for a license to practice law because she was a married woman. In his concurrence, Justice Bradley noted that women's lack of legal existence separate from their husbands demonstrated that family harmony was "repugnant to the idea of a woman adopting a distinct and independent career from that of her husband." (*Bradwell v. Illinois*)

Justice Bradley's judgment that "[t]he paramount destiny and mission of women are to fulfill the noble and benign offices of wife and mother" applied equally to women seeking to enter the health professions. According to a 1909 editorial by a Chicago medical school official, "Women do not have the courage or strength to endure the hardships incident to a successful physician's life. I have never known a woman to make what I call a success of the practice of medicine. I fear that the great majority of them are abortionists, which gives them their greatest source of revenue." ("Women in Medicine," 189–90) Dr. Holmes likewise believed that "[w]omen in their business relations have not a keen sense of right and wrong." (Holmes 1904, 29) Thus, the physicians' campaign against midwives was bolstered by stereotypes about women's incapacity to work successfully outside the home.

These negative gender images were no doubt reinforced as well by anti-immigrant sentiments directed at midwives. Whereas most of the physicians belonging to the Chicago Medical Society were native-born whites, 97 percent of the midwives in Chicago during this period were foreign-born. (Reagan) In its 1908 exposé on midwives in Chicago, the Committee on Midwives determined that just over half of Chicago's midwives were German or Polish; the remainder were primarily Swedish, Bohemian, Russian, or of other Western European origin. (Bacon et al.) Leaders of organized medicine in Chicago, aware of the overwhelmingly immigrant makeup of Chicago's midwife population, spoke with disdain about the "foreign element" that brought this practice to U.S. shores. (Holmes 1920, 28) Sinclair's portrayal of the unscrupulous midwife Madame Haupt in *The Jungle* likewise emphasizes her ethnic origins. The description begins by noting that she was a Dutch woman; she speaks with a heavy accent. When she shouts at Jurgis after fatally botching the delivery, "you pays me dot money yust de same! It is not my fault dat you send for me so late I can't help you vife," she embodies stereotypes about midwives' greed and insensitivity as well as those about immigrants' ignorance and vulgarity.

It took the committee only a few months—and no research—to conclude that the epidemic of criminal abortion was created primarily by midwives. In 1908, physicians from the committee declared, "[i]t is generally conceded that midwives are the chief agents in procuring these abortions." (Bacon et al, 1349) At its 1904 Symposium on Criminal Abortion, the committee shone its spotlight almost entirely on midwives. Cook County Coroner John Traeger painted a tragic image of young women who came to the big city to obtain an abortion at the hands of midwives:

> The young girl in the small town who is led from the straight and narrow path and to hide her shame is compelled to come to a large city. . . . She either leaves the house of the midwife a physical wreck or finds a resting place on a marble slab in the Cook County Morgue. . . . I never did and never will show mercy and I consider the brightest page of my record as coroner of Cook County, the one containing a list of the midwives I assisted in sending to Joliet Penitentiary for the practice of criminal abortion in Cook County. (Traeger, 37)

So extreme was the committee's targeting of midwives that it prompted one of the two lone female physicians who spoke during the gathering to remark, "Anyone who listened to the discussion this evening, who does not know the facts, might carry the impression that it is only the midwives who are guilty of criminal abortion." (Ladova, 45)

The committee pursued its mission by instilling in all physicians a duty to use their influence to bring offenders to justice. This role was a major departure from the common attitude among those in the medical profession that it was "no part of the duty of the physician to play detective for the authorities." (Will, 508) The committee engaged in educational outreach to doctors to teach them about the laws related to criminal abortion, training them to be more effective gatherers of incriminating evidence. It investigated physicians and midwives suspected to be performing criminal abortions in the city.

In addition to collecting information from Chicago daily newspapers, the Committee sent female investigators undercover to try to trap alleged abortionists by getting them to agree to perform the operation. (Bacon et al.) Frustrated when the grand jury failed to indict Constance Anderson for the death of Mrs. Morris Swanson, Dr. Rudolph Holmes undertook to investigate the midwife. Speaking with fellow physicians, he collected "written data of three women who died as a result of criminal operations at Constance Anderson's hand." (Holmes 1904, 34) Dr. Holmes' tenacity in tracking Anderson probably contributed to prosecutors' success in indicting her twice over the next several years.

A particularly effective strategy was to cement its ties with government offices involved in the detection and prosecution of criminal abortion, including the Cook County Coroner's Office, the State Board of Health, and the Cook County States Attorney's Office. The Criminal Abortion Committee operated like an unofficial arm of the State that reinforced government efforts to expose and punish abortionists. The committee and the coroner's office collaborated in creating "how-to" literature on abortion prosecutions for hospitals and medical schools and in sharing access to each other's files. Their main point of cooperation was the coroner's inquest. At inquests of deaths that appeared sudden, accidental, or violent, the coroner, along with a jury of six good men, made the crucial determination whether or not to charge and hold a suspect to the grand jury for formal indictment. In 1904, the state's attorney's office cited lack of evidence against criminal suspects as the main reason so few cases made it past the coroner's office. (Dobyns)

The circumstances that led Mrs. Alide Koester to her death in 1904 while attempting to abort her pregnancy are unclear. According to accused midwife Maria Jahnke, Mrs. Koester sought the midwife's help only after trying to perform an abortion upon herself with a lead pencil. (Bacon) Mrs. Jahnke claimed to have unsuccessfully tried to repair the mortal damage, most likely a punctured uterus or blood poisoning. But the jury at the Cook County Criminal Courthouse rejected Mrs. Jahnke's story, choosing to believe instead the testimony of a prominent Chicago physician, Dr. C. S. Bacon, president of the Chicago Medical Society and chairman of the Criminal Abortion Committee. Dr. Bacon testified that Mrs. Koester, a patient he had treated in the past, had made a dying declaration to him, which accused Mrs. Jahnke of performing the lethal operation. Despite conflicting evidence presented at trial, Dr. Bacon's testimony was unassailable because he knew as a result of the committee's training to include precisely the elements of a dying declaration required to make it admissible in court.

At the suggestion of the Criminal Abortion Committee, the coroner began immediately calling the committee when he became aware of a suspected abortion death. The committee provided the coroner general information about the suspect or, if it could investigate quickly enough, about the particular facts and circumstances of the case. A member of the committee was present at almost every inquest, usually serving on the jury. Committee members frequently took over the inquest, questioning witnesses about the victim's death. (Minutes of Chicago Medical Society Meeting, January 9, 1912) The committee's relationship with the state's attorney's office was equally intimate. Committee members supplied evidence on abortionists, gave expert testimony at trial, and pushed for prosecution of particular offenders.

The Criminal Abortion Committee's most celebrated victory was the 1908 conviction for murder by abortion of the notorious midwife Lucy Hagenow, a.k.a. Louise Hagenow, a.k.a. Dr. Sucy, a.k.a. Ida Von Schultz, by far the most often indicted health practitioner at the time. The *Journal of the American Medical Association* reported in its Medical News section that Mrs. Hagenow had been brought to justice not by the Cook County State's Attorney, but "through the efforts of the Chicago Medical Society, headed by Dr. Rudolph W. Holmes." ("Medical News," JAMA) Were it not for the Criminal Abortion Committee, the case of Annie Horvatich, who died in Mrs. Hagenow's care, might have ended with the burial of Miss Horvatich's body on the south side of Chicago. Instead, a full week after Horvatich's death, Coroner Peter Hoffman became aware of the incident and ordered that the body be disinterred. Hoffman made his standard immediate call to the Criminal Abortion Committee and Dr. Holmes made the post-mortem examination according to the evidentiary requirements for a criminal prosecution.

Not only did Dr. Holmes testify against Hagenow at her trial, but his committee supplied evidence of Hagenow's prior acts as an abortionist to prove that she operated on Miss Horvatich with the intent to induce a criminal abortion. It supplied a dying declaration against Hagenow made years earlier in a separate case, testimony by a prominent physician who claimed to have treated a prior victim of Hagenow, and testimony by one of the committee's investigators that Hagenow had confessed to performing abortions during one of their conversations. (*People v. Hagenow*) The committee's evidence that Hagenow performed the abortion that killed Miss Horvatich and that Hagenow lacked any therapeutic intent convinced the court to convict her of murder and to sentence her to twenty years in the Joliet Penitentiary.

abortions; they were subjected to them. (Reed) Rather than deciding to have an abortion, they were compelled by their unfortunate situations "to submit to the ordeal." (Traeger, 37) At the 1904 Symposium on Criminal Abortion, Cook County Coroner Traeger characterized the victims of abortionists as "the young girl in the small town who is led from the straight and narrow path and to hide her shame is compelled to come to the large city." They deserved not scorn, but sympathy: "To these poor victims of circumstance I have but a pitying tear," he exclaimed. (Ibid.)

Doctors also deemed the women who died from abortions to be innocent because they did not posses the ability to reason about the predicament they found themselves in. One doctor pled for "justice and charity for the unfortunate girl who with unreasoning animal feeling attempts to escape her exposure and humiliation by abortion." (Reed, 29) Another described abortion victims as "girls or women who are led astray though their ignorance, foolishness, or misguided affection." (Ladova, 44) Dr. Holmes attributed abortion to women's debilitated moral judgment: noting women's lack of judgment in business matters, he concluded, "If this is true, I am sure that her mind has an analogous bias when she is considered in relation to her desires to be aborted." (Holmes, 29) Holmes recognized that this moral lapse was a departure from the gender norm that ordinarily ascribed moral superiority to women. "It is sad parody on the high virtue and purity of women," he lamented, "that they do not see the evil they do when they seek, and only too often secure, a criminal destruction of their unborn children." (Ibid.)

If women who died from abortions were vulnerable victims, then midwives were the villainous predators who took advantage of them. Painting midwives as vicious and violent criminals, the press referred to them as a "girl murder ring." (*Tribune*, May 30, 1915) They portrayed midwives as literally preying on women. The Cook County Coroner, for example, described these abortionists as "human vultures that thrive off the shame and disgrace" of innocent women. (Traeger, 37) In their investigative report on midwives in Chicago, the physicians of the Committee on Midwives called for the inspection and regulation of a midwife's business after the practitioner had been "turned loose, so to speak, on an ignorant and credulous community." (Bacon et al, 1350)

The women's alleged moral weakness was met by midwives' moral depravity. To begin with, the Chicago Medical Society's Committee on Midwives described midwives as incompetent in matters of health and illness, illiterate, and "filthy beyond description." (Ibid., 1346) "Secure in the fact of her legal right to practice," the committee explained, "she may become as lax in her methods as she chooses, and by her carelessness or overconfidence, endanger the lives of hundreds of mothers and their babes." (Ibid., 1350) In his paper on sepsis, a well-known physician and professor of obstetrics at Northwestern University Medical School described the hands of midwives as "responsible for fevers." (De Lee, 150) He created the impression that midwives, as a class, were too careless or ignorant to take sanitary precautions to protect their patients from infection.

But the disparaging image of midwives went beyond their lack of medical skill to a lack of virtue. Doctors attributed midwives' motivation for performing abortions to their greed and heartlessness; it was their conniving and manipulating nature that allowed them to take advantage of their vulnerable victims. Like *The Jungle's* Madam Haupt who insisted on payment even after killing her patient, the picture painted by Chicago physicians—and the mainstream media aiding the physicians' crusade against midwives—underscored midwives' cruel extortion of sums that their victims could hardly afford. Midwives, they claimed, based the quality of their services according to the amounts they received. One Chicago woman, the *Chicago Daily Tribune* reported, died because "she only had $2.50":

> Ms. S., a midwife, has the reputation of being a "good" abortionist, but when Mrs. M of West 15th St. visited her she had only $2.50. This amount evidently wasn't enough to bring out all the skill of the midwife, and Mrs. M developed blood poisoning. She died." (*Tribune*, June 1, 1915)

The evil of midwifery was deemed irremediable. As the Committee on Midwives concluded, "No permanent reform can be secured with uneducated, untrained, and vicious midwives." (Bacon et al, 1350)

Physicians as Victims of Villainous Women

When it came to physicians charged with murder by abortion, Chicago doctors performed an amazing rhetorical feat. When confronted by their own participation in criminal abortion, the same society of physicians turned the rhetorical paradigm they used against midwives on its head. Instead of casting these more prestigious abortionists as villains as they had midwives, the doctors painted their colleagues as innocent victims of conniving women who sought the operation. Thus, the very women they had portrayed as victims of midwives became the villains in this elite version of the criminal tragedy. Unlike midwives, who were painted as scheming predators, the physician's role in abortions was that of the reluctant participant motivated only by his desire to help. It was the physicians charged with criminal abortion who were victimized not only by the law, but by the very women they campaigned to protect from unscrupulous midwives.

Most often, organized medicine claimed that its physicians had taken no part in the abortion at all. It cast criminal prosecutions of physicians as unjust proceedings against faultless Samaritans who became implicated in fatal abortions only because they reported or tried to repair the damage already inflicted by incompetent midwives. (Holmes 1904; Will) A common defense when the doctor reported an abortion performed by a midwife was that the shrewd woman had falsely named the doctor as the abortionist in retaliation against his revealing her secret.

Physicians who did perform the operation blamed their female patients for compelling them to do it. They claimed that they were at the

Dr. Amante Rongetti. Sentenced to die for performing illegal abortions.
(*Chicago Daily News* negatives collection, DN-0087173. Chicago History Museum.)

75

mercy of women who wielded irresistibly persuasive powers. As one physician put it, "No one dare say her nay. She is responsible to nothing and no one . . ." (Will, 507) Another compared women who implicated doctors in criminal abortion to a "ravenous lion that goes forth seeking whom he may devour." (Reed, 28) Doctors also described these women as "faithless" women who had immorally abandoned their maternal nature. "Among the wealthy society women the evil is the most pronounced, as here the best and the highest human instinct—motherhood—is sacrificed on the altar of vanity and social dissipation." (Ladova, 44) When it came to criminal abortion, argued members of organized medicine, doctors were merely the victims of "the designing intrigue of a faithless woman." (Will, 511)

Doctors described an arsenal of tactics employed by these designing, faithless, abortion-seeking women. Some women used tears to wear down physicians' resolve. Other women supposedly resorted to blackmail, threatening to destroy the doctor's practice if he did not meet her demand for the operation. One doctor described women as so calculating that they used the legal exemption of women from prosecution "as a shield for designing malice and blackmail." (Will, 507) "When it is considered that the testimony of one thus herself immune . . . is competent as against the physician or anyone else," the doctor explained, "it may readily be seen what a pitfall has been prepared for the unsuspecting medical attendant. Indeed, he is placed absolutely at the mercy of any woman whom he attends in a case of abortion." (Ibid.) The same women who were passive and irrational victims of midwives became controlling and designing manipulators of doctors who wielded the power to destroy a doctor's career with their "malicious mischief." (Ibid.)

Physicians also claimed that they experienced unfair treatment in the courts. Jurors could not understand the difficult choices physicians had to make when treating women with unwanted pregnancies. One physician complained that as regarded criminal abortion cases, "the doctor is always 'between the devil and the deep sea' . . . no matter what course he pursues he is amenable, in both opinions and acts, to the untutored judgment and sentimental capriciousness of the average jury. . . ." (Will, 511) Nor could juries fairly assess the evidence against doctors who had merely helped women suffering from midwives' shoddy work. "Physicians, from the very nature of their calling, may be exposed to suspicion, or even be placed in jeopardy by attending women who have had criminal operations performed by others," wrote this same doctor. (Ibid.) He argued that doctors should therefore be entitled to a special evidentiary standard: "As circumstantial evidence may throw suspicion on the innocent physician in the strict performance of professional duty, such evidence cannot have the weight as in other criminal procedures." (Ibid.)

Conclusion

The Chicago Medical Society's remarkable rhetorical strategy likely played a critical role in both increasing the prosecution rates of midwives for murder by abortion and in decreasing the prosecution rates of their colleagues. While portraying midwives who performed abortions as villains and the women they performed them on as their victims, the medical establishment cast doctors as innocent victims of conniving women who sought the operation. Taking advantage of prevailing gender, race, and class stereotypes and norms, physicians deployed this rhetorical tactic to cement their dominance over reproductive medicine. Thus, the Chicago Medical Society campaign against midwives at the turn of the twentieth century provides an illuminating case study of the ongoing relationship between the right to abortion and women's role in society.

References

_____. "End murders by abortions, council order: health committee will start investigation of baby slayers," *Chicago Daily Tribune*, June 2, 1915, 1.

_____. "Lucy Hagenow exposes girl murder ring; guilty midwives pay protection money, says woman convict," *Chicago Daily Tribune*, May 30, 1915, 1.

_____. 1908. "Medical News." *Journal of the American Medical Association*. L: 1356.

_____. 1904. Minutes of Chicago Medical Society Meetings. (Original minutes available at the Chicago Historical Society.)

_____. 2005. Northwestern Historical Homicide Project. (Available online at *http://homicide.northwestern.edu*.)

_____. "Widow dead; new abortion mystery seen," *Chicago Daily Tribune*, June 1, 1915, 1.

_____. 1909. "Women in Medicine (editorial)." *Illinois Medical Journal*. XV: 189–190.

Bacon, C.S. 1904. "The Duty of the Medical Profession in Relation to Criminal Abortion." *Illinois Medical Journal*. VI: 18–24.

Bacon, Charles S., Hamilton, Alice, Hedger, Caroline, Holmes, Rudolph W., and Stowe, Herbert M. 1908. "The Midwives of Chicago." *Journal of the American Medical Association*. L: 1346–1350.

Bradwell v. Illinois, 83 U.S. 130, 16 Wall. 130, 21 L.Ed. 442 (1873)

De Lee, Joseph B. 1906. "Obstetric Asepsis and Antisepsis." *Illinois Medical Journal*. X: 150.

Dobyns, Fletcher. 1904. Comment in "General Discussion," from Symposium presented to the Chicago Medical Society on Criminal Abortion. *Illinois Medical Journal*. VI: 40–42.

Frazier, Carolyn. 2002. "The Efforts of the Chicago Medical Society's Criminal Abortion Committee to Prosecute Murder by Abortion, 1904–1913." (Unpublished paper on file with the authors.)

Holmes, Rudolph Weiser. 1904. "Criminal Abortion; a Brief Consideration of its Relation to Newspaper Advertising. A Report of a Medico-Legal Case." *Illinois Medical Journal*. VI: 29–34.

Holmes, Rudolph W. 1920. "Midwife Practice—an Anachronism." *Illinois Medical Journal*. XXXVIII: 27–31.

Keyes, A. Belcham. 1906. "The Sociologic Duty of a Medical Society to its Members," *Illinois Medical Journal*. X: 498.

Ladova, Rosalie M. 1904. Comment in "General Discussion," from Symposium presented to the Chicago Medical Society on Criminal Abortion. *Illinois Medical Journal*. VI: 43–45.

Olsen, Frances E. 1983. "The Family and the Market; A Study of Ideology and Legal Reform." *Harvard Law Review*. 96:1497.

People v. Hagenow, 236 Ill. 514, 86 N.E. 370.

Petchesky, Rosalind Pollack. 1990. *Abortion and Woman's Choice: The State, Sexuality, and Reproductive Freedom*. Boston: Northeastern University Press.

Reagan, Leslie J. *When Abortion Was a Crime: Women, Medicine and Law in the United States, 1867–1973*. Berkeley: University of California Press.

Reed, Charles B. 1904. "Therapeutic and Criminal Abortion." *Illinois Medical Journal*. VI: 26–29.

Schoen, Johanna. 2005. *Choice and Coercion: Birth Control, Sterilization, and Abortion in Public Health and Welfare*. Chapel Hill: University of North Carolina Press.

Siegel, Reva. 1992. "Reasoning from the Body: A Historical Perspective on Abortion Regulation and Questions of Equal Protection." *Stanford Law Review*. 44:261.

Sinclair, Upton. 2001 [1906]. *The Jungle*. New York: Penguin Putnam/Signet Classic.

Traeger, John E. 1904. "Criminal Abortion as it Comes Before the Coroner's Office." *Illinois Medical Journal*. VI: 35–37.

Will, O.B. 1900. "The Medico-Legal Status of Abortion." *Illinois Medical Journal*. I: 506–511.

Yarros, Dr. R.S., discussion following presentation of Walter B. Dorsett, "Criminal Abortion in its Broadest Sense," 1908. *Journal of the American Medical Association*. LI: 961.

Ilana Diamond Rovner

Law and Passion: Cases Involving People in Extreme Emotional States, and the Consequences

When I sat on the United States District Court for the Northern District of Illinois, that is, the federal trial court, I presided over many cases that touched me deeply. Now it is not that I am not emotionally touched by the cases I hear on the appellate court, the United States Court of Appeals for the Seventh Circuit, but there is a very different dynamic. On the court of appeals we almost never see the defendants in criminal cases, or in the civil cases, for that matter.

It is all done on the briefs, on the papers, and we see and hear only the lawyers. On the trial court, I saw the defendants—sometimes for weeks on end, sometimes for months, and even over a period of years. And in viewing these individuals, and often times their families and their friends, I had a far more intimate view of them than would ever be possible in the court where I now sit.

My reflections come directly from one of those cases in the trial court. It is a case about emotional, not physical, violence. On the bench for twenty-one years, I have dealt with every hateful crime known to humankind, but this case is one of those that has stayed with me. It involves a middle-aged woman who, from extremely humble beginnings, rose to be manager of a very large and prestigious bank in Chicago. She was well educated, having earned a masters degree in finance. The crime she admitted and pled guilty to was a straightforward one—embezzlement from her employer. Embezzlement of a *lot* of money.

It all had to do with a man. As she explained it, there was nothing she would not have done for her lover. *Absolutely nothing.* And so, when he wanted a Mercedes Benz, she found a way to buy him a Mercedes Benz. When his mother wanted to open up a boutique, she found a way for the woman she thought of as her mother-in-law to buy a boutique. As she explained it, when the money went so did he, along with the putative mother-in-law.

At her sentencing, I blathered something, as judges are wont to do, about finding it difficult to understand a more misguided approach to relationships, followed by some nonsense about how surely she must have understood that she could not go undetected, or that sooner or later, she would lose her job and face criminal charges and time in a federal penitentiary.

She took it all in, and then she apologized to her family, to me, to the bank, to the world at large, and said: "I was blind with passion. The only thing I cared about in this world was André. He was everything to me."

When the sentencing was over and she was about to be led away to prison and the court reporter had turned off her equipment, I stood up to leave the bench and said, "Good luck. Do the best you can."

And in response she said, "Oh, judge, if only I had killed him."

Sometimes I think about all the things that I have had to consider in relation to all the men and women that I have sent to prison, or kept in prison, who were propelled by their passion—individuals who seemed just like the people we pass on the street and see in the subway who, until gripped by extreme emotion, would never dream of doing anything that would lead to a prison cell. I would not know where to begin counting the individuals I have seen, up close and personal, who have committed crimes ranging from the nascently devious to the incredibly heinous because of something uncontrollable they called love.

I view families in a very nontraditional way. We all understand that the nuclear family makes up a small percentage of what we have come to know as families. The vast majority of the defendants I have seen in the courts are not part of families in the traditional sense of the word, but often view themselves as being part of a family. They are close in every way—physically, emotionally, and if we can call it that, often professionally.

It is not difficult to understand why the vast public is fascinated by true-life sagas of passion gone mad. Fascinated and repelled, we become voyeurs into places where we do not belong. But judges are voyeurs whom society has decided *do* belong. Probation reports (what we judges refer to as "sentencing memoranda") often read like the steamiest of novels, allowing the reader—the judge—to view an individual's life in the most minute detail. Both repelled by and drawn to these true-life manuscripts, I am never more aware than at sentencing of the fact that there is always something new that has the capacity to surprise and shock.

So let us think about my defendant's statement, "If only I had killed him."

What was she saying? Instead of taking responsibility for her actions, was she blaming it all on André? Was she saying that if he had not been in her life none of her aberrant behavior would have occurred? Or, was she saying that if she had killed him it would have been better for her—even if it meant a lifetime in prison, rather than a few years? Did she think that if she had killed him, she would not have had to obsess about him any longer? That he would be gone forever? *Dead?*

In the final analysis, does it really matter? We regard people as being answerable for their criminal acts. Society does not care about the root of the defendant's obsession. We think that although obsession purports to have an object, obsession is actually about the obsessed. After all, it was she who chose André, thus intertwining her passion and her obsession with her crime.

As a judge, I am forced to dissect a person's crime and reach a particular judgment of responsibility so that society will say: "Good. Justice has been done." In his novel *The Reader*, as certain terrible revelations became more damning, the author Bernhard Schlink wrote:

> I had to point at Hanna. But the finger I pointed at her turned back to me. I had loved her. Not only had I loved her, I had chosen her. I tried to tell myself that I had known nothing of what she had done when I chose her. I tried to talk myself into the state of innocence in which children love their parents. But love of our parents is the only love for which we are not responsible.[1]

In our federal system, because of the federal sentencing guidelines, we are given a narrow range of months and years within which to punish. We are asked to put people in mathematical boxes. How much money did you steal? Four points. Did you use a gun to commit the crime? Two more points. We add up the points and the total tells us how serious a crime was, and how long a sentence should be. One's guilt can thus be calculated and categorized so that the sentence is not dependent on the judge alone, but is objectively "fair." Blame and punishment are measured out like a recipe.

Society may say "Good," but there is no way to explain how unsatisfactory that is for me as the judge, because the law can almost never assign blame properly. The crime is not necessarily the person. The person has a history, a family, disadvantages, privileges, loves, hates, fears, and hopes. As the last person that a defendant sees before being sent away, it is as if all of society's assignment of blame is being translated through the person of the judge. Although there is not a form of violence that I have not dealt with over the years, it is always the emotional violence that I encounter that fascinates me.

It is no wonder that I am taken with the story of Adele H., the daughter of Victor Hugo, the great French writer. Her encoded diaries were discovered in 1960. They give us a look into a young woman's obsession with a handsome army officer who is also a shameless blackguard. Her obsessive and irrational love led her to follow him to what in 1863, was one of the ends of the earth—Nova Scotia. Adele wrote to her father and mother telling them that she had married the lieutenant—a total fabrication. Indeed, her journals are filled with delusional descriptions of the life she only fantasized. Many of her actions would have put her in a prison today. She was the dictionary definition of a stalker.

What is so powerful about the story of Adele H. is that it is true—every word of it. She completely debased herself, believing that by doing so, she could gain the love of a gold-digger, a gambler, and womanizer. I am not certain how many of the women whom I have encountered in criminal cases would have recognized the name of Victor Hugo, let alone that of Adele Hugo. But I can think of quite a few who had a lot in common with her. There is not anything they would not do in order to appease the objects of their passion.

In an article a number of years ago, Joe Morgenstern reminded us that "[o]ne section of the current California criminal code, dealing with malice aforethought, contains a poetic phrase left over from English law that aptly describes obsession's source: 'an abandoned and malignant heart.'"[2]

Lest you believe that my view is that only women are obsessed, I assure you that through the years I have seen many obsessed men. One person who would recognize the names of Victor and Adele

Hugo is the former Chief Judge of the New York State Court of Appeals, Sol Wachtler, who stalked both his ex-lover and her daughter, and for that crime, served fifteen months in prison by order of a federal judge.

Julie Carlstrom, a Los Angeles family therapist, has said:

Blame should be a legal or political issue. The therapeutic issue should be health and safety. It may seem terribly unfair to take someone who's truly being victimized and say, "You have to look at your own part in this," yet it's the only way to protect the person and to help her protect herself. At the least, you have to resolve the reason why someone continues to tolerate or excuse dangerous behavior, or they'll very likely be sucked right back into the same dynamic.[3]

Well, it seems as if we judges and the criminal justice system have found a way to keep these individuals from being sucked right back. We put them away. And with the federal sentencing guidelines that I mentioned earlier, we put them away for a long time. In doing so, we do not think of them as romanticized versions of Adele Hugo. Instead, in the cold, sparse daylight of a courtroom, it goes something like this:

You have admitted devising and executing a scheme that defrauded the Northern Trust Company of a total of 566 thousand, 864 dollars and fifteen cents. What you did was an absolutely stunning crime. You were a woman who simply could not say "no" to someone you cared about. Your need to please him has simply overwhelmed and ruined your life. I am very hopeful that you will get the psychological care that you obviously need to deal with your emotional problems.

And then, a bit later:

I hereby sentence you to 60 months in the custody of the Attorney General of the United States, to be followed by three years of supervised release. As a special condition of your supervised release, you will be ordered to pay restitution not in excess of 566 thousand dollars, which can realistically never come to pass unless you win the lottery. You have the right to appeal your sentence.

These are not the romantic words of novels, these words are the exact antithesis of passionate literature. But these words assign responsibility and these words allocate blame in the society in which we live.

Notes

1. Bernhard Schlink, *The Reader* 170 (Carol Brown Janeway trans., Vintage Books, 1st intl. ed. 1997).

2. Joe Morgenstern, *Obsession. (psychopathic behavior in men toward women)*, *Playboy*, Dec. 1, 1994 at 82.

3. Julie Carlstrom, as quoted in Morgenstern, *supra*, n. 2.

Marianne Constable[1]

Chicago Husband-Killing and the "New Unwritten Law"

In April 1919, the *Chicago Tribune* reported that Mrs. Emma Simpson shot her husband, from whom she was separated but refused to divorce, in court, in proceedings concerning alimony payments. Mrs. Simpson told a reporter that she would defend herself. "I will need no attorney—the new unwritten law, which does not permit a married man to love another woman, will be my defense. It will save me." And, she continued, "I will tell my whole story to the jury and they will free me. I am perfectly confident of that."[2]

Mrs. Simpson was wrong, it turns out, on several counts. Rather than defending herself, she retained Clarence Darrow as her attorney. He indeed defended her by arguing to the all-male jury, "You've been asked to treat a man and a woman the same—but you can't. No manly man can." The jury deliberated only half an hour, however, before finding Simpson, at the prosecutor's urging, insane *and* guilty.

If Emma Simpson thought the new unwritten law would save her, others wanted to save Chicago from the new unwritten law. A June 1912 article in the *Chicago Inter-Ocean* asked:

> Can a woman be convicted of murder in Chicago? Has some intangible defense taken growth that renders her immune from the treatment that would be accorded a man under similar circumstances? . . .

The questions have nothing to do with the probable guilt or inno-
cence of any certain fair defendant. It has been the cumulative ef-
fect of year after year of acquittals that has forced on [readers']
minds a suspicion of the existence of a new "unwritten law," hold-
ing a protecting wing over the heads of the weaker sex.[3]

The article refers to "almost a score" of Chicago women, charged
with murdering their husbands or some member of their families, who
were acquitted. The article also mentions "an almost equal number of
women, originally hail[ing] from Chicago, [who] have been arraigned on
charges of like crimes committed in other portions of the country"—one
of whom was said even now to be living in a flat on the South Side of
Chicago.

What was the "new unwritten law"? Cook County police records
suggest that 265 women killed their husbands (including common law
husbands) in Chicago between 1870 and 1930; of these only about 24
were convicted and some of these convictions were vacated.[4] Of 17 con-
victions of white women between 1875 and 1920, according to Jeffrey
Adler, one woman's sentence was remitted, two were found criminally
insane, and two were sentenced to terms of only one year.[5] From 1921
to 1930, only 12 of the 186 women who killed their husbands seem to
have been convicted and to have served their time. Even before women
were allowed on juries in Illinois then, and contrary to received wisdom,
all-male coroner's juries, grand juries, and petit or trial juries, at least in
Chicago, exonerated most wives who killed their husbands.

Perusal of New York and St. Louis newspapers suggests that
Chicago's articulation of concern over husband-killer acquittals was
unique, although the fact of such acquittals may not have been.[6] In any
event, Chicago husband-killing cases were "spectacular" in both senses
of the term. The woman journalist who covered some of the cases in the
mid-1920s for the *Chicago Tribune* wrote a play that later became the
basis for the recent hit musical and film "Chicago." Husband-killing
cases appear throughout the twentieth century in many forms of popu-
lar culture: as short stories, plays, silent film, musical drama, film.

But what exactly was Chicago's new unwritten law? Available
documents for the most part reveal what it was not: formal legal records
indicate when the so-called new unwritten law—as the exoneration of
women who killed their husbands (or other intimates)—failed. Grand
jury indictments, for instance, occur when coroners do not free a sus-
pect. Prosecutors go to trial when grand juries fail to discharge an ac-

86

cused. Prison records (and those of probations and pardons) exist when defendants are not acquitted. And yet it is to these writings and others that one must turn to explore "the unwritten." The unwritten, in these cases, is a "law"—at least occasionally in name—which, like all modern American positive law, raises questions about the doing of justice and the transmission of law through texts.

A Legal Right?

In the only scholarly article I have found that mentions the new unwritten law directly, Jeffrey Adler writes that "The new unwritten law gave a woman the right to use lethal force in resisting an abusive husband." Claiming that "The overwhelming majority of the women who looked to this affirmative defense did not claim that adultery had occurred, and none of these killers had caught her spouse in flagrante delicto," he argues that

> In order to secure an acquittal (on the ground of self-defense), the woman had to demonstrate that she had been the victim of wife beating. Having established a history of abuse, she was then legally justified in killing her husband, according to this theory.

Adler goes on to quote Emma Simpson's case—leaving out the phrase "which does not permit a married man to love another woman."[6a]

Was the new unwritten law a formal legal right and affirmative defense, as Adler suggests? Might it have been a battered women's syndrome defense for its time? Was it somehow analogous to—or, better, a distortion of—the "old unwritten law" or honor defense used by men who, upon finding a wife, daughter or sister in flagrante delicto, killed the other man? Was "new" a way of referring to the novelty of women invoking particular legal defenses? Or was it a reference to women becoming beneficiaries of what was also considered an "unwritten law," that of jury nullification or the right to negate official law?

Unfortunately, Chicago (Cook County) criminal court records for 1902 to 1927 have all been destroyed. It is therefore impossible to confirm that the phrase was used at trial. So far, perusal of pre-1902 and post-1927 files don't indicate its use. (The post-1927 files are especially interesting because they contain, for cases with jury trials, both the instructions given and those requested but denied.) Further, because the trials resulted largely in acquittals, there is but one appellate case; the

Nitti case, as one would expect, is quite atypical, and does not seem to include the phrase. (The issues in the 1923 trial and appeal of Italian immigrants Isabella Nitti and her new husband Peter Crudelle for the murder of Sabelle's first husband, about which more will be said later, provide hundreds of pages that reveal more about the state of legal practice in Chicago at the time than about the new unwritten law.) Based on newspaper accounts, coroners' records, grand jury indictments, and the few trial and appellate materials that exist, though, there are still four—nonexclusive—interpretations of the new unwritten law.

One interpretation of the new unwritten law—that apparently invoked by Emma Simpson when she speaks of finding her husband in a hotel room with another woman four years earlier and to which she refers when she says that the new unwritten law "will not permit a married man to love another woman"—takes the new unwritten law to be analogous to the "old unwritten law" or the nineteenth-century custom, apparently inherited from Europe, whereby a man who found his wife, sister, or daughter *in flagrante delictoe*, had a heat-of-passion or provocation defense should he kill the woman's lover. Clarence Darrow, who represented Emma Simpson, later refers to the unwritten law (neither "old" nor "new") in the context of a 1932 Hawaii case, which he lost, in which he defended a husband whom he acknowledged was "legally" guilty, for killing the men who accosted his wife. As in Maurine Watkins' 1926 play, "Chicago," the old unwritten law applied to men who killed their rivals, rather than the objects of their ostensible affections. (In Watkins' play, which later became the basis for several works including the recent blockbuster musical film, "Chicago," a husband kills a man whom he does not know is his wife's lover and the "unwritten law" defense is said to be unavailable to him.)

The new unwritten law, unlike the old unwritten law then, concerned the killing of a spouse or partner rather than the rival. As Emma Simpson understood it though, it protected the woman who killed a husband who had betrayed her. Betrayal however actually was seldom an issue in cases, unlike Simpson's, where acquittals occurred. Husband-killing cases where "jealousy" or "betrayal" or the granting or receiving of "attentions" were mentioned (according to the CHHP or in newspaper articles) tended to be cases that led to conviction, rather than exoneration or acquittal. This becomes especially clear in the 1920s.

During the 1920s, numbers of husband-killings grew. Of course, so had Chicago's population. And so did the use of guns in such killings. In the last three decades of the nineteenth century, according to the

CHHP, 18 wives and mistresses killed their partners, three of whom were police officers. In the decade from 1900 to 1909, 22 women killed their partners; from 1910 to 1919, 35 did so; from 1920 to 1929, 169 did so, 23 in the year 1929 alone. This figure would be matched only by the 24 husband-killings of 1930. Of the twelve convictions that were not vacated in the 193 husband-killings that took place during the eleven-year period from 1920 through 1930, jealousy was an issue in at least five of the disputes. Grace Pearl shot her husband in a "fit of jealousy," according to the police record; Marcelle Hernandez shot her husband during "a domestic quarrel due to jealousy"; Beulah Conner's "motive" for shooting was said to be jealousy. Tillie Evans stabbed her husband "in the home of another woman"; Angeline Clark stabbed her common law husband "for speaking to another woman on the phone." Jealousy and betrayal certainly did not provide grounds for exoneration under a new unwritten law, although some—like Emma Simpson—perceived it to be so.

A second interpretation of the new unwritten law, closer to that claimed by Adler then, takes the new unwritten law to be an early version of something like a battered women's syndrome defense. Like men's justified provocation to anger under the old unwritten law, the new unwritten law might be thought to cover instances in which another emotion—of "fear" of a man—provoked a woman to kill. Indeed coroner's records confirm that many of the killings occurred during the course of one of many struggles, where a possibly intoxicated husband came home to a waiting wife. Weapons were usually guns—but also kitchen knives, pokers, stove pipes; killings took place in kitchens, drawing rooms, bedrooms—clearly "domestic" violence. Both coroner's records and newspaper articles time and again speak of witnesses testifying as to the violent quarrels and fights between women and the husbands they killed.

Whether and how during this period a woman's state of mind was linked to her abuse, as is often an issue in contemporary cases, remains to be investigated. The coroner's jury record (through 1911) does not seem to touch the issue. Coroner's records most often describe the cause of death in medical terms and in passive voice. Hence, Thomas Barker's death was "due to Fracture of Skull, said fracture received caused by being hit on the head with a piece of a stove held in the hands of and thrown by one Mary Ann Barker." Ollie Mitchell came to his death "from shock and hemorrhage due to an incised wound in the chest, said wound inflicted with a knife held in the hand of one Delilah Mitchell . . ." A coroner's jury could recommend that a woman "be held to the Grand Jury until discharged by due Course of law," although it seems to increasingly have stated its "opinion that the accused was justified in protecting her life and the lives and her children" or its belief that "her act was one of self defense. We therefore recommend that she be released immediately from police custody."

Even when the six-man coroner's juries did not exonerate women who had been subjected to brutality, however, grand juries failed to indict; should grand juries continue the case, prosecutors filed no bills; and when they did so, judges as well as juries acquitted the women. As Judge Kersten declared in the 1905 Hopkins case:

> The evidence in this case clearly establishes the fact that the deceased was in the habit of maltreating, abusing and beating this woman . . .[7]

The assistant state attorney's speech to the trial jury in the case of Virginia Troupe—the one white woman to be convicted of manslaughter and sentenced to the minimum penalty of 14 years in the penitentiary before 1920—bespeaks the threat that a defense grounded in a wife's having been beaten posed: "If this jury sets the precedent that any woman who is attacked or is beaten by her husband can shoot him, there won't be many husbands left in Chicago six months from now."[8] (The 19-year-old Mrs. Troupe, by the way, had admitted that she and her husband were quarreling over attentions, to which her 15-year-old brother-in-law testified, that she had received from another man.[9] She ultimately served eight years in the female penitentiary of Joliet Prison.[10])

One conviction of a husband-killer that did not mention jealousy or betrayal reverses the usual spouse-beating roles. Mrs. Hilda Exlund, described as a woman "of powerful physique" who had been "a husband beater for years," was convicted of murder in 1919 (she too was sentenced to 14 years at Joliet Prison). The foreman of the trial jury of 12 married men who convicted her, claimed that "The fact that she was a woman did not enter into our discussion or deliberation. She was guilty and should be punished."[11] Neighbors called as witnesses had said that the defendant, "a large woman," "continually abused her husband," who was described as "a small man," and "called him names."[12]

A third interpretation of the new unwritten law then, a variation on the second, conceives of it less as a battered women's syndrome defense for its time than as self-defense in the case of women. Acquittals of wives—like exonerations earlier in the process—may have been based on self-defense. Not only do jury instructions available in post–1927 cases bear this out, but as early as 1905, Judge Kersten states (of the Hopkins case) that:

> . . . [The evidence] clearly establishes that on the night in question [the deceased] made a brutal and vicious assault on her, and she had a right, under the circumstances, if she honestly believed she was in great danger of losing her life, or of receiving great bodily harm, to use such force as was necessary to protect herself; and what was necessary, under the circumstances, no person on earth could tell but herself.

And as Kersten put it:

> A woman, when married, does not become the chattel or slave of her husband. She has the same rights that her husband has, and her husband is bound to preserve these rights to the same degree that she is bound to preserve his.

Six of Kersten's colleagues also commented on the Doyle holding for the press. They noted that women were no longer men's property—"A woman is not a man's slave because she is wedded to him"—and that women had the right to defend themselves—"The law of self-defense applies to women as well as it does to men." The *Record-Herald* noted that "the result of the [Hopkins] trial was no surprise . . . The surprise came in the fact that the coroner's jury had not previously exonerated her." Already in 1902 in fact, in an early husband-killing case, the wife's acquittal was simply reported as a matter of self-defense. (Compare the much earlier 1867 trial of unmarried Mary Cosgriff, aka "Irish Mollie" Trussell, however, for whom the new unwritten law was apparently not yet available. In what the *Chicago Times* in its report portrayed as a spectacularly sentimental case, Cosgriff's self-defense claim failed. Eleven of the jurors who convicted Cosgriff of manslaughter for shooting George Trussell, "a gambler and 'sporting' man," her long-time lover, and the father of her ten-year-old son, wrote the governor after the trial, however, petitioning for her pardon. The state's attorney, having "examined the daily morning papers of this city published on last Saturday and Monday containing an account of the trial," declared that the newspapers "contain a substantially correct statement of the evidence." With the trial judge's concurrence, these articles were forwarded the governor. They provide the only trial documentation in the file of Cosgriff's pardon, which the governor granted.)

If the "unwritten law" in the cases above refers to self-defense (as it also does in a short story by Nelson Algren in the 1930s), the "new" of the new unwritten law seems to apply to the extension of self-defense to women during a period in which emergence of—and anxiety over—the "new woman" was paramount.

A fourth interpretation then is that while "new" may refer to women, "unwritten law" refers more broadly to jury nullification or to what was not perceived as formal or official law at all. In law review articles of the time, "unwritten law" refers to any instance of what we *now* call "jury nullification." Legal and political justifications for "jury nullification" in the United States seem to shift from a grounding in natural law or morality in the mid-nineteenth century, to due process concerns in the early twentieth. The "new unwritten law" could mark a moment of similarly shifting understandings of women's roles and rights. As women became visible in the legal system, the new unwritten law could refer to an as-yet unresolved and yet clearly changing situation, made explicit in husband-killing cases, in which terms for the articulation, in positive law, of women's place in society ultimately shifted from moral language concerning the domestic sphere to a procedural language of rights.

The four interpretations above suggest that rather than being, as Adler suggests, a formal legal right or affirmative defense as such, the new unwritten law was how the popular press referred to what was apparently widely perceived as not being official law at all. The four interpretations are not incompatible. Jurors seemed to some, if not to many, to be carving out exceptions to the formal law for women, even as women's roles were changing and judges were insisting that perceived exceptions were in keeping with official articulations of the law of self-defense anyway.

The Right Story?

Despite claims such as those of Judge Kersten, the perception that male juries and the male-dominated system of the time somehow failed to properly apply the law to women persists today in various forms. In 1917, before women were allowed on juries in many jurisdictions and well before the first woman served on an Illinois jury in 1940, Susan Keating Glaspell wrote a prize-winning short story, "A Jury of Her Peers," about a woman who kills her husband. The story, resurrected in the 1970s by the movement to valorize and reclaim women's voices in literature, is usually read as an indictment of the male-dominated legal system. Glaspell based the story on a one-act play, "Trifles," that she had written two years earlier. The play itself was apparently inspired by the first (April 1901) trial of Margaret Hossack, accused of having murdered her husband, which Glaspell had covered as a reporter in Iowa.[14]

The story tells of a visit by two women to the home of a widow whose husband had been found strangled in bed the day before, with a rope around his neck. The women have come to fetch an apron and shawl for Minnie Wright, who is now in jail. They accompany their husbands—the sheriff and the farmer who found the man's body—and a county attorney (or prosecutor), who are inspecting the dreary house and property, the scene of the crime, for clues. The men, who seem to think that Mrs. Wright did kill her husband, find nothing to suggest a motive. They make fun of the women who are occupied in the kitchen with the mundane things of Wright's life—the interrupted task of pouring sugar and wiping down the table, preserves that have spilled over, an oven that does not work properly, quilting pieces that are stitched more erratically than the rest. As they gather Mrs. Wright's much-mended affairs, the two women notice a broken bird cage. Looking, on their own initiative, for Mrs. Wright's sewing scissors to bring her, they find underneath the things in her quilting basket, a pretty box. Wrapped in red silk in the box is a canary whose neck has been wrung. At the end of the story, Mrs. Hale, the farmer's wife, and Mrs. Peters, the sheriff's wife whom the attorney describes as "married to the law," take and hide the dead bird, the only evidence that seems to provide a motive.

The 1900 murder that inspired this story occurred, not in the urban wilderness of Chicago, but in rural Iowa.[15] At the coroner's inquest and at Hossack's first trial, which resulted in a life sentence of hard labor, the prosecutor insisted on entering evidence of family disputes to establish Hossack's motive for murder. Neighbors and others testified as to John Hossack's cruelty, threats, and rage toward his wife and children, even as they suggested that such family matters should have been kept private. The defense, by contrast, continually (and largely unsuccessfully, it seems) objected that such evidence was irrelevant. Hossack herself refused to testify as to any maltreatment by her husband—in her silence hiding, as did Minnie Wright's peers for a different reason, what we, again like Minnie Wright's peers, would tend to consider a crucial aspect of her case.

In contrast to Hossack's Iowa trial, in which beatings were perceived to establish a wife's motives and lead to conviction, during the first three decades of the twentieth century in Chicago, beatings seem rather to justify women's lethal responses and to lead to their exoneration. Clearly, differing expectations and perceptions—in Chicago and in Iowa, in fact and in fiction—of violence and justice, of women's roles in marriage and in public, are at issue. They emerge both in what is said and what is unsaid in various texts. How is one to understand these differences given the sometimes contradictory messages of public records and written texts, however? What are we to make of the silences and speech of various sources?

In Chicago, at least one Cook County prosecutor or state's attorney argued that women should be allowed on juries. He argued in 1912 for women's jury service, not—as Glaspell might be thought to suggest—because of women's greater understanding of or insight into their sisters' experiences, but because he thought that women would see through the wiles and manipulations of their fair husband-killing sisters. Men "can never overlook the sex element and judge impartially and without emotion. The defendant need not be beautiful; if she merely appears feminine on the stand, she is safe," State's Attorney Wayman suggested.[16] Was Wayman's position yet another manifestation of the male-dominated legal system in which women were relegated to particular stereotypical roles? And if so, what of it? What links can be made between views like his and the eventual extension of jury service to women?

Even women lawyers—women were admitted to the bar in Illinois long before they had the right to vote or to serve on juries—were not above manipulating—or claiming to manipulate—the system. Helen Cirese, an extremely fashionable and photogenic Italian-American lawyer and, at age 20 in 1920, the youngest woman to graduate from De Paul Law School, reflected in a 1940 interview on her work on a team of Italian-American attorneys seeking a retrial in the 1923 Chicago case of Isabelle Nitti-Crudelle. According to Cirese, who also successfully defended Chicago husband-killer Lela Foster in 1921, the fact that a string of beautiful women had all been acquitted of killing their husbands suggested to her that Nitti had only to be taught English and dressed up for her appeal to succeed. How does this public recollection seventeen years after the fact square with the hundreds of printed pages on record that constitute appellant's briefs and dwell on the procedural inadequacies of Nitti's earlier trial—and in particular on mistakes by her trial attorney?

These are only a couple of the many issues surrounding stories of Chicago husband-killers and the new unwritten law's ambiguous boundaries between fact and fiction. A "law" at least in name, the unwritten law makes its somewhat paradoxical appearance in writings. In the silences and speech of its texts, in their facts and fictions, the new unwritten law emerges as one early twentieth-century possibility of justice—and, of course, of injustice—which has yet to be more fully explored. Traces of the new unwritten law offer the possibility of a history of law, in which what is mundane and everyday—like a dead canary—can not only be hidden, but can be found— and perhaps hidden—again. In the transmission and transformation of traces of the new unwritten law, law's dynamic character emerges as a subversive legacy—the story of finding and hiding and perhaps finding and losing justice again.

Afterword on Sources

Additional information and background on homicide cases from the Chicago Historical Homicide Project can be found in the archives of the Chicago History Museum, the Chicago Public Library, The Newberry Library, Northwestern University Library and other collections. Appellate case records and, for some cases, trial transcripts may be preserved in the archives of the Illinois Supreme Court. The Illinois State Archives include additional sources for prison records, such as the Joliet Prison historical records. Coroner's records may be found through IRAD, the Illinois Regional Archives Depositories. Details can be found on the Chicago Historical Homicide Project website: www.homicide.northwestern.edu under *references*.

Notes

1. Thanks to Leigh Bienen, Leslieanne Cachola, Shannon Jackson, Sara Kendall, Janisha Sabnani, and Shalini Satkunanandan, for help with these preliminary formulations of this material.
2. April 26, 1919, Chicago Tribune
3. "No Chicago Woman Convicted of Murder; Scores of Fair Sex Arraigned and Tried for Killing but In Every Case Jury Has Failed to Hold Guilty," *Chicago Inter-Ocean*, June 22, 1912.
4. Much of this data comes from the Chicago Historical Homicide Project (CHHP), supplemented by other sources. Many thanks are owed to Leigh Beinen at Northwestern University School of Law School for making accessible a database of a Cook County police log, maintained consistently from 1870 to 1930, that records more than 11,000 homicides. The log contains names and situations of all the victims of killings that po-

lice were called in on, including information about suspects and, often, the outcomes of legal actions.

5. Jeffrey S. Adler, "'I Loved Joe, But I had to Shoot Him': Homicide by Women in Turn-of-the-Century Chicago," *Journal of Criminal Law and Criminology* 92 (2002): 867-897, using records from note 4 and others. I am indebted to this incredibly informative article. Adler found that "every white woman who killed her husband between August, 1905 and October, 1918 was exonerated or acquitted, totaling thirty-five consecutive cases" (884; note that two women were never charged or tried and a third committed suicide). See also Jeffrey S. Adler, "'We've Got a Right to Fight; We're Married': Domestic Homicide in Chicago, 1875-1920," *Journal of Interdisciplinary History* 34 (Summer 2003): 27-48.

6. In a study of prosecutorial records of late nineteenth-century New York, Carolyn B. Ramsey argues that wife-killers and other institutionally and politically marginal types who killed were convicted in disproportionately high numbers. "The Discretionary Power of 'Public' Prosecutors in Historical Perspective," 39 Am. Crim. L. Rev. (2000) 1309. Elsewhere she argues that legal treatment of wife killers between 1880 and 1920 in New York and Denver differed from that of husband killers. Women were treated more leniently than men and evidence of past abuse was viewed sympathetically in female defendants' cases, but not in male defendants' cases. "Intimate Homicide: Gender and Crime Control, 1880-1920," Univ. Colo. L. Rev. 77 (2006): 101-191.

6a. Adler, "Loved Joe," 882.

7. Rec-Her, Tu 3/21/1905.

8. *Inter Ocean,* W 1/10/1906.

9. *Chicago Tribune,* Aug. 10, 1905.

10. Joliet Prison records.

11. *Chicago Tribune,* Jan. 17, 1919.

12. *Chicago Tribune,* Jan. 15, 1919.

13. *Chicago Record-Herald,* March 21, 1905.

14. See Ben-Zvi, Linda, "'Murder, She Wrote': The Genesis of Susan Glaspell's Trifles," in Ben-Zvi, Linda, ed., *Susan Glaspell: Essays on her Theater and Fiction* (Ann Arbor: Univ. of Mich. Press, 1995) and many others on the origins of Glaspell's story, as well as its later reception.

15. Patricia L. Bryan, "Stories in Fiction and in Fact: Susan Glaspell's A Jury of Her Peers and the 1901 Murder Trial of Margaret Hossack," 49 Stan. L. Rev. (1997) 1293. Information in this paragraph about the Hossack trial comes from Bryan, "Stories," 1303, 1317-1325, 1330-32, 1339-41.

16. See "Women Jurors to Try Feminine Murderers," Vol. XX, No. 11, p. 328 (Nov. 1912), (https//: www.law.stanford.edu/library/wlhbp/articles.html accessed 11/17/03 at 3:30 pm.)

Jana Harris

The Laundress by the Lake, 1892

The Hardest Thing
Butter Creek Schoolhouse, 1873

From a sod floor beaten to hardpack
By use, we watched Miss Teacher sweep
Loose grit, putting down
Gunny bag carpet except for a square
Near the stove for us to scratch
Our letters and numbers into the ground.
During the first year, she
Boarded at our house
As part of her pay. At night
We tried not to stare as Miss
Teacher climbed into bed
With all her clothes on,
Changing under the covers.
We rode, three to a horse,
The four miles to school.

Neither blackboard nor books, only
Tattered Bible and ancient almanac
To practice geography and spelling.
Our only light, the open door until
Hollowed potatoes made perfect

Candlesticks. Light or dark,
We mapped St. Paul's missionary journeys
Compared with equal distances down
The road to home: If Columbia Gorge
Was our Jordan, then
Mount Hood our Sinai and
—without question—Umatilla Landing
(with Spanish dance halls and
Twelve liquor emporiums)
The Wilderness of Sin. But
When Miss Teacher made us hold
The scratching stick like a pen,
Pretending to drip the ink,
Now blot, blow dry

—that was the hardest thing.

Jana Harris, *The Dust of Everyday Life*, an Epic Poem of the Pacific Northwest

The Laundress by the Lake, 1892:
Using Historical Documents in Creating Fictional and Poetic Narratives with an Eye toward Re-evaluating the Evidence

For years I have been writing fiction and poetry about the day-to-day lives of Northwest frontier women and children who lived more than a hundred years ago. In doing this, I have felt myself to be conducting a writerly investigation of people and events which otherwise would have been forgotten. The fiction, not surprisingly, came out in the novel form; the poetry in the form of linked dramatic monologues—a sort of confluence of historical narrative and poetic imagery. My work is informed by travel and archival materials including photographs, diaries, journals, household and personal artifacts, newspapers, reminiscences, interviews, obituaries, court reports, maps, legal files and documents, school records, scrapbooks, and whatever else might fuel the imagination. In one mental pile I collect the elements of narrative—the fuel of fiction; in the other I collect striking images—the life's blood of poetry. Until I find a suitable vehicle, odd images, narrative fragments, and bits of language get stuck in my head for years.

My first poetry book in this vein centered on the women who immigrated to the Okanogan Valley in north-central Washington State between the years of 1886-1893, and was titled *Oh How Can I Keep on Singing? Voices of Pioneer Women*. While doing research for this collection—as well as for a novel concerning a nineteenth-century woman prospector—I stumbled upon the infamous silver mining town of Ruby, which was, for a brief time, government seat of the newly organized Okanogan County, Washington Territory. Memoirist Guy Waring dubbed Ruby Camp "the Babylon of the West." Indeed, the more I read about Ruby, the more its legal code (or lack of it) intrigued me. The goings-on in this silver mining town leapt out from the archives and seemed to strongly resemble many allegedly democratic governments run like personal fiefdoms.

These are some of the known statistics concerning Ruby, Washington Territory: In 1886, after the Columbia Indian Reservation, commonly known as the Moses Reservation, was returned to the public domain (meaning it was taken away from the Native Peoples, the Sinlahekin, Moses, and the Okanogans among them), the isolated high desert of the Okanogan Valley west of the Okanogan River, east of the Cascade Mountain Range, and south of the Canadian border was opened up to mineral claim and white settlement. In a nutshell, the indigenous people who had lived, gathered, and hunted in the area, some for time immemorial, were *enticed* to move elsewhere. As one might imagine, this caused them considerable consternation.

Ruby City, as the camp came to be called, was founded in 1887 and flourished until 1893 when the gold standard was initiated and the price of silver plummeted forcing the nation into further economic depression. By 1899 Ruby was a ghost town. The camp was named for the Ruby Mine located on Ruby Hill on the eastern slopes of the Cascades, the camp springing up in a forested canyon near the banks of Salmon Creek. During its short life the town of Ruby was ravaged by fire, destroyed by flood, and devastated by snow slide.

To get to Ruby City from the Pacific Coast, a prospector would have to walk east from Seattle for about six days crossing the Cascades to Wenatchee, then walk north for two more days. Crossing the Columbia River at Wild Goose Bill Condon's ferry, the prospector continued in a northwesterly direction, crossing the Okanogan River at "Pard" (short for "Partner") Cummings' ferry to the settlement of Alma after which followed a thirteen-mile trudge into the mountains. If a prospector came from the East Coast, he would ride the rail line across country to its terminus in Sprague, forty miles south of Spokane, then journey by stage or wagon one hundred and fifty dusty miles west to Ruby a.k.a. Mudtown.

Ruby's main street stretched north and south for a quarter of a mile. At its peak, the town boasted of twenty saloons, dance halls, and card rooms including one faro hall; a bank owed by one of the saloonkeepers; six general stores and a post office, which was located in a store operated by Judge George J. Hurley; a newspaper; a schoolhouse, which doubled as a community dance hall; a brewery; a jail; a county auditor's office; an assay office that weighed and determined the value of precious metals; an unrecorded number of brothels; two to three hotels, which housed mining investors, engineers, and visiting dignitaries; and a concentrating mill (which reduced the amount of ore shipped to smelters) connected by a mile-long aerial tramway up to the Second Thought Mine on Ruby Hill. The town government consisted of a county auditor who registered mineral claims; a sheriff (Philip Perkins); a U.S. marshal, coroner, and justice of the peace (Richard Price), a mayor and five councilmen. Memoirists claim that either a shooting or a robbery occurred

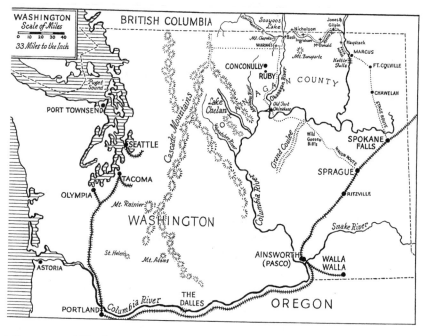

The state of Washington.
(Frontispiece to the book, *My Pioneer Past*, by Guy Waring (Boston: Bruce Humphries, Inc. 1936.))

almost once a week. Guy Waring remembered few criminal convictions and most pertinent documents pertaining to this period were destroyed if indeed they ever existed. Prostitution in Ruby appears to have been legal and it was the mind-set of the Victorian era that only by the provision of bordellos could *modest* women retain their virtue. In his memoir, Guy Waring reported that every conceivable crime was committed in this town except for "interfering with virtuous women." Sexual assault has always been underreported.

One of the few professional women living in Ruby was a madam by the name of Little Ella (no last name given). Described as a large fleshy woman, Ella murdered without remorse one of her clients, then escaped prosecution by "taking a sudden visit to Spokane." The history books put forth these theories concerning a possible motive: a) the victim, a miner, had given Ella's girls a social disease, b) the victim had argued with Ella, and she shot him in an effort to have the last word, and c) Ella had had a headache and had been annoyed by the victim—none of which seem to add up to the kind of rage that would prompt a homicide. In any case, Ella returned to her establishment a few months after the murder and resumed business as if nothing had happened. The incident is documented only because either Ruby's sheriff or the county auditor—accounts vary—stumbled over the body when leaving Ella's establishment the morning after the shooting and felt compelled to report the miner's death.

During the short life of this Bret Hart-like mining camp, few women of any sort resided in Ruby. At its height, the town's population boasted of anywhere from five hundred to a thousand males and fifty females most of whom were employed in the brothels. The mayor was often in the saloon business. The sheriff's duties, in addition to keeping what peace was possible in a community where claim-jumping inflamed tempers, alcohol flowed freely day and night, and everyone carried firearms, was the collection of licensing fees from the saloons, mercantiles, and dog owners, in order to fund municipal works. The town treasurer kept these fees in a baking powder tin buried in someone's backyard rather than in the Ruby bank. The actual disposition of city funds is unclear. Town maintenance was bare bones and consisted of grading and watering Main Street to keep the dust down in summer and the construction of a raised plank walkway to avoid the mud during the remainder of the year. Construction of a municipal water system was undertaken but never completed. Payment for these projects was made by warrants issued by the city council in the form of promissory notes, which proved unredeemable and valuable only as souvenirs.

Ruby's was a contentious population at best. Civil War veterans held midnight shoot fests, Union vs. Confederate. Custer had met his fate only fifteen years before, Sitting Bull had recently been assassinated, and news of the massacre at Wounded Knee was still in the headlines. Veteran U.S. Cavalry Indian fighters who'd come to seek their fortunes in the mines did a good amount of race-baiting among the already outraged native population. Lynchings were not unheard of. Freighters, stage drivers, and mail carriers had to be tough and quick-witted to survive gangs of highwaymen. (One freighter acquired the sobriquet "Cranky Frank," because he was always in such an ill humor than no one dared to molest him.) A healthy drug trade flourished; opium and cocaine, though expensive, were not illegal. The first and one of the few residents to die of natural causes was said to have been a mayor-bartender named "Shaky" Pat McDonald who succumbed to delirium tremens. Local lore has it that when the beloved McDonald was mayor of Ruby, his saloon was used as a courtroom. Jurors were paid with "liquid refreshment" and when a juror fell off his barstool, an alternate juror was substituted.

Though the main industry of Ruby was mining, trappers selling beaver and bear skins passed through town, as did farmers who brought their truck of vegetables to town to sell. The reminiscences of one old-timer have it that the animal pelts were used for "base purposes" though this, like so many other activities and commerce in Ruby, was never elaborated upon; the reason given was that such stories were "unfit for print." Though no great mining fortunes were made in Ruby City, a great many fortunes were spent. Precious little of that money, however, went to fund civic necessities.

The schoolhouse, for instance, was built with illegally acquired public funds. Virginia Hancock Grainger Herrmann, a five-foot-tall redhead, educated at the University of Washington, was the superintendent of schools. Mrs. Herrmann, then Mrs. Grainger, was the first female superintendent of schools in the territory. A direct descendent of John Hancock, Mrs. Grainger also claimed to be related to Chester A. Arthur and Robert E. Lee. The tale of Ruby Schoolhouse in District 3 is substantiated by county documents and enhanced by the twice-divorced Mrs. Herrmann's reminiscences published in the Okanogan Independent in the mid 1920s, and later in her biography.

Here's the thumbnail sketch: In the Ruby school district there were thirty prospective students, although only fifteen to twenty attended regularly as the population was described as "floating." In Virginia Grainger's opinion, the current one-room school building suited the needs of the community. The powers that be in Ruby, however, wanted to bond a new schoolhouse large enough to serve as a community hall: four schoolrooms downstairs with a dance hall on the second floor. Virginia refused to sign the bond, which was passed by Ruby's citizenry. She also refused to sign the construction contracts. No matter; the town fathers overrode her and building commenced without legal technicalities. Judge George J. Hurley of Ruby pointed out that as a woman Mrs. Grainger was ineligible to hold public office and the county commissioners sent an emissary to demand that Virginia hand over the books of the Superintendent of Schools. She refused, saying she would continue to do her job until God or the Supreme Court directed her otherwise. All the same, the illegally funded Ruby schoolhouse was built.

While teaching in District 3's new facility, Virginia arrived one morning to find four of her younger students lying drunk on or beside the walkway. One of the schoolrooms had doubled as a cloakroom for a dance the night before and the following morning the children had indulged in the litter of half-empty bottles of intoxicants. Virginia was not paid for her duties as teacher in Ruby for nearly ten years. District 3 went bankrupt and the school construction bonds eventually had to be paid off by the state. Later, a school built in the nearby town of Okanogan (formerly the settlement of Alma) was named for Mrs. Grainger.

By and large, civic activities in and around Ruby were, like the building of the community hall, self-serving if not downright dishonorable, and in 1890—about the time of schoolhouse fiasco—civic-mindedness in Ruby took on an even darker hue: Late one night in October shortly after Ruby had, due to its legal shenanigans, lost its position as county seat, twenty mounted men—who to this day have remained unidentified—gathered in Ruby, then rode north, storming the jail at the neighboring mining town of Conconully (formerly Salmon City), the new seat of county government. After overpowering the jailer and his assistant, the twenty masked men removed a fifteen-year-old Indian boy who had been in custody there and took him as their prisoner. Though the boy had only been a possible witness to the murder of a freighter named Samuel Cole, he was lynched that night as the perpetrator.

His people on the Colville Reservation across the Okanogan River were outraged. Loud mourning rites followed. Many, though certainly not all, of the white settlers had a morbid dread of their Native American neighbors and feared an uprising. The farmers and ranchers had never gotten along with the miners, so the homesteaders were surprised and relieved when the Ruby City fathers came to their aid by offering to barricade all women and children in one of Ruby's deepest holes, the Fourth of July Mine. No uprising occurred. The only skirmish that broke out happened when a band of Rubyites rode to Alma to help protect "Pard" Cummings' trading post from native attack; the white forces at Cummings's fired on the band from Ruby, thinking them Indian invaders. The murderer of Samuel Cole was never apprehended nor were the men who lynched Steven prosecuted. Later, souvenir chips of the hanging tree were sold on the infamous streets of the mining camp.

Given the facts of this stranger-than-fiction town, I had to read between the lines of historical events, personal memoirs, and legal documents, reinterpreting them, an act I have come to think of as a writerly kind of forensic accounting.

Reaching for artistic form while using real events as springboards, I hoped to cast light on the ordinary and/or to see the event from an unexpected vantage point. Take that lynching, for instance. The history books represent it this way: An Indian boy named Steven (no last name supplied) was lynched supposedly because the local white population did not understand the difference between a material witness and a perpetrator. Even without the perspective of a hundred years distance, this

Town of Ruby City, around 1896.
(Courtesy of the Okanogan County Historical Society.)

104

is difficult to swallow. But to continue: The white population felt that if matters hadn't been taken into hand, the Indian lad who had been brought into custody would be tried for this crime, and if convicted, given a light sentence. Local sentiment was that Indians who were outlaws were not sufficiently punished for their crimes against the white population, though it is not clear now nor was it then that Steven was to be charged for the murder of Samuel Cole.

At the time of the lynching the population of Ruby was approximately five hundred souls; the population of the entire Okanogan County not even two thousand. The idea that the entire posse of twenty men could forever remain nameless taxes my credulity. What seemed very possible to me when I first read these accounts, and what still seems possible to me today, is that one or more of the twenty vigilantes had a hand in the murder of Samuel Cole—which probably began as a robbery—and feared that they might be identified by Steven. If that were to happen, the perpetrators might have been tried not in Ruby, but in a state court in Spokane where a conviction, though not a foregone conclusion, was at least possible. Nowhere is this theory put forward by historical accounts or mentioned by the personal references to these events.

But where to start a novel or a narrative poem set in Ruby City?

Its strange brand of justice aside, Ruby was first and foremost a boomtown and during its heyday the mood must have been expansive, even heady. The smell of pine-scented snow and dry mountain air was the smell of destiny; the constant clamor of mine activity the sound of boundless possibility. As a storyteller, I wondered: What would it have been like for a woman to live in such a place? And what would she be doing there? With the exception of the intrepid Mrs. Grainger, "decent women" didn't venture into Ruby and children, especially girl children, were forbidden by their parents to go there. I imagined a female character swept into Ruby by circumstance; she might be the daughter of immigrants—intelligent and street smart, but lacking in formal education. Or she might be educated, but—like Virginia Grainger—from a family whose fortune was destroyed by the Civil War and the economic downturn that followed. Perhaps she had "married badly" or for some other reason had to make her own way in life alone. At the time a woman could not vote; if she was married, her wages and her property were her husband's to dispose of as he wished. Certainly she would have had to possess both enormous personal charm and a high entrepreneurial aptitude to survive. The history of Ruby, however, is so enmeshed in larger-than-life narrative imagery and incident that the creative writer has the problem of choosing what might, in a novel or a dramatic monologue, be believable and build toward universality.

Although I have published two novels and many short stories, I consider myself first a poet and then a prose writer. I think in lines of poetry. And so I began to explore "character" with the help of a poetic line. Supposedly Sinclair Lewis wrote a biography of each character before he began his novels and, in this spirit, I began to write a book of linked narrative poems concerning the women who immigrated to the Okanogan Valley beginning in 1886. Given the factual background of Ruby Camp, I considered the character and circumstances of the local laundress. The position of laundress was considered a plum job for a Victorian woman who needed to earn a wage as it represented a steady flow of income without the necessity of leaving the home. As a literary device, having a central character who was a laundress interested me because a laundress would have an entrée to almost every character who passed through town, as well as having legitimate access to the community's dirty linen, literal and otherwise. With the inspiration of legal documents, memoirs, and reminiscences of such women in other late nineteenth-century Northwest mining towns, I began my writing about Ruby City with the following poem about a fictional laundress in Ruby:

The Laundress by the Lake, 1892

Dorwin, the saloonkeep, brought me the news,
asking: could they use my tent for the service?
His establishment had suffered
a shootfest and was unfit for funerals.
I wasn't the least surprised,
in fact relieved. I thought it was word
of an accident in the shaft.
Dorwin said he'd sent to Wallula for a preacher
—a special occasion.

Husband, a sensible man when sober,
until he came down with Western Fever
and bought by mail a trading post.
There's no describing this place:
3 days' journey by riverboat, 2 walking

Loop Loop Canyon trail with a tree
tied to the back of our wagon
for a brake, only to be swallowed by mire
at the bottom. Ruby City known as Mudtown.
No water, no lights except tallow dip
barely making darkness visible;
8 saloons, little Ella's Dance Hall, a livery,
bank, blacksmith, and an assayer who's better
at sampling spirits than ore.
Living Quarters: mainly tents,
Log cabins for those who've struck a vein.
Plank sidewalks traverse the side
of a mountain plagued by snowslide.

The water? 20 cents a bucket hauled
by Chinamen. Turns my laundry drab
and is not without metallic fragrance, though
most in Ruby never tasted it.
Few wells dug, on account of lot jumping.
So far five have been charged with killings
attributed to boundary disputes. All acquitted.
The court? Upstairs in Mr. Dorwin's saloon.
The jury often sequestered to ponder
pressing questions unfathomable anywhere
except at barroom footstools.

Laundry by the Lake my shingle says.
Not really a lake, but the end of a ravine
dividing North Main from South,
though Mayor "Shaky" Pat called it that
when he'd look in on me.
One would have thought his familiarity
with whiskey would have been a bar
to political preferment, but when the votes
were counted Mr. Dorwin's candidate
had defeated Little Ella's, two to one.

How's the mister? Shaky would ask,
even his florid face consumed by tremens. Well
the mister recovered from injuries

sustained when hauled up the shaft
in a bucket and a chain link broke.
Fell 50 feet, broke every bone
in his knee. As if the Glory Hole
hadn't already eaten all our pay.

When we lost the trading post,
husband went full time to the mines,
I took in miners' laundry. A dollar a load,
mending's extra, not to mention
Little Ella's blouses: high-necked, long-sleeved,
and a sinful amount of silk decoration.
Takes me an hour each, pressing
the tiny scallops with the point of my iron
warmed on the cookstove.

This morning when the Saloonkeep brought
the news, I was ironing Ella's chemise
starched to specifications, recalling

Husband's recuperation: so hungry
I ate starch to keep my stomach from gnawing.
When Dorwin asked for use of my tent
—and though I was truly saddened—
I knew the little rent would help.

"The Honorable 'Shaky' Pat McDonald
has succumbed," he said, head bowed.
"The first in Ruby to die of natural causes."

In camps such as Ruby, while men were busy with the pressing work
of mining in the hope of making fortunes overnight, the laundress often
doubled as the undertaker, laying out the dead. In the next poem, I
probe the laundress's psyche by exploring her day-to-day life as seen
through the lens of her other duties:

The Laying-Out

Of the Mayor "Shaky" Pat McDonald
By the Laundress, Ruby City, 1892

His last words:
"Move my bed closer to the stove."
For a moment he'd come back from
the Dakotas, harvesting buffalo bones
to be made into plaster, his bed
six inches from the fire.
Shook himself to death, saloonkeep Dorwin said.
The doctor, a four day's ride away.

So cold the night he died the azure sky
sharpened stars to pin pricks.
Dorwin put him out back,
laid across a plank propped up on feed sacks for lack of lumber.
The alley so filled with privies and whiskey
no wolf would trouble him.

Come white-breathed morning,
streetmud froze brick solid.
Dorwin (his beard pointed as a pitchfork)
bore Shaky to my tent
so stiff I balanced him between
stumps of stovewood without the plank
which was needed for a coffin.

Hands crossed over his sunken chest,
I comforted them with silk violets
from a hat he gave me
in payment for his laundry,
unlike Mr. Dorwin who applied what I was owed
to Husband's bar bill.
I sent word to Little Ella's, could she
give a petticoat or purple
flounce to line the casket?
With laundry soap I washed the body,
my hands puffy lobsters, I remembered

his gift of bag balm. Next,
lathered and shaved his cantaloupe rind face,
powdered his ashen cheeks with clay,
shined his hair with lampblack.
Two new pennies held his eyelids closed
—my last week's tip from Little Ella.
A fistful of silver nuggets
(here in this pillowcase, I saved
every tip he gave me) rounded out his cheeks.
His upper plate made of silver money,
missing, though he'd had it Friday.
When he dropped in, I was knitting socks
(a dollar-fifty each, used as legal tender);
his foot wagged in time to my fingers
working ivory sticks. I wondered
how a man could open-shut his mouth so much
it did not make him weary.

The assayer's black horse drew the wagon,
we followed carrying our chairs.
It was a pick and powder-blasted grave
we lined in budless willow.
The horse harness unhitched,
reins threaded beneath the coffin
lifted down to Ecclesiastes,
to *We shall meet, but we shall miss him,*
and other words concerning
the future of the dead.
Dust to dust—before someone took up a shovel,
I spread straw across the coffin,
to soften that haunting noise.

Tomorrow while I'm boiling water,
tendering fat and ash and lye to soap,
tomorrow while I grate trousers across
board and batten, my tent strung
with lifeless laundry shapes,
there'll be no one to praise the Glory Hole,
no assurances Husband will yet make good.
Tomorrow when I carve *P. McD.*

on the wooden head slab,
who will wag his foot in time
as my fingers work the chisel?
Morning sun shining through the canvas roof,
bright, but without warmth.

I left the laundress's tale behind for a moment and went on to explore the character of a miner, one who might be sympathetic to women. In the next poem, inspired by his photograph, I try to get inside the head of "Chickamin" Joe Hunter, a miner in the neighboring town of Nighthawk.

In Answer to The Question: Why'd You Do it?
"Chickamin" Joe Hunter,
Nighthawk, 1892

The railroad ended at Billings.
I walked the rest of the way, wore out
my only pair of shoes. I'd stopped
cursing by then. It was winter,
the trail empty except for dark blue
sky and sprinklings of stars. At dawn
sun flooded the snow white enough
to blind me. I neared a teepee
upholstered in old wagon covers.
The door flap opened to
hungry magpies screaming
from a naked willow.
As I passed, there she stood
—a familiar picture.

"Tillicum," she said,
offering herself for ten cents.
Her hair ragged, her voice shallow
as a puddle, she never looked me in the eye,
a Siwash custom. I didn't want her,
I did have ten cents. Still
she followed, carrying a digging stick.

I called her Sparrow Face,
her shoulders wrapped
in an ancient tablecloth begrimed with clay
—an immigrant's shroud?
I didn't want to know.

I heard her weep like lapping water:
At week's beginning, the blizzard broke,
she'd eaten one camas-flour biscuit,
a curl of deer fat. Next day
she found a rockrose root shaped like
a cloud trailing across the hard blue sky.
She drank ice-melt,
ate her last Olalla berries.
She'd had no food since and longed to eat
—the word "longed" drawn out
like a breeze caught
in wind-topped pines.
She was maybe thirteen.

The same age as when I left Iowa.
My stepfather knocked
me out of bed each morning:
Don't work, don't eat.
My first chore to milk the cow.
Winter I had no shoes.
I'd make the cow get up,
warmed my soles where she'd been lying
—her bedding steamed with dung.
Next I fed Buck and Ben,
straightening their harness left on
all winter, else it froze.
When I got back,
Stepfather held his nose,
grabbed my milk pail,
locking the door against me.
I stole some rags, bound my feet
and left—his name, a curse word.
At the Union post, I got work
carrying water,

Had my picture taken
wearing high boots and a warm blue uniform.
The war ended.
The railroad took me to Wyoming.
I got camp jobs that taught me
how to cook.

Opening my pack, I wanted
to do something for her.
She lightly drummed my gold pan.
I gave her the grub kit,
trying to explain:
Always speak professionally
of garnish and spice.
Put on decent clothes and tidy up when
you enter a kitchen.
You can learn to make pies as well as
any white man if you leave out deer fat.
I demonstrated the coffee pot:
A miner prefers his hot and with few
grounds as you can manage.
Before you serve, ask,
boiled or unboiled?

Her eyes fixed on my
withered yellow apple.
Cracks in her lips glistened.
I could not watch her eat. She sang
and chewed the way a baby sometimes does.

I had one nickel, carried all the way
from Billings. When we got to "Pard" Cummings'
trading post, I gave it to her for a box of apples.
As is the Siwash custom,
She said not good-bye or thank you.

I walked to Nighthawk's many tents
at a bend in a river too angry to ice up.
The sun set early behind rose-hip glaciers.
Darkness ended a trail of gnats, though noises

of blasting powder louder than battle
raged as I made a new pot with a wire handle
from discarded lard pails.
Grinding beans between stones,
I could not shake the thought of
little Sparrow Face.

That was five years past.
Within months I got enough of a stake
to file a claim, which, in the excitement of '88,
sold for eighteen-thousand dollars.
By then I'd built a cabin, acquired
kitchen gear, enough shirts to go
three weeks of mining,
enough rope for line to dry them.
On a night so cold I wore all my socks
on both hands and feet and two
wool caps at once, I dreamed of her
ragged hair, hand clutching a tablecloth
to her breast. "I long to eat" howled
through the wall chinks.

Come morning, I bought by mail-order
enough coffee pots for every
Siwash woman in the county.

Some stored dried Olalla berries in theirs,
some kept rockrose root
in the shape of clouds,
a few learned to make miners' coffee.
They called me "Money" Joe.
As was their custom, none said, Thank you.
None asked, Why?

Continuing with the development of local characters, in the following poem I used a crime as a springboard. With the help of diaries and legal documents outlining one of the countless thefts near Ruby, I constructed a composite:

Dutch Jake's Hell-Time Calendar, 1887-89

March—began keeping diary.

With mule and dog, forded the Okanogan
looking for agricultural pursuits.
Met Sar-sept-a-kin and several Nespelem
who offered nine horses for a bottle of whiskey
before concluding their entreaties were in vain.
Eyed my father's gold watch brought
from Frankfurt-on-Main.

Near Broken Spoke Ranch met a Tacoma man,
claimed to have sold a share in the Tough Nut Mine
at Ruby City for $11,000!

Today bothered by boils: face, neck, and elsewhere.

May 30—Made camp. Mosquitoes so thick
they could be taken from the air by handfuls.
Broke camp about midnight to escape.
Climbed the hills toward Salmon City,
spread my blankets only to find
an army of rattlers. Evacuated
after killing fifty reptiles. Moved on
a few miles to Soda Creek,
slept peacefully in rye grass as tall
as the mule's shoulder. Dreamt of cutting
fifteen tons with a scythe.

In the morning grouse so thick
they could be killed with a stone.
Deer plentiful and did not stir
at the sound of my gun. Crickets
kept me awake the following night.
An abundance of yellow jackets.
Boils more painful, but draining.

June 6—Pitched a tent, tilled two acres
for truck. Difficulty in getting seeds.
Trading post proprietor's wife
at Wild Goose Condon's Ferry
suggested hot compresses.
Bought onion sets and horseradish root.

Aug. 9—an army of crickets came
from the north, devastating my crop.
Insects so thick they filled the trail ruts,
their shells oozing out of the mule's feet.

September—Arrived Salmon City
en route to silver fields of Ruby.
Settlers few—legal land claims impossible due
to questions of statehood.
Three or four tents. A "sooner" named Moss
had a log establishment.
Built a board shack: improvements, $30.
Sold it for eighty to a Frenchman
who admired my watch. *April*—
Packed the mule and headed for Ruby.

Met Sar-sept-a-kin who recommended
groundhog oil for various purposes,
including balding and boils.
Traded him a bottle of Old Number Seven.

May—Returned to newly elected county seat,
Salmon City, made claim on the *Quantum Sufficit*.
Sar-sept-a-kin, who was there with a quantity
of corn, waited for me to supervise
sale and collection of money.

Boils improving. Bought my shed back for $25.
Planted truck in the yard from seeds
Sar-sept-a-kin gave in exchange for whiskey.
Buried Father's watch in a baking powder tin,
north end, second row of beets.

October—Mercury dropped, so cold the ink froze
as I made this entry, despite a hot fire.
Dog shivering. All blankets and extra clothing
used to cover truck. Boils completely gone.

January 1—Today an eclipse of the sun
occurred from twelve until three.
Dog howled, mule off his feed.
A report came into Moss's Saloon:
Washington soon admitted to the Union.

July—Left the dog and gold watch
with the saloonkeep, Mr. Moss—Ruby too wild
for safety. Sar-sept-a-kin offered
(for a bottle) to keep an eye on the proprietor.

Mule packed with squash and red cabbage.
Followed prospector's trail, tracing
ore veins and pay ledges. On the outskirts
soon learned that Ruby people did not
patronize Salmon City-ites due to
the county seat question which brought
white head from their mouths.
Gave the vegetables away. To develop Q.S.,
watch will have to be sold.

Returned home directly.
Learned Moss had been killed by
skull fracture, his saloon set fire over him.
An Indian was suspect and chased
as far as Wild Goose Condon's ferry where
the Frenchman pulled him from his horse
by the hair and he drowned due to intoxication.
Moss's body found, but the mystery
of the gold watch could not be explained
—though the dog fled unharmed.

Boils returning: face, neck, and elsewhere.

After writing about a hundred pages of poems such as these, I
had compiled enough characters and details to begin my novel. I had

my main character, the laundress, and I named her Pearl. She had no experience as a laundress, but she was young and female; in Ruby that was all the recommendation she needed to set up business. My Pearl did, however, have aspirations. She had staked a mineral claim, which she worked in her spare time, hoping that the ore will buy her a medical education. She was an accomplished seamstress and on this merit was hired by the local physician as his apprentice. Doc had lost his glasses and had trouble repairing wounds. Pearl lived on the edge of town in a tent attached to a piano crate given to her by the actual mayor of the town, "Shaky" Pat McDonald. She hired an imagined laundry assistant, a mixed-race woman, named Mary Red-dawn who was married to a Chinese laborer—not an uncommon coupling. In my attempt to explore the forces of evil in Ruby, one of the antagonists took the form of Dutch Jake, the speaker in the earlier poem. In my fictional permutation of this character, he became a manipulator, card shark, and bully. Jake owned the town livery; thus he controlled local transportation. What I wanted to do in this novel was plumb the character of the man behind Ruby's mayor, sheriff, and town council. The public officials who made up Ruby's "saloon government" would have been popular glad-handers, not necessarily individuals of strong moral character. Jake would have been the prickly personality who knew how to instill courage in these men—if not a personal courage, then certainly the courage of the mob.

Here early in the novel *The Pearl of Ruby City*, Jake appears at Pearl's tent ostensibly to pick up his laundry. His feathers have been ruffled after an encounter with the schoolteacher Carolina, based on the character of Virginia Grainger Herrmann. In the progression of linked dramatic monologues to a novelization of the rise and fall of Ruby City, the characters, who in the poetry book only spoke to the reader now can and must speak to one another. A note on my use of "damaged" language—words such as "squaw," "Siwash," and "half-breed": These words were the diction of the time, and I chose not to change them for the sake of present day political correctness. I wanted my dialogues and stream-of-consciousness internal monologues to be representative of what might have been everyday thought and speech patterns. I did, however, try very hard to use each piece of damaged language advisedly. What follows is a conversation in the novel between Pearl, the laundress, and Jake, the livery owner:

Jake Pardee strutted in, his large blond features filling up every nook and cranny of my tent. Without being asked, he sat down on one of the two crates pulled up to my little table and put his muddy boots on the other, leaning back against the canvas wall.

"I come for my clothes," he said, chewing on a pine twig. His sheepskin jacket fell open, exposing a vast shirtless torso. The heaviness in my stomach churned. "At fifty cents a shirt, the least a man could get is prompt service," he growled. "Whatcha do with all your money, anyway?"

I stirred the tea. The tension in the air felt as thick as bread dough.

"Cat got your tongue, Pearly?"

"I've been called to tend the sick and finished no work today," I told him in my most polite but frozen voice. "They're soaking as you can see," I motioned to the buckets of laundry next to the stove.

"My ma used to say that a scrub board 'n' elbow grease worked wonders."

"You'll have to be patient," I answered.

"Just tryin' to help. Soaking's no way to get a job done." He leaned back farther, as if he planned to stay all night. Jake was an expert on everything, even woman's work.

Mary Reddawn moved back into the corner where I kept the potatoes I made into laundry starch. She split bits of kindling with the hatchet she always carried in her belt. Mary had a way with fire and could coax even the greenest log into a blaze. With each ring of her little blade, I imaged her dismembering a piece of Jake our town's livery owner.

"I don't know why Carolina does me that way," he said, chewing thoughtfully. "I like ladies to behave as ladies, not talk you blind with questions. Her and her haughty ways," Jake said, stretching out, putting his hands behind his head. "But you, Pearly . . . I could watch you write in your notebook all day. I'll bet that's what you was doing instead of my shirts. But I'm a broadminded soul. I could watch your hand like a finch flying across them pages for hours."

Jake was speaking of my medical journal, I supposed. "I've been tending Shaky, as I said." I put an extra bite into my words, hoping to cover my lie.

"What sense in that? He's near gone and I'm in need of my flannels."

"Don't speak that way, please." I wished I was the hot-headed murdering sort redheads are supposed to be. I wouldn't give him time to say his prayers.

He eyed Shaky's potion brewing on the stove. "If there's anyone who needs tending to, it's me. I could use a little warm tea."

I didn't like the look in his eye. My hands busied themselves, clanking pots.

"I try to help you out," he said, lowering his voice. "I make a special trip here to get my clothes so your tiny feet won't have to tramp up the ravine to bring me my laundry. But instead of washin', you're writing all day or out working your Lost Cause Mine."

"Last Chance Mine," I corrected.

He continued undaunted, "I tell you, Pearly, my fortune's made. You'd do well to say a kind word to me. Why, I'd marry you any day over that nose-in-the-air Carolina."

I could not help but raise my voice. "I'm already married, as is Carolina. My name is Mrs. Ryan, you might recall."

"So you say, but I ain't seen any sign of a husband." With that he rose to his feet and muscled his way through the doorway. He turned to Mary as if he'd just noticed her, "Well, if it ain't my favorite hangs-around-the-town half-breed." And with that he fled my establishment.

As Mary gathered warmed stones in a pot and covered them with a blanket, I heard her mutter, "Pokamiakin mamaloose Stinktail someday."

Mamaloose, I learned soon after arriving in Ruby, was Chinook for "to make dead." "Stinktail" was trapper talk for "skunk" and the Indians' name for Jake Pardee. Pokamiakin was Mary's cousin and the only man, white or copper, who'd sworn to get even with Jake. "Pokamiakin" could also be translated as Rabid Coyote or shortened to Poka Mika, meaning anything from "I fight you" to "I poke you," to words that shall not be mentioned. Whites thought him a desperado; Indians considered him an under-chief. In any case, he had crossed bloodshot eyes and was the most frightening-looking Siwash I'd ever met—though he always favored me due to the fire color of my hair.

Of course things are not as they first appear and Jake proves to be less evil than other more "benevolent" residents of Ruby. For me, it was far easier to develop the amoral personae in fictional form than it was to develop such a character in the poetic monologue. Ruby's more tragic-comic and ironic details lent themselves to the novel far more readily than to verse. In part, this is because poetry demands a tighter economy of language, whereas in a novel it is permissible for the writer to sprawl and digress—though admittedly in a controlled way.

Coloring in documents from the perspective and distance of a hundred years, fleshing out the story and the back story, reinventing what was unsaid and unwritten because it was not fit for print, these are the tasks of the writerly investigator. And what to do with the results of this forensic accounting? If the documents did not provide me with a narrative framework, then they provided a hook that caught my writer's eye, a hook that would not be dislodged. Under the guise of narrative fiction and poetry, the creative writer can shed sudden light into various nooks of past legal anomalies, bringing them back into the fore for re-examination, a sort of trial by reader followed by new judgments on long past and forgotten events. Further, a re-evaluation of the evidence might open our eyes to similar if not parallel situations of the present.

Afterword on Sources

Few documents exist concerning life in Ruby. Many were destroyed by fire in the mid-1890s or by the flash flood which temporary leveled Conconully, in 1894. During territorial days, and shortly after statehood, the laws of Okanogan County were carried out by county commissioners, the first three appointed by the territorial governor when Okanogan County was organized in 1888; later the commissioners were elected by the citizenry. Most elections were a contest between miners (Democrats) and ranchers (Republicans). These first commissioners appointed the first county officials and elected Ruby as the seat of government. On November 11, 1889, Washington acquired statehood.

One of my major sources is the memoir of Guy Waring, chair of the first three commissioners. Arriving in the Okanogan near what is now the town of Loomis in 1884, Waring was from Massachusetts and graduated from Harvard ('82) just behind Theodore Roosevelt; the two were life-long friends. Waring and Roosevelt were also Harvard classmates of Owen Wister who wrote the first American Western, *The Virginian* (which became the movie "Shane"). Wister visited the Okanogan largely because of Waring's encouragement, and many of Wister's Okanogan experiences and characters were incorporated into his famous novel. Before Ruby became county seat, court was sometimes held in Waring's house and trading post. When, much to Guy Waring's dismay, Ruby became the seat of government, Waring had to travel from his cattle ranch to Ruby where court convened. He feared for his life both en route and on the way home.

Another of my sources is the memoir of Ulrich E. Fries, a Danish immigrant who homesteaded near the Okanogan town of Brewster. In addition to being a cattleman, Fries was a mail carrier. In the early 1990s, I interviewed three of U. E. Fries's six children: his son Emil in his mid-nineties, his eldest child Signe at age 101, and his youngest Louise in her 80's. Ulrich Fries and Guy Waring were acquainted; Fries delivered mail to Waring. Though Waring and Fries seem to have been two of the few educated and morally upright citizens of the area, the men appear to have disliked each other. Part of the problem, I suspect, was that the polished well-spoken Waring was American-born and possessed a keen sense of Yankee entitlement. Fries, on the other hand, was a foreigner who, though he read several languages, spoke fractured English.

According to Ulrich Fries, many legal trials were carried out by the local Justice of the Peace who sometimes had no knowledge of the law whatsoever. Sometimes a defendant would ask his neighbor to serve as his lawyer. It seems to me that all concerned with the judicial system often made up or parroted the law as they went along. Fries recounts one murder trial in Ruby, which took place in the out-of-doors and late at night. According to Fries, Richard Price, who served three government positions simultaneously—justice of the peace, U. S. marshal, and coroner—spent a considerable amount of time in a Ruby saloon before finally gathering together an impromptu jury of six men.

If a defendant was ever found guilty (which was unlikely, since most of the jurors were probably his associates), it was not unheard of that the defendant escaped. The escape was made possible by the prisoner's friends who were either deputized to arrest him or escort him to the state penitentiary. Escape in the middle of nowhere on the way to prison in Walla Walla wasn't difficult. The following excerpt from Ulrich Fries's memoir illustrates the legal process even after the county seat was moved from the unruly Ruby to the more law-abiding Conconully.

> In case of an arrest, a jury trial was no guarantee of justice, for often there were jurors whose own records were not above suspicion, or

who sympathized with the accused. I served on the jury three times while the county seat was at Conconully [1889–1914], under three different judges, Taylor, Martin, and Pendergast.

The case under Judge Martin was known as the Pearson Case. Eight head of cattle had been stolen from British Columbia, brought across the boundary, and sold in the town of Republic. The case was given to the jury at 10:30 P.M. and not until five-thirty the next morning did we reach a verdict of conviction. One man said he could not bear the thought of taking liberty away from a man. It was he, who, when we finally decided the man guilty, went to a corner of the jury room and wept. Another juror refused to make a decision but simply kept still, giving in only after long heckling by the other jurors. The defense appealed the case, procured a new trial, and got Pearson acquitted. (page 367)

Many of my characters are composites. The details of their lives, however, were cribbed from the real lives of others of the same period and of a similar place. As to an explanation of some of the details in the poems printed above: In territorial days, a "sooner" was a settler or homesteader who occupied on a piece of land before it had been surveyed by the government. Because the land had not been surveyed, the settler could not legally file a claim to the property he/she occupied. "Bag balm" was and is a medication used to treat chapped udders on milk cows. Both frontier men and women used bag balm to treat chapped hands. And regarding the purchase of a trading post by mail: it was not uncommon for someone to buy a trading post, the forerunner of the general store, or any business venture for that matter, sight unseen from an advertisement in an East Coast newspaper, then trek three thousand miles west in the hope of setting up business. These establishments were seldom as advertised and some were totally nonexistent.

When using a factual character—Joe Hunter for instance—I tried as much as possible to stick to the particulars of what I knew of his or her life. Joe Hunter was purported to have donated eighteen thousand dollars from the proceeds of his mining efforts so that the Native females of Okanogan County could each purchase a coffee pot. How might a man become so sensitive to the plight of others who, at the time, were often considered less than human? According to the various physiologists I consulted, he was probably orphaned or the child of a single mother and abused as a child. I researched memoirs of men of the Western Migration who were treated cruelly by stepfathers or guardians and in my writing borrowed from their childhoods. Though I supplied the events of Hunter's early life and his trek west, I did not make them up. The minute details were appropriated from the lives of still others of that era. I don't know that Joe Hunter ever met a young native Okanogan woman whom he called Sparrow Face, but he might have. She and her circumstances are described by Ulrich Fries in his memoir. Fries was the fifteenth of eighteen children, his father, a blind Lutheran minister, died when Fries was a child. It was Ulrich Fries who bought the starving young Indian girl the box of apples.

Regarding the central character, Pearl, in my novel *The Pearl of Ruby City*, and her establishment, the Laundry by the Lake: There was no lake in Ruby, the body of water in question was a bog or a tributary of Salmon Creek, the concept of a "lake" was meant to be ironic. This tributary or swamp, I believe, separated North Ruby from South Ruby. South Ruby was the graveyard—founded by . . . I forget his name, but he died in a boundary dispute as did many other Ruby-ites. The particulars of the life of my "laundress by the lake" were borrowed from the life of an actual mining camp laundress in Alaska.

And finally, it was a stroke of luck that I knew what my historical characters, their children and pets, their homesteads and towns, landscape and livestock looked like. Many of the aforementioned were photographed just after the turn of the twentieth century by an enigmatic photographer, Frank Matsura. As a young man, Matsura immigrated to Seattle from Japan where he had been well educated and worked as a schoolteacher. It is not known why he came to the United States, but he probably settled in the Okanogan for his health. Matsura worked as a dishwasher's assistant and launderer in Conconully. In his spare time, he set up a photographic studio in the town of Okanogan (formerly Alma) where he took photographs of weddings, pioneer picnics, Fourth of July celebrations, the native population, the coming of the railroad, school children and their teachers. He died suddenly in 1913 of tuberculosis at the age of 36. Without Matsura, I wouldn't know what Judge George Hurley or other players in Ruby politics looked like. I have often fantasized that the faces of some of the twenty anonymous horsemen who lynched the Indian boy Steven hide in Matsura's black-and-white compositions.

Bibliography

A *Davis Family History*, The story of the W.L. Davis Family (privately published, 1988) Compiled by Georgene Fitzgerald.

Fries, U.E., *From Copenhagen to Okanogan*, the Autobiography of a Pioneer (The Caxton Printers, Ltd., Caldwell, Idaho, 1949).

Her Mark, the Story of Virginia Grainger Herrmann (XI Chapter of Alpha Sigma State, Delta Kappa Gamma, 1951).

Matsura, Frank S., photographer, *Images of Okanogan County* (The Omak-Okanogan County Chronicle and Okanogan Historical Society, Okanogan, Washington 2002).

Ramsey, Guy R., *Postmarked Washington, Okanogan County* (Ye Galleon Press, Fairfield, Washington, 1977).

Roe, Joann, *Frank Matsura, Frontier Photographer* (Madrona Publishers, Seattle, 1981). *Told By the Pioneers, Tales of Frontier Life as Told by Those Who Remember the Days of the Territory and Early Statehood of Washington*, Vol. I, II, III (State of Washington, Olympia, 1937–38).

Waring, Guy, *My Pioneer Past* with an introduction by Owen Wister (Bruce Humphries, Inc. Boston, 1936).

Washington State Archives: Friendly Visiting Program, State Department of Public Welfare, 1936, unpublished interviews.

Wilson, Bruce A., *Late Frontier*, A History of Okanogan County, Washington 1800–1941 (Okanogan County Historical Society, Okanogan, Washington, 1990).

Wister, Owen, *The Virginian*, (Macmillan & Co., New York, 1902).

Woody, O. H. *Glimpses of Pioneer Life of Okanogan County*, Articles published 1923–24 in the *Okanogan Independent*.

Relevant Texts by Jana Harris

Oh How Can I Keep on Singing? Voices of Pioneer Women, Poems (Ontario Review Press, Princeton, 1993).

How Can I Keep on Singing? Video 56 min (Moving Images, Seattle, 2000) melissa@movingimages.org.

The Pearl of Ruby City, a novel (St. Martin's Press, New York, 1998).

The Dust of Everyday Life, an Epic Poem of the Northwest (Sasquatch, Seattle, 1997).

Lan Cao

Laundrymen, Chinatown

From the rich database containing records of homicides during the 1870–1930 period, it is clear that Chicago was a city transformed by immigration. The Germans, Swedes, Irish, Poles, Italians, Jews, and the "unassimilable" Chinese came to Chicago to work and live in great numbers. I examined the cases from the Chicago Historical Homicide Project data set involving Chinese victims and noticed a persistent pattern in these cases. For the Chinese immigrants ("Chinamen" as they were called), their lives centered around certain essential facts. They lived and worked in Chinatown; they owned or worked in a laundry; they were involved centrally or marginally in tongs, ethnic self-help groups that over time transmogrified into criminal organizations. In many of the cases I examined, their deaths also centered around these facts. Many of the victims died in Chinatown, in their laundry or restaurant, with the specter of tong involvement looming somewhere in the background.

Chinatowns, laundries, and tongs. An entire history of the Chinese presence in the United States can be woven around those words. And so can a compelling work of fiction. To illustrate this point, I propose to provide a sampling of both. In Part I of this essay, Laundrymen, I examine the historical background and ask why so many Chinese men laundered clothes—why so many performed traditional women's work? And what was the role of the law in imposing this reality on their lives. In Part II, Chinatown, I look at the same facts but do so by telling a story, a part in a chapter of a novel about Chinatown, set in a large American city.

126

I. Laundrymen

Chinese immigrants created a niche—an ethnic niche—in San Francisco in the mid 1800s at the start of the Gold Rush. Most of the immigrants in San Francisco, as in other large Western towns, were disproportionately male. This was because many of the men expected to stay temporarily in the United States, make money, then return home to China. Thus many did not bring wives with them. Additionally, when the Chinese Exclusion Act was passed, Chinese immigration was drastically reduced, making it almost impossible for the men who decided to stay in the United States to bring their wives into the country to join them.

Chinese men had no choice but to perform women's work. In cities such as San Francisco, laundering was considered inappropriate for a white man. Spanish-American and Native American women ran "Washerwomen's Lagoons" and charged exorbitant fees for their washing and laundering services. With the influx of single men into California during the Gold Rush and the demand for laundering skyrocketing, it was in many cases cheaper to throw away a dirty shirt and buy a new one than to launder it. The Chinese saw an economic opportunity and began to open local laundries. By 1850, Chinese competition drove down the price for washing shirts. This was the beginning of a Chinese niche in laundries that continues to this day.

Because the laundry operators were men doing "women's work," they were particularly susceptible to certain charges. In sparsely populated places such as Montana, whites charged Chinese laundrymen with usurping laundry opportunities from widows and single women. In urban areas such as San Francisco, the Chinese were charged with disrupting white families when they performed tasks traditionally reserved for housewives. Furthermore, because the Chinese laundrymen were either bachelors or had left their wives in China, wild rumors of sexual misconduct were often directed against them, for example, unsubstantiated claims that the Chinese lured little girls to their laundries for illicit sexual purposes. As late as 1902, in his Congressional testimony, "Some Reasons for Chinese Exclusion: Meat vs. Rice, American Manhood Against Asiatic Coolieism—Which Shall Survive?" Samuel Gompers, the leader of the American Federation of Labor, charged that the Chinese planned on converting little boys and girls into "opium fiends" and that children were kept as sex slaves in the back of Chinese laundry houses.

In addition to laundering, the Chinese also prospected for gold. Their success and the news of their good fortune led to a surge in Chinese immigration to the United States, from slightly more than 2000 in 1851 to 20,000 in 1852. The success of the Chinese provoked hostility among white miners, who fanned false rumors that the Chinese coming to the United States were competitive only because they were nothing more than cheap, malnourished coolie laborers.

White miners also persuaded the state legislatures to pass legislation to discourage Chinese competition. California levied a three-dollar-per-month tax on all foreign miners and then subsequently amended the law to increase the tax and to make it applicable only to the Chinese. The white miners also used violence against their Chinese competitors, causing many Chinese to leave the mines.

Many Chinese who left the mines found work building the Central Pacific Railroad. Approximately 83 percent of the 12,500 railroad construction workers were Chinese. The railroad's completion in 1869 left these workers without a job. From 1867 to 1869, successful strikes by white mineworkers caused many mining companies to ban Chinese miners from underground work and also from all mining jobs. In cases where the strikes were not successful, miners and union workers resorted to violence to keep the Chinese out of mining.

Many Chinese gave up mining and entered the laundry business, either as workers for other Chinese or as owners. In the latter case, they set up laundering houses outside mining camps and in cities throughout California and the West. The laundrymen did not have laundering experiences in China—it was considered women's work there as well. But many established laundries in the United States because they identified a profitable niche and others followed, learning the trade by apprenticeship with established laundrymen.

Anti-Chinese sentiments were vehemently directed against Chinese laundries. False charges were directed against them, for example, that they cheated customers or that they sprayed water and starch from their mouths—in other words, that they spat—onto clothes as they ironed, thus spreading disease. In reality, the Chinese used a special process whereby air was blown through a tube filled with water. In January 1877, the San Francisco Board of Supervisors appropriated $1500 to the Citizen's Anti-Chinese Committee to fuel a "Chinese Must Go" campaign. Many other jurisdictions in the West passed facially neutral laws aimed against Chinese laundries. Maximum hours laws, zoning laws, licensing laws, tax laws, et cetera were enforced selectively against Chinese laundries.

For example, in the 1880s, Chinese laundrymen often worked ten-to sixteen-hour days. Many laundries operated twenty-four hours per day as well. San Francisco laundries often shared space and facilities by alternating their signs, with laundrymen of one laundry working the morning shift and laundrymen of another laundry working the night shift. In 1882, the San Francisco Board of Supervisors prohibited the laundering of clothes between 10 P.M. and 6 A.M. When the law went into effect in January 1883, the city arrested one hundred Chinese laundrymen for violating it. Although lower courts declared the law unconstitutional, a three-judge panel of the Supreme Court of California upheld it, declaring that it was not discriminatory because it applied to "all persons" in the laundry business. The United States Supreme Court, in Barbier v. Connolly,[1] unanimously upheld the ordinance as a legitimate exercise of state power.

Chinese ghettos, Chinatowns, were also forcibly created. For example, in 1890, San Francisco's Bingham Ordinance prohibited any Chinese from locating, residing, or operating a business anywhere outside a designated area. Those who did at the time had sixty days to move. Although the ordinance was subsequently declared a violation of the United States Constitution and of treaties with China, anti-Chinese zoning laws proliferated in California. In 1892, the town of Chico in California required an individual to receive a written permit from the town's board of directors before opening a public laundry outside two designated areas. Additionally, the permit could not be granted unless the applicant obtained the written consent of a majority of the real property owners within the block on which the proposed laundry was to open as well as of those within the four surrounding blocks. This law was declared unconstitutional by the California Supreme Court in Ex Parte Sing Lee,[2] which noted that the ordinance interfered with the applicant's right to engage in a lawful occupation.

Legislatures continued to pass anti-laundry zoning ordinances despite the courts' rulings. Sacramento's ordinance, which was upheld, prohibited laundry owners from renting out space in a building not exclusively used for a laundry. This effectively drove small Chinese laundries from the downtown area. White-owned laundries were not affected because most owned their facilities.

The existence of Chinatowns was not due merely to the personal preferences of the Chinese but rather also due to repressive laws mandating segregation of the Chinese. The California legislature enacted a law in 1879, later declared unconstitutional, requiring towns and cities to remove the Chinese from city limits. Landlords and realtors refused to rent and sell to Chinese outside the boundaries of Chinatown. In 1885, in Tucson, a concerted campaign was begun to force the Chinese into a "Chinatown," so they could be monitored.

Ironically, the Chinese were able to leverage their situation—limited opportunities and forced segregation—into an economic asset. First, as I mentioned earlier, immigration restrictions meant Chinese men could not freely bring their wives to the United States. This meant many ended up performing "women's work," including opening laundries. Second, given the hostility by whites to Chinese entry into mining and to the Chinese generally, the Chinese established their own ethnic economy (Chinese hiring other Chinese), ethnic niche (laundering), in an ethnic enclave (Chinatown). Like other ethnic groups faced with external hostility, the Chinese created their own economy to ensure the group's economic survival. Ethnic economies are based on personal relationships and ethnic ties, allowing group members to utilize group norms of solidarity and trust to lower the screening, monitoring, and enforcement costs of intra-group transactions and to further intra-group economic needs. Because the Chinese had developed a niche in laundering and other businesses such as Chinese restaurants and shops selling "exotic" Chinese specialties that catered not only to Chinese but also non-Chinese consumers, the Chinese ethnic economy was not limited to the ethnic market but extended to the general market with greater opportunities.

Additionally, the segregation of the Chinese into Chinatowns also resulted in the spatial or locational clustering of Chinese businesses. These businesses employ Chinese workers who have the benefit of an ethnic network characterized by ethnic characteristics and geographic proximity. In other words, ethnic neighborhoods such as Chinatown were the spatial anchor of the Chinese community, often close to or part of the Chinese economic enclave. Business concentration within an economic enclave geographically close to ethnic neighborhoods created synergy between businesses and residences. Such "agglomeration of economies" encouraged the proliferation of ethnic businesses. It furthered the cultural presence of the area and promoted its visibility as an ethnic market. It may also, as in the case of the Chinese, create an export platform from which ethnic firms may expand beyond their ethnic customer base.

Being part of a common locational enclave also allowed the Chinese to establish cultural associations and schools based on common geographic origins and clans. For example, in response to demands by Chinese parents for their U.S.-born children to attend public school, the San Francisco School Board allowed the Chinese School to be opened as a "separate but equal" public school in San Francisco Chinatown in 1859. When the Chinese School was closed in 1871, Chinese cultural associations funded by Chinatown merchants organized and ran Chinese language schools.

In the face of intimidation, threats and harassment, the Chinese turned inward and relied on their own institutions. They created the Chinese Consolidated Benevolent Association, also known as the Chinese Six Companies, a hierarchy of fraternal, district, family, business, and charitable organizations to promote community economic development and self-help. District associations or tongs served as ruling bodies that settled differences between Chinese of various backgrounds. Family societies, such as the Lee Association or the Wong Association, served as credit unions for extended kin and even now provide support for the infirm and the elderly. Tongs, as the community's cultural and economic cornerstones, proliferated, but some transmogrified into secret, criminal associations specializing in prostitution, gambling, and other illicit activities.

Image of Frank Moy (called King of Chinatown), leaning against a desk in a room in Chicago, Illinois, surrounded by a group of men.
(*Chicago Daily News* negatives collection, DN-0003451. Chicago History Museum.)

In sum, the Chinese experience in the United States can be succinctly summarized with three words: laundries, Chinatowns, and tongs. Laundries represent the community's development of an ethnic economy and ethnic niche—as a reaction to anti-Chinese animus. Chinatowns represent white segregation of the Chinese as well as the creation by the Chinese of an ethnic economic enclave that would produce synergy between Chinese residents and businesses. Tongs represent self-help associations. Tongs also symbolize the capture of these associations by criminal elements in Chinatown for illicit purposes.

II. Chinatown

The following is a selection from a novel of mine that weaves together this history and present reality about Chinese immigration to the United States. It is an excerpt from *Song of the Yellowbird*, a novel-in-progress.

The main character is Nibao, a twenty-something young man from Fujian Province, who arrived in New York City's Chinatown in 2001 on a ship run by a secret criminal organization. At the time of the novel, he is working with a present day tong in Chinatown that is smuggling Chinese into the U.S. to work in the underground economy in Chinatown. Since this is a novel, a work of imaginative fiction, the story is about him and also told through him. Some of the events are seen through his eyes, but more importantly, his experience is the emotional center of the novel.

One month after the ship crashed, Nibao stood in a small, dim shop. Whose shores, what continent were they in?

This was Canal Street, New York City Chinatown.

Not long ago, he had been in a dark abyss deep in the ship's hull, huddled for months below deck—intercontinental phantoms smuggled by the Snake Heads of Fujian Province for a sum of $35,000 American dollars, to be paid off by many years of hard work. Nibao thought of it as his version of Mao's Five-Year-Plan: gold pieces to be accumulated in America, then sent back to his family in Fujian. He was among the lucky ones. His family in Fujian would soon be living in brick houses from American gold pieces while the rest of them would still be huddling in damp, crumbling huts because, unlike Nibao, they had not been chosen by the Snake Heads for migration to the Gold Mountain. He had heard the stories, of gold-paved streets in cities across water, of Meiguo, "beautiful country," of men becoming wealthy after a few short years of hard work, breathing in white steam from backroom laundries and menial savings.

This was the beginning of his indentured future here. He reassured himself that history was on his side, that he was not alone. So many men before him had made this voyage, men who had glided their boats across the Straits of Formosa: men who, years before Christopher Columbus crossed the Atlantic, had been sent by the Ming emperor to explore faraway places, in vessels that were four hundred feet long and one hundred and sixty feet wide. His people had discovered America long before Columbus did. The voyages continued in big and small ships, manned by traders, fishermen, pirates, even when new emperors made seafaring a crime, burned all ocean-going vessels, and ordered that all transgressors be decapitated. They continued even now, as stories came back with the currents.

Yes, he was among the lucky few.

Cleaver steels. Glossy Peking-roasted ducks hung upside down on hooks. Nibao cleaved flesh and bones, split breasts, sorted viscera into a bowl. On the floor were bins of salmon, tuna, crabs, and other fishes whose names he had never heard of. He was to clean and descale them, pack them on top of ice buckets to be ogled by blue-eyed tourists. The sooner he finished, the sooner the wages would be earned, the sooner his debt to the Snake Heads would be paid. No late payments. This was the beginning of his years as apprentice butcher, waiting for the final tolling of the bell when the Five-Year-Plan ended and his freedom would then be permanently bought. He could forego instant dignity for possibilities in the future.

The Snake Heads, Nibao knew, ran a sprawling, mobile empire. With their secret connections and coordinates, they had brought thousands and thousands from Fujian, each with calamitous stories, and turned them into backroom pluckers and gutters of chicken and ducks. Nibao learned soon after his arrival in New York City that almost everyone in the Fujianese section of Chinatown owed the Snake Heads something. Some who came several years before Nibao already made it big in the city, sending coins back to native villages to care for ailing parents and other relatives. Years of sleeping on shared cots in New York Chinatown meant that in small Fujian villages, swamps would be filled and paved over, forests would be hacked away to make room for flamboyant villas. All with American dollars saved and sent by those the Snake Heads brought.

Nibao was both lucky and unlucky, his boss, Mr. Wong said. He was both cursed and blessed. Nibao had to agree. He believed that things follow a certain preordained route but that sometimes extraordinary events could set a different force in motion, creating a bend in the path, taking lives on that path in a wholly different direction and giving them wholly different incarnations. Once he could almost hear the lychee roots ripping their way through the Fujian soil. Now because of the Snake Head's benevolence, he was standing on a concrete floor in the middle of New York City Chinatown, visible but yet invisible, in a shadow world tourists do not see, in an America only people like him ever inhabited. This was America viewed from the wrong end of the telescope.

Here in Chinatown among other refugees and outcasts, deportees and guest workers, illegals and undocumented, it was all understood that even the most zigzag, most circuitous route may no longer lead to American shores. Not for a long time perhaps. Before, it was difficult and arduous but possible: improvised crews, decrepit trawlers, contrabands like them transported around the African coast, through the constellation of Caribbean islands, then deposited in safe houses in American cities. But now it was almost impossible to get in. The Blue Police swinging heavy nightsticks were on alert, guarding American waters and American airspace. Nibao could almost hear the thwock thwock of their batons—succulent whacks—against bare skin. There was talk of torture in jail, even American jails. This was America after September 11, people whispered. Sudden raids. Electrodes, canes, scars. He would have to be all the more cautious. Do the Blue Guards make a distinction between illegals from Fujian and those from Arabia and, still yet, men who flew planes into buildings? All around him, the talk was about Osama Bin Laden, about catastrophic politics, crazy terrorists. Afghanistan would explode in a few months, maybe even weeks. The Taliban would be smart to leave while they could. Borders north and south were monitored. The country had understandably developed a low tolerance for aliens.

Nibao closed his eyes, remembered the day when his new world changed forever. Before it happened, the towers were already his personal compass, tall and confident, side by side, shoulder to shoulder against the skyline. In the crazy network of crooked Chinatown streets and alleyways, he relied on them to know whether he was going north or south. The bright summer sun threw its dappled light against their mirrored glass. He liked looking at them, remembered the time when he was in Fujian and first saw them in a picture postcard. Those returning to Fujian from a visit to America would undoubtedly position themselves squarely before the towers for pictures, as if to provide proof that they had indeed been to New York City. To him, they were New York City itself, seductive, out of reach. When he walked the Chinatown blocks, feeling terribly lost, he felt their presence, twins, looking out for each other, and this thought was strangely comforting to him. Sometimes when he felt lonely in this teeming city seething with aliens, he looked up at the sky, at the two of them, and somehow felt less alone.

That morning, he was ten blocks away, at the Happy Meat and Fish Shop. He heard the first plane bury itself into the first tower. Boom. A concussion that reverberated in the earth's interior flesh. The second plane he actually saw, over and over, on multiple replays, disappear into the building itself, only to reemerge with a long plume of fire on its tail. Up until then, it could still have been an accident. Boss Wong's friend from the Fujianese Congregation Hall had rushed into the store and flipped on the television. "What do you mean, something terrible?" Wong had asked. He was frantic. His body went slack, face glistening with sweat. His daughter worked in a restaurant on the top floor of one of the towers. "You mean a bomb?" "A hijacking?" Up until then, no one had thought of this as a possibility, to aim a passenger plane as if it were a deadly rocket into a building. Fire trucks from the Chinatown firehouse rolled past, carrying firemen in leather boots with steel shanks, bunker pants, leather helmets, coils of rope, hooks, crowbars. Fire poured out of a black hole in the sky. The twins were still standing, his spiritual connection, two dark, quivering metallic shadows. Nibao blinked, could not believe this was happening in America. And then there was the terrible sound of concrete, glass and steel collapsing, the smell of jet fuel, like burnt kerosene. Before the towers fell, there was still hope.

Afterward, everything changed.

Once upon a time, or so it seemed, he could see the tour buses. Tour number nine from Big Apple Tours would take the tourists both uptown and downtown, which included the World Trade

Center, Chinatown, Battery Park City, and the United Nations. The sidewalks were colorful with visitors from all over the world, even America. The ruts on Canal Street meant heavy traffic, prosperity. "This is so smashing! Everything in Chinatown is one big sale, no?" Pictures were snapped of wives next to hawkers, of husbands holding their poses beside bins of live salmon, red snappers, and crabs. "Take one more, just in case."

But Chinatown after September 11 was unlucky. Off-limits. Streets were cordoned off. The Holland Tunnel was closed to civilian vehicles. Flashing lights, sniffer dogs, police checkpoints. Few tourists came. Restaurants went out of business and garment factories closed. Those that were still alive had to cope with the swelling demands that came from being one of the few businesses that were still left. Nibao was both lucky and unlucky that way. He worked at one of the remaining meat shops that catered not only to Manhattan Chinatown restaurants but also to restaurants in the outer boroughs of Queens and Brooklyn, where enclaves of new Chinatowns had begun to sprout. He had plenty of work to fill his long day, even more so than before. Every week, Boss Chin would send him to Ground Zero with boxes of takeouts, moo shoo pork, roast chicken, red-lacquered duck, fried rice to feed the firemen and other workers there, ostensibly because the Happy Meat and Fish Shop and other participating restaurants had their part to play in Chinatown's contribution to the city's recovery and clean-up efforts. But Nibao also sensed that Wong was doing it for his daughter, who remained among those still missing in the wreckage. Nibao could barely look at the sight, the remains of the twin towers, their nicked, burned, scarred bodies scattered in muddy pits, twisted scaffolds of metal like skeletons hauntingly etched against a gray background of soot and smoke. The sky itself seemed utterly empty and at the same time strangely blemished, tortured. He continued walking, nursing the terrible calm coursing through his flesh.

It was after nine when Nibao began to make his way up the sidewalk of Canal Street, Chinatown. The walk from the basement lair to the butcher shop was a constant reminder of the unlucky crash months before. Manhattan too felt like a vessel plowed into earth and rock, its barnacle belly torn asunder. A rattling chamber that dizzied his senses. Neon lights, darting bodies, high-pitched human voices speaking foreign languages and even Chinese dialects he did not know. Laughing fu dogs for sale in open carts. Bok choy and rambutan, longans and lychees. Mickey Mouse T-shirts and red-lacquered shrines. Hand-knit sweaters hawked by Guatemalan Indians. Each metal screech and black-fumed cloud, each object hawked and peddled and haggled over assaulted his five senses much more accustomed to the quiet pace of Fujianese village life. But here in New York City, people from the world over came here to take up lives of danger, risk, and invention.

Nibao walked past the famous Bank of China on East Broadway, stopped and looked. He had heard about the small building across the street. Boss Wong had mentioned it, and the services it offered he had seen advertised in Chinese-language papers and leaflets stacked on crates at the Happy Meat and Fish Shop. According to Wong, the Snake Heads owned the building as well, along with "this" and "this" and "that," Wong boasted, pointing to dots on a makeshift map drawn up for Nibao's sake. Nibao looked at the sign hanging outside the building—import/export. So this was where the Snake Head performed his "fai chen," or flying money services. Nibao smiled at the thought that someday he too would have enough coins to send back home. He would come to this building, plunk down his stash of cash. In the meantime, Boss Wong warned him to keep everything hush hush because the Blue Police did not appreciate their system of underground banking— banking that leaves no traces, banking without names, papers, or records. Nibao understood. Those like him who survived intercontinental migration and phantomed their way through this new world, stalked by the ever-present Blue Police, had no paper or record that would qualify them for business with the Bank of China. The Bank of China was for people with identities. There are aspects of Chinatown life that the Americans will never comprehend.

Flying money was what they needed, this ancient system from the Teng Dynasty, exported in its new and improved version for use in America. Thousands of years before, merchants and traders who traveled the perilous Silk Road used flying money instead of carrying large sums of cash to avoid being robbed. Today in Chinatown, an undocumented man like him could walk through the door, hand over a bundle of cash, $500 dollars, for example, to the secret banker, ask that money be transferred to even the most remote place in a Fujian village, and within two days, the cash would be delivered by another secret banker in Fujian to the person with the correct password. No questions asked. No written contract. Just simple, ordinary trust. Between the two secret bankers, the debt would be settled later through their import/export connections. The secret banker in Chinatown could sell, for only 500 dollars, 1000 dollars worth of goods from his export business to the secret banker in Fujian. The magic was in the invoice, of course. Altered invoices.

But after September 11, the Blue Police, ever-more vigilant, were on the increased lookout. They were used to a different role and looked uncomfortable in their new role combating not ordinary criminals but invisible terrorists. There would be more organized raids. Army guards walked the streets in boots, camouflaged uniforms, carrying rifles, ammunition. The men who flew those planes into the twin towers had been financed with money wired through the Arabic underground network, their version of Chinese flying money. It was something the Arabic traders had picked up from the Chinese along the Silk Road long ago.

And so, just to be safe, flying money services would no longer be advertised. Just word of mouth from now on, Boss Wong said. Still, crackdown or no crackdown, the Snake Heads would continue to rely on this secret, underground bank to lend money to those in Fujian who could not afford down payments. And those in Chinatown would still come here to order flying money services for relatives back home. This nondescript building in front of him was one of the hubs of Fujianese Chinatown. Even American laws could not change this fact. Boss Wong snickered, "The Bank of China took three weeks, charged a bad foreign-exchange rate and delivered the cash in yuan. The Snake Heads delivered the money in hours, charged less, and paid in American dollars. Where would you go even if you had a choice?" Things became so bad that the bank began offering color televisions and prizes to those who used them for money transferring. Boss Wong said, "No one came."

Nibao continued walking the crooked streets of Chinatown, seemingly caught in its twists and turns. On his right was the Chinese Merchants Association, the On Leong Tong—"Peaceful and Virtuous Association"—with its pagoda roof and gold balconies. Nibao stared. It was one of the strongest tongs in the city. Different groups, merchants, workers had their own associations. Each carved out its own fiefdom. Each had local chapters all over, in Houston, Dallas, Atlanta, Washington D.C., and along the West Coast. The tongs were simply part of life, originally meant to be

138

protection societies for weak family associations and as old as Chinatown itself. They gave money to Sun Yat-Sen's revolution. Even Chiang Kai-Shek once had his own triads, secret societies on which today's tongs were modeled.

Now, On Leong Tong ran the Ghost Shadows Gang and controlled Mott Street. Hip Sing Tong did its business on Pell Street, was affiliated with the Flying Dragons Gang. There was Tung On Tong and its Tung On Boys Gang on Division Street, and the Fukien American Association with its Fuk Ching Gang on East Broadway. Like other new arrivals, Nibao had learned this well. It was important to know when a man was trespassing.

Rumor had it that the Snake Heads operated from one of these tongs. Certainly they had a tough business to run. With the risks and expense involved in shuttling human contraband, the distance between the points of departure and destination, the need to cultivate virtually a mini United Nations of underground facilitators, some on a permanent retainer basis to run safe houses, and a list of other unspecified urgencies, one could see why rules had to be enforced and tong power applied to those who strayed. After all, most of the city's Fujianese understood that the economy of smuggling must be run on a tight, orderly basis.

Even in Fujian, the party chiefs cooperated with the tongs and directed the police to "open one eye but close the other." And why not? Take a look at Changle, Tingjiang, and Lianjiang, the three centers of power near Fuzhou for the Snake Heads. As long as the Snake Heads did well, the Fujian construction business, specializing in mansions complete with marble staircases, English turrets, and Jacuzzi thrived. The provincial government also thrived. Rumors had it that with 500-million American dollars in remittances each year, it was natural for the local guards to enjoy a cut. This would be in addition to the coins dropped in secret coffers to ensure safe transit from Fujian ports.

The Snake Heads were feared, yes, but also revered. Some of the Snake Heads were also charitable. If someone died on the journey, free passage could be given to a relative.

With them in charge, this was not a place where things failed to happen. The way Boss Chin put it, "If people do not pay the money they agreed to pay, then of course the Snake Heads will have to take some measures."

And so they all understood more than they let on about tong

power. They worked full shifts and took few breaks. They took no chances. An oral contract was the most binding, understood. "No need to explain." The tongs had no need to use actual threats. Their sai low, little brothers, as the foot soldier enforcers were called, only had to say, "My big brother needs a hundred dollars, can you help?" Or "I want to sell you an orange tree," and then demand many more than the orange tree was actually worth. It was also understood that the contract that had to be honored was the unwritten one. Neither Chinese nor American, lives such as Nibao's, indentured lives, were expendable.

Nibao was almost home. This was where he will live for years— Mott Street, Chinatown, where bedrooms routinely doubled as terraces, refuse rooms, wash lines, stand-up beds, and where even narrow sidewalks served as illegal sublets for shopkeepers eager to charge vegetable peddlers $2000 a month for their own patch of cement.

And so oceans away from Fujian, he lived his life in shifts. Nibao worked days and slept nights, bunked with twenty other day workers in a Mott Street tenement building that the Snake Heads had purchased with cash. While he sharpened knives and slashed and sliced fish and meat, other coolies who worked the night shift took their place, sleeping and living in a mirror world. Nibao never saw these day ghosts. He left for the shop before their home rotated.

Tonight as he crawled into bed, all he could smell on his pillow was the sweat and musk oil of the day ghosts he had yet to see.

Notes

1. 113 U.S. 27 (1885).
2. 31 P. 245 (Cal. 1892).

Bibliography

Himilce Novas and Lan Cao, *Everything You Need to Know About Asian Americans* (Penguin Plume) (2d ed. 2004).

Lan Cao, *The Diaspora of Ethnic Economies: Beyond the Pale?* 44 *Wm & Mary L. Rev.* 1521 (2003).

Paul Ong, *An Ethnic Trade: The Chinese Laundries in Early California*, J. *Ethnic Stud.*, Fall 1981.

*Deborah W. Denno**

Death Bed

I am sitting in the witness stand of a courtroom in Frankfort, Kentucky, facing David, a young defense lawyer at Kentucky's Department of Advocacy. David is standing at a podium questioning me. It is April 18, 2005. We have been waiting for this moment for a very long time. I am the first of a dozen expert witnesses to testify in *Baze et al. v. Rees et al.*,[1] a bench trial concerning the constitutionality of Kentucky's lethal injection protocol. Lethal injection is this country's most widely used method of executing death row inmates. I am testifying on behalf of the plaintiffs, Ralph Baze and Thomas Bowling, two condemned inmates who are claiming that the Kentucky protocol constitutes cruel and unusual punishment under the Eighth Amendment of the United States Constitution and Section 17 of the Kentucky Constitution. The three defendants involved in this trial are most responsible for how Kentucky's executions are handled. They are the Commissioner of the Kentucky Department of Corrections, the Warden of the Kentucky State Penitentiary, and the Governor of the Commonwealth of Kentucky.

For months, David and his colleagues have been preparing for this trial. I am here because I have studied lethal injection, indeed all of this country's execution methods, for nearly fifteen years while a professor at Fordham University School of Law in New York City. The topic of execution methods has so troubled me that I have continued to follow it during my entire legal career, in spite of other professional interests and commitments. To me, the problem with execution methods symbolizes nearly everything that has gone astray with the death penalty in this country.

This courtroom scenario in Frankfort is not what people typically think of when they hear the word "trial" in the popularized television sense of that word. Everything about the setting projects smallness and understatement. Frankfort, the state capital, has a population of less than 30,000 people. The city's courthouse is a miniature of all the ones I have ever seen. There are only two courtrooms in the entire building. There is no Starbucks. Most certainly, this is no place for a *Boston Legal* episode where trials seem like packed fish bowls viewed by hundreds. As I sit in this courtroom, however, I am continually reminded that some of the most significant cases ever decided in this country started in locales that many Americans would consider quaint. We merely watch, not experience, *Law & Order* lives.

A civil bench trial is also very different from a criminal jury trial. In a civil bench trial, there is no direct involvement of the inmates' peers by way of a jury vote. A prosecutor and defense attorney do not battle over the guilt or innocence of the inmates. There is little interest in the original facts of the case. The inmates have already been convicted of murder and sentenced to death. They are not appealing their sentences and are not even present in the courtroom. Indeed, because this bench trial is a civil matter and a lawsuit, the inmates, who were previously called defendants in their criminal case, are now called plaintiffs.

Regardless, the "how" of Kentucky's executions is the heart of the plaintiffs' case. The constitutionality of execution methods is also of burgeoning significance throughout the country as medical investigations continually reveal the troubling, and all too latent, aspects of lethal injection. The concern is highly democratic within the death row inmate population. The risks of an inhumane lethal injection affect every inmate equally, no matter their color, their class, the quality of their legal representation or the purported social value of their victim. Each inmate has been designated by the state to die in the same way. In this bench trial, we are wrangling over how exactly that death will occur.

David and I both believe that lethal injection is not what the public and many lawmakers think it is—a serene and soothing way to die, like putting a sick animal to sleep. We think the process is inhumane and tortuous, the result of medical folly, political compromise. We want to convince the Kentucky judge of this. The attorneys representing the Commonwealth of Kentucky want to convince the judge that we are wrong. They claim that lethal injection is in fact a humane and suitable way to die.

This trial will be a battle of experts, but also a battle of words, said and unsaid. All exchanges will take place within predetermined legal limits. The challenge is, how can we convey our arguments within the imposed structure of this hearing and its rules?

The message that will unfold cannot be imparted like a standard story. Rather, it must reveal itself within the context of three parts: a series of questions that David will ask me and the other experts on direct examination, what the Commonwealth's attorney will then ask us under cross examination, and then what David may want to clarify during redirect examination. This procedure enables the admission of evidence, rules that have been set out and refined over hundreds of years of tradition in the British-American legal system. The process is exciting for me, an academic, accustomed to the hallowed Socratic method, in which I, as Professor of Law, relentlessly question my students. Now, I am in the role of answering questions, not asking them. I relish this role.

In the past few years, there have been a number of evidentiary hearings on lethal injection across the country. From lethal injection's inception in 1977, the method of execution has been continually under constitutional attack. Yet, lawyers have also always had a great deal of difficulty finding out the specifics of how a lethal injection is conducted and what protocols or guidelines have been and are used to ensure that executions are conducted humanely. The lack of information has made it impossible to have a thorough challenge to the method's constitutionality. Over the years, however, a committed group of academics, lawyers, and doctors have chipped away at the shell of secrecy, releasing forward a bounty of new information on a wide range of issues. This 2005 trial in Kentucky brings a fresh message: it is the fullest and most sophisticated investigation of lethal injection ever conducted.

A Note on the Lethal Injection Process

In most states, including Kentucky, lethal injection involves having an executioner syringe three chemicals into the body of an inmate sentenced to death: *sodium thiopenthal*, an "ultrashort" acting barbiturate intended to put the inmate to sleep; *pancuronium bromide*, a paralytic agent used to immobilize the inmate; and *potassium chloride*, a toxin that induces cardiac arrest and hastens the inmate's death. These injections

143

are to occur sequentially, while the inmate is strapped to a gurney, a padded stretcher typically used for transporting hospitalized patients. There have been photos of the execution gurney so artfully shot that the gurney does indeed look like a bed, an inviting place where a person would want to stretch out if not for the fact it is to be used for a killing.

I use the term "death bed" to depict this execution scenario even though these words have not been applied in this context before, either by legal practitioners or academics. Typically, deathbed connotes the last few hours of a dying person's life or the place from which a dying person makes a final statement. An inmate on an executioner's gurney, however, is strapped down, not free, and is dying not because of failed health but because the state has determined the inmate should be punished to death.

In 2002, I published an article in a symposium issue of the *Ohio State Law Journal* focusing on the problems associated with lethal injection. The article contended that lethal injection was unconstitutional under the United States Supreme Court's interpretation of the Eighth Amendment's Cruel and Unusual Punishment Clause for a range of reasons: the procedure involved the "unnecessary and wanton infliction of pain," the "risk" of such pain, "physical violence," the offense to "human dignity," and the contravention of "evolving standards of decency."

My conclusions were supported by a large study I conducted of the most up-to-date protocols for administering lethal injection in all thirty-six states, which, at that time, used anesthesia for state executions. The study focused on a number of factors that are critical to conducting a lethal injection humanely, such as: the types and amounts of chemicals that are injected; the selection, training, preparation, and qualifications of the lethal injection team; the involvement of medical personnel; the presence of witnesses, including media witnesses; as well as details on how the procedure is conducted and how much of it witnesses can see. The fact that executions are not typically conducted by doctors, but by execution technicians, is a critical aspect of the process.

In the article, I argued that many of the problems with lethal injection could be attributed to vague lethal injection statutes, uninformed prison personnel, and skeletal or inaccurate lethal injection protocols. When some state protocols provide details, such as the amount and type of chemicals that executioners inject, they often reveal striking errors, omissions, and ignorance about the procedure. Such inaccurate or missing information heightens the likelihood that a lethal injection will be botched and suggests that states are not capable of executing an inmate without violating the prohibition against cruel and unusual punishment.

Over the decades, there have been many drawbacks associated with lethal injection, all of which contradict the public's perception that injection is a peaceful way to die. First, evidence suggests that some inmates are given insufficient amounts of the initial chemical, sodium thiopental, and therefore regain consciousness while being injected with the second and third chemicals. In this situation, the inmate will suffer extraordinary pain while the second chemical, pancuronium bromide, takes its paralytic effect, preventing the inmate from moving or communicating in any way. Then when the third chemical, potassium chloride, is administered to cause death, the paralyzed inmate will experience a burning sensation likened to a hot poker inserted into his arm, which spreads over his entire body until it causes the heart to stop. It is striking that the American Veterinary Medical Association has condemned the use of pancuronium bromide and potassium chloride for the euthanasia of animals because the paralyzing effect of the pancuronium bromide would mask the excruciating pain that the animal was experiencing from the potassium chloride. These chemicals are too horrifying for killing animals but they are routinely used to execute human beings.

The vagueness of the protocols also results in executioners often ignoring an inmate's particular physical characteristics (such as age, body weight, drug use), factors that have a major impact on an individual's reactions to chemicals and the condition of their veins. Physicians have problems finding suitable veins for injection among individuals who are diabetic, obese, or extremely muscular. Heavy drug users, who constitute a significant portion of the death row population, present particularly difficult challenges because of their damaged veins and resistance to even high levels of lethal injection chemicals.

All of these difficulties are compounded for untrained executioners, who are the ones typically carrying out the protocols. For example, executioners having trouble finding a vein because of obesity or drug use may insert a catheter into a sensitive area of the body, such as a groin or hand. In some cases, if a vein can still not be found, executioners will perform a "cut-down" procedure, which requires an incision to expose the damaged vein. The cut-down procedure is used with disturbing frequency in lethal injection executions, while it is only a memory to modern day anesthesiologists, who have far more feasible alternatives. The cut-down problem has even caught the eye of the Supreme Court. In May 2004, in *Nelson v. Campbell*,[2] the Court unanimously held that an Alabama death row inmate could file a civil rights suit to challenge the state's proposal to execute him with a cut-down procedure. *Nelson* is the first case where the Court has addressed the lethal injection issue. While the *Nelson* case did not concern the merits of lethal injection, it appears the Court may have already come to terms with the broader aspects of the procedure because the Court was willing to call into question one aspect of it.

The Kentucky Trial's Rules and Constraints

This backdrop puts perspective on the bench trial in Frankfort and the issues concerning the lethal injection protocol in Kentucky. Three days before the trial, I flew to Lexington, Kentucky, to stay at the home of my friend and colleague, Roberta Harding, a professor at the University of Kentucky School of Law. Roberta and I had met some years ago while working together on a death penalty issue and she was closely involved with some of the cases handled by the Kentucky Department of Advocacy. My early arrival in Lexington gave me the opportunity to prepare, to confer with Roberta who would also be attending the trial, as well as to have a few moments to take in the Kentucky countryside.

The rolling hills of bluegrass were never more glorious than during our Monday morning drive to Frankfort, timed so that Roberta and I could reach the courthouse sufficiently early to touch base with the attorneys beforehand. Although the drive was only forty-five minutes, it was an amazingly refreshing trip given the abundance of greenery and the burst of a spring season that had not quite yet arrived in New York. The city of Frankfort was surrounded by all things rural, and I could not help but envy its residents.

The state capital since 1792, Frankfort has a charming, small town feel. Its buildings and homes are gorgeously historic, a snapshot of the early architectural wonder of our country. The Frankfort courthouse is an aptly elegant structure for holding such an important trial. But my feelings of awe in this setting were quickly marred by the reality of the circumstances of our visit—as though the city's gentility was on a collision course with the ugliness of our purpose for being there. To me, the death penalty and lethal injection in particular were reminders of all the damage that people can do to one another no matter what the blessings of their surroundings. It was as though we as a society felt that we did not quite deserve such harmony, such beauty, and therefore had to go and foil it in some was by scavenging for our more brutal natures. Were

146

we truly meant to be such two-sided beings or did we simply fail to appreciate what we had been given? No matter. Brutality seemed to be abounding that day. I had no time to pick apart my thoughts. We had work to do. Up the courthouse steps we went.

Of course, the outcome of a bench trial is heavily dependent on the judge. I had heard good things about Judge Roger L. Crittenden, the Circuit Court judge whose courtroom demeanor and decisions would be so important to our case. Judge Crittenden, a registered Democrat and graduate of the University of Kentucky School of Law, was a Franklin District Court judge from 1980-1991, before becoming a Franklin Circuit Court judge in 1992. With over 25 years total on the bench, he seemed to have a solid foundation for evaluating the evidence. But this was a case with political overtones. At the time of the trial, Judge Crittenden was one of three candidates Kentucky's governor was considering to fill a vacancy on the heavily Republican Kentucky Supreme Court. Ultimately, Kentucky's governor selected a Republican nominee for the vacancy, an outcome that the press viewed as predictably political. At the time of this writing, Judge Crittenden had expressed "disappointment" with not being asked to take the post but had not yet indicated that he would seek election to the Kentucky Supreme Court in 2006.

It was difficult to tell if these circumstances would have any impact on the outcome of the bench trial. In news reports, Judge Crittenden has characterized his decisions as more conservative than liberal. A number of commentators had noted, however, that Judge Crittenden does not show a clear discernible pattern in his voting record. Judge Crittenden himself had stated that he approached all issues on a case-by-case basis. This reputation made the outcome in our case seem even less predictable.

I learned before my travels to Frankfort about the constraints on the substance of my testimony. These rules inhibit an expert's language, the specific words they can use, and the ways their statements can be phrased. And, such restrictions make the process of testifying somewhat more difficult.

David detailed the constraints the Commonwealth's attorneys specifically requested for my testimony. First, I cannot talk about the Eighth Amendment's Cruel and Unusual Punishment Clause or how it is to be interpreted or has been interpreted. This is understandable. The judge decides the law, not the expert.

Second, I am forbidden to give a medical opinion about the chemicals used in a lethal injection execution. Again, this limitation makes sense. I am not a medical doctor and have no experience working with these chemicals, even though I have read a great deal about them. Any discussion of cut-down procedures is also barred, presumably for the same reason.

Next, I am prohibited from mentioning Fred Leuchter. I find this request most perplexing. Until 1990, Leuchter was the creator of most of this country's execution machinery. I had written earlier about Leuchter's grip on the execution methods industry and long ago, I had even had a lengthy discussion with him. But Leuchter's story involved far more than just execution methods. He was an unrelenting public speaker who denied the existence of the Holocaust and was obsessed with the revisionist movement.

Leuchter's controversial side garnered him a spotlight. Jewish groups took notice, discovering that Leuchter was not the "engineer" he claimed he was but rather only the holder of a bachelor's degree in history—in other words, no more educationally qualified to build execution equipment than the typical arts and sciences graduate, no matter how self-taught in the area he professed to be. Leuchter told me the revelation destroyed his business. No warden would go near him publicly although privately wardens still called him for advice because there was simply no one else available with Leuchter's execution methods expertise. Further, no person or corporation was rushing to fill the gaping hole in such a socially repellant enterprise.

There is so much more I could say about Leuchter and his false representations that my account of him here is a sugarcoating. I suppose that the Commonwealth's attorneys thought that Leuchter's well-documented revisionist antics would be highly prejudicial, that his purported pro-Nazi leanings would distract from the merits of the lethal injection arguments. Of course, I have always thought that Leuchter exemplified in his own bizarre way the true underbelly of the execution methods business. Directly or indirectly, he is responsible for how the great majority of inmates in this country have been executed and how they will be executed. The fragile state of the execution methods industry is highlighted by the fact that wardens continued to depend on Leuchter despite all that has been exposed about him.

Lastly, I could not discuss the topic of electrocution. Again, this seems to make sense to me although I can see how the topic could creep into this trial on grounds of relevancy. On March 31, 1998, the Kentucky legislature voted to switch the state's method of execution from electrocution to lethal injection. However, like a number of other state legislatures that voted to change from electrocution to lethal injection, the legislature did not entirely eliminate electrocution as a method of execution for some inmates. If the condemned inmate was sentenced to death before the March 31, 1998 date, he can still be executed by electrocution if he makes it an affirmative choice. Under the principles of *ex post facto*, a state legislature may decide to leave an option available so that an inmate may not be worse off by any legislature's enacted change after the date of his crime. There are still nearly thirty Kentucky inmates remaining who can choose between electrocution or lethal injection.

Still, it is one of the many contradictions in this area that Kentucky or any state allows such a choice between execution methods for some inmates but not for others, based upon the date when the newer and presumably more humane method was legislated and the date of the commission of the inmate's crime. This compromise tactic is not atypical, however. And, for some states, the situation can get even more complicated. For example, South Carolina has a unique choice provision with no apparent purpose apart from some odd compromise based upon statutes in other states. As of June 8, 1995, all inmates in South Carolina can choose between electrocution and lethal injection as a method of execution no matter when they were sentenced to death. The differences come for those inmates who fail to choose either method, and therefore are assigned by default the method prescribed by statute. Those inmates sentenced to death before June 8, 1995, are executed by electrocution if they do not choose lethal injection; those inmates sentenced to death after June 8, 1995, are executed by lethal injection if they do not choose electrocution. While this statutory scheme is one of the more weirdly convoluted, in a very basic way, all the schemes are.

One reason for such a peculiar approach to selecting execution methods is a concern that all state legislatures have when it comes to the death penalty: If the legislatures introduce a new method of execution, such as lethal injection, the old method, typically electrocution, will be presumed unconstitutional. Some state statutes go so far as to make certain that the old method of execution (such as electrocution) is not rendered unconstitutional simply because lethal injection has been introduced. With this kind of statutory jig, state legislatures attempt to ensure that no method of execution will ever become unconstitutional, thereby barring any suggestion that the death penalty in general is vulnerable to constitutional attack. Like all death penalty jurisprudence, the topic of execution methods is rife with irony, double-think, irrationality, and obfuscation. Thus, it is endlessly fascinating.

The Kentucky Trial Begins

With these and other constraints in place, the trial begins. Because I am the first witness, I must wait outside in the hallway during the initial proceedings, until the judge calls my name and a bailiff comes to get me.

I am sitting in a chair near the water fountain, yearning to testify. I feel as though two inmates' lives are hanging in the balance along with potentially every other death row inmate in the country. I believe that much of this trial is about how death penalty politics get in the way of justice and, in this particular case, even common sense.

But I am not the only one waiting in the hallway. There are several other witnesses lined up to be called. Out of curiosity, I try to overhear their conversations as a group of them stand in the corner to the right of me. I think that they are prison administrators, most likely there to be questioned about the lethal injection procedures during their earlier tenure at the Kentucky State Penitentiary.

In the corner to my left, a reporter is questioning a pastor about the death penalty. The pastor clearly thinks lethal injection is unconstitutional and is telling the reporter his views with great passion. I turn once again to my right and look at one of the prison administrators who is speaking the loudest in the group. I believe he says to his colleagues that he did not want to come to the trial this morning. In a way, I can understand his line of thinking. He was delegated a role he should never have been given. The legislatures make such important decisions initially about the death penalty, only to pass on the actual implementation of their choices, such as what execution method to use, to prison personnel who have no training or expertise to carry them out. This process does not seem fair to those on the lowest level of the political hierarchy, much less to the inmates who bear the brunt of such an irresponsible degree of delegation.

The door to the courtroom opens and I look up expecting to see a bailiff. Instead, I see one of the defense attorneys who is coming out in the hallway to drink from the water fountain. He looks at me and chuckles, "Now I get to see a law professor on the stand." It is a funny comment for this setting, and I grin in response to it. Of course, the attorney is referring to the fact that the tables are turned. I represent "every law professor" who has ever administered the Socratic method to a student in class—an experience all law students abhor, no matter their veil of seeming arrogance when questioned, no matter how kind the law professor attempts to be.

Modern-day law professors no longer try to emulate the famously sadistic Professor Kingsley in *One-L*, Scott Turow's poignant account of first year law school. We make an effort to be gentle, realizing that no good, and certainly no pedagogic value, derives from embarrassment. The rewards of such professorial concern, however, have an airtight cap. It is the experience itself that students fear—that perilous verbal test before dozens of their peers—that marks their intellectual reputation in class and provides life-long fodder for the inevitable law school yarns. Everyone who has been a law student knows those Socratic professor nightmares; they never go away.

Oddly, these thoughts spur my desire to get into the courtroom with the hope of setting the record straight. I have the Socratic method down. Being grilled does not concern me. The door opens once again and the bailiff calls me in.

I walk into the courtroom for the second time that morning. I had wanted to see the room before I testified, so that I would have my bearings, no atmospheric surprises. The courtroom is sunny and relatively modern, obviously refurbished from its original appearance. At my first viewing, I was crushed to see that it looked so new and cheap, from the synthetic paneling of the jury box to the institutional beige walls and rugs to the moveable video cameras off to the side. I had wanted to see the original structure, thinking how magnificent it must have been at one point. I had envisioned, say, mahogany walls, an antique gold clock, intricate weaves. Now the scene appears Wal-Mart-like, a jarring contrast to the historic loveliness of the city around it.

I cannot help but think that this redone setting will have an effect on the outcome of the case, as though it is not just the architecture that was covered in bland courtroom "modernese" but our ideals and values as well. There is something very unnerving about the sterile, medicalized, guise of lethal injection that makes it seem as though it is progressive, when in fact it is anything but that. Rather, it is medical technology gone awry, used for a goal that was never intended. From this perspective, then, perhaps the decor of this courtroom is actually much more appropriate for the subject matter of this bench trial than the grand design of yonder years. After all, it does seem as though our criminal justice system has become covered in thick ugly plastic.

I am surprised at how many people are sitting in the courtroom gallery and by the sizeable number of reporters who have appeared. It is clear that a contingent of individuals is very interested in this issue, and I sense that they share my side. After all, lethal injection advocates need not make the effort to attend such a trial. They are still winning this war.

The bailiff is kind and makes sure that I am seated before he leaves my side. As I turn to take the oath, Judge Crittenden greets me with a nod and smile before swearing me in. I appreciate the gestures. I am not accustomed to such cordiality in this context. I have testified as an expert before and, when judges have already made up their minds, they can make it clear that your presence is not wanted.

Questions and Answers

I glance up and there is David, looking very serious. It is only the second time I have ever seen him. As with all hearings, David's questions start with addressing my qualifications. *What is your current profession? How long have you been a professor of law? Where have your previously testified in court concerning lethal injection?*

My answers are short and clipped, basically one-liners. They have to be. In 1997, I had testified in two evidentiary hearings on lethal injection. One hearing was in Texas (the first such hearing in the country), the other in Connecticut, which, in 1997, had not yet executed anyone by lethal injection. During the Kentucky trial, I knew that it was considered relevant only to say the names of the states and the years. But I wanted to have been able to say more.

I would have liked to have noted that the Texas and Connecticut hearings occurred eight years ago and that a great deal more information and more scientific data on lethal injection had emerged since that time. Only those individuals studying the process for many years would realize this evolution. The opinions from the 1997 hearings were not openly published, so no outsider would ever know about them or the dearth of knowledge then before the courts. Looking back on the first hearing in Texas, I realize in retrospect how little we knew about lethal injection. Modern evidence has only confirmed our earlier statements about the worrisome application of the chemicals, and has revealed even more problems.

The next set of questions David asks me concern what I have written on the topic and for how long. *As a law professor, have you researched* lethal injection? When did you begin to research lethal injection? How many texts or articles on lethal injection have you published?

I give the titles of five publications. David asks me to go through each of them and discuss what they are about. Unfortunately for the purposes of my testimony, each article has a substantial analysis of the Eighth Amendment and how the doctrine may apply to execution methods. The Eighth Amendment was one of the areas I was prohibited from mentioning in my testimony. When I briefly gloss over the substance of this discussion, the Commonwealth's attorney immediately objects, reminding me that I cannot reference the Eighth Amendment. I find out by virtue of his objection that I cannot even *mention* that I discussed the Eighth Amendment in an article. It is as though the topic is profane.

My statements are strictly confined to repeating some of the more technical aspects of my articles, most particularly my 2002 *Ohio State Law Journal* publication on the survey of lethal injection protocols. Although my 2002 article has been introduced into the record, one purpose of my testimony is to demonstrate how Kentucky in particular fares relative to other states as well as to emphasize aspects of the article that are particularly relevant to this bench trial.

The Eighth Amendment cap in the trial reminds me of how rarely the substance of the amendment is addressed, even in the professional, legal literature. The Eighth Amendment is widely applied in practice, but peculiarly skirted in academia. For example, the principles of the Eighth Amendment are typically not examined in detail in mainstream constitutional law or criminal procedure books. The doctrine also falls through the cracks in law school classes unless a professor specifically focuses on the death penalty, which is usually covered in a seminar. A comparable kind of neglect is shown when state and federal cases apply the amendment, as they commonly do in a range of circumstances. In the execution methods context in particular, citations to legal doctrines arising from the Eighth Amendment—or the phrase "Cruel and Unusual Punishment"—are commonly truncated and often inaccurate and incomplete.

David now focuses on my 2002 publication, which examined the results of my survey of lethal injection protocols. *How did you go about researching and reviewing execution protocols, procedures, and the chemicals used in lethal injections?*

I explain that at the time the survey was conducted, thirty-six states had statutes authorizing anesthesia for a state execution. My research assistant first checked to see if the protocols for these thirty-six states were publicly available, that is in public venues beyond what was designated in a state statute, such as information set out in Web sites, described in court cases, or provided in some other kind of hard copy documentation. For those protocols that were not publicly available, my assistant would usually call the state's department of corrections or another state agency to gather necessary information, particularly details on the types of chemicals used and the qualifications and training of executioners. State officials would provide us with all or some part of this information we were seeking, either over the phone or by e-mail.

I point out that for seven states, the information on lethal injection chemicals was declared unavailable. Officials in four states said that the information was confidential (Nevada, Pennsylvania, South Carolina, and Virginia); three additional states said the information did not exist (Kansas, Kentucky, and New Hampshire). I hone in on the following point that particularly distinguished Kentucky's "nonexistent" information. When my assistant called Kentucky's Department of Corrections, he was told that while there was a statute that describes the use of the death penalty, Kentucky did not have a protocol or policy to implement executions by lethal injection. My assistant was informed that the protocol would be applied on a case-by-case basis. This fact has great relevance to the reasons for this trial.

Of course, David is trying to show that even though Kentucky now has a somewhat publicly available protocol, none existed in the fall of 2001, when I conducted my survey. Indeed, the Department of Corrections' representative told my assistant over the phone that "[t]he protocol would be dictated by each case as it comes up." This procedure screamed out an absence of care and planning on the part of the Department of Corrections. There was no documented format for an attorney to investigate or challenge.

David's next series of questions tie this information about Kentucky to the broader history and procedure of lethal injection, focusing specifically on the kinds of chemicals Kentucky now says it will use in the future. *How many states currently have the death penalty?*

I say, 37 states, noting that New York recently abolished the death penalty.

How many states currently use lethal injection as a method of execution?

I say, 36 states, excluding New York. What I do not say is that Nebraska is the only state left that does not use lethal injection. The

Nebraska legislature has, however, considered a number of bills proposing that the state switch to lethal injection from electrocution, now the state's only legalized method of execution.

With the next series of questions, David planned to delve into the history of lethal injection and how it began to be used in this country. *Which state was the first to adopt lethal injection?* I say, Oklahoma. *In what year?* 1977. *How did Oklahoma go about adopting lethal injection as a method of execution?*

My answer to this question is deceptively short out of necessity and deference to the boundaries that are imposed upon me by the proceedings. In the trial I tell how in 1977, the now-deceased Senator Bill Dawson of Oklahoma asked Dr. Stanley Deutsch, then head of the Department of Anesthesiology at the University of Oklahoma Health Sciences Center, to recommend a manner of executing inmates by way of an injection of lethal chemicals. Senator Dawson was concerned about the high cost of fixing the electric chair that Oklahoma already had or building a new gas chamber, which could cost thousands of dollars. Besides, Dr. Deutsch had informed him that lethal injection was a viable means of execution. In a short, typo-ridden, letter to Senator Dawson dated February 28, 1977, Dr. Deutsch made some recommendations for how a lethal injection might take place. His recommendations included the use of two different kinds of chemicals for an injection.

That is where the story ends for purposes of the trial but there was far more to tell about how Oklahoma's lethal injection statute was written. What I had to leave out of my testimony was that in May, 1977, three months after Dr. Deutsch had sent his letter to Senator Dawson, Oklahoma adopted a lethal injection statute based in large part on Dr. Deutsch's letter suggesting employment of two types of chemicals. Indeed, Oklahoma's lethal injection statute, which has been copied by many other states, repeats nearly verbatim the terms that Dr. Deutsch wrote in his letter to Senator Dawson.

Dr. Deutsch's letter stated that unconsciousness and then "death" would be produced by "[t]he administration . . . intravenously . . . in [specified] quantities of . . . an ultra-short-acting barbiturate (for example, sodium thiopental) in "combination" with a "nueormuscular [sic] blocking drug[ ]" (for example, pancuronium bromide) to create a "long duration of *paralysis.*" Oklahoma's lethal injection statute, which tracks the language of Dr. Deutsch's letter almost word for word, states that "[t]he punishment of death must be inflicted by continuous, *intravenous administration* of a lethal *quantity of an ultra-short-acting barbiturate* in *combination* with a chemical *paralytic* agent until *death* is pronounced by a licensed physician according to accepted standards of medical practice." It is a disturbing thought indeed that a statute of such extraordinary significance for people's lives, and deaths, is based on such a short and informal correspondence.

David's next few questions probe more specifically into how Oklahoma came up with the particular types of chemicals that the state's Department of Corrections selected for its protocol. Since the publication of my 2002 statewide study of lethal injection protocols, lawyers have been able to acquire, through the Freedom of Information Act, Oklahoma's initial 1978 protocol, as it was originally written.

What chemicals did Oklahoma use in its first lethal injection protocol? I say, sodium thiopental and a paralytic agent. There was more information I could not divulge because it was not relevant for the purposes of answering this particular question. Oklahoma's 1978 protocol specifically mentions sodium thiopental as the ultra-short-acting barbiturate, but includes a possible choice of three paralytic agents: "either *tubo-curarine* or *succinylcholine chloride* or *potassium chloride*." Dr. Deutsch's letter mentions "succinylcholine" but not tubo-curarine or potassium chloride.

This revelation about the choices of three paralytic agents in Oklahoma's 1978 protocol is astonishing. It has always been a mystery how potassium chloride ever became the third chemical to be employed in a lethal injection procedure. Potassium chloride's inclusion as a paralytic agent in Oklahoma's protocol, and the fact that this formula was then unthinkingly copied in other states, is one possible explanation.

In order to emphasize the fact that it was problematic for the Oklahoma Department of Corrections to select these chemicals, David uses the next set of questions to establish that at no time was any research conducted on the effects of any of these drugs on the human body in the context of an execution. The lack of any kind of study has always been one of the more shocking discoveries about the lethal injection procedure. Of course, it is impossible to test directly a mechanism for killing people. Further, the kind of experimentation that was carried out in the 1800s on animals to determine the effectiveness of electrocution on humans would most likely be prohibited today. At the same time, it is clear that more thorough research could have been attempted on the potential impact of these lethal injection chemicals on the human body given what we know about their use for other purposes.

Did your research reveal the reason why these particular chemicals [sodium thiopental and pancuronium bromide] were to be used [by Oklahoma]? My answer: Other than Dr. Deutsch's letter and its recommendations, my research revealed no other basis for Oklahoma to have chosen these particular chemicals.

What if any medical or scientific studies on the effects of these chemicals when used for a lethal injection were conducted before Oklahoma adopted the chemicals for lethal injection? My answer: No such studies were ever conducted.

What if any medical or scientific studies on whether these chemicals caused pain when used for a lethal injection were conducted before Oklahoma adopted the chemicals for lethal injection? My answer: My research revealed no such studies were conducted.

What if any medical or scientific studies were conducted before Oklahoma adopted lethal injection to determine whether other chemicals could be used? My answer: No such studies were conducted.

Oklahoma became the first state to adopt lethal injection as a method of execution in 1977. How many states since have adopted lethal injection as a method of execution? My answer: 36 states.

Out of the 36 states, from how many have you reviewed execution protocols or other information concerning their lethal injection procedures? My answer: 28 states.

Why did you not review the protocols of all 36 states? My answer: At the time of my study in 2001, Alabama had not yet adopted lethal injection. And seven states, as I mentioned, either informed me that the information about protocols was confidential or that it did not exist. In sum, 28 states (with lethal injection) + 1 state (Alabama, which did not have lethal injection) + 7 states (with missing information) = 36 states.

How many of these states use the two chemicals originally adopted in Oklahoma? My answer: 27 states. Also, there may be others since seven states did not disclose their procedures or protocols.

Which states follow Oklahoma? My answer: Arizona, Arkansas, California, Colorado, Connecticut, Delaware, Florida, Georgia, Idaho, Illinois, Indiana, Louisiana, Maryland, Mississippi, Missouri, Montana, New Mexico, New York, North Carolina, Ohio, Oregon, South Dakota, Tennessee, Texas, Utah, Washington, and Wyoming.

Based on your research, what if any medical or scientific studies on the effects of these chemicals were conducted before these states adopted the chemicals for lethal injection? My answer: There were no studies conducted.

What about whether the chemicals cause pain? My answer: There were no studies conducted.

What about other chemicals that could be used? My answer: There were no studies conducted.

At this point, David starts focusing on the third chemical, potassium chloride, as well as on the two states that deviate from the typical three-chemical lethal injection pattern. The purpose of this line of questioning is to highlight the peculiar origins of the use of potassium chloride and how it too has questionable applicability to an execution by lethal injection.

Which, if any, states do not use sodium thiopental and pancuronium bromide? My answer: New Jersey.

What does New Jersey use? My answer: The applicable statute indicates that sodium thiopental and potassium chloride are to be administered. What I do not say because it is not deemed relevant to this line of questioning is that the New Jersey Department of Corrections has noted consistently over the years that when it does execute an inmate, it plans to use three drugs, including one to stop breathing. This tactic suggests that state statutes may not reflect the actuality of an execution when decision-making power is delegated to prison personnel. In the case of New Jersey, contrary to statute, prison officials have said that they actually plan to inject pancuronium bromide or a paralytic agent that is similar to it.

How did potassium chloride come to be used in lethal injections? My answer: There are three plausible sources. First, Oklahoma's original 1978 protocol mentioned potassium chloride under its list of potential paralytic agents to be employed in an execution. Second, advising doctors, some of whom were involved in developing state execution protocols, such as New Jersey's, added potassium chloride although it is not clear when or why. Third, Fred Leuchter may have suggested including potassium chloride.

My answer about Leuchter is short because it had been stipulated that I not mention him. Yet, his role was clearly relevant to answering the question that David asked me. What I did not say was that, according to Leutcher, the New Jersey doctors agreed with his recommendation that potassium chloride be included as the third chemical in the lethal injection machine that Leuchter had created for New Jersey's executions in the early 1980s. Because the medical literature did not specify what dosages of the chemicals were adequate to be lethal, Leuchter said that he relied on information that was available for the slaughtering of pigs and estimated the dosages accordingly.

Which states use sodium thiopental, pancuronium bromide, and potassium chloride in lethal injections? My answer: The 27 states mentioned previously, apart from North Carolina, which injects only sodium thiopental and potassium chloride.

Which, if any, of these states conducted any scientific or medical studies on the effects of these three chemicals when used in combination for lethal injection? As I started to answer this question, the Commonwealth's attorney objected, explaining that this same kind of question had already been asked. The judge agreed and David moved on.

The next line of David's questioning concerned North Carolina, which was apparently one of the states officials at the Kentucky Department of Corrections investigated to develop the protocol that Kentucky had at the time of the bench trial in Frankfort. During the four-year period between when I examined Kentucky's protocol in my 2001 survey and the time of the 2005 bench trial, Kentucky officials had developed a protocol. The reason why David mentioned North Carolina in his questions was because North Carolina was one of the nine states in my 2001 survey that disclosed the exact dosages for chemicals executioners injected into the inmate. The dosage of sodium thiopental was of particular interest because of evidence that executioners did not inject sufficient amounts of it in order to successfully anesthetize inmates. Therefore, an inmate would still be conscious while he was paralyzed by the pancuronium bromide and thus be unable to express pain. In the Kentucky protocol, officials listed that inmates be administered three grams of sodium thiopental, two grams less than the amount North Carolina said it administered in my survey. David was attempting to document this strange discrepancy in amounts between North Carolina and Kentucky.

Did you review North Carolina's execution protocol in preparing your 2002 article? Yes.

What anesthetic do they use? Sodium thiopental.

At the time of your article, what quantity of anesthetic did North Carolina administer? Five grams.

In preparation for your testimony today, have you reviewed Kentucky's lethal injection protocol? Yes.

According to the protocol, what chemicals are administered in a lethal injection execution in Kentucky? Sodium thiopental, pancuronium bromide, and potassium chloride.

Are the first two chemicals used in Kentucky's lethal injections the same chemicals that were originally adopted in Oklahoma? My answer: Yes.

This ended the direct examination. Of course, it is only a very small part of the whole lethal injection story. A cross examination of my testimony also followed but, it is too lengthy and uninformative to recount here. As it turns out, with respect to my testimony, Judge Crittenden's final opinion primarily relied on the evidence revealed during my direct examination. Because of the inadequacy of the cross examination, this outcome did not surprise me.

The Aftermath

As soon as I finish testifying, I leave the courtroom and speak briefly with some reporters in the hallway who are writing stories about the bench trial. I then head back into the courtroom, this time to listen to the testimony of two of the prison administrators who were waiting in the hallway with me beforehand. The administrators' ignorance of the lethal injection procedure and their lack of documentation of how the technique was developed seem very clear to me as they speak. At the same time, both witnesses are articulate and straightforward about how they conducted their duties. I am impressed by them. Again, I cannot help but feel that they and their counterparts in other states are the victims of legislatures' statewide romance with lethal injection—the details of which are left to the imagination of ill-informed prison personnel.

I would like nothing more than to hear the next four days of testimony by the remaining expert witnesses. However, I must catch a plane back to New York that afternoon. I am sorry to leave the tranquility of Frankfort. And I hope to return to the city, but only as a delighted tourist.

The next day I read news coverage of the Frankfort trial. I can already tell that the topic of the trial affects people very emotionally. In the course of a few hours, three strangers have e-mailed me their opinions about my testimony (see the Appendix). They are critical of what I said and what they think I am trying to achieve. Facets of all three e-mails represent standard views in this country toward the death penalty and lethal injection specifically.

What is most striking, however, is the extent to which the e-mails go beyond the issues at hand. For example, I would expect the commentators to emphasize typical pro-death penalty themes: the perception that the victims and their families are neglected, that inmates are coddled and will be set free, and that people testifying against lethal injection are simply against the death penalty in general. But e-mailer #1 uses comparisons to Hitler to emphasize how he feels about my views, claiming that "[t]he skilled American Judiciary creates more individual horror than Adolph Hitler could possibly imagine. . . . [W]ith the predominance of maggot mentality on both sides of the bench that exist in contemporary judicial circles, I fear the worst!" In turn, e-mailer #2 presumes that "people like [Professor Denno] would claim they [the inmates] have been rehabilitated, and should be returned to society." Of course, this subject had nothing to do with the bench trial and has never been a topic I have addressed publicly. E-mailer #3 analyzes my views on the death penalty in the context of his strong political leanings and even his opinions toward gay marriage: "When my president George Bush keeps appointing more conservative justices to the courts during the remaining [sic] of his administration the liberal groups will find great difficulty if not impossible [sic] to change certain laws concerning the death penalty and gay marriage." Likewise, "[a]s our population [sic] the baby boomers ages they become more conservative and a huge voting block to be reckon [sic] with. Remember it's the 'Red States' that count!"

I am not surprised by these kinds of sentiments. As a death penalty researcher, I have received heatedly negative correspondence before. I have no fruitful way to respond to those who write, except to thank them for expressing their views, because I believe the mailers' perspectives deal with a conglomerate of matters often having no direct relevance to the death penalty. What concerns me most, however, is how similar types of more publicly voiced opinions may affect the outcome of death penalty cases—perhaps even the bench trial that I just attended in Frankfort.

The Final Opinion

On July 8, 2005, Judge Crittenden released his decision. With one exception, he upheld the constitutionality of Kentucky's lethal injection procedure. I was very disappointed with this outcome, of course. But I also thought the press accounts of this bottom line conclusion belied the details and true significance of all that Judge Crittenden actually wrote. For those of us in the death penalty trenches, a close read of the opinion reveals some extraordinary and unprecedented statements about the flaws of the lethal injection procedure, as well as recommendations for how it should be improved.

It is remarkable, for example, that Judge Crittenden states that one part of Kentucky's protocol was indeed unconstitutional. He held that it was cruel and unusual for the Kentucky protocol to allow Department of Corrections personnel to insert a catheter into the condemned's neck. No judge has ever made such a finding about lethal injection. Judge Crittenden appeared to be particularly influenced by the testimony of a medical doctor with the Kentucky Department of Corrections. That doctor stated that he would refuse to perform the neck injection procedure and that those who would be performing it are insufficiently trained to do so. Judge Crittenden's perspective on this matter is very clear: "The Plaintiffs have demonstrated by a preponderance of the evidence that the procedure where the Department of Corrections attempts to insert an intravenous catheter into the neck through the carotid artery or jugular vein does create a substantial risk of wanton and unnecessary infliction of pain, torture or lingering death." (pp. 12–13)

Judge Crittenden also made novel findings of fact in response to a number of important points raised during the bench hearing that I think will be critical in future litigation on lethal injection, or it should be. First, Judge Crittenden fully accepted arguments that two of the chemicals (sodium thiopental and pancuronium bromide) used in lethal injection executions derived directly from Dr. Deutsch's recommendations to then-Senator Bill Dawson in 1977. Further, the opinion emphasized that there was "scant evidence" that any of the states that have since adopted lethal injection, including Kentucky, engaged in any research on lethal injection to justify their decision to follow Oklahoma's lead. "Rather, it is this Court's impression that the various States simply fell in line relying solely on Oklahoma's protocol from Dr. Deutsch in drafting and approving a lethal injection protocol. Kentucky is no different." (p. 2)

Likewise, Judge Crittenden accentuates the lack of research and study in other aspects involved in the creation of lethal injection protocols. He notes, for instance, that "[t]hose persons assigned the initial task of drafting the [Commonwealth of Kentucky's] first lethal injection protocol were provided with little to no guidance on drafting a lethal injection protocol and were resolved to mirror protocols in other states, namely Indiana, Virginia, Georgia, and Alabama." (p. 6) For example, Department of Corrections personnel "did not conduct any independent or scientific or medical studies or consult any medical professionals concerning the drugs and dosage amounts to be injected into the condemned." (p. 6) Such reluctance to seek expertise continues to the present day, a revelation that was made especially noteworthy when the Kentucky Department of Corrections decided to up its dosage level of sodium pentathol. As Judge Crittenden explains, "[n]or were any medical personnel consulted in 2004 when the lethal injection protocol dosage of sodium thiopental . . . was increased from 2 grams to 3 grams." (pp. 6–7)

Judge Crittenden's decision also makes clear that the Kentucky Department of Corrections instituted three major improvements in its lethal injection process in preparation for the Frankfort bench trial. These kinds of changes demonstrate that the Department of Corrections was well aware that aspects of its protocol were vulnerable to constitutional attack, particularly since Judge Crittenden makes a point of rewarding the Department for these three alterations. "[D]uring the course of this litigation the protocol has been amended by the Department of Corrections to increase the dosage of the short acting barbiturate, to drop one procedure (the cut-down), and the Department's medical personnel have agreed that any injection in the neck is inappropriate. The unilateral actions by the Department are commendable." (p. 12)

To the unknowing death penalty observer, such preemptory moves on the part of the Kentucky Department of Corrections may seem minor, even expected. However, in the context of over a quarter century of litigation on lethal injection, these changes are amazingly substantial and revealing. There is no evidence that the department would have taken such extreme steps to implement these protective measures had the Frankfort bench trial not taken place. The department's behavior also acknowledges its awareness of Judge Crittenden's concern that important safeguards for lethal injection be instituted. Thus, it becomes apparent that inmates' challenges against execution methods can have an impact irrespective of how a court finds the method's overall constitutionality.

But Judge Crittenden's expectations for lethal injection safeguards do not stop with these three alterations. His opinion also spotlights his belief that Kentucky's protocol should be made public so that it can be scrutinized. As Judge Crittenden emphasizes, "[t]he citizens of this Commonwealth are entitled to know the method and manner for implementing their public policy." (p. 13) Likewise, Judge Crittenden notes that the reasons the Department of Corrections had previously used to justify the "confidential nature" of the protocol no longer exist. (p. 12) Therefore, "[t]he Department of Corrections should amend the current protocol to eliminate the need to protect its contents from public view." (p. 12) In particular, "[s]ince the nature of the drugs used and the method for administering those drugs during an execution have been discussed publicly in this action, there seems to be little reason why the Department of Corrections cannot publish a lethal injection protocol that does not compromise the security of the institution or the personnel involved." (p. 13) I feel particularly vindicated by this aspect of Judge Crittenden's decision. During the time of my lethal injection survey, my assistant and I had made a concerted attempt to acquire Kentucky's protocol and were unable to do so. We felt there was something very wrong about a procedure that could never be known, and therefore never be judged.

I did think Judge Crittenden's decision rang of naiveté in some places. He seemed to put more medical trust than is warranted in the Department of Corrections personnel, despite his recognition of their lack of qualifications. For example, Judge Crittenden noted that "the current lethal injection protocol requires the Warden . . . [t]o reconstitute the Sodium Thiopental into solution form prior to injection [and] [t]he Warden has no formal training on reconstituting the drug" (p. 7); yet, Judge Crittenden did not consider this medical ignorance on the Warden's part to be problematic. Judge Crittenden stated that the drug manufacturer's instructions are sufficiently straightforward to follow and "there would be minimal risk of improper mixing [of the drugs], despite converse testimony that a layperson would have difficulty performing this task." (p. 7) Likewise, Judge Crittenden acknowledges that sodium thiopental and pancuronium bromide can precipitate and clog the tubes distributing the chemicals to the inmate's body and also that the Department of Corrections provides no device to monitor the level of an inmate's consciousness. Again, however, he states that the risks of these occurrences are minimal. I think he is wrong. Such seemingly minor indications of ignorance concerning the lethal injection procedure have been linked to major lethal injection botches in this country. I have confidence that another court will address these kinds of problems in the future.

Overall, however, Judge Crittenden provided an impressive opinion. I do think the holding would have been more consistent with the other points and clarifications Judge Crittenden makes had he declared lethal injection unconstitutional. Regardless, Judge Crittenden's decision is a far bolder declaration than the press seems to have realized and its conclusions make great progress in the direction of reforming the lethal injection procedure.

Departing Comments

Of course, I want lethal injection to be abolished as quickly as possible. Since 1976, there have been 973 executions in the United States. A total of 805 (83 percent) of those executions, the great majority, have been carried out by lethal injection. In my mind, nearly every inmate who is to be executed in this country risks facing a torturous death.

Pro-death penalty commentators often say that critics of lethal injection are just using this issue as a ploy to eliminate the death penalty entirely (recall, for example, the comments of e-mailer #2 labeling me a hypocrite for this very reason). Yet, there is no basis for such an accusation. Regardless, that characterization does not apply to me. In theory I do not oppose the death penalty. I can envision how the punishment of death may make a socially worthy statement when applied to those whose existence is clearly too despicable for us to even consider them human.

But I do question whether the criminal justice system can ever select out those who deserve death in a fair, bias-free way and then execute them according to the standards of the Eighth Amendment. Indeed, there is no evidence that the death penalty can be inflicted in a consistently constitutional manner. In sharp contrast, there is a great deal of evidence showing the brutality and incompetence of the lethal injection procedure, so much so that I cannot comprehend anyone condoning it, no matter what their views on capital punishment.

Both Justices Harry Blackmun and Lewis Powell ultimately concluded that the death penalty should be abolished because it could never be administered equitably or meaningfully under any set of rules. I feel the same way. And if people find this approach hypocritical then I suppose those people and I do not share the same vocabulary. As I mentioned previously, death penalty issues involve a battle of words, both said and unsaid. Perhaps this is the time to say less—and do more—in order to bring meaning to how we define justice.

Appendix

E-mailer #1: I am appalled at your endeavors to obliterate lethal injection as a means of execution. How is it that those who kill people in the most brutal ways possible are deserving of painless death in the most humane way possible? Perhaps if you were forced to suffer the maceration of the most intimate part of your body and then forced to endure death by strangulation, what I have stated might have significance.

The skilled American Judiciary creates more individual horror than Adolph Hitler could possibly imagine. Consider for a moment, the level of compassion and consideration a child molester has for a young victim he has just raped and then killed by choking him or her to death. How is it that those individuals are entitled to years of adjudication [over] victim expense? I am hoping that the Courts will reject your case. However, with the predominance of maggot mentality on both sides of the bench that exist in contemporary judicial circles, I fear the worst!

E-mailer #2: You might consider the cruel and unusual punishment meeted [sic] out to the two police officers and their families and the two robbery victims and their families before you complain about their murderers suffering for a brief period from a leathal [sic] injection. Your client's pain will be momentary, the families' pain is perpetual.

You obviously oppose capital punishment, but to base that opposition on the pain a murderer might suffer is specious, to say the least. Make your case against capital punishment on honest grounds, not this hypocracy [sic].

Incidentally, I would like to see these two spend the rest of their lives behind the walls, since death is too easy and too quick. My only concern is that after a few years people like you would claim they have been rehabilitated, and should be returned to society. No one ever seems to care about the victims or their families, do they?

E-mailer #3: I read with interest about you trying to have the death penalty as we know it in this country overturned, especially lethal injection. I am an avid supporter of the death penalty. Lethal injection is the most humane way to end a condemned persons [sic] life. The laws in this country are a derivative of the Judo Christian ethics and law. I also believe that executing a condemn [sic] person is not a deterrent for future crime, but it does provide supreme closure for the victims [sic] family to the extent that this evil person will never ever again do another evil atrocity. I truly believe you are supporting a loss [sic] cause, with the public news media broadcasting more heinous crimes to gain television ratings every day the [sic] will be an ever increasing public cry for more stiffer punishment including the death penalty. When my president George Bush keeps appointing more conservative justices to the courts during the remaining [sic] of his administration the liberal groups will find great difficulty if not impossible [sic] to change certain laws concerning the death penalty and gay marriage.

If you believe that lethal injection is inhumane, lets [sic] try [the] firing squad or a public hanging for the public broadcast networks to air, especially in high definition. Now that in and of itself could be a vast deterrent for future heinous crime. Prisons are full and taxpayers that have been paying the tab for lifetime incarceration [and] angry. As our population [sic] the baby boomers ages they become more conservative and a huge voting block to be reckon [sic] with. Remember it's the "Red States" that count! I respect your opinion just as you respect mine.

Afterward: For Further Reading

Deborah W. Denno, "When Legislatures Delegate Death: The Troubling Paradox Behind State Uses of Electrocution and Lethal Injection and What It Says about Us," 63 *Ohio State Law Journal* 63–260 (2002).

Deborah W. Denno, "Getting to Death: Are Executions Constitutional?" 82 *Iowa Law Review* 319–464 (1997).

Deborah W. Denno, "Is Electrocution an Unconstitutional Method of Execution? The Engineering of Death over the Century," 35 *William and Mary Law Review* 551–692 (1994).

Linda L. Emmanuel & Leigh B. Bienen, "Physician Participation in Executions: Time to Eliminate Anonymity Provisions and Protest the Practice," 135 *Annals of Internal Medicine* 922–924 (2001).

Neil J. Farber et al., "Physicians' Willingness to Participate in the Process of Lethal Injections for Capital Punishment," 135 *Annals of Internal Medicine* 884–890 (2001).

Roberta M. Harding, "The Gallows to the Gurney: Analyzing the (Un)constitutionality of the Methods of Execution," 6 *The Boston University Public Interest Law Journal* 153-178 (1996).

Jacob Weisberg, "This Is Your Death," *The New Republic*, July 1, 1991, pp. 23–27.

Notes

1. Baze et al. v. Rees et al., No. 04-CI-1094, Franklin Circuit Court, Kentucky (July 8, 2005), was a bench trial because it was a civil matter. The two condemned inmates, who are plaintiffs, brought a suit challenging the constitutionality of lethal injection as a method of execution in Kentucky. The defendants are the Commissioner of the Kentucky Department of Corrections, the Warden of the Kentucky State Penitentiary, and the Governor of the Commonwealth of Kentucky. The remedy sought was a declaratory judgment. Before the trial started, a preliminary injunction had already been granted by Judge Crittenden, barring the use of lethal injection.

2. Nelson v. Campbell, 541 U.S. 637 (2004), was an unanimous opinion delivered by Justice Sandra Day O'Connor.

Acknowledgments

* I am most grateful for the helpful comments provided by Daniel Auld, Leigh Bienen, and Roberta Harding. I thank David Barron for the questions asked during the testimony.

Austin Sarat and Nasser Hussain

The Literary Life of Clemency: Pardon Tales in the Contemporary United States

> Turning a terrible action into a story is a way to distance oneself from it, at worst a form of self-deception, at best a way to pardon the self.

> Natalie Zemon Davis

Writing in 1788, Alexander Hamilton set out to explain and defend what seemed to his contemporaries something of an anomaly in America's new constitutional scheme, namely lodging the power to grant "reprieves and pardons for offenses against the United States" solely in the President of the United States.[1] That power was then and remains now one of the great prerogatives of sovereignty as well as one of the most vivid expressions of mercy.[2] Indeed the original definition of sovereignty in the West comes from the Roman law maxim—*vitae et necis potestatem*—the power over life and death. Thus the opening sentence of Michel Foucault's final section of the *History of Sexuality. Volume One* says that "for a long time, one of the characteristic privileges of sovereign power was the right to decide life and death."[3]

While such a power is, in a constitutional democracy like the United States, no longer associated with a king, the continuing existence of capital punishment in the United States gives witness to the fact that the sovereign power over life is far from being extinguished. Much has been said and written about the power to kill within the confines of modern law; the punishment of death has been regarded as of a different order, as the most robust and terrifying of law's power, of its essential dealings in pain and violence. Such a sustained focus on the right to impose death sometimes eclipses the essential corollary of the definition of *vitae et necis potestatem*: the sovereign right to spare life.

In a modern political system this power to spare life remains in the form of executive clemency. Clemency, as the authors of a recent report on its use in non-capital cases say, is a general term for the power of an executive to "intervene in the sentencing of a criminal defendant to prevent injustice from occurring. It is a relief imparted after the justice system has run its course."[4] In capital cases executive clemency is distinctive in that it is the only power that can *undo death*—the only power that can prevent death once it has been prescribed and, through appellate review, approved as a legally appropriate punishment.

Like all sovereign prerogative, clemency's efficacy is bound up with its disregard of declared law. John Locke famously defined prerogative as the "power to act according to discretion, for the public good, without the prescription of the Law, and sometimes even against it. . . . [T]here is a latitude left to the Executive power, to do many things of choice, which the Laws do not prescribe."[5] As a monarchical prerogative, or executive action in a democracy, clemency appears to be something essentially lawless, "the raw exercise of power against the law itself." This fact may have prompted Blackstone's observation that "in democracies . . . this power of pardon can never subsist; for there nothing higher is acknowledged than the magistrate who administers the laws."[6] It may also give rise, in a society dedicated to the rule of law, to tension, doubt, anxiety about clemency.

Perhaps clemency's anxiety-arousing status explains why, unlike the president's power as commander-in-chief of the army and navy, a constitutional provision the propriety of which, in Hamilton's view, was "so evident in itself . . . that little need be said to explain or enforce it,"[7] the President's power to pardon needed explanation and defense. Like the king acting "in a superior sphere . . . ," lodging the power to pardon exclusively in the president meant that the fate of persons convicted of crimes would be dependent ultimately on the "*sole fiat*" of a single person. This was hardly the image of a government of laws and not of persons that Hamilton sought to defend. Yet defend it he did, while also claiming that what he called "the benign prerogative of pardoning . . .

(unlike almost every other government power in the new constitution) should be as little as possible fettered."[8]

Hamilton constructed his defense of the pardon power around several propositions. First he noted that without such a power "justice would wear a countenance too sanguinary and cruel."[9] Second, he argued that having such awesome power lodged in one person would inspire in the chief executive "scrupulousness and caution." Third, Hamilton focused particularly, and revealingly, on the political uses of executive clemency, paying special heed to the power to pardon in cases of treason which he rightly describes as "a crime leveled at the immediate being of the society." Hamilton worried that "treason will often be connected with seditions which embrace a large proportion of the community."[10] And it is a "well-timed" offer of clemency, Hamilton contended, deriving neither from the "dilatory process of convening the legislature" nor its fractious deliberations, which in the "critical moments" of "seasons of insurrection or rebellion . . . may restore the tranquility of the commonwealth; and which, if suffered to pass unimproved, it may never be possible afterwards to recall."[11]

While, to a twenty-first-century audience, some of Hamilton's arguments may seem quaint, or outdated, the need to explain and defend executive clemency appears to be as pressing today as it was in Hamilton's time. One result of this need is that clemency has had, and continues to have, a rich discursive and literary life. In one or another form, those who exercise that power regularly respond to a compulsion to speak, to narrate, to produce pardon tales, to give what the sociologists Marvin Scott and Stanford Lyman call "accounts."[12]

Accounts, like the pardon tales we will be examining, are linguistic devices "employed whenever an action is subject to valuative inquiry . . . to explain unanticipated or untoward behavior . . . [They] recognize a general sense in which the act in question is impermissible, but claim that the particular occasion permits or requires the very act."[13] In clemency what is untoward or impermissible, in need of explanation and defense, is its lawless quality, its status as "the power of doing good without a rule."[14]

In this essay we focus on the speech and writing that surrounds clemency and on the accounts governors construct to justify its uses in capital cases, in which by a stroke of the pen they can spare life, or by standing silent, acquiesce in its extinction. Through this examination we focus on narrative's special relationship to violence and death, what Professor Peter Fitzpatrick says is law's horizon both as "supreme stasis" and "the opening to all possibility that is beyond affirmed order."[15] We take up the discursive and literary life of clemency, focusing in particular on how chief executives enlist narrative in their confrontation with law's violence, on how they use rhetoric and narrative to cope with the emotionally charged decision to spare a life or to let someone die.

In our view, one of the central preoccupations of the literary life of clemency is the effort to domesticate this power and, in so doing, render it compatible with democratic politics. Contemporary pardoners try to do so by speaking to background expectations against which sovereign prerogative in a constitutional democracy might seem to be acceptable. As Terri Orbuch observes, "[P]roducing their accounts, actors are displaying knowledge of the ideal ways of acting and ideal reasons for doing what they have done."[16]

When taken out of isolation and placed next to one another, pardon tales begin to emerge as a *genre* with certain distinct generic properties. The first of these has to do with the structural position of clemency as a discretionary power lodged finally in the office and person of the chief executive. Thus in each of their accounts we encounter the governor as a solitary figure wrestling alone with an enormous responsibility. But executive clemency is not only a personal discretion but a virtually unreviewable power by either the people or the courts. This leads to two other generic qualities in pardon tales: an effort to demonstrate the gravity of the decision making process, and some rhetorical trope that connects what is in the end a personal choice with larger cultural and political values. These generic conventions are addressed to an audience imagined to be anxious and doubtful about the way the power to spare life is used. In this essay we ask how do pardon tales respond to the pervasive cultural anxiety that necessarily attaches to a power that cannot be subject to rule? What rhetorical and literary strategies do they employ? Can and do these narratives provide consolation and calm that anxiety?

Our inquiry into contemporary pardon tales owes much to the work of Natalie Zemon Davis who, in *Fiction in the Archives*, turned to letters of remission authored in the hope of securing the king's grace for what they revealed about the narrative conventions of sixteenth-century France.[17] Here we alter Davis' perspective, moving from analysis of the literary productions of those seeking clemency to the rhetorical and literary work of those with the power to grant it. However, just as Davis argued that appeals for mercy were, several centuries ago, particularly good sources for understanding "contemporary habits of explanation, description, and evaluation,"[18] we think that the same is true of modern pardon tales. They provide one fruitful resource for examining the capacity of narrative to soothe anxiety and quiet doubt, to suture the breach between law and sovereign prerogative, between our culture's desire for rule-governed conduct and the ungovernability of mercy.

George Ryan: "I Must Act"

One of the most recent, and one of the most interesting, of those pardon tales was delivered in January, 2003 by Illinois Governor George Ryan when he commuted 164 death sentences. Ryan's act was the single sharpest blow to capital punishment since the United States Supreme Court declared it unconstitutional in 1972 and appeared, at first glance, to be a rare display of mercy in distinctly unmerciful times. As a humane, compassionate gesture in a culture whose attitudes toward crime and punishment emphasize strictness not mercy, severity not compassion, it seemed to run against the grain of today's tough-on-crime, law and order politics. Because Ryan pardoned or commuted the sentences of sadistic rapists and murderers as well as more sympathetic candidates for mercy and people about whom there was a continuing question whether they were guilty of the crimes for which they were convicted, his decision produced an explosive reaction.

People for whom death is both a morally appropriate and necessary punishment demonized Ryan and denounced his clemency in the strongest possible terms, claiming along the way that he had dishonored the memory of murder victims, inflicted great pain on their surviving families, made the citizens of Illinois less safe, and abused his power. Opponents of capital punishment, not surprisingly, made Ryan into an instant hero. They treated his decision as a turning point on the way toward what they hoped would be the demise of state killing. That Ryan acted with two days left in his term of office and in the face of vocal opposition from citizens, the surviving families of murder victims, prosecutors, and almost all of Illinois's political establishment only compounded the drama surrounding his decision.

Nothing in his personality, or in prior political record, suggested that George Ryan ever would become a significant anti-death penalty activist. Indeed throughout his career in government he had been an outspoken supporter of capital punishment, and in his gubernatorial campaign he had restated his belief in the appropriateness of the death penalty. "'I believed some crimes were so heinous,'" Ryan recently said of his long held position on capital punishment, "'that the only proper way of protecting society was execution. I saw a nation in the grip of increasing crime rates; and tough sentences, more jails, the death penalty—that was good government.'"[19] Yet by the winter of 2003 Ryan had indeed become a key player in the national debate about capital punishment.

While his pardon tale, delivered the day he announced his mass clemency, gave voice to some of the most important of today's arsenal of anti-death penalty arguments, as a rhetorical performance Ryan's 22 page, hour long, "I Must Act" was both deeply personal and yet flatly bureaucratic, presenting, as its title suggests, his decision as if it were "compelled," an act of duty not a personal choice. In addition, his speech was, as law professor Robert Ferguson says of judicial rhetoric, "self-dramatizing. It has, in effect, no other choice. Judges often solve this difficulty by stressing the importance of a decision only they can make."[20]

In terms of its substance, Ryan's pardon tale had two different registers, and was riven along the important and pervasive distinction between an individual grant of clemency and a mass commutation. If the first is more amenable to a language of compassion and largesse, then the second is inexorably systemic and speaks more in the discourse of institutions and the distribution of powers amongst them. In both he sought to speak to a variety of background assumptions in the presence of which his exercise of clemency might be forgiven, if not applauded.

In this regard, Ryan's rhetoric was designed to convince his listeners that, in spite of his mass clemency, he shared their values and commitments, their compassion for victims, their belief in fairness, and their desire to be tough on crime. In terms of the last of these values and commitments he recounted the story of one inmate who did not want his sentence commuted. "Some inmates on death row," he told his listeners,

> "don't want a sentence of life without parole. Danny Edwards wrote me and told me not to do him any favors because he didn't want to face a prospect of a life in prison without parole. They will be confined in a cell that is about 5-feet-by-12 feet, usually double-bunked. Our prisons have no air conditioning, except at our supermax facility where inmates are kept in their cell 23 hours a day. In summer months, temperatures in these prisons exceed one hundred degrees. It is a stark and dreary existence. They can think about their crimes. Life without parole has even, at times, been described by prosecutors as a fate worse than death."[21]

Though his clemency was a merciful reduction of punishment, his pardon tale was, in fact, less a story of mercy than initially meets the eye.

Indeed, how could Ryan's act be merciful when it was directed not to particular individuals, but toward everyone on death row? Mercy, after all, is not a wholesale virtue. As the philosopher and critic Martha Nussbaum notes, mercy requires singularity and attention to particulars. It demands, she says "flexible particularized judgment." To be merciful one must regard "each particular case as a complex narrative of human effort in a world full of obstacles."[22]

As if to alleviate any shred of doubt, the language of mercy played little role in Ryan's account. In fact, in the course of the speech announcing the clemency decision Ryan mentioned mercy only twice, and both times the language of mercy was used in quotations, through the deployment of someone else's words. This rhetorical gesture meant that he could grant mercy while, at the same time, keeping it at a safe distance. Thus he told his listeners, without further elaboration or comment, that, "The Most Reverend Desmond Tutu wrote to me this week stating that 'to take a life when a life has been lost is revenge, it is not justice.' He says 'justice allows for mercy, clemency and compassion. These virtues are not weakness.'" Second, reaching back into American history, he quoted Abraham Lincoln's admonition that "'mercy bears richer fruits than strict justice.'"

Ryan's wholesale clemency was less an act of grace, or of forgiveness, than a concession to inadequacies of a death penalty system gone awry and to a political system unwilling or unable to address those inadequacies. "Ultimately," law professor Dan Kobil claims, "Governor George Ryan was persuaded to grant clemency to every person on Death Row not as a grand gesture of forgiveness, but because his faith in the ability of the Illinois system to give only deserving defendants a sentence of death had been destroyed by a series of blatant errors and mistakes."[23] He tried to appeal to his audience's sense of fairness, their imagined revulsion at the prospect of executing the innocent. When his speech did display compassion, its compassion was directed to the surviving families of murder victims rather than to the murderers whose lives he spared. Clemency without forgiveness, mercy without being merciful, these attributes are crucial in the contemporary pardon tale.

As we will see, unlike governors before him who in their own pardon tales attacked the death penalty, per se, criticized it as immoral, and called for its abolition, Ryan provided no such critique. Instead Ryan's "I Must Act" explains his decision through two somewhat contradictory stories. Both serve to ground his clemency in a set of shared cultural and political concerns. Far from a majestic act, Ryan put clemency into discourse to demonstrate his engagement with and fidelity to those concerns.

The key element in this effort is a story of victims and their suffering. So important was this element that it seems safe to say that Ryan's account gave further evidence of an important trend in our political culture, namely that "We have become a nation of victims, where everyone is leapfrogging over each other, competing for the status of victim, where most people define themselves as some sort of survivor."[24] In his second story he examined institutions and their failures. While the first expressed a commitment to the interests of the victimized, the other embraced a retributive theory of clemency.

Ryan's account was less an effort to reconstruct the stories of those who had petitioned him for clemency or to plot his efforts at revisiting these crimes—although he did do some of that—but more a narrative to the extent that it invoked and represented cultural tropes that would hopefully soften those who might disagree with the governor, and place his decision in a wider context of shared ideas. The trope that animates Ryan's account more than any other is that of victims.

As if not able to say it enough times, Ryan repeatedly tried to assure his listeners that he had indeed heard the voice of victims. "I have conducted private group meetings, one in Springfield and one in Chicago, with the surviving family members of homicide victims. Everyone in the room who wanted to speak had the opportunity to do so. Some wanted to express their grief, others wanted to express their anger. I took it all in. . . . I redoubled my effort to review each case personally in order to respond to the concerns of prosecutors and victims' families." Ryan portrays himself as according victims a deep and respectful attentiveness. He takes in their grief and anger, again rhetorically refiguring himself into a victim. Ryan's account is grounded not in sovereign grace, but in the need to pay homage to suffering. In his embrace of victims as a rhetorical touchstone for his clemency he displays the frail sovereignty of a democracy, desperately seeking grounding in a shared conception of citizenship in which we are bound together by our common suffering and victimization.

In the story of institutional failure, Ryan appears as a committed retributivist using clemency to do the work that justice, not mercy, requires. "The facts I have seen in reviewing each and every one of these cases," Ryan observed, "raised questions not only about the innocence of people on death row, but about the fairness of the death penalty system as a whole. If the system was making so many errors in determining whether someone was guilty in the first place, how fairly and accurately was it determining which guilty defendants deserved to live and which deserved to die? What effect was race having? What effect was poverty having?" Instead of a system finely geared to assigning punishment on the basis of a careful assessment of the nature of the crime and the blameworthiness of the offender, Ryan, quoting Justice Blackmun, concluded that "'the death penalty remains fraught with arbitrariness, discrimination, caprice and mistake.'"

Finally, in Ryan's pardon tale, like others of its genre, clemency is an agonizing burden thrust on him by the duties of his office rather than an awe-inspiring power wielded with pleasure. "My responsibilities and obligations," Ryan noted, "are more than my neighbors and my family. I represent all the people of Illinois, like it or not. The people of our state have vested in me the power to act in the interest of justice. I know," he said, "that my decision will be just that—my decision . . ."

Ryan continued, as if his listeners would derive satisfaction from seeing him suffer for his lawless act. "Even if the exercise of my power becomes my burden I will bear it . . . ," he said. In addition, he described the extreme personal cost, the anguish that accompanies the exercise of the sovereign power to spare life. Thus, Ryan shared with his listeners his concern that "whatever decision I made, I would be criticized . . ." and his worry that he would "never be comfortable with my final decision . . ."

When Governor Ryan issued the mass commutation of death sentences in Illinois he spoke to, as well as stirred up, our national doubts and anxieties about executive clemency. Attending to his rhetoric, to his explanation of this decision, shows Ryan desperately trying to allay those doubts and calm those anxieties. Yet despite Ryan's efforts to ground and authorize his acts in the suffering of victims and the systemic flaws of the capital punishment system, he could not resolve the contradictory elements, which, as far back as Alexander Hamilton, register democracy's need for, and yet discomfort with, prerogative power.

Edmund G. (Pat) Brown: *Public Justice, Private Mercy*

George Ryan spoke to, and through, a genre of pardon tales the presence of which was marked by his invocation of the name of Edmund G. (Pat) Brown, former governor of California who, during his eight-year term of office, commuted almost two dozen death sentences and whose 1989 book, *Public Justice, Private Mercy*, is a widely recognized classic in the contemporary literary life of clemency.[25] In his speech Ryan took heed of Brown's warning that "'no matter how efficient and fair the death penalty may seem in theory, in actual practice it is primarily inflicted upon the weak, the poor, the ignorant and against racial minorities,'" and noted this book's broad indictment of the death penalty on the grounds that "'it has neither protected the innocent nor deterred the killers. Publicly sanctioned killing has cheapened human life and dignity without the redeeming grace which comes from justice metered out swiftly, evenly, humanely.'"

Yet, Brown was by no means a consistent opponent of capital punishment. Before his 1959–67 service as Governor of California, he was a district attorney who strongly supported it.

He was, however, troubled while prosecuting two men who had killed a service station owner during a robbery. The defense lawyer declared that Brown was handling the case personally because, if the men received the death penalty, Brown would be re-elected as district attorney. The defense lawyer was right. Brown, with his re-election in mind, had told his staff to "get me a lead-pipe cinch."[26] Apparently conscience-stricken by his adversary's remark, he asked the jury to recommend life in prison without possibility of parole. They did so. Pat Brown was at best ambivalent about the death penalty for many years thereafter. While he supported it as attorney general of California and when he was first elected governor, he ultimately turned against it.

As the quotations used by Ryan suggest, *Public Justice: Private Mercy* chronicles the evolution of Brown's views on capital punishment. At the same time, it offers a narrative account of the clemency decisions he made during his time in office, a narrative which is rich and engaging in its detail, even if a bit repetitive. The book's chapters each tell the story of a different case in which Brown decided whether or not to commute a death sentence. They lay out the principles and individual circumstances that moved him one way or the other and, in so doing, draw attention to the uniquely individualized nature of Brown's clemency considerations.

Throughout the book Brown portrays himself as deeply engaged in the clemency process and conscientious in the discharge of his clemency powers. Indeed he writes as if these attributes would reassure his readers that his clemency decisions were, even if lawless, nonetheless responsible. He writes as if seeking forgiveness for decisions with which his readers might strongly disagree. Thus, early on in the book, he reminds us that "I inaugurated the practice of personally conducting executive clemency hearings in every death case,"[27] and "I insisted on conducting every clemency hearing myself, often sending out investigators to collect more information if I thought some area still needed clearing up."[28]

To drive home the point about his engagement and conscientiousness, he draws an explicit contrast between his careful consideration of each case and a blanket clemency issued by the governor of New Mexico three years before the publication of his book. "[U]nlike the recent governor of New Mexico," Brown writes, "who was so opposed to the death penalty that he refused to let *anyone* be executed . . . , I refused the clemency requests of thirty-six condemned prisoners during my eight years in office . . . For each of them, no matter how hard I searched, I couldn't find a compelling reason to go against the judgment of the court and the law of the state."[29]

Brown's emphasis on an individualized approach to clemency also serves as a kind of repudiation of what Ryan would do some time later. Writing about his last days in office, Brown says "[T]he pressure on me to make some parting gesture against capital punishment was great—pressure from church groups and other opponents and also from inside that part of me which felt that whatever I'd done over the years really hadn't changed anything . . . But it's also true that I never seriously considered giving blanket reprieves or commutations to all sixty-four on Death Row."[30]

Explaining why he refused these entreaties, Brown seems to be very aware of the conundrum of clemency's lawful lawlessness, and, as if refuting the charge that his clemency decisions disrespected and/or damaged the law, he goes out of his way to tell his readers of his commitment and fidelity to law. "I had been elected twice," he says, "by a majority of the people of California in a pact or trust to uphold their constitution and their laws, and I wasn't about to break that pack or violate that trust now that a few hundred thousand votes had shifted the other way."[31] Or, as he put it earlier in the book, "[T]he death penalty was the law of the state, one of the laws I was sworn to uphold. If I disagreed with a law, it was my job to try to change it through the legislative process, not by evading my responsibility and refusing to enforce it."[32]

Brown reassures his readers that he understood that clemency is "an extraordinary power" in a constitutional democracy and that he set a very high burden of proof for its use. It is, he wrote, "to be exercised only when justified by *compelling* circumstances."[33] Elsewhere he says that in order to grant clemency "I as governor had to look for some *extraordi-*

nary reason why the defendant should not be executed. (emphasis added)"[34]

As he describes his reasons for commuting death sentences in twenty-three cases, several things stand out. First, he takes every chance to acknowledge the special nature and limited focus of his clemency decisions, as if he were acting in a posture of deference to the proper jurisdiction of other branches of government. "[T]he section of the Constitution that granted the governor the power of clemency," Brown writes, "had little to do with guilt or innocence or even with the finer points of the law."[35]

While admitting that he "was trying to move beyond legal limits as I looked for reasons to commute," there seems little room for mercy in Brown's story. Indeed most of the reasons he gives for commutation have nothing to do with compassion or mercy. They sound vaguely legalist, e.g. addressing new evidence, an inability to resolve questions about actual innocence, redressing unequal penalties, et cetera. "As the last stop on the road to the gas chamber," he wrote, "it was up to me to make sure that the law—even if I disagreed with it—was being fairly applied."[36] Or, giving an accounting of his reasoning in granting clemency in the cases where he did so, Brown notes the frequency with which he found "examples of unfairness and injustice that even the hardest heart couldn't ignore."[37] Like Ryan, Brown's story repeatedly distances himself from mercy and forgiveness, assuring us time and again of his disgust at the crimes that put people on death row.

Yet in each of these moments he also is the hero of the piece battling against those feelings to do what his office required of him. "Some crimes," he says, "were so terrible that I could fully understand and sympathize with the judges and juries who sentenced those who committed them to death. But during the clemency process I had a different kind of decision to make . . ."[38] Or, in another place he notes that "Reading those case reports filled me with as much anger at the killers as any man alive, but anger is a luxury that a governor can't afford."[39]

In several ingratiating moments of candor, Brown makes reference to his other duties as governor, duties which required him to balance the value of doing the "right thing" in clemency cases against the collateral, political costs that granting it almost always imposes. Thus in the first clemency case to reach his desk Brown acknowledged that he "thought for a long moment about my priorities as governor, about the fair employment bill I wanted to get through, the water and education bills I had in the works. Was the Crooker case," he asks, "really worth putting those things on hold and perhaps in jeopardy?"[40] Later he again confessed that as he made his clemency decisions he considered "what impact my decisions might have on my reputation, or on the spectrum of bills we were trying to enact."[41] These are refreshing moments in the genre of contemporary pardon tales, moments in which Brown wins his readers trust by showing himself to be something other than an otherworldly do-gooder, candidly owning up to his human and political interests.

Yet these moments quickly disappear as Brown recounts his success in resisting the temptation to give in to narrow political calculations. Here the story reverts to, what in contemporary pardon tales is, the familiar portrait of the solitary man wrestling with his conscience, seeking to do the right thing under very trying circumstances. Thus Brown says of his clemency decisions, "They didn't make me feel godlike . . . : far from it; I felt just the opposite." Referring to the power over life and death that supplies sovereignty's very definition, Brown writes, "It was an awesome power that no person or government should have . . ."[42] Far from enjoying his exercise of sovereign prerogative, Brown argues that removing the clemency power would be "more humane and compassionate than forcing (any governor) constantly to decide on the life or death of an individual."[43] And, in this invocation of compassion, not for the condemned, but for those with the power to spare life, Brown joins Ryan in presenting himself as a kind of victim. "[E]ach decision," he says, "took something out of me that nothing—not family or work or hope for the future—has ever been able to replace."[44]

Public Justice, Private Mercy, written when Brown was eighty-three years old, more than twenty years removed from office, reads like the dying declaration of a man unable to put to rest decisions made decades before. It reads as if it were written less to convince his readers of the grounding and purpose of his clemency decisions than to convince, and pardon, himself. "I am eighty-three years old as I write these words. I've done many things during my life that have given me a great deal of pleasure and pride and a few things that I'd either like to forget or to have another chance at. But the longer I live, the larger loom those fifty-nine decisions about justice and mercy that I had to make as governor."[45]

Ultimately, Brown's book poses what he calls a "selfish question," namely, "Have my decisions on Death Row really made any difference?"[46] This unanswered, perhaps unanswerable question, haunts the text, leaving its readers to ask what kind of difference in Brown's use of clemency would make a difference to us or whether any account of it could help us rest easier with its lawful lawlessness.

Michael DiSalle: *The Power of Life or Death*

From Ryan's recent speech and Pat Brown's 1989 book, we look back several decades to another governor, Michael DiSalle and his pardon tale. DiSalle, who served as Governor of Ohio from 1959–1963, was the oldest of seven children. Born in New York City on January 6, 1908, when he was three years of age the family became residents of Toledo, Ohio, where the future governor attended public and parochial schools and served a quiet term as mayor. His subsequent term as governor was, however, anything but quiet, leading one reporter to observe that Di-Salle "did not know how to pick his fights, and warred unproductively with everyone from newspaper editorial boards to the legislature. He did not know how to capitalize on his successes or avoid blame for public relations failures on his watch."[47]

Unlike Ryan and Brown, DiSalle was a long time and consistent opponent of capital punishment. "I have long felt," he reports, "that only the Giver of Life has the right to take away life. I do not believe we achieve justice by practicing retribution . . ."[48] He believed that "'punishing and even killing criminals may yield a grim kind of satisfaction . . . But playing God in this way has no conceivable moral or scientific justification.'" Thus during his term as Governor he commuted six death sentences. Yet, somewhat surprisingly, he also allowed six others to be carried out.[49] Two years after he left office, in 1965, DiSalle turned clemency into literature, publishing an account of the decisions he made in each of the twelve capital cases that came to his desk.

The Power of Life and Death is, in many ways, a remarkable book, straightforward in its exposition, lucid in its prose, revealing in its rhetoric. It is fictive in the way Davis describes the pardon tales of the six-teenth-century citizens of France as fictive, namely in its "forming, shaping and molding elements: the crafting of a narrative."[50] As Davis explains, the "shaping choices of language, detail, and order are needed to present an account that seems to both writer and reader true, real, meaningful, and/or explanatory."[51]

DiSalle deploys language, detail, and order to tell a story of conflict between his conscience and his duty, his moral principles and the oath of office that binds chief executives to faithfully execute the law of the

182

land even when they find it morally abhorrent. Like Ryan's and Brown's pardon tales, DiSalle's relies on the trope of anguish, the agony of the person forced by circumstance to wield Godlike power on the basis of fallible human judgment. And, like Brown's *Public Justice, Private Mercy*, one of the most revealing aspects of this book is its primary narrative device, a series of detailed accounts of each of the twelve instances in which DiSalle considered clemency in a capital case.

Page after page he recounts the details of the crime, of the life and circumstances of the criminal, of the legal processing of the case, and of his own efforts to get at the truth and reach a judgment that would heal the rift between his moral objection to capital punishment and Ohio's embrace of it. Each of the cases is introduced by a hackneyed headline or transparent play on words—"The Lovesick Den Mother," "The Equality of Justice Is Not Strained," "The Four-Angled Triangle," and "The Bookie and the Wise Guy," et cetera. As he moves from the headline through each case, DiSalle is didactic and, at the same time, defensive, trying both to encourage more informed and rational responses to crime and criminals and also to provide a convincing accounting of each of the decisions he made.

His use of minute detail functions as a device to reassure readers of veracity and conscientiousness. Here we are reminded of Thomas Laqueur's analysis of a different cluster of narratives from the eighteenth century onwards, autopsy reports, the parliamentary inquiry reports and so on, which he calls the humanitarian narrative.[52] And while Laqueur seeks to discover the rhetorical conditions by which these accounts arouse pity, we are in particular intrigued by his insight that an exacting level of detail is used as a means to assure competence and veracity. These accounts, Laqueur tells us, are all heirs to the scientific and empiricist revolutions of the seventeenth century. "This aesthetic enterprise," he notes, "is characterized by its reliance on detail as a sign of truth."[53]

Presenting the detailed story of each of the twelve cases in which he considered, or granted, clemency, DiSalle offers evidence against which his decisions can be judged. Unlike Brown whose pardon tale seems to be a self-referential look back through time at the meaning and impact of his clemency decisions, DiSalle's book is written as if he were putting himself on trial in the here and now, calling himself before the bar of public opinion to defend against an accusation frequently made during his term as governor, namely that in his use of the clemency power he set himself above and outside the law, arrogantly and irresponsibly deploying a power that should be used more sparingly than he used it or that it should not be used at all.

Indeed, over and over again DiSalle reminds his readers of accusations contained in newspaper stories and letters addressed to him. He enfolds the voices of his critics in his story, often characterizing them in sweeping terms, e.g., "Most Ohio newspapers cried out in editorial horror and indignation each time I exercised clemency; they spoke in whispers each time I allowed a man to die,"[54] or, as he puts it, in response to his first commutation, editorial writers "excoriated me," DiSalle says, "for having set myself above the conclusions of the courts and jurors . . ."[55]

In other places he quotes particular criticisms communicated directly to him. For example, "We no longer need police, courts, juries or judges. The great DiSalle will see that justice is served."[56] Or as another outraged citizen wrote, "It is difficult for an ordinary Ohio voter to understand how an elected Chief Executive can allow his beliefs to cause him to overrule the judiciary . . ."[57]

As to its avowed purpose, DiSalle says that his book was "written in the hope that judges, prosecutors, criminologists, law enforcement officers, and the ordinary citizen . . . will make a sober, disinterested judgment, when passions are not raised to a fever heat by inflammatory headlines blazing the news of some monstrous crime."[58] A sober, disinterested judgment of what? Or, of whom?

At first glance one might think that the object of this admonition is crime and punishment policy, but as the book unfolds it is clear that it is written as a reply brief to the charges he has so scrupulously documented. And, explaining his use of "case histories," he exclaims, "Let the reader judge."[59] Reader sovereignty substitutes for popular sovereignty, placing the once powerful governor within the frame of a kind of democratic community. The reader's imagined judgment is a stand-in for the verdict of history itself.

In the course of his pardon tale, DiSalle, like Ryan, attempts to reassure his readers that though his exercise of clemency, like all such exercises, was a kind of lawful alegality, authorized, but not governed by law, it was, in every case, grounded in values and beliefs he shared with the citizens of Ohio. And, like Brown, he writes as if trying to persuade his readers that his use of clemency was less a majestic moment of sovereign prerogative, than just the kind of thing that they too would have done had they been in his shoes. In this way his pardon tale domesticates and diminishes prerogative even as it details its exercise. To do so it tells two different stories, one substantive, the other procedural.

First, DiSalle's seeks to convey to his readers that, while they might disagree about particular judgments, his exercise of power was grounded and disciplined by principles deeply rooted in the legal and political culture. The first of these is that clemency is appropriate when "the inflexibility of legal procedure prevented the entire truth from reaching the jury."[60] Second, DiSalle explained that clemency should be used to insure equal treatment under the law as in instances when "there was an obvious inequity of justice in administering punishment."[61] Third, clemency is appropriate when particular factors, e.g. youth or mental incapacity, "mitigate guilt."[62]

These principles are, in the first instance, legalistic. They position clemency as merely a corrective for some deficiency in the legal process. However, the third does leave space for mercy, albeit on limited grounds. As if authoring his own constraining jurisprudence, these principles are said by DiSalle to supply the only "legitimate reasons" for granting clemency. Where one or more were present, clemency would be granted; where none were present, clemency would be denied. As DiSalle informs his readers, "[F]or the six who died I could find no extenuating circumstances, no unequal justice, no questionable legal procedure, no reasonable doubt, to justify my reversing the sentences of the courts."[63]

It is worth noting that in these principles there is little of the kind of concern for victims and their suffering that played such a large role in Ryan's pardon tale. This difference registers a profound change in the background assumptions to which pardon tales must speak if they are to do their justificatory work. It registers change from a time when criminal justice was thought to be public justice to today when victims have succeeded in contesting what Professor Danielle Allen calls "the near-total erasure of the victim from the process of punishment."[64]

In any case, when they do appear in DiSalle's pardoner's tale, victims appear mostly as an abstract category. Thus, early in the book DiSalle says, "[T]he time to show concern for the victims of crime is long before the shot is fired or the blow struck—by seeking a sensible way of eliminating the causes of crime rather than by trying as we now do, futilely, after the fact, to eradicate crime by punishing the perpetrator."[65]

Here DiSalle, like Ryan and Brown, offers a pardon tale that displays mercy without being forgiving. It is as if DiSalle wanted, like Richard Celeste, another Governor of Ohio, to say about those who were the beneficiaries of his commutations, "I didn't forgive them. I did not forgive them." Moreover, as he describes it, DiSalle's use of the power to pardon is, in Jacques Derrida's sense, conditional rather than unconditional. As Derrida puts it, "It is important," he says, "to analyze at base the tension . . . between on the one hand the idea . . . of the unconditional, gracious, infinite aneconomic [sic] pardon, accorded to the guilty precisely as guilty, without compensation, even to one who does not repent or ask for pardon, and on the other hand . . . a conditional pardon, proportionate to the recognition of fault, to remorse and the transformation of the sinner who asks, then, explicitly, for pardon."[66]

In addition to the substantive grounds on which DiSalle's pardon tale seeks to reassure its reader-judges, it repeatedly details the process he employed in reaching his clemency decisions. DiSalle seeks to persuade both that his decisions were made with great care and that there were great personal costs associated with each and every instance of clemency. While Ryan's narrative task was to account for a use of clemency that refused to draw distinctions and make individual judgments, DiSalle's book is filled with stories of uniquely, almost obsessively, individualized judgment.

In each of these stories DiSalle presents himself as an engaged and active participant, reviewing extensive case files, reading pleadings, asking questions, and in several instances going to death row himself to interview the person whose fate he would ultimately decide. As he notes in regard to one of the cases in which he granted clemency,

> In due course I received an application for executive clemency, and gave it long and serious consideration . . . I was left with no alternative but to conduct my own investigation. I spent weeks researching the legal and philosophical basis for executive clemency. I spent more weeks digging into the archives for the result of clemency appeals in cases, particularly in the state of Ohio, in which people found guilty in the same crime received different sentences. I went to the gray stone fortress that is the state penitentiary to talk to the principals in the case.[67]

In another case he tells his readers that he went "to see the physical layout of the scene of the crime so that I could understand what really took place."[68] In still another he says, "I pursued my own investigation into the question of responsibility. The day before Nelson was to die, I drove to the penitentiary to talk to the condemned youth."[69]

Not only does his narrative seek to bridge the gap between himself and his reader-judges through an appeal to shared principles and a demonstration of the care with which he used his clemency power, in the end, like Brown's *Public Justice, Private Mercy*, it recounts the substantial personal pain which acting beyond rules imposes on those who wield life or death power. DiSalle writes of the "harrowing days" on which he had to "go into a long executive session with his conscience" when he decided on clemency petitions in capital cases.[70] In so doing he turns clemency into melodrama, reminding his readers at the outset that his story comes from "someone who . . . had the final word on whether or not a fellow man was to die . . ."[71]

The Power of Life or Death describes DiSalle as an agonizing and agonized decision-maker, as if by recounting the pain associated with his clemency decision he could enlist some measure of sympathy and convince his readers that his use of sovereign prerogative was reluctant and responsible. Describing each of the days on which an execution was carried out as "a waking nightmare," he said that "I could never get used to the idea that a man would die—even a man guilty of the most incredibly inhuman behavior—because I had not exercised the power that was mine as long as I was governor, the power to keep him alive."[72] In another place DiSalle writes, "Even when I was convinced of the man's guilt, doubt haunted my unconscious long after the warden had notified me that the prisoner was dead."[73] Conjuring a metaphysical imagining, he says that when he refused clemency he "owed the whole human race an apology" and that he "could not bear to see the imagined reproach in anyone's eyes."[74]

In the end, despite his effort to bridge the gap between himself and his readers through an appeal to common principles, a demonstration of the care he took in making his decisions and of the agony associated with them, he worries about narrative's inability to supply the materials for truly empathetic judgment. He warns his reader-judges, and reminds himself, that inevitably they must judge him from a distance that no set of stories, or narrative conventions, can close. Finally giving into the impossibility of the task he set for his pardon tale, DiSalle concedes that "No one who has never watched the hands of a clock marking the last minutes of a condemned man's existence, knowing that he alone has the temporary Godlike power to stop the clock, can realize the agony of deciding an appeal for executive clemency."[75]

Conclusion

The impulse to narrate, to provide accounts of our actions, Hayden White writes us, is "so natural . . . [and] so inevitable . . . that narrativity could appear problematical only in a culture in which it was absent . . ."[76] Or, as Peter Brooks puts it, "Our lives are ceaselessly intertwined with narrative. . . . We live immersed in narrative, recounting and reassessing the meaning of our past actions, anticipating the outcome of our future projects, situating ourselves at the intersection of several stories not yet completed."[77] Surely White and Brooks are right; putting events into narrative, creating stories to record and speak about those events, and turning deeds into justificatory rhetoric is ubiquitous.

Our immersion in narrative, stories, accounts is, however, not free of history or context. Each lives in history and has a history of its own. At some times, and under some conditions, each flourishes; at other times they atrophy. In some places and in response to some situations they find a home; in others they seem strangely absent. In this essay we turned to executive clemency as one site to examine the generation of narrative, stories, and accounts.

Yet, as DiSalle reminds us, pardon tales may be unable, in the end, to bridge the gap between sovereign and citizen and do the justificatory work they seek to do. This may be because, as Jacques Derrida suggests, the pardon always undoes any account offered for it.[78] In *The Century and the Pardon*, Derrida turns to the universalization of apology and forgiveness, both personal and historical, that mark our post-traumatic times. Exploring diverse manifestations of the pardon from the Japanese apology to the language of forgiveness in the South African Truth Commission to the role of pardon in the mitigation of punishment, Derrida locates at the heart of the pardon an illuminating paradox, as much a result of a Christian tradition as of a modern secularized theology: the pardon is at once an act of grace without logic or reason, and yet is equally inscribed in a conditional, even contractual exchange, where one party repents and the other forgives. It is this paradox that produces for Derrida a deep conundrum about pardon and the accounts offered to explain it, namely: "it is necessary it seems to me, based on the fact that, yes, there is the unpardonable. Is this not in truth the only thing to pardon? The only thing that calls for the pardon."[79] Derrida's analysis dramatizes for us the limitations that inhere in any accounting of a pardon. What account, what narrative, what set of rhetorical devices can satisfactorily account for this aporia? For the pardoning of the unpardonable?

Perhaps the real work that pardon tales do is less to provide such an accounting and more to console those who exercise sovereign power in a world in which that power takes and spares life. Perhaps this is why the impulse to narrate flourishes in the face of the death penalty. The history of narrative is, in fact, a record of the way humans respond to the violence and pain which always threaten to undermine and destroy our carefully constructed, but fragile, webs of signification. Pardon tales are one way that their authors confront those conditions.

In the face of clemency's lawful lawlessness and its seemingly anomalous place in a constitutional democracy, contemporary pardon tales provide some semblance of order by connecting sovereign prerogative and the lived experience of readers in a democratic culture. In the face of the uncertainties of judgment that accompany mercy beyond law, they are produced to provide closure, if not for their readers than for their authors. As Natalie Zemon Davis writes about pardon tales several centuries ago, "Turning a terrible action into a story is a way to distance oneself from it, at worst a form of self-deception, at best a way to pardon the self."[80]

It may be that all pardon tales can do is to provide some assurance for those with the power to spare life that meaning can be made and that it can survive in a world of violence and pain.

Notes

1. Alexander Hamilton, "Federalist 74," *The Federalist: A Commentary on the Constitution of the United States*, New York: The Modern Library, 1956, 482.
2. As the law professor Robert Weisberg puts it, "the commutation of a death sentence (is) the most dramatic example of mercy." See Robert Weisberg, "Apology, Legislation, and Mercy," 82 *North Carolina Law Review* (2004), 1415, 1421. The association of clemency and mercy has roots that extend as far back as the Roman Empire. There Seneca, in one of the great essays on clemency, says that "of all men . . . mercy becomes no one more than a king or a prince." Seneca, *Moral and Political Essays*, edited and translated by John Cooper and J.F. Procope. Cambridge: Cambridge University Press, 132. Mercy, as Seneca defined it, "means 'self-control by the mind when it has the power to take vengeance' or 'leniency on the part of a superior towards an inferior in imposing punishments.' . . . We might speak," he continues, "of mercy as moderation that remits something of a deserved and due punishment." 160.
3. Michel Foucault, *The History of Sexuality. An Introduction.* Robert Hurley trans. New York: Viking, 1990, 135.
4. *Clemency for Battered Women in Michigan: A Manual for Attorneys, Law Students and Social Workers* http://www.umich.edu/~clemency/clemency_manual/manual_chapter02.html.

5. John Locke, *Second Treatise on Civil Government*, edited with an introduction by C. B. Macpherson. Indianapolis, Ind.: Hackett Publishing,1980, Sections 159–160.

6. William Blackstone, *Commentaries on the Laws of England: A Facsimile of the First Edition of 1765-1769* Chicago: University of Chicago Press, 1979, 4: 397–402.

7. Hamilton, "Federalist 74," 482.

8. *Id.*

9. To the framers, the power to pardon was necessary because in the England of their day it was common for minor offenses to carry a sentence of death, with pardon by the King being the only way to avoid that punishment. Judges often applied a death sentence, having no choice, but at the same time applied for a Royal Pardon in the same breath. This is what Hamilton had in mind when, in Federalist 74, he mentioned "necessary severity" and "unfortunate guilt."

10. Hamilton, "Federalist 74," 483.

11. *Id.*

12. Marvin Scott and Stanford Lyman, "Accounts," 33 *American Sociological Review* (1968), 46.

13. *Id.*, 48.

14. John Harrison, "Pardon as Prerogative," 13 *Federal Sentencing Reporter* (2000-2001), 147, 147.

15. Peter Fitzpatrick, "Life, Death, and the Law–And Why Capital Punishment is Legally Insupportable," 47 *Cleveland State Law Review* (1999), 483, 486.

16. Terri Orbuch, "People's Accounts Count: The Sociology of Accounts," *Annual Review of Sociology*; (January 01, 1997).

17. Natalie Zemon Davis, *Fiction in the Archives: Pardon Tales and Their Tellers in Sixteenth Century France*. Stanford: Stanford University Press, 1987.

18. *Id.*, 4.

19. See Norman Greene et. al., "Governor Ryan's Capital Punishment Moratorium and the Executioner's Confession: Views From the Governor's Mansion to Death Row," 75 *St. John's Law Review* (2001), 401, 406.

20. See Robert Ferguson, "The Judicial Opinion as a Literary Genre," 2 *Yale Journal of Law & the Humanities* (1990), 201, 207.

21. This and the following quotations are from Governor George Ryan, "I Must Act," January 11, 2003. Speech at the Northwestern University College of Law. Found at http://www.deathpenaltyinfo.org/article.php?scid=13&did=551.

22. Martha Nussbaum, "Equity and Mercy,"22 *Philosophy and Public Affairs* (1993), 103.

23. Daniel Kobil, "How to Grant Clemency in Unforgiving Times," 31 *Capital University Law Review* (2003), 219, 227.

24. See Ofer Zur, " Psychology of Victimhood: Reflections on a Culture of Victims," *http://www.drozur.com/victimhood.html*. Also Susan D. Moeller, *Compassion Fatigue: How The Media Sell Disease, Famine, War And Death* (New York : Routledge, 1999).

25. Edmund G. (Pat) Brown with Dick Adler, *Public Justice, Private Mercy: A Governor's Education on Death Row*. New York: Weidenfeld & Nicolson, 1989.

26. *Id.*

27. *Id.*, 45.

28. *Id.*, xii.

29. *Id.*, 106.

30. *Id.*, 142.

31. *Id.*

32. *Id.*, 36.

33. *Id.*

34. *Id.*, 10.

35. *Id.*, 135.

36. *Id.*, 121.

37. *Id.*,

38. *Id.*, 135.

39. *Id.*, 121.

40. *Id.*, 10.

41. *Id.*, 154.

42. *Id.*, 163.

43. *Id.*, 105.

44. *Id.*, 163.

45. *Id.*

46. *Id.*, xvii.

47. Jack Lessenberry, "Book Review: DiSalle's True Potential Unfulfilled," (May 16, 2004), http://www.toledoblade.com/apps/pbcs.dll/article?AID=/20040516/ART02/405160312.

48. Michael V. DiSalle with Lawrence G. Blochman, *The Power of Life or Death*. New York: Random House, 1965, 6.

49. As a commentator noted sometime later, while conservatives attacked DiSalle for his opposition to the death penalty, "there were more executions carried out in Mr. DiSalle's one term than in the administrations of the next four governors combined!" Lessenberry, "Book Review: DiSalle's True Potential Unfulfilled."

50. Davis, *Pardon Tales* . . . 4.

51. *Id.*

52. See Thomas W. Laqueur, "Bodies, Details, and the Humanitarian Narrative" in Lynn Hunt ed., The New Cultural History. Berkeley: University of California Press, 1989.

53. *Id.*

54. Michael V. DiSalle with Lawrence G. Blochman, *The Power of Life or Death*, 27.

55. *Id.*, 39.

56. *Id.*

57. *Id.*, 54.

58. *Id.*, 4.

59. *Id.*, 28.

60. *Id.*

61. *Id.*

62. *Id.*

63. *Id.*, 5.

64. Danielle Allen, "Democratic Dis-ease: Of Anger and the Troubling Nature of Punishment," in *The Passions of Law*, Susan Bandes, ed., New York: New York University Press, 1999, 191, 204.

65. Michael V. DiSalle with Lawrence G. Blochman, *The Power of Life or Death*, 4.

66. Jacques Derrida, "The Century and the Pardon," *Le Mondes des Debats*, No. 9 (December, 1999), 5. Found at www.excitingland.com/fixion/pardonEng.htm.

67. Michael V. DiSalle with Lawrence G. Blochman, *The Power of Life or Death*, 52.

68. *Id.*, 87.

69. *Id.*, 80.

70. *Id.*, 83.

71. *Id.*, 3.

72. *Id.*, 83.

73. *Id.*, 6.

74. *Id.*, 83.

75. *Id.*, 5.

76. Hayden White, *The Content of the Form: Narrative Discourse and Historical Representation*. Baltimore: Johns Hopkins University Press, 1987, 1.

77. Peter Brooks, *Reading for the Plot: Design and Intention in Narrative*. New York; Alfred Knopf, 1984, 3.

78. Jacques Derrida, "The Century and the Pardon," *Le Mondes des Debats*, No. 9 (December, 1999), 2. Found at www.excitingland.com/fixion/pardonEng.htm.

79. *Id.*

80. Davis, *Pardon Tales*, 114.

Annelise Riles

Wigmore's Shadow

Part I: The Fictions of Law

The pull of the image, into the past. As you enter the Chicago Homicide Project website, you experience it right away. A lady in a feathered hat, perched on the corner of a desk, waiting, we are told, to testify. What is that look on her face—apprehension? Amusement? Anticipation? And that street in the background, behind the child with the ball—isn't that around the corner from here, where the market stands now? Leigh Bienen's visionary project is a project that celebrates the visual, and the story, and the capacity for the visual to tell stories about the law.

As I click through the pages of the website, those images pull me into several other pasts, all in a sense my own. The site mentions a certain John H. Wigmore, professor and Dean of the Northwestern Law School at the turn of the century. It tells us that Wigmore was one of the founders of *The Journal of Criminal Law and Criminology*, the institutional host of the first academic articles from the Chicago Homicide Project, in 2002. I imagine how much Wigmore would have enjoyed this website, how he would have wanted to contribute objects from his own collection—the personal effects of Al Capone, or materials from his early experiments in new forensic techniques from handwriting analysis to fingerprinting, or his carefully preserved and indexed clippings of newspaper accounts of famous Chicago trials. Most of all, I think how much Wigmore would have approved of this harnessing of the pull of the image.

Wigmore arrived in Chicago in 1894, the year after the World Columbian Exposition. He was an outsider, an import from the East Coast, brought in to preach a newfangled Harvard-style legal education on the intellectual frontier. Truth be told, he probably would have preferred to stay in the East, but he himself was something of an outsider to the Boston Brahmin culture, and so his best hope was to focus his tremendous energies on building something new, elsewhere. From the beginning, he had an outsider's appreciation, a taste and flair for the exotic brand of justice administered on the streets and in the courts of Chicago. He was no missionizing critic; on the contrary, the rough and tumble of it all fascinated and energized him. Taking on the fedora as his own signature piece, he embraced Chicago, enjoyed it, helped build it. In no time he was the darling of the legal establishment and counted several prominent Chicago financiers as his personal patrons. It was a good life, a fun life, I imagine.

The website celebrates Wigmore, then, as a kind of institutional forefather. But that is not how I met John Henry Wigmore. I met him rather, through the pull of his images.

1996. I have just landed in Chicago to take up my first academic post, a post-doctoral fellowship at the American Bar Foundation. The only person I know in town is Leigh Bienen, the woman who years before at Princeton University had dazzled me with her dual life as both a fiction writer and a courtroom lawyer, each identity kept intricately hidden from the other, on two tracks, under the sign of two different names even, each feeding each other silently, secretly, in ways known to her alone, a kind of practical joke on the world that seemed to keep her continually amused. She had held up the only example of a life in the law that I could imagine for myself. For me, that had led to zigzags back and forth between graduate school in anthropology and law school, between periods working on legal reform projects in far flung places and periods of anthropological fieldwork in others. And now, in 1996, here I am. I will be teaching two law courses at the Northwestern Law School to supplement my fellowship stipend. The day before, just before catching the shuttle bus to Heathrow Airport, I turned in my doctoral dissertation at the University of Cambridge, and throughout the flight to Chicago I have been sitting on my hands, trying to resist the urge to open the thing and find all the errors and omissions that surely lie between those covers. When I arrive at Northwestern Law School, I haven't opened a law book in three years.

I drop my things at the rooming house where I will be staying and walk past the shiny glass buildings, down one of those movie-set-like Magnificent Mile streets with its immaculate gardens and glamorous women pulling along equally glamorous dogs, toward the Northwestern Law School, to pick up my keys. I am anxious. I am a foreigner to Chicago, and I know enough to know that it would take years to understand a city like this one. After three years of graduate school in anthropology, half of which I spent in the Fiji Islands conducting research, the rest spent furiously typing on my own inner world of the keyboard, I also fear I am now a foreigner to the law. I pull open the heavy glass door of the law school, step onto the vast marble floor, and glance at the students chatting, books in hand. I suddenly become aware of myself, my long frizzy anthropologist hair, my billowing skirt. I slowly climb the enormous staircase. At the top, a long glass case, the length of the corridor, displays the publications of members of the faculty—I read off the titles, sinking into my shoes. Technical subjects in securities law, corporate law, the law of evidence, contracts; some I can't even decipher. I grasp back into my law school past, trying to remember what the words in those titles mean. I try to picture the men and women behind those texts, and a wave of panic hit. I wish I could lie down, right now, in front of this enormous glass case and fall into a deep, dark sleep.

A year later, and outwardly, life is transformed. I have joined the Northwestern Law School faculty as an Assistant Professor of Law and traded my boarding house room for a respectable apartment. I wear neat suits and carry a briefcase. In daily life—classroom, committee meetings—I am a well-disciplined subject, dutifully doing what needs to be done, not overreaching.

But as a scholar, I am still the girl in front of the glass case. I am unwilling to give up what I do, I know that, but I am struggling to find a place for myself, for my work in that case, among those articles. "Why should anyone care about Fiji?" I have heard enough times so that I no longer mention it. I cringe at faculty meetings when people call me out, jokingly, for example in response to a problem with the central administration: "maybe Annelise knows some witchcraft we could use," to wide chuckles. I panic when a colleague asks, good-naturedly, what I am working on, and I develop elaborate techniques of deflection, ways of changing the subject. I work furiously, round the clock.

One night, when I am working alone in the law school, I stumble down the hall to the faculty lounge for a cup of coffee and loiter back to my office, procrastinating. I stop in the hall in front of a dark stone object, some eight feet tall, and more than a few feet around, in a glass box, by the potted plants. I have passed it a thousand times before. "This is a replica of the Code of Hammurabi, brought back from France by John Henry Wigmore," the Chair of the Appointments Committee had said, as he gave me the mandatory tour of the building on the day of my interview for a permanent position. I had been far too preoccupied to allow that to sink in, and we had moved on, chatting about my research agenda, and about plans for expansion of the school.

The Code of Hammurabi? A *replica* of the Code of Hammurabi? What is it doing here? In what is now a dark early morning hour, the presence of this enormous object, by the potted plants, seems like some kind of preposterous joke, both wildly impossible and just right. Almost in the same instant, I catch myself wondering; and also pulling back— no time for dilly-dallying. I have to finish this thing; whatever it is I'm working on, it's late already, et cetera, et cetera.

I walk down the hall, back toward my office. It is a dark, wood paneled hallway, built when Wigmore was dean. It has always felt cold and slightly depressing to me. Boring, old, conservative, alien territory. For the first time, I slow down enough to glance at the lithographs hung at three-foot intervals on the walls. A series of cartoons from English newspapers lampooning the courtroom, barrister and judges. Some are honestly quite funny. I end up spending most of the night wandering the halls, noticing the cartoon-like spoofs of crests of arms, with the names of legal scholars who would have been Wigmore's contemporaries, in the moldings, or the imitation facsimile of the American Declaration of Independence posted in a case. Downstairs, in the original foyer of the building, a sign is posted, so that every student would confront it on his way through the doors: "Lex Delicto, Lex Contracto, THIS—IS—LAW!" On the facing wall, a giant stone is engraved with the following slogan: "If Bologna, that Capitol of Sausage, can become the Seat of Legal Theory, Why not Chicago, the Capitol of Corn?" How could I never have noticed these things before? I wonder at the absurdity of us all, students and faculty, going on our business in the midst of this circus of statements and images. And I wonder what my colleagues would think if they saw me lurking around the building like this in the middle of the night . . .

John H. Wigmore came to Northwestern fresh from three years in Japan. After graduating from the Harvard Law School, he floundered a bit, did some work for Brandeis, and then got sent off to Japan through an arrangement between the President of Harvard University, Charles Elliott, and the venerable Yukichi Fukuzawa, one of Japan's most illustrious Meiji era intellectuals, and the founder of Keio University.

Fukuzawa wanted to import the new Harvard methods of law teaching to Japan, and so in 1889, Wigmore was sent to Japan, much as he later would be sent to Chicago, to do the job. But from the letters and accounts of his wife and lifelong confidante Emma, one gets the sense that something happened to the man almost from the moment of that sail into Yokohama harbor. Wigmore found himself riding in rickshaws, having tea with British consuls, playing shortstop on Japan's first baseball team. He wrote articles on flower arranging and architecture and ethnology, as well as on the new Japanese Civil Code. He discovered abandoned records of the customary law of "Old Japan," as he called it, and initiated a major project to organize, translate, and publish these. He took an interest in Buddhism. He traveled.

How does all this shoehorn itself into a professional life, when a person returns? In inhabiting Wigmore's carnivalesque palace of legal studies, I began to realize that Wigmore and I shared a set of secrets, passions, maybe even anxieties (it was hard to tell on the latter point with Wigmore). Wigmore seemed to deal with it all by collecting things. Every summer Wigmore and his wife Emma traveled and brought back from foreign lands, images and pictures and other representations of law. Wandering through the basement of the library, I encountered his books, probably unopened since his death—the enormous tomes of decisions of the highest appeals of Japan, signed in the emperor's own vermillion brush; even the case law and statutes of Fiji and Tonga, and Trinidad; and many other places he surely had never visited. One day, the librarian, who knows of my developing obsession, brings me two legal seals discovered in a box under the staircase, with a note from Wigmore stating that they are Mesopotamian relics, dug up in the Middle East somewhere. Reading the records of his elaborate instructions to his travel agent, I imagined him plotting his summer escape, through one European, African and Asian city after another, by every possible mode of transport, back into that other world of adventure and no questions asked, all bankrolled, of course, by his devotees among the Chicago elite.

I admired him, for trying to bring the unrestrained, omnivorous passion for the outside world he had discovered, to the profession: his published "list of legal novels," for example, distributed to every Northwestern law student, admonished lawyers to learn something about human nature, and about ordinary people's perception of their profession, through fiction (John H. Wigmore). I smiled at the first line of his book, A Kaleidoscope of Justice, itself, a collection of images, stories, songs about the law in different jurisdictions of the world, interspersed with kaleidoscopic images, drawn by Wigmore, that depict differences among legal systems as permutations of one another, like pieces in a kaleidoscope.

> READER! This work is not offered to you as a piece of scientific research, but mainly as a book of informational entertainment (John Henry Wigmore, A *Kaleidoscope of Justice: Containing Authentic Accounts of Trial Scenes from All Times and Climes*)

I made a point of walking through the old foyer of the law school, where Wigmore had installed a chime that played one of his favorite limericks, a song he delighted in playing for the students at the annual talent show, each morning. In the foyer, up high, perched there in the corner where the ceiling meets the wall, a wooden sculpture about three feet tall looked down at us. At the Northwestern archives, I learned that Wigmore, a lifelong skeptic of all organized religion, had discovered to his delight the existence of a Catholic patron saint of lawyers, St. Ives. With characteristic gusto, he had organized a delegation of Chicago lawyers to France to make an offering to the saint, and the group had brought back this shoddy replica as a souvenir.

There were rumors that he and Emma kept a Shinto shrine in their living room in Evanston, among other oddities. More than once, I found myself straying up Lake Shore Drive, to sit in my car, across the street from the house I had seen in the photos in the archives, now probably occupied by a professor who had never heard of Wigmore, imagining him and Emma, sitting on that porch debating one silly question or another, with gusto. Where did the energy, the compassion, the stories, the words, the courage to bring those worlds together come from?

I should add also that there were problems in our relationship from the start. Wigmore refused to be shoehorned into the role I sometimes seemed to concoct for him, as fairy godfather of humanistic legal studies. For one thing, I had to admit that he was basically a despicable character. He came to class each day dressed in his World War I military uniform and insisted that his students call him "The Colonel" (in retrospect, I wish I had summoned the courage to try this). He wrote diatribes against labor unions and lambasted Sacco and Vanzetti in print during their trial—something which cost him the friendship of numerous luminaries of the legal academy. He praised the lack of due process in the Japanese criminal justice system and criticized American justice as excessively soft on crime. I remember confiding to Leigh Bienen about my newfound interest in Wigmore. Amused and perplexed, she pulled out an article she had written many years earlier critiquing Wigmore's claim that young women could not be trusted to give proper evidence in a court of law on matters of sexual abuse since by definition they were incapable of telling the truth.

Wigmore is known as the father of American comparative law for an article in two parts he published in the *Harvard Law Review*, the first article in comparative law in a major American law journal (John Henry Wigmore, "The Pledge Idea: A Study in Comparative Legal Ideas"; John Henry Wigmore, "The Pledge Idea: A Study in Comparative Legal Ideas. II."). The article traces the evolution of modern markets from "primitive" systems of barter to the evolution of the legal institution of collateral and accompanying creditors' rights. As I only later learned, the article includes, among other things, an extensive discussion of Japanese law. The underlying message concerns the role that law plays in supporting the development of markets, and the role that comparative law plays in understanding the contributions of law. It is a highly technical, torrid piece of work. I read it quickly and paid little attention to the argument, concluding it belonged to that other side of Wigmore that held no particular fascination for me.

But for a while I ignored all this and took the Wigmore of the elaborate performances, the strange objects, the limericks, and the travel as a kind of ready-made justification—not so much to be emulated as invoked, St. Ives-like.

As it turned out, my own life and research took me to Japan, to conduct ethnographic research among regulators of the derivatives market. That was the end of my relationship with Wigmore, I thought—he had served his purpose, we had had some fun. I didn't imagine he would catch up with me.

As it turned out, the topic of the moment, in the regulation of the Japanese derivatives markets, was collateral. With the economic downturn, Japanese banks had to post collateral with their counterparties in New York or London in order to enter into swap transactions. Those counterparties in turn wanted to have rights to sell the collateral, or to use it somehow, before the completion of the swap, when they would then return the collateral to the Japanese bank. This is legal under New York and UK law, but it seemed that it was not legal under Japanese law (which among other things affords higher degrees of protection to creditors). Regulators, academics, and lawyers working for the banks debated how to amend or interpret Japanese law to bring it into line with so-called "global standards."

Some time into my fieldwork, one of my research subjects, a lawyer in private practice, brought up the name of John Henry Wigmore. I expected to discuss Wigmore's time in Japan, or his research in Japanese law, but my interlocutor instead asked what I thought about the details of Wigmore's argument about the evolution of the institutions of collateral. In particular, he noted, Wigmore had analyzed two technical schemes—a collateral security scheme and a so-called "sale with option to repurchase scheme"—as legally distinct but functionally equivalent from the market-participants' point of view. What did I think—was Wigmore right about this? It mattered because one of the options on the table to resolve Japan's collateral problem might be the adoption of a version of a sale with option to repurchase.

Stunned and embarrassed—I had never paid attention to those details—I realized that for all my cheerleading, I had not taken Wigmore seriously as an interlocutor. I listened quietly as my friend evoked Wigmore to me in a new way, as a contemporary of a kind, not an image from the past.

The past in the present: methodologically and theoretically, the article itself is a fairly straightforward application of the evolutionary theories of law prevalent in the nineteenth century (for example, in the work of Henry Maine and Lewis Henry Morgan) but already falling into disrepute by the time of Wigmore's publications in the *Harvard Law Review*. The point of this breezy romp through Scandinavian and German law, followed by Jewish, Japanese, and Hindu law (the latter in one paragraph) is precisely the past in the present. Each of these legal systems followed the same trajectory of development, Wigmore argues, toward the modern system of collateral. It is the sort of argument I would date as belonging in the past—mid-nineteenth century. And yet what is most confusing about my Japanese interlocutor's invocation was precisely his pulling of that article into the present, his enrollment of it in a very prescient, modern-day dispute. Thinking back to that glass case in the corridor of the Northwestern Law School, I remembered that several respected colleagues had, to my confusion, tried to engage me seriously about the details of Wigmore's research in this way—"he had some interesting things to say about the Commons in Scandinavia . . ." Like my Japanese friend, my colleagues had treated Wigmore as a kind of contemporary, a scholar in the next lane, so to speak. Moreover, for these colleagues, it was the other side of Wigmore's work that mattered. The underlying political premise of that work—law in the service of markets—conformed with their own views. The underlying method—evolutionary theory—was also now back in vogue in the legal academy.

My talisman, it turned out, had been on the other side all along. Or more to the point, my colleagues' pulling of Wigmore into their own present—as a kind of contemporary and co-conspirator in the cause of the technocratic rationalization of the law in light of the needs of the market, seemed somehow much more efficacious than my invocation of Wigmore as an image, through his images, as a kind of excuse for explorations of fiction, performance, parody, meanings, stories, in short a set of law and humanities moves and interests defined parasitically but ultimately weakly by the sheer fact that they seemed to be what technocratic legal instrumentalism was not. I couldn't really blame Wigmore. That article had been there all along, but I had been, ironically, too flat-footed in my sophisticated high-heeled performances, to take it seriously.

So here is a question for my fellow travelers in the humanistic studies of law. Might there be anything of interest to us in this other Wigmore—the Wigmore of technical legal doctrines, of law in the service of the market? To culturalists such as ourselves, the technical details of law are mundane, almost inherently uninteresting. The obsessive focus on law as a technical tool is precisely the problem; it obscures all else, makes it difficult to talk about other important and interesting questions. As James Boyd White put it long ago,

> Law then becomes reducible to two features: policy choices and techniques of their implementation. Our questions are 'What do we want?' and 'How do we get it?' In this way the conception of law as a set of rules merges with the conception of law as a set of institutions and processes. The overriding metaphor is that of the machine; the overriding value is that of efficiency, conceived of as the attainment of certain ends with the smallest possible costs. (White 686)

One way of putting this point is that as experts in meaning, we find nothing particularly meaningful about these technicalities. They are mere tools. There is nothing much to capture our fantasies here; no wonder I skipped over The Pledge Idea on my way to the Panorama and the Kaleidoscope. Engaging the question of what to make of the technicalities requires a different modality, precisely not storytelling and images. And so, like the Colonel, I slip into a different costume now.

Part II: Legal Fictions

The Pledge Idea is a dense, highly technical article. Although the evidence on each point is scanty, the legal questions are baroque, and the argumentation intricately woven. But if we take it as a work of legal theory, the article concerns one principal kind of legal technicality, one device, the legal fiction. As the mid-twentieth-century legal theorist Lon Fuller put it, a legal fiction is "either (1) a statement propounded with a complete or partial consciousness of its falsity, or (2) a false statement recognized as having utility" (Fuller "Legal Fictions" 369). A fiction differs from a hypothesis, for example, because there is no question of proving its truth—it is known to be false. But a legal fiction differs also from a lie because "it is not intended to deceive" (Fuller "Legal Fictions" 367). Fuller's many examples include the notion that a corporation is a person, or the doctrine of coverture, which held that at marriage husband and wife merged into one person, the person of the husband.

Wigmore's account of the evolution of collateral is an account of the evolution of one such legal fiction. To simplify dramatically, Wigmore aims to show that in more primitive times, if one person loaned something to another, he or she would keep something of value belonging to the debtor until the debt was repaid. In such a scenario, the object, the *res*, was the creditor's only recourse—if the debtor failed to repay, the creditor could do as he pleased with the *res*—and this was all the creditor could do. Over time, however, both sides learned to act as if the lender kept the asset, and to treat the *res* as more and more collateral to the underlying transaction between the parties. In a modern mortgage, for example, the parties act as if the bank has possession of the property until the mortgage is paid, although the debtor actually remains in possession. This legal fiction—the fiction that the lender, the bank, actually possessed the *res*—allowed modern commercial relations to flourish, Wigmore argues. Wigmore provides dozens of examples of such legal fictions bundled together in the singular, and seemingly straightforward technical device of modern collateral. Although he does not explicitly say as much, concentrated as he is on the details, one could read his larger account as a story about the emergence and growth of an intricate relation of fictions in an emerging body of commercial doctrine.

As a subject, legal fictions ignite lawyers' passions. Some ardently defend the legal fiction as the very engine of progress in the law. Sir Henry Maine, for example, celebrated the contributions of legal fictions to the evolution of law from Roman times to the present. For him, legal fictions were one of three key political institutions, alongside courts of equity and legislatures, by which the law changed itself in order to keep up with changes in society. For example, the legal fiction of adoption allowed Roman citizens to incorporate foreigners into their communities while preserving the premise that kinship defined political allegiances. Fictions "satisfy the desire for improvement, which is not quite wanting, at the same time that they do not offend the superstitious disrelish for change that is always present," he argued (Maine 31). Without legal fictions, in other words, the law would stagnate—and hence would hold society back by refusing to recognize in law changes long since recognized in society.

But the legal fiction has equally powerful adversaries. Jeremy Bentham, for example, considered it the height of lawyerly obfuscation, the very opposite of ethical, transparent government:

> It has never been employed to any purpose but the affording a justification for something which otherwise would be unjustifiable. . . . It affords presumptive and conclusive evidence of the mischievousness of the act of power in support of which it is employed. . . . In every case, and throughout the whole field of government, these instruments of mis-rule have had, as they could not but have had, for their fabricators, the fraternity of lawyers." (Bentham and Bowring: v. IX, pp. 77-8)

The legal fiction is a device used by lawyers to pull the wool over everyone else's eyes, on the way to furthering their own class interests, in other words. If lawyers wish to change the law, they should do so through their legislature, where the public has at least some degree of access, instead of with a lawyerly wink and a nod. Bentham's position has powerful contemporary advocates. The constitutional theorist Cass Sunstein, for example, has plainly argued that we need "principles, not fictions"—that legal fictions are "unhelpful and in fact harmful to legal reasoning and results. Fictions are not indispensable. The law would be better off without any of them." (Sunstein 1256)

This brings us back to the symposium's theme, violence. The very choice of the word violence—violence, in contrast to crime, in the context of the Chicago Homicide Project—seems to gesture toward an analogy between the literal forms of violence documented in the Chicago Homicide Project database, and more figurative forms of violence—forms of violence that do not, at first glance, seem like violence at all. The law and the humanities movement—and law and literature in particular—has long sought to draw out the mundane violence of the law in this way. The great dean of humanistic studies of law Robert Cover, for example, famously claimed that "the subject matter of constitutional interpretation is violence" (Cover 818)—incarceration, the death penalty, the coercive authority of the State—and hence "constitutional law is . . . more fundamentally connected to the war than it is to the poetry" (Cover 817).[1] Here, ironically, although Bentham himself drew a sharp distinction between "poetry and truth," and condemned "the mischiefs which have resulted from this magic art" that serve only "to gratify those individuals who are most difficult to be pleased" (Bentham and Bowring v. II, p. 258), when it comes to legal fictions, humanists seem squarely on Bentham's side.

But there is no doubt that we can think of many terrifying examples of the violence perpetrated with the help of this device. Take for example the fiction of *terra nullius*, of empty land, by which colonial authorities gained legal recognition for their dispossession of indigenous peoples of their lands and hence legal title over those lands. Or the fiction under English Law of coverture, of a wife's "covering" (the word also means disguise, deceit, pretense) during marriage, whereby on the day of their marriage, women lost the capacities to contract and own property that they enjoyed as single women.

Here, in fact, Wigmore himself sides with Robert Cover. He emphasizes the foundation of the legal fiction of collateral on the availability of state-sanctioned violence. In "primitive" situations, in which citizens rely only on self-help to enforce their will upon one another, he argues, the creditor in effect holds the *res* hostage for the period of the debt. Only once the creditor believes she can harness the capacities of the state to commit violence, in the service of her dispute with the debtor, will she feel confident releasing the *res*, and allowing the debtor to remain in possession of it for the time being. So here Wigmore seems to suggest a point of humanistic engagement with the technicalities of law—a kind of extension of already familiar themes of legal violence to a new set of subjects, legal technicalities. Along with Wigmore, and Bentham, we might unmask the hidden violence of the law.

On the face of it, this seems like a plausible project. But at least for myself, I have a problem with it as an intellectual vocation. First, one hardly needs humanists to make the point. Bentham himself said it all, one hundred and fifty years ago, and in language far more scathing than most of us would probably dare muster today. Even Wigmore, the champion of law in the service of the evolution of markets, could see the point, although true to form, he remained tantalizingly ambiguous about what conclusions the reader should draw from his observations. Mainstream doctrinalists like Cass Sunstein have roundly taken up the cause of exposing the political injustices of legal fictions. Do we need further critique and unmasking?

I have to admit that I feel increasingly dissatisfied with the pull of images and the parallel humanistic critiques of technocratic legal knowledge. The unmasking of the violence of legal fictions and other technicalities certainly have their place, and still can be fun to do. But what I like about Wigmore's gluttonous immersion in the intricacies of one set of legal fictions is that it owns up to Wigmore's own insider status, his participation in the technocracy as a lawyer, a teacher of law, a law school dean. There is nothing wrong with denouncing the violence of law, of course, as long as one acknowledges that it is not some other, "The Law," that is violent, as long as one is willing to say, "I am also violent, I am the Law" (Kennedy).

That is, the search for alternative stories to tell about the law, from the outrageous to the ludicrous, appeals to humanists partly because they are not outrageous and transgressive *for us*. On the contrary, they reconfirm our deepest faiths, that law is a set of performances, that its categories are arbitrary and yet constitutive, that hidden beneath the smooth surfaces of technicalities is a ferment of violence and politics. As I think about my relationship to Wigmore, and through him to both objects in the Northwestern Law School foyer—the Code of Hammurabi and the glass case with the technical legal articles on display, I wonder if it might be possible to engage the legal fiction in a way in which the destabilization begins here, with me.

I will come back to this question at the close of this essay. For the moment, instead, I want to consider what makes a legal fiction distinctively legal. What exactly is the difference between a legal fiction and a literary fiction, for example? Most commentators from Henry Maine on simply assume an obvious difference and concentrate instead on highlighting some surprising similarities—on drawing analogies between the disparate realms of fiction and law. Some commentators suggest that the difference lies in the audience's reception of the fiction: the reader of literature knows that he encounters something false in fact, and knows that the falsehood, the telling of a story that never happened, serves to reveal a higher order of truth, the essence of the story. In contrast, in this view, only some parts of the audience of a legal fiction—the expertly trained lawyers—understand that the fiction is not true in this way.

Personally, I think this distinction, and its underlying critique of legal fictions, protests too much. First, reader response theory (Iser) and ethnographies of fiction readers (Reed) conclusively demonstrate that readers have a far more subtle and engaged relationship to fiction than a simple understanding of a story as an untruth at one level in the service of demonstrating truth at another level. Reed, for example, speaks of readers' experience of being captured, possessed by the author of the novel in a way that obviates the very question of truth or falsity. Conversely, the suggestion that lay persons are incapable of understanding, for example, that the law's treatment of mortgaged property as in possession of the bank for the period the mortgagee pays off the mortgage is a fiction seems quite implausible. Moreover, with Nomi Stolzenberg, and, as she shows, with Bentham also, one would want to appreciate how the legal fiction is itself performative and legislative—how the legal treatment of women "as if" they were subsumed in the personality of their husbands for legal purposes alters the husband and wife's conception of themselves and the marriage, even if they understand that this is only an "as if" (Stolzenberg). But nevertheless, even this simple distinction between literary and legal fictions seems inadequate.

So then what distinguishes literary and legal fictions? I want to suggest now that it is the particular character of the legal fiction as an *explicit instrument*, a device with a clearly defined purpose, a means to an end. A legal fiction is a fiction with a purpose explicitly attached, whereas a literary fiction, like all art, has no other purpose but its own existence. It is supremely purposeless without utility. For Maine, for example, legal fictions serve the venerable purpose of legal reform. For Bentham, in a parallel way, the problem with legal fictions is that they serve no rational purpose: "[The fiction] has never been employed but to a bad purpose. It has never been employed to any purpose but the affording a justification for something which otherwise would be unjustifiable" (Bentham and Bowring: v. IX p.77). The two agree in other words on the purposeful quality of the fiction and even on the nature of the purpose; they disagree only on whether the ends justify the means. Lon Fuller, likewise, focuses on the legal fiction's tool-like quality when he argues that at least one purpose of the legal fiction is as technical abbreviation, a "convenient shorthand" (Fuller, "Legal Fictions Part II" 537), a marker or place-holder for the points at which legal theory reaches the limits of its own capacities. To treat human embryos as "quasi-property," for example, is not so much to imagine them as actually part human and part property as to create a placeholder for the fact that we do not yet know how to imagine embryos, in relationship to existing legal categories of person and property. The legal fiction is an instrument for getting over these kinds of humps—a tool for leap-frogging over our own conceptual limitations. Although other kinds of fictions (most notably, fictions in the sciences) can be tools, they need not be always and explicitly imagined by their users in this way.

Here we can see a kind of divide between the humanistic and technocratic studies of law—between the Wigmore of the Code of Hammurabi and the Wigmore of the law in the glass case. The humanistic studies of law have to a large extent defined their project as an attempt to broaden the range of stories one could tell about law, precisely to overcome this hegemony of purposes and instruments, of technical reckonings of relations of means to ends. The legal fiction, from this perspective, is just another technical device.

But is it? Having considered what distinguishes legal fictions from literary fictions, that is, its status as instrument, let's turn to what differentiates this particular instrument in the lawyer's toolkit from others, that is, its fictional status. A legal fiction is a particular kind of tool, after all: it is a statement, a story a judge or a lawyer tells, while simultaneously understanding full well—and also understanding that the audience understands—that the statement is *not fact*. It is a legal conclusion, in other words, that takes the form of a factual statement: At law, a wife's property and personhood merge into those of her husband at marriage; at law, an embryo "is" quasi-property.

In *The Philosophy of "As If,"* Hans Vaihinger describes fictions, or "as ifs," as the fountain of all knowledge (Vaihinger and Ogden). An "as if" is knowledge that is consciously false, and as such irrefutable. It differs from a hypothesis because the point is not to check the claim against some wider and more authoritative reality but rather to turn inward, away from such reality. It differs also from a lie, since the author of the As If makes no attempt to hide its falsity. Vaihinger draws attention to the delicate epistemological stance of the As If—to its subtle, ambivalent, "tension." The As If is *neither* true nor not true, but rather is itself the tension between true and not true. Vaihinger's insights have had some currency in debates about legal fictions. Lon Fuller ignored Vaihinger's own insistence that his theory was "diametrically opposed in principle" to American pragmatism and enthusiastically embraced Vaihinger as the greatest of all pragmatist thinkers about the law: "I am firmly convinced that a study of Vaihinger will make one a *better* legal thinker" (Fuller "Legal Fictions Part III" 880 n. 177).

One of Vaihinger's principal insights is that the fiction is, on the surface, a means to an end. But he emphasizes what he terms "the law of the preponderance of the means over the end":

> It is a universal phenomenon of nature that means which serve a purpose undergo a more complete development than is necessary for the attainment of their purpose. In this case, the means, according to the completeness of its self-development, can emancipate itself partly or wholly and become established as an end in itself (Vaihinger and Ogden xlvi).

The "tension" of the legal fiction, then, is as much a tension of the means and the ends as a tension between truth and fiction. From this point of view we can understand Vaihinger's insistence that, despite all this talk of means and ends, his "fictionalism" is definitely not American pragmatism.[2]

I raise all of this in order to suggest that Vaihinger proposes to us a different avenue for humanistic engagement with the technicalities of law such as legal fictions, those aspects we have either critiqued from the outside as "violence," or have ignored altogether. Vaihinger shows how, at the heart of the instrument, the relation of means to ends, the binds of the tool progressively loosen over time as lawyers begin to appreciate the means as means, for its own sake (Riles "Property as Legal Knowledge: Means and Ends"). Indeed, one could say that such an appreciation of the means, of the qualities of a good legal fiction, of its clever and yet appropriate deployment, is the craft of legal knowledge. It is a special kind of craft, performed and appreciated *as if* it were simply a device for balancing opposing political interests, or rendering the market more efficient, or improving human rights standards, or conditions for scientific research. Heidegger called such things—the art at the heart of technical instrumentalism—*techne* (Heidegger). More recently, Giorgio Agamben has compared the punctuation of the means to the place of gesture in dance—something that happens in the course of moving across the stage, of getting from here to there, but that cannot be reduced to that purpose. Agamben sees in these "means without end" emancipatory possibilities (Agamben). And indeed, perhaps Wigmore found some of the same emancipatory delight in puzzling through the technicalities of legal fictions as a young man as he found in collecting outrageous and ironic images and stories of law as an older man. Perhaps we could think of the pull of techne, of the *means*, as something on par with the more readily apprehensible pull of images exemplified so beautifully by the Chicago Homicide Project website.

From this point of view, the legal fiction, with its delicate preponderance of the means over the ends, begins to look like a challenge worth taking. What would it take for me, as a humanist, to abandon my search for *alternatives* to that glass case in the Northwestern Law School foyer, or again to give up the somewhat sanctimonious performances of transgression and critique, and instead to find some other register—a register of response, in kind, appropriate to, even empathetic of the delicate As If?

One final thought: I have circled back, as it were, followed Wigmore's trajectory in reverse, beginning where he left off and ending up where he began. This begs a question: why did Wigmore abandon the legal fiction in the second part of his career for the fictions of law? I wonder if it has something to do with the turn legal theory took at the midpoint of his career, that is, the advent of modernism. I have described elsewhere how Wigmore's career began at the twilight of the era of classical legal formalism, and how he himself played a crucial role in ushering in a new style of legal thought by discovering and enthusiastically promoting young modernists (later known as Legal Realists) such as Roscoe Pound (Riles "Encountering Amateurism: John Henry Wigmore and the Uses of American Formalism"). One of the wedges between classical formalism and legal realism, in the realist imagination, was a new scientific, or rather engineering-like quality of modernist theories of law, as opposed to what the realists painted as the amateur character of classical legal formalism. As I describe elsewhere, the realists embraced the banner of law as a "means to an end" and promoted themselves as expert technicians in the construction and deployment of legal instruments.

From this point of view, Wigmore's panoramic evolutionary account of the rise of a "legal idea" like collateral—with its weak sourcing, its broad brush strokes, and, equally importantly, its emphasis on the semi-autonomy of legal ideas rather than its explanation of law as the effect of social and material forces seemed quite outdated, and judging from Wigmore's own embrace of the principles of realism, one must assume that he agreed.

But what is interesting in this context is that although Wigmore abandoned the collateral project, this did not mean that he turned to producing scholarship in the traditional modernist mold. On the contrary, he goes even further in the other direction, pushes the envelope, produces a book that actually announces that it is a "Panorama" and that it is not serious scholarship but entertainment. It is a bold, and quite clever act of resistance to a new orthodoxy, a refusal of both dominant positions—classicism and realism—that seems to show up their similarities, their intimate relation, the symbiotic nature of their dispute.

This leads me to ask, what would count as the analog to Wigmore's bold move, his careful and calculated, yet celebratory, omnivorous act, that refuses both sides of the dominant opposition? Today, the crucial opposition is not between classicism and realism—in retrospect historians agree that the hard edged difference between those two positions is best appreciated as a kind of legal fiction of its own. Today, the dominant opposition, the key debate, is between "cultural approaches" to law—law and literature, law and the humanities, legal history, legal anthropology, approaches working under the sign of Wigmore's faux Hammurabi Code—and self-consciously instrumentalist, technocratic approaches—law and economics, law and psychology, doctrinal scholarship, work that submits to the constraints and also enjoys the privileges of that glass case. From this point of view, Wigmore's performances are no longer transgressive as they once were; rather, they are just one side, one position, in a well-buttressed debate. In order to recapture the sprit of Wigmore's intervention we will have to do something other than just extend it, or notice it—we will have to replicate it onto our *own* terrain (Miyazaki).

And so what I ultimately take from my friend Wigmore is that to choose either of these positions, humanistic or technocratic, cannot possibly be the answer. Wigmore seems to stand rather for the need to find a third place that is not yet so easily contextualized in existing discourse, that makes visible the commonalities and that obviates the now-naturalized fault lines, that must work to create its own context. And I also take from Wigmore the law of the preponderance of the means over the end in our own work as much as in the law. That is, the project for the sheer passion of it, its own reward, not simply a means to some other professional end.

Notes

1. Here, ironically, although Bentham himself drew a sharp distinction between "poetry and truth," and condemned "the mischiefs which have resulted from this magic art" that serve only "to gratify those individuals who are most difficult to be pleased" (Bentham and Bowring: v. II, p. 258), when it comes to legal fictions, humanists seem squarely on

Bentham's side. With the exception of the subtle work of Nomi Stolzenberg, who rescues Bentham from caricature. Nomi M. Stolzenberg, "Bentham's Theory of Fictions—a 'Curious Double Language,'" *Cardozo Studies in Law and Literature* 11 (1999).

2. Vaihinger's own phrasing of the distinction is telling:

> Fictionalism does not admit the principle of Pragmatism which runs: "An idea which is found to be useful in practice proves thereby that it is also true in theory, and the fruitful is always true." The principle of Fictionalism, is as follows: "An idea whose theoretical untruth or incorrectness, and therewith its falsity, is admitted, is not for that reason practically valueless and useless; for such an idea, in spite of its theoretical nullity may have great importance. But though Fictionalism and Pragmatism are diametrically opposed in principle, in practice they find much in common. Thus both acknowledge the value of metaphysical ideas, though for very different reasons and with different consequences." Hans Vaihinger and C. K. Ogden, *The Philosophy of as If, a System of the Theoretical, Practical and Religious Fictions of Mankind*, International Library of Psychology, Philosophy, and Scientific Method (London, New York: K. Paul, Trench, Trubner & Co. Harcourt, Brace & Company, inc., 1924) viii.

References

Agamben, Giorgio. *Means without End: Notes on Politics*. Minneapolis: University of Minnesota Press, 2000.

Bentham, Jeremy, and John Bowring. *The Works of Jeremy Bentham*. Edinburgh, London: W. Tait; Simpkin, Marshall, & co., 1843.

Cover, Robert. "The Bonds of Constitutional Interpretation: Of the Word, the Deed, and the Role." *Georgia Law Review* 20 (1986): 815-33.

Fuller, Lon L. "Legal Fictions." *Illinois Law Review* 25.4 (1930): 363-99.

—. "Legal Fictions Part II." *Illinois Law Review* 25.4 (1930): 513-46.

—. "Legal Fictions Part III." *Illinois Law Review* 25.4 (1930): 877-910.

Heidegger, Martin. *The Question Concerning Technology, and Other Essays*. 1st ed. New York: Harper & Row, 1977.

Iser, Wolfgang. "Indeterminacy and the Reader's Response in Prose Fiction." *From Reader Response to Literary Anthropology*. Baltimore: Johns Hopkins University Press, 1989. 4-5.

Kennedy, David. *The Dark Sides of Virtue: Reassessing International Humanitarianism*. Princeton, N.J.: Princeton University Press, 2004.

Maine, Henry Sumner. *Ancient Law*. Classics of Anthropology. Tucson: University of Arizona Press, 1986 (1861).

Miyazaki, Hirokazu. *The Method of Hope: Anthropology, Philosophy, and Fijian Knowledge*. Stanford, Calif.: Stanford University Press, 2004.

Reed, Adam. "Henry and I: An Ethnographic Account of Men's Fiction Reading." *Ethnos 67, no 2* (2002): 181-200.

Riles, Annelise. "Encountering Amateurism: John Henry Wigmore and the Uses of American Formalism." *Rethinking the Masters of Comparative Law.* Ed. Annelise Riles. Oxford; Portland: Hart, 2001. 94-128.

—. "Property as Legal Knowledge: Means and Ends." *Journal of the Royal Anthropolgical Institute* (N.S.) 10 (2004): 775-95.

Stolzenberg, Nomi M. "Bentham's Theory of Fictions—a 'Curious Double Language'." *Cardozo Studies in Law and Literature* 11 (1999): 223-49.

Sunstein, Cass. "Principles, Not Fictions." *University of Chicago Law Review* 57 (1990): 1247-58.

Vaihinger, Hans, and C. K. Ogden. *The Philosophy of As If, a System of the Theoretical, Practical and Religious Fictions of Mankind.* International Library of Psychology, Philosophy, and Scientific Method. London, New York: K. Paul, Trench, Trubner & Co.; Harcourt, Brace & Company, inc., 1924.

White, James Boyd. "Law as Rhetoric, Rhetoric as Law: The Arts of Cultural and Communal Life." *Chicago Law Review* 52 (1985): 684-702.

Wigmore, John H. "A List of Legal Novels." *Illinois Law Review* 2 (1907-08): 574-93.

Wigmore, John Henry. *A Kaleidoscope of Justice: Containing Authentic Accounts of Trial Scenes from All Times and Climes.* Littleton, Colo.: F.B. Rothman, 1983.

—. *The New Wigmore: A Treatise on Evidence.* New York: Aspen Law & Business, 2002.

—. "The Pledge Idea: A Study in Comparative Legal Ideas." *Harvard Law Review* 10.6&7 (1897): 321-417.

—. "The Pledge Idea: A Study in Comparative Legal Ideas. II." *Harvard Law Review* 10.7 (1897): 389-417.

ArLynn Leiber Presser

The Ghost Light

There is a letter. I have never seen it. I'm pretty sure that it was de-
stroyed. It was kept hidden long enough to do its damage. I was almost
three years old when it was sent and I wasn't thinking about letters. I
was thinking about the light—standing in the hallway of a Cape Cod
home in Western Springs, a bedroom community outside Chicago. I
watched the sun fall down outside a window swathed in ruffled chiffon.
I thought "this yellow golden palace is where I will come to live soon—
this will be my home." I felt very important because a woman in a very
nice suit drove me to this house several times to visit the family that
would be mine and she always told me how special I was. I was chosen.
I was to be "specially adopted"—meaning that of all the children this
new family could have adopted, they had decided upon me. Special, spe-
cial me. And special, special them that they were given the privilege of
choosing their new daughter.

My new mother told me that my name was Lynn and that what I
thought was my name—ArLynn—was actually just referring to "our
Lynn." So now my name was Lynn, just Lynn. But there was something
about the situation that troubled me. I would figure out precisely what
on the next visit with the lady of the very nice suits—being adopted by
the new family meant that I had to leave the old one behind. As an
adult, I've heard how I cried and screamed and ran down the hallway of
the agency offices to scratch at the doorway of the office where my
Mother—my old mother—dropped me off for the last time.

But the letter. It still existed while I stood in the doorway of the bedroom of the yellow-gold house. It had been mailed by my father to my grandfather Fritz Leiber who lived far away in Pacific Palisades, California. Fritz wrote science fiction and did the occasional movie—he and his wife were character actors presiding over a group of actors, writers, filmmakers, and creative types with parties that lasted days and sometimes weeks. It was the sixties, they were daring and they were on top of the world. The letter caught Fritz by surprise: my father Justin admitted failure. Twenty-three years old, the prodigy working on his doctorate in linguistic philosophy, married and a father, he wrote "We are putting ArLynn up for adoption. If you want to stop this process and raise her yourself, you need to take her now."

Fritz looked at his wife Jonquil, an actress, occasional writer, and a drunkard—as he was—in the days before there was a forgiving therapeutic label. She had an added fondness for Phenobarbital. I had been sent to live with them for several months when I was an infant, and Fritz had come home one day to find me covered with wounds from a diaper pin which could not find purchase and was inserted again and again into my flesh before Jonquil gave up altogether on diapering me. I had been shipped back to my parents. And with this letter, Fritz decided on a course of inaction. He put it in a desk drawer without responding or passing it along to Jonquil. Weeks later, another letter: She is now gone. A shock to be sure, but when Jonquil found the first letter in his desk months later, there was a rupture in the Leiber family.

This was in the sixties, and there was a shortage of couples to adopt, an abundance of available children—a reversal of our current adoption marketplace. Most prospective parents did not want toddlers—babies handed over in the hours after birth were most prized, even more so than they are now, because more parents chose never to tell adoptees that they were in fact not biologically related. So it was not so much that I was "special" as that the new family was willing—they were the best the agency could find for a three year old. The new family had been rejected by other agencies because there was a problem—well, actually two.

The first was my new father, who had suffered several major heart attacks in his thirties and was not expected to survive past his fortieth birthday. The second was a little more subtle: my new mother who gave me cookies and told me my new name had been subjected to a hysterectomy when she was seventeen. In those days, hysterectomy was an accepted medical response to mental illness and to venereal disease.

I shudder when I write this, but almost immediately after my adop-

214

tion, my new father was sent away on business for several years, only to commute home on the occasional weekend. My new mother fell apart. She had a violent and unpredictable temper. She had few friends, no family to rely upon, and she had no idea how to be a mom. I spent days and sometimes weeks locked in the basement of that yellow-gold house after the lady with the nice suits stopped visiting. For crimes that now seem trivial. I stole food. I asked for toys at the drugstore. I dallied returning home from school. I did all the things kids can do and want to do.

This new not mother spent days and sometimes weeks in her own prison above my own, the second floor master bedroom. Never changing out of her bathrobe, seldom washing her hair, leaving the house only fleetingly and reluctantly. There was violence of an utterly baffling and vengeful nature. I remember my new father's belt collection and being kept home from school for a week when the backs of my legs were a mess of red welts. I remember the rush of electricity when I was electrocuted in a bathtub. I remember accusations and furniture being thrown. But the locking up was the most frequent form of punishment, and it's where I learned everything I know about the world, facing a blank concrete wall dappled with mold, shadows, and spider webs.

Socrates claimed that all he did was draw from the student the knowledge that already existed within—and I made my own exploration of the world in the basement of 4207 Linden Avenue. I concocted number games, counting the steps that led to the first floor. I learned how to count in binary on my hands but could not articulate "base two" until an eighth grade unit on the matter. An exploration of my feet made me understand the contraction/release of opposing muscle groups—a first step in elemental anatomy. I imagined worlds where our most cherished assumptions were found to be untrue—the "what if" was worth hours of thought. I made up stories and pondered, in that delightful sophomoric way kids do, the Great Questions of the Universe. Why are we here? Is there a God? Are there other universes in which every choice I make is a fork in the road leading to an infinite number of other futures? I went to school nearly every day and got good grades. I was polite and very quiet. I didn't have friends and I didn't leave my house on weekends or after school. I remember thinking there was a gap between "good kids" and me—and I couldn't figure out how I could be good enough to have friends, get toys for Christmas, go out for ice cream on a summer day.

The first time I read Plato's Allegory of the Cave was a revelation. Those who were in chains were simply inventing their own world, making their own way, were just like me in the basement, and shouldn't be condemned for peaceably sharing a communitarian vision. They had every right to ignore and distrust the individual who claimed to have walked out of the cave to live among the Ideal Forms. As it is, I was a teen, so let's just say that I misinterpreted the thoughts and motivations of those who were chained and faced the shadows as well as the heroism of the one who correctly saw the wondrous beauty of the Platonic Ideals. And, of course, was killed for his efforts. All I knew was that I didn't want to be the one walking out of the cave even as I did want to be the one walking out of the basement.

I tried to escape sometimes and was punished with more time. Then my not mother hit upon a system—I wouldn't try to escape if I were naked. I was humiliated and sometimes the neighbor children would drive their bicycles up the driveway to peer in the windows. I would hide—often up under the stairs in the furnace closet. This not mother created her own storyline in which my eight years older sister, adopted at birth and so very imprintable and submissive, was the Glenda to my Wicked Witch. My sister spent hours ironing in the basement just so that she could keep me company—our family had very well-pressed clothes.

When my not really father returned for a night, he was given the assignment of going down to the bottom of the basement stairs to give the Big Lecture. He told me I was bad, I promised better behavior and it was pretty clear we didn't know what we should do next. One night, as he spoke, I was sure I heard a noise an animal would make. Not a dog, exactly. Not a mouse, precisely, since I was familiar with that sound. Not a wolf, surely. A something like a bark, a whine, a growl, and then silence. I tried to concentrate on my repetition of better behavior promises and then the animal noise would interrupt. I didn't want to be in the basement with a big animal—spiders and mice were bad enough. I said, "I hear a dog." He said, "We don't have a dog."

True enough. But then there was more barking/howling/snarling, not to be ignored. I followed my not father into a part of the basement behind the furnace closet and there we discovered my so possibly crazy not mother. She had somehow snuck into the basement unbeknownst to us and was seated on a work bench, rocking back and forth as she howled. Her face was distorted, muscles slack in some places and taut in others. She stopped long enough to ask if I were scared. Well, yes, of course. And she said that if I was scared enough of the basement, I would learn my lessons and be a better girl. There was a lesson, yes, but it was this: I looked to my not father, he looked at her, and I realized that he would not, could not help me. He had no idea what to make of her transformation into an animal.

When I was twelve, and my good sister left home, all hell broke loose.

And it was Hell that was at issue. Hell and Heaven and the very fate of the Earth. My so not mother concluded that I was in league with Satan—and I don't think it was a coincidence that this belief reached its maturity as I body-slammed menarche, acne, and breasts. To be possessed by Beelzebub would suggest that I was a victim, like Linda Blair of the twisting head and pea soup projectile vomiting, but this was not quite the same. No, no, I was the architect/friend/muse/partner of Lucifer. He worked his evil to please me. I guided him on the path of destruction. She forbade me to go to church because she feared the wrath of God if I did—she said the Lord knew that my presence in church was merely to taunt him. That He knew I was secretly laughing at him while I prayed. This was the end of me and the Baptists.

She described couples who came to our front lawn to have sex as homage to my partnership with Satan. After a rainstorm, a child drowned in the creek near an aunt's home and this not mother believed that it was I who had caused his death—I can still remember her making me come see his cold, white body laying on the grass after the recovery and my horror that I had caused this.

I was terrified that I provoked evil in our world but that I did not know how to stop it. I had trouble understanding that there were no couples having sex on the front lawn of our suburban home, the drowning was not caused by me but by a swollen creek, and Satan doesn't have me on his speed-dial. But I worried—could this be true? Could Satan take his orders from me? Could all that is terrible in the world be my problem? In better moments, the absurdity would strike me. But, in those better moments, it was almost worse because I saw the coming danger. Because my not mother had a responsibility to save the world.

I had (and still have) an extraordinary instinct for survival and as I entered high school was as certain of her murderous intentions as you are that the sun will rise tomorrow morning. She intended to kill me and was at war with herself about it—murdering one's child is an act that requires courage and deliberation. I watched her, listened to her, weathered violent confrontations that hinted at a tectonic shift and I believed I would not survive the summer between my sophomore and junior year in high school. I would be isolated, I would be vulnerable, I would be a victim. The war in her head over whether, when and how to do it would not end well.

This was before Jerry Springer, before mandatory reporting laws, before domestic violence was in our vocabulary. How could I explain to anyone that I knew my not mother well enough to know that she intended to save our world with my blood? How could I dissuade her? How could I escape? I felt the visceral fear of Hell, which would be my destination in the afterlife.

I believed there was a family out there—the one that gave me up, the one I had no memory of, this family that could have saved me this, the family I could be part of. We would love each other—or would have—if I were rather average. Sort of normal. Oh, let's be quite honest—I decided this other family was perfectly, wondrously, exceptionally Ralph Lauren normal.

Oh, Normal! A family with favorite board games and anecdotes and road trips and memories and hugs. Cable knit sweaters and postcards from vacations. Church on Sundays and pot roast dinners afterwards. Grandmothers with favorite cookie recipes. Family reunions and the fight over what makes a second cousin or a first cousin once removed. I was (still am) mesmerized by Norman Rockwell and I adored (still adore) every detail of his *Saturday Evening Post* covers. *Ladies' Home Journal* magazines thrilled me. I discovered Emily Post and was sure that outside the yellow-gold house everyone used finger bowls and fish forks. Normal people who weren't afraid of Hell because they were certain they would arrive in Heaven. I was attracted to Normal Boys and Normal Pleasures and the Platonic Ideal of Normal—and I'm sure that Normal has never felt that same attraction for me. From outside the yellow-gold house, it must have looked just that Normal—although I've since had conversations with former neighbors who have said they knew something was weird but never sure what. Still, in all of our neighborhoods, in our own little towns, there are houses that are like that.

My house has no more and no fewer secrets than yours or your neighbors. I have a husband who teaches at Northwestern Law School. He has testified in an advisory capacity in front of Congress several times and is occasionally a talking head for news programs. Sometimes people will meet me and say they've heard of him. I have two boys who live at home. They perform in local community theater and they have done small, independent movies. They don't necessarily think I'm cool but they don't mind that this year I put pink highlights in my hair or that I give them hugs in public. I think they don't do drugs or drink, but like any other parent of teenagers, I could be deluding myself. I am a re-covering attorney, having practiced commercial litigation for four years and deciding it was not for me. I published twenty-seven romance nov-els before deciding I wanted to move on to a bigger, better fiction for-mat—haven't found it yet, so I may very well be a has-been writer. But I have other interests: I am the president of our local Rotary Club, I write and direct the PTA benefit show, I give dinner parties, both for-mal and not.

I left that not home when I was fourteen and spent several tense months trying to live independently or, in the vernacular of delin-quency, on the streets. Utterly incompetent, I turned out to be better at working the system—foster homes, group homes, a stint at a juvenile de-tention center—until a caseworker decided that I could take a stab at college. I took the S.A.T. with less than two years of high school com-pleted, but with a strong determination to make something of myself. I got accepted by a YMCA school that proved the adage you never want to be in a club that would accept you as a member. I worked hard, got good grades, and transferred out to a real college the next year.

I hired a private detective when I was fresh out of law school and over the course of that Bar Exam Summer, we had lunches, we met for coffee, he spoke of progress but there was never anything substantial. On the precipice of August, I endured two days of sweating, hyperventilat-ing, second guessing, insomnia, vomiting—and the Bar Exam madness—and, afterwards, I got into one of Western Civilization's better bubble baths thinking that if bears hibernated through winter surely I could spend a season in the tub. The detective called, interrupting, wanting to know if I were finished. Yeah, sure. He then allowed as how he had been in contact with my father for two months but he had worried that I might not do well at the bar if I were consumed by family issues.

"Your grandfather is a famous novelist," he said. "I read all his works when I was younger. Meet me at my office tomorrow morning. Could you get him to autograph one of his books for me?"

James Michener!

I leapt about the hallway of the YMCA where I lived, giving very wet, soapy hugs to every person I came upon. James Michener—the only old-enough novelist I could think of. I didn't know Sidney Sheldon and I didn't think J.D. Salinger had any children. Somerset Maugham and P.G. Wodehouse were dead.

My grandfather wrote *Hawaii*!

Boy, was I disappointed the next morning when he said Fritz Leiber.

"Who?" I snarled. There had to be a mistake.

I had to give up James Michener for a (to me) complete unknown who wrote about swords and sorcery and alternate universes and witches and warlocks and—well, couldn't a girl do better? At least someone with a few movies under their belt?

"*Conjure Wife* has been done a number of times," my detective said. "Joan Collins starred in one version. And he just came out with another book—it's called *The Ghost Light*."

I believe all science fiction is ultimately the Allegory of the Cave. The individual out of sync with his community, the community being out of sync with reality. The story of the escape, the triumph, the defeat, the struggles of the individual breaking out of the cave and into the light is the science fiction model. At all costs, no matter how threatening or fantastic the cave dwellers, no matter how improbable the escape—*The Stars Our Destination, Do Androids Dream of Electric Sheep, 2001: A Space Odyssey*—over and over the individual makes a daring attempt to live the authentic life, to bust loose, to get outside the cave.

And it may also be that the writer is merely a person who has escaped from the cave into another world, a world more or less real than our own. And certainly, that was Fritz's experience as a man and as a writer—

In 1969, his wife Jonquil died of an apparent alcohol/barbiturate overdose. Fritz found her dead after a night of such drunkenness that he blacked out and he hesitated about calling the authorities. Blacking out was a daily occurrence. Arguments between them were common and violent. He believed that he killed her, most likely strangling her. And this belief was made manifest in *The Ghost Light*, in which a husband awakens beside the cold body of his wife. He straightens the house, unaware she is dead or perhaps very aware that she is dead.

"Next he remembered, or thought he remembered, waking in the dark in bed and talking and then sleeping with, and then arguing with Helen and shaking her by the shoulders (or maybe strangling her! he wasn't sure which) and then passing out again," the troubled science-fiction writer of the story confesses. A friend who is called in counsels: "For God's sake don't talk about strangling Helen when the doctor comes unless you're really sure you did it!" The author avoids a full investigation of his wife's death by reminding the police and attending physician of two earlier overdoses his wife had survived and by keeping quiet about his self-doubts.

And on the wall of his living room hangs a portrait of the deceased wife, and the story concludes with the wife's ghost flaking the paint from the portrait, creating a blizzard within the house, suffocating and burying her husband.

So much of Fritz's real life experience was contained in that single story: his drinking, his blackouts, the doubts about what happened, the possibility of murder, the diversion of the police from investigating. He considered himself a man of reason as well as a man not bound by convention or the petty morals expressed in law and in religion. Fritz told the story of the cave over and over, successful with forty-two books and countless short stories, Hugo and Nebula awards, many fans and readers. He wrote about the individual who breaks free of convention—but look what he did with that in his personal life.

I wasn't sure I wanted to meet Fritz.

My father was the first relative I met and I think he was extraordinarily brave to come to the city for a weekend. He was astonishingly open, and in fact, told me so much of himself in the cab coming in from the airport that I felt overwhelmed. His wives, his diseases, his foibles, his fears, his everything. He left me with lots of books—his, Fritz's, his mother's, Jonquil's. I began a telephone relationship with Fritz. He lived in San Francisco with Margot Skinner in adjoining apartments and, while he had given up alcohol a few years after Jonquil's death, she was quite a drinker. I teased them that they should marry and she took that as license to make many drunken calls over the next months to tell me how desperately she wanted and deserved that wedding.

As summer turned to fall, I had changed what I thought of myself. Sure, I had an office but I didn't think of myself as a real lawyer. I didn't think of myself as someone lost without a family even as I still hadn't met everyone. No, I now thought of myself as a member of a family of actors, writers, and artists.

Then I met my mother, a contract public defender who could not support herself very well.

Meeting her made family even more complicated: the storyline of the two parents diverged sharply. My father had told me a story in which they had prepared to divorce and she wanted nothing to do with me— he had asked his parents in that letter to stop the adoption process only because he thought he could not raise a child on his own. She told me that they were preparing to divorce and he wanted nothing to do with me—and so he wooed her with the story that if they put me up for adoption, they could concentrate on preserving their marriage, a marriage from which he bolted coincidental to the close of the six-month waiting period on finalizing an adoption. Neither story is correct and both are true.

I could not forget the letter to Fritz, and I could not forget my mother's timeline, which family photographs seemed to corroborate. I could not think of my dad as a monster, and I couldn't see my mother as quite as awful as all that. I should explain that many, many recovered families have an issue of entitlement between them: whichever relative is the poorer feels that it is only right that the richer should share. After all, they're family. My father's wife had worried that I would put that pressure to bear on their family—she rewrote her will the week before my father flew up to meet me. And my mother, as it turned out, very much put that pressure on me. For a while, I sent money and when I stopped, she terminated the relationship. A second rejection but one that I wasn't unprepared for.

I finally met Fritz at Thanksgiving dinner at my father's home. From photographs and articles, I knew that he was well over six feet, but the man I met was so deeply stooped that he was no taller than my five-six self. (I met my maternal grandmother last year and she's stooped as well—nobody in my family has good posture but they all seem to have very good teeth and everyone keeps their hair.) I still harbored concerns about the death of my grandmother. But seeing this frail man, I could not sustain any sense of his power. And I could not begrudge him the choice he made to put the letter in his desk drawer. He had difficulty walking—he shook violently when he coughed—and his fingers were stained from cigarettes. He drank cups and cups of coffee. The morning after turkey dinner, a day trip was proposed and my father divided the family between two cars.

"Fritz has asked that you drive with him because he has something very important to share with you," my dad said.

Wow, I thought. A family secret. An important part of my history. I can't wait. The drive to the ocean was a little less than two hours, punctuated by four stops to find Fritz a bathroom. He had to be helped from the car and carefully folded back in. I waited, quietly but not very patiently. As we neared the shore, the houses on stilts on either side of the highway, he announced that he had been thinking for a long time about something he needed me to know.

"Margot," he said. "I can never marry Margot."

Marry Margot?! Like I really care one way or another!

"I can't marry her because I can't be monogamous," he continued. "There is a dominatrix who sees me. She doesn't charge me. She's very good."

"Really?" I said conversationally.

"She's got a big clientele but she makes time for me because she reads my books."

I didn't know much about dominatrices. Didn't have a clue about their pricing structure or their commercial practices. But I figured whatever the dominatrix was doing with Fritz, it probably involved his brain more than his body. Just a guess. And I realized that I had better be okay with the Not Normal. And that he still thought of himself as outside convention, apart from it all.

My dad parked in the beach lot. We pulled Fritz from the car, an operation very much like the "jaws of life" thing paramedics do. The beach was empty, it was a cold November day and there was a forecast of storms rolling up from the Gulf. I walked with Fritz to the water's edge. I didn't say much and neither did he—but we held hands, whether out of necessity or affection I couldn't say. He looked out at the roiling clouds, and I thought he was much the outsider looking at the wall. Baffled, because being a science fiction writer meant that he was always looking outside the cave. Stooped, having lost his power, impotent against the storm.

"She couldn't do it," he brayed. "She couldn't raise you. So I had to keep the letter. I thought you were going someplace better."

Okay. No Ralph Lauren moment. But as close as this family's going to get. We watched the clouds, we watched the ocean, we walked back to the car.

One last note about Fritz: several years later, I was married and had two children when I got a call from Margot. They had been at a science fiction convention in Toronto and had taken the train into Chicago. Fritz was desperately ill. I met them at a hotel near the train station. They were accompanied by two twenty-something fans who were serving as assistants—Fritz always had fans nearby. Margot was concerned that he might have suffered a mild stroke and we discussed our options—Margot was phobic about flying and so we had to consider that the fastest way to get back to San Francisco would not necessarily be what she would consider. I glanced over at the bed. Fritz sat with my youngest, an infant, on his lap.

My older son, five years old, leaned against him talking about Teenage Mutant Ninja Turtles, his obsession of the moment. Fritz was engrossed by both boys. But I could be just imagining, projecting, chasing the Normal, a grandfather in love with his great grandchildren— and I returned to the problem at hand. We sent Margot and the fans back to San Francisco on the next train. Fritz spent several days in a Chicago hospital before my father flew up to accompany him on a final flight back to San Francisco. Fritz died less than a month later and his funeral service was at the Neptune Club in San Francisco. It was a sprawling, drunken, hedonistic, loving farewell to a man who had trav-eled outside the cave by other cave dwellers—he was propped with a cigarette in one hand and a bottle of whiskey in the other and a woman clad in leather kissed him goodbye on the lips.

Regina M. Schwartz

The Price of Justice and Love in
The Merchant of Venice

At the dawn of the process of secularization, during what historians now refer to as the early modern period and some literary critics still call the Renaissance, the medieval religious worldview began to erode and concerns that were once clearly governed by religious institutions, rituals, and doctrines gradually became the purview of secular thought and practice—including the law and the drama. When religious certainties were unmoored, many of the hard questions once addressed by religion—like justice and love—were taken up by secular cultural forms like the court and the stage. Here, I turn to the _Merchant of Venice_, composed in about 1598, to ask what was gained and what lost in that transition toward secularization. In the _Merchant of Venice_, both love and justice are subjected to modern contractual thinking. Promises are made contractually, vengeance is sought contractually, social healing is instigated contractually, and in all cases, the solutions offered by those contracts fall far short of the aspirations of either love or justice.

While many of Shakespeare's plays are preoccupied with justice, and he often draws heavily upon both legal and religious thought to animate the problem, in the _Merchant of Venice_, he puts versions of both Jewish and Christian ideas of justice into explicit dialogue, and as if that were not complex enough, he heaps common law and equity into the mix. Hence, we find both of the following declarations of excess in the critical literature: on the one hand, "in this play, the advocate of Shakespeare's exceptional Biblical knowledge will find more material than in any others,"[1] and on the other hand, "over the centuries, the *Merchant of Venice* has spawned more commentary by lawyers than any other Shakespeare play."[2] Still more, the play interrogates the relation between love and property and how to understand these in relation to both human desire and dignity. The climax of all of these forces is dramatized in the amazingly condensed trial scene.

The criticism on the *Merchant of Venice* is a tribute not only to the complexity of the play but also to how fruitful criticism can be: for centuries, scholars have engaged in a lively debate on the legal, religious, social, and political dimensions of the play. For Harold Bloom, "The play, honestly interpreted and responsibly performed . . . would no longer be acceptable on a stage in New York City, for it is an anti-Semitic masterpiece, unmatched in its kind."[3] For Daniel Kornstein, "Rather than anti-Semitic, the play can be read as pro-minority rights. It shows how inequality before the law breeds dangerous and divisive discontent."[4] The *Merchant's* performance history notably includes stagings in Nazi Germany as well as in the newly forged state of Israel. Portia has been embraced as a paragon of skill, wit, and learning who commands authority as both lawyer and judge in a man's world—Sandra Day O'Connor was referred to as "the Portia who now graces our court,"[5] and Portia has been reviled: "In addition to her hypocrisy and vindictiveness, we see her as a bigot, and not just a minor-league bigot, but a world-class, equal opportunity hate monger."[6] In the early nineteenth-century, William Hazlitt dissed Portia more politely, but as definitively: "Portia is not a great favorite with us."[7]

Still, thus far, the weight of criticism has been in Portia's favor, and along with affirming her victory, many critics read the play as an endorsement of Christian triumphalism—showing how Christian love and mercy must supercede Jewish justice. Critics have by and large focused on either the religious or the legal discourse, but when we are attentive to both—as indeed the play is—something more complex happens: the Christian mercy argument blurs into equity law which then seems to "win" in a contest with civil law. On this reading, equity courts are an effective mechanism to grant clemency, while a strict adherence to a contract looks less forgiving: a court of equity may well forgive the penalty clause of a pound of flesh, but Shylock anticipates that the Venetian court will enforce it. Indeed, even Antonio imagines that possibility at the time of their agreement: trying to convince Shylock to make the loan, Antonio says, "But lend it rather to thine enemy, who if he break, thou mayst with better face exact the penalty." (I. iii. 132–4) Clearly, according to the play, this is an enforceable contract. *Pacta sunt servands*, promises are meant to be kept: there is a moral duty to keep one's word. This explains why in civil law, contrary to common law, the typical remedy for breach of contract is specific performance instead of damages.[8] "To ensure that the promisor will fulfill his end of the bargain, the civil law not only allows, but also encourages the addition of a penalty precisely to do what the common law abhors: to compel performance . . . To make this point clear, Article 1226 of the French Civil Code defines a penalty as '[A] clause by which a person, in order to ensure the performance of an agreement, promises something in case such agreement is not performed [by him].'"[9]

Civil law and equity are not the only law codes that govern the world of Venice in the Renaissance. In its transition to modernity, it is not an altogether secular world: Jewish law and Christian logos have their roles. Some critics have lumped together Judaism, justice, law and pitted them against faith, love, and charity, seeming to echo Paul. Others have argued that Jewish law should not be altogether dispensed with, only mitigated by the Christian charity that supersedes it. This logic is akin to keeping the Hebrew Bible, but calling it the "old" testament. John Coolidge summarizes, "The Law, justice, and their concomitant 'wisdom' are not simply rejected, then. What is rejected is their finality. They must be bound to love. To choose that love is to find their true meaning, but to choose them without love is to be a 'deliberate fool.'"[10] Sounds good, but this is ultimately, as its author confesses at the start, a reading of the *Merchant* as "a work of Christian apologetics"—and perhaps too of "equity apologetics."[11] Such a reading, it seems to me, oversimplifies the complexities of this play's stunning multilayered critique, one which extends to Christianity—after all, the challenge of Christian justice, "love thy enemy" is not achieved in this drama, Judaism—Shylock's retributive justice knows no forgiveness, equity—which favors the aristocracy, civil law—which can be brutally literal, and commerce—which reduces love to transactions and inevitably broken promises.

The pivotal trial scene produces the most haunting image in the history of literature for reducing the human person to property: the pound of flesh that Shylock demands as payment for a forfeited loan. His determination to seek justice, that is, damages—here, retribution—in the form of this obscene payment makes a travesty of damages in contract law. Portia, disguised as the wise lawyer, hoists him on his own petard, famously pushing his literalism about the payment owed to him even farther than he does:

A pound of that same merchant's flesh is thine,
The court awards it, and the law doth give it.

. . .

And you must cut this flesh from off his breast,
The law allows it, and the court awards it.

. . .

Tarry a little, there is something else.
This bond doth give thee here no jot of blood;
The words expressly are 'a pound of flesh'.
Take then thy bond, take thou thy pound of flesh,
But in the cutting it if thou dost shed
One drop of Christian blood, thy lands and goods
Are by the laws of Venice confiscate
Unto the state of Venice.

. . .

For, as thou urgest justice, be assured
Thou shalt have justice more than thou desir'st.

IV.1. 296–314[12]

Flaunting any interest in verisimilitude, the play quickly turns Shy-
lock from a plaintiff in a civil suit into a defendant in a criminal trial—
and by doing so brilliantly represents the confusion wrought by seeking
justice through a measurable compensation. Intent upon murdering An-
tonio out of revenge for all of the degradations he has endured from him
and his Christian friends—including the theft of his daughter by a
Christian—Shylock intends to use the law to execute that vengeance.
But while it is Shylock's, how far is this murderous literalism being as-
sociated with Jewish law—hence, with Judaism? Are we seeing Paul's
dictum dramatized that the "letter (that is, the old law of Moses) killeth
but the spirit (the new law of Christ) maketh live"?

Judaism is hardly silent about killing. From the story of the first two
men, Cain slaying Abel, on through the revelation of the law in Exo-
dus, Levitical legislation, and biblical prophecy, killing is expressly for-
bidden. Surely, this is not "Jewish justice." In Amos, injustice is defined
with the prophet's outrage: "you sell the righteous for a pair of shoes."
But Paul's characterization of Pharisaic literalism fueled anti-Semitism
in the Renaissance and doubtless contributed to this portrait of the

Jew—as not only the avaricious cheating moneylender, but the legalistic one. To ensnare Shylock in his understanding of justice, Portia pushes the letter of the law, literalism, to its utmost extreme:

> Therefore prepare thee to cut off the flesh.
> Shed thou no blood, nor cut thou less nor more
> But just a pound of flesh. If thou tak'st more
> Or less than a just pound, be it but so much
> As makes it light or heavy in the substance
> Or the division of the twentieth part
> Of one poor scruple, nay, if the scale do turn
> But in the estimation of a hair,
> Thou diest, and all thy goods are confiscate.

> IV. i. 321–329

Shylock's insistence on literal justice is aligned in the play to common law: after all, he is not seeking redress from rabbinic law, but from a secular Venetian court of law, and his working assumption is that if his claim is not honored, then the entire legal structure that protects all of Venice's international commerce will crumble. In his opening speech at court, he notably commingles allusions to oaths and curses in Judaism with the secular court and state:

> By our holy Sabbath I have sworn
> To have the due and forfeit of my bond.
> If you deny it, let the danger light
> Upon your charter and your city's freedom!

> IV. 1. 36–39

If the dominant critical commonplace that sees the play representing Pauline theology were right, then the dead letter of the law, literalism, is not only embraced by Judaism, but also by common law: and both are being subjected to critique. Several legal studies—including those by Mark Edwin Andrews, Maxine McCay, and W. Nicholas Knight—have read Portia's victory in the trial as an endorsement of Shakespeare's belief that common law's over-strict justice needs to be mitigated by equity.[13] In that reading, Christian mercy trumps Jewish justice, it is exercised by equity courts, and Portia is its spokesman.

But critics who are especially sensitive to the economic and political context in which the play was written have offered another perspective, commercial: "as the complex, large-scale financial operations of early capitalism began to emerge in the middle years of the sixteenth century, its practitioners became acutely aware of the value of a comprehensive and predictable legal system that offered protection from arbitrary interference . . . The common law, particularly after it began to recognize and incorporate the jurisprudence of the increasingly important international mercantile legal system, was clearly the law that best offered this protection."[14] Nonetheless, if the common law protected economic activity, it also protected its profits from exploitation by the crown and the landed aristocracy. The social conflict between the interests of the crown and landowners on the one hand and those of the rising merchant class, on the other, forms the socioeconomic backdrop of the play. This is a profound play about commerce—it is called the *Merchant* of Venice, not the Jew of Venice (and it could have been, Marlowe gave us the *Jew of Malta*). In its world of nascent global capitalism, the activities of the rising merchant class were protected by common law. In this light, "while the immediate stakes in the conflict between the two groups were financial, the ultimate prize was much greater: the ability of the independent rising class to use the common law to thwart the sociopolitical will of the ruling class."[15] Equity courts became the chief means by which the landed class and monarch could exercise its prerogatives; with the language of mercy, they allowed landholders to slip out of the reach of common law.

It is likely that Shakespeare's audience would not have heard Portia's famous speech on mercy as the timeless embrace of transcendent Christian ideals that later audiences have. Even in recent productions, many directors slow the speech down to make her seem to intone eternal verities; in film versions, close ups seem irresistible.

> The quality of mercy is not strained,
> It droppeth as the gentle rain from heaven
> Upon the place beneath. It is twice blest,
> It blesseth him that gives and him that takes.
> 'Tis mightiest in the mightiest, it becomes
> The throned monarch better than his crown.
> His scepter shows the force of temporal power

IV. 1. 181–187

The speech is immediately undercut by talk of "mitigating justice"—the language of equity, not the language of Christian mercy. Shakespeare's audiences would have understood that this language of "mitigating the law" was an aristocratic prerogative that flowed from the doctrine of divine kingship and that unlike "the gentle rain that droppeth from heaven," it does not fall on everyone. Instead, it protected the landed nobility. In this light, Shylock is not only espousing the value of law, but also the rights of minorities to be protected by law. The Jewish Shylock, as the archetypal outsider in Christian Renaissance Venice, is asking for protection from the ruling class. Portia speaks of mercy, but indulges instead in the strictest interpretation of the law, and far from grant mercy, indicts Shylock as a criminal, strips him of his property, and endorses his forced conversion. This she does by recourse to the old Alien Statute of Venice, a statute that allows the state to take all of the property of an alien who makes not only direct but also "indirect attempts" on the life of any citizen—and even to execute him.

Mercy does not mitigate justice, it cancels the demand for it. In the course of Portia's speech, what begins with pious talk of God becomes degraded to the instrument of the aristocracy. Furthermore, this speech, so often taken as an exemplum of Christian virtue—even if it is the preamble to a hideous mercilessness—is, ironically enough, drawn from the "Old" rather than the "New" Testament: Deuteronomy 32:2, Ecclesiasticus 36:19, and Ecclesiasticus 28:1-4 are its chief inspirations: "My doctrine shall drop as the rain, my speech shall distil as the dew, as the small rain upon the tender herb, and as the showers upon he grass" (Deut 32:2); "O how fair a thing is mercy in the time of anguish and trouble! It is like a cloud of rain, that comes in the time of a drought" (Eccles. 36:19).

Clearly, the play is thereby questioning or at least "putting under quotation marks the customary equation of the Old Law with strict judgment and the New Law with spiritual mercy."[16] Once the trial ends with no mercy for Shylock, we see how fully the potentially inspiring biblical language of mercy had been manipulated by Portia. When Shylock names Portia a veritable Daniel—the name meaning God is my Judge or the judgment of God—he flatters her far more than she deserves. The biblical Daniel was a wise interceder who questioned the witnesses separately at the trial of Susannah and "convicted them of false witness by their own mouth." (Susannah 48) But if Daniel saves the innocent through judicious use of law, Portia condemns Shylock to poverty and forced conversion. But her real name is not Daniel—this is the Jew's hope, that he will be treated justly. Her name, Portia, may have rung another bell from the Apocrypha: I Esdras, where there is a description of the captive exiles returning to Jerusalem and seeking their "porcion." "These also are they of Iewry, which came vp and turned Agayne vnto Ierusalem, out of the captiuyte that Nabuchodonosor ye kynge of Babilon ad brought vnto Babilon. And euery man sought his porcion agayne in Iewry, his cite, they that came wt Zorobabel, and with Iesus, Nehemias, Saraias, Raelaias, Elimeus, Emmanius, Mardocheus, Beelserus, Mechpsa, Rochor, Oliorus, Emonias, one of their prynces."[17] (Coverdale Bible, 1535) Portia offers not even a portion of justice/love.[18] Furthermore, Shylock reminds his hearers that Christians possess slaves while Jews free all bondsmen, according to the Levitical law. Perhaps even Renaissance audiences could apprehend Judaism as equally merciful.

I am not the first to suggest that so-called Christian mercy is really the inheritance of Jewish mercy. But while it may ironically question received notions of Jewish justice and Christian mercy, this play's purpose—for all its sympathy to Shylock as an alien who does not enjoy the protection of Venetian society—is surely not a defense of Judaism. For if Portia reduces mercy to mitigation to ruthlessness, Jewish law suffers a similar degradation by Shylock: surely demanding justice while intending vengeful murder is contrary to every version of the law—and there are many—that the Hebrew Bible offers. In Exodus 34:26, the law against murder takes a particularly poignant turn when Moses is summarizing the law and concludes with the sublime metaphor for injustice: "you shall not boil a kid in its mother's milk." Far from the kind of legalistic prescription that Paul would have made of this about dietary laws and how a particularist community embraces them while sacrificing true justice, Moses is insisting, according to the rabbis, that you should not deal death with the vehicle for life. "Don't boil a kid in its mother's milk" is not a bad way of thinking about the law—use this potential instrument for social health, for life, instead of for social injury, vengeance, and death.

When the religious covenant that binds justice to law is stripped of its transcendent underpinning and becomes secular contract, it risks being reduced to literalism. Similarly, when the mercy that structures the doctrine of grace in Christianity is reduced to courts of equity, it can be reduced to protecting landowners' interests, rather than granting universal mercy. Religious rhetoric—including mercy, law, justice, faith, and oaths—can be readily hijacked for political purposes and economic interests, especially at the disenchantment of the world from the belief that its order is founded and governed by transcendence. So is Shakespeare's play suggesting that the secular law—both common law and equity—falls short of religious law? I doubt it. For both law and religion are subjected to critique. When Portia's suitor Bassanio chooses the casket of lead over the gold and silver ones in this play to win her—the ancient theme of the three caskets is bound in this play to the plot about usury, received from the Italian source Ser Giovanni, Il Pecorone—he offers a speech that many critics have taken as a kind of moral summary of the play: appearances deceive; all that glitters is not gold. Shakespeare says this better:

> So may the outward shows be least themselves—
> The world is still deceived with ornament—
> In law, what plea so tainted and corrupt
> But being season'd with a gracious voice
> Obscures the show of evil? In religion,
> What damned error but some sober brow
> Will bless it, and approve it with a text,
> Hiding the grossness with fair ornament?
> There is no vice so simple, but assumes
> Some mark of virtue on his outward parts;

III. 2. 73

If law and religion can both be degraded and misused on the side of evil, what then is the ground we can appeal to for justice? What is the moral grounding in the world of this play? One religious world-view has an answer: transcendence. Morality is God-given: when Jefferson opened the Declaration of Independence and based the declaration of rights on "we hold these truths to be self-evident, that all men are created equal," the presupposition of a creator-god who made all humans equal was supposed to guide all subsequent interpretation. Nonetheless, appeal to the justice of that creator-god did not prevent interpreting "all men are created equal" as all males, all white males, indeed, all propertied males.

The play seems acutely aware that once the religious worldview that anchored right and wrong, good and evil, are unmoored, and a commercial worldview takes hold instead, we should be wary of the results. Moreover, it explores the price of reducing the world, life and love, to economics. No ascetic, Shakespeare was a businessman who was among the first to organize his players into a company in which he owned the principal share. That company, the Chamberlain's Men, took out loans in order to build their theater, the Globe, and it was encumbered by interest payments. According to court records, Shakespeare's father was

233

brought to court for demanding too much interest (English law provided that ten percent interest was acceptable). While the Bible and the church fathers condemned usury, Calvin thought it inevitable in the modern world. Perhaps because Shakespeare enjoyed the advantages of capitalism as much as he did the legal system, he issues the caution that both economics and law can be powerful instruments of injustice, especially against the interests of aliens and minorities. These deadly instruments are cloaked with hypocrisy: legal codes are used to mete out vengeance, the language of mercy is used to degrade, promises of love issue in acts of hatred.

The two plots of the play—the courtship/marriage plot at the beginning and end, and the loan and bond of flesh plot that take up the center—are like a Möbius strip, together exploring the economics of human relationships, of giving and receiving.[19] In Renaissance literature, love was frequently spoken of in commercial terms, as free agents giving and receiving with the expectation of increase, the "natural interest" of breeding happiness together. This was joined to a theological discourse of giving a gift with no expectation of return, of neither interest nor principal—giving recklessly, as Christ did, as Antonio does by offering his life as the bond, and as the message of the lead casket conveys: he who chooses me hazards all. The fact that matrimony is a legal contract adds to this picture. But while love can include a contract, an economic transaction of dowries, et cetera, surely it is more than that. That reduction of love to economics is satirized when Shylock learns that his daughter has fled with a Christian and stolen his money: "My daughter, O my ducats, O my daughter!" (II. 8. 15–22) While justice is, in theory, protected by law, perhaps justice, like love, must exceed economics and law—else we would use the law to murder.

But this should give us pause, for it raises a difficult question: Does justice exceed the capacities of the law? Is injury to a person's dignity beyond the purview of law to repair? In the trial scene, law is manipulated by Shylock to get revenge on the enemies who have degraded him, and law is equally manipulated by the enemies not only to disarm Shylock but also to humiliate him. This most famous trial scene in literature may even be hinting toward legal nihilism. But Shakespeare does not sound like a nihilist—at least, not here—for his engagement in social critique suggests his fervent embrace of underlying values. Surely this play suggests that human worth is not measurable or translatable into economic terms—my daughter, o my ducats, o my daughter—and further, that commerce, for all its advantages, has a dangerous price—a kind of imperialism or infection that reduces all to its terms. Everything is bought and sold in the mercantile world of Venice, especially love.

The vocabulary in the first act is laced with terms like "fortunes" "worth" "means" in a web of double entendres. When Bassanio, Portia's suitor, first describes his love for Portia, it is in relentlessly economic terms:

> In Belmont is a lady richly left,
> And she is fair, and fairer than that word,
> Of wondrous virtues . . .
> Nor is the wide world ignorant of her worth,
> For the four winds blow in from every coast
> Renowned suitors . . .
> [she attracts international buyers]
> O my Antonio, had I but the means
> To hold a rival place with one of them,
> I have a mind presages me such thrift
> That I should questionless be fortunate.

I.i. 161–176

In such a world, where people are bought and sold, justice is inevitably crafted to compensate economically, for in a world of commerce, this is all we have to redress our injuries. More than a critique of the law, this play is a critique of the mentality that reduces all persons, all value, to economic terms. We seek damages for repair of injury. Shylock seeks injury in lieu of damages. A pound of flesh cannot rectify anything; it only destroys. It offers no penance, no forgiveness, no love—only economic punishment.

What would satisfy Shylock's demand of justice if not the life of Antonio? I asked my students this question, and they said, profoundly enough, an apology. This is the logic—that confession and contrition mean something, but perhaps not enough—that informed the Truth and Reconciliation Commissions in South Africa. But how do we compensate Muslim prisoners that we torture? With an apology? With money? When law or, for that matter, love succumbs to economy, perhaps it begins to lose some of the value of performing justice . . . easy to say, for how can law be responsive to injury outside of economic terms? If law can protect against social hatred, should law be in the business of promulgating social health, and if so, to what extent and how? Do we need a minimal approach, a protection of our rights: do not steal, do not defame, do not kill? Or do we want to throw into the mix a positive valuation of the other: respect, concern, even love? What kind of law has the biblical tradition given us when it asks that we love our neighbor?

One of the reasons these questions are urgent is that in secular modernity, we have fallen under precisely the spell that Shakespeare anticipates in the *Merchant of Venice:* the economic model of social relations. This is seen not as tragic, not as a loss of our humanity, not as terrible compromise of our moral life, but is rather fully embraced as efficient, useful, even, amazingly enough, just. The influence of a thinker like Richard Posner, who followed his disturbing enough *Economics of Law* with his outrageous *Economics of Justice* is a symptom of how widespread this cultural blight has become. I need not critique the particulars of his work—economic and legal theorists have done an excellent job, showing how making the accumulation of wealth a normative principle for justice simply does not hold.[20] Posner fails to distinguish positive economics from efficiency, consequently the important difference between the work of legislators and judges, between makers of policy and upholders of law, and his debt to utilitarianism is far deeper than his superficial distinction would have it—he substitutes the maximization of wealth for the maximization of happiness. His claim that "reason" or "scientism" grounds his embrace of the highest good as the maximization of wealth could not offer a better example of the failure of the modern scientific paradigm to protect the moral good. What is most reasonable, for Posner, is to assess, rationally, the costs and benefits of each interaction. These include rape, racial discrimination, even revolution. All have assessable costs and how each is adjudicated can be discerned through the reasoned assessment. In an astonishing conflation of the value of charity with wealth, he writes "even altruism (benevolence) is an economizing principle, because it can be a substitute for costly market and legal processes."[21] In his economic stupor, he has clearly lost his bearings: when charity is cost-effective it is no longer charity. Besides, *caritas,* translated as charity and love, is an intrinsic measure of worth, while price implies an extrinsic one. For Posner, corrective justice serves wealth-maximization, "an act of injustice [is] an act that reduces the wealth of society; . . . a failure to rectify such acts would reduce the wealth of society by making such acts more common."[22] Converting social hatred into an economic calculus, an injury into a penalty clause, is precisely what the play mocks in its central image of the pound of flesh.

Why does the central plot of the *Merchant of Venice* focus on a contract, a perverse one? Decidedly not to teach us either the right way to make one, assess one, uphold one, or determine the costs and benefits of one. The comic-tragic exaggeration of the penalty clause of a pound of human flesh exposes the contract itself it as ludicrous at best, and dehumanizing at worst. The contract, made in the context of social hatred, cannot have any assessable value for the "price" of the Christian hatred and the rage it inspires in Shylock are boundless. Similarly, far from reducing his daughter to his ducats, Shylock's anguished juxtaposition has the effect of reminding us precisely that the loss of his daughter is incommensurable, i.e., cannot be measured in ducats. During the trial scene, Shylock demonstrates forcefully how untranslatable his pain and his rage are into any price: offered a huge fortune, he insists instead upon the literalism of his contract—the pound of flesh, the life of Antonio. But this is obscene, and the obscenity deepens when Portia thrusts this logic back at him: not one drop of Christian blood can be shed with the pound of flesh or Shylock loses his life. Far from offering an economic norm for justice, The Merchant of Venice constantly holds out prices only to reject them: from the suitors' quest for Portia to Shylock's revenge, from Antonio's love for Bassanio to Bassanio's love of Portia. The gold and silver caskets, the rings, the ducats, the loan, the contract, the ventures of the merchant, the confiscation of Shylock's property: each only suggests in its own way that the world of Shakespeare's imagined Venice, and perhaps by extension, of Shakespeare's very real London, is afflicted with moral and spiritual depravity. Portia's father explicitly sought to eliminate those who would attach a high payment (or price) to her—and Bassanio's misguided efforts to do so nearly result in the death of his pining friend. When Portia does give her love the price, of a ring, it is only to discover how readily her husband gives it away. While Antonio loses his fortune at sea, he admits repeatedly that this is meaningless to him. Jessica's theft of her father's ducats pales before the horrid news that she has sold her mother's ring for a monkey; here, the pricelessness of Shylock's beloved Leah is contrasted to the wretchedness of his daughter's exchange. If the Merchant of Venice has anything to teach us, it is that the economic understanding of justice is spiritually bankrupt. In a world defined by ventures, usury, contracts, a world of "merchants" in the deepest sense, there is only exploitation.

Love, of the neighbor, of the other, of the brother, romantic love—let alone human compassion—have no place in this economic calculus. In the midst of this critique, does Shakespeare offer any hope, a recommendation, however faint, of an alternative understanding of justice?

charity. To remain faithful to the revelation is to engage in acts of justice toward the other. This other as not just another person, nor others in the sense of the infinite diversity of humanity, nor God as Being, but far more radically other, in the sense of incomprehensible to me and hence uncontrollable by me, not subject or subjected to my instrumentalization. For Levinas, this otherness is best understood as a transcendence that breaks into our world to call us to a new order, the order of responsibility: this is the transcendentally given Law. God is present only in the face of the other person. The State has to answer not only to justice, but justice must answer to a prior Law, of charity, that is, of love. Moreover, Levinas' ethics is not grounded in a limitation of evil but the command of a positive good.[24] For Levinas, "love is originary."[25]

With Paul, the understanding of love takes a different turn: fidelity to Revelation demands spreading the good news of Love, exemplified by proselytizing, converting, political organization. This is the work of Love. For Levinas, fidelity to the Revelation means living according to its command of assuming responsibility for the other: "Truth—the knowledge of God—is not a question of dogma . . . but one of action, as in Jeremiah 22 . . . That is our universalism."[26] This in turn widens into other differences: Badiou, seeing Paul as exemplary in his community-building by conversion, is willing to run the attendant risks of totalitarianism and fundamentalism. Levinas, fearing totality with its connotations of intolerance and fascism, would be faithful to Revelation without any attempt to convert others. This is not an indifference to truth, on the one hand, nor embracing a private truth or mysticism, on the other, for what follows from the Revelation at Sinai is a rigorous concept of the collective life, the political life. This is indeed a new universal—not the empire (ancient near eastern or otherwise) that insists on fidelity on pain of destruction—but a universal in which each person acts in accord with his apprehension of a revelation, a revelation of responsibility—not of resurrection. In Paul, being faithful requires speaking that truth, persuading others of that truth, organizing it politically—only then is it universal. For Levinas, the universal truth of revelation issues in a completely different regard for the other: he is not the object of persuasion, he is the one for whom I am responsible.

Obviously, neither Posner nor Levinas's theories of justice had been elaborated in Shakespeare's day. Still one cannot help but wonder if Levinas' understanding of the religious Law—not as superceded by love but as Love to begin with, is not the lesson that his Daniel strains to teach, despite his/her failure to reach it, for the Levinasian alternative, the justice of love, is a radical ethical alternative to the maximization of wealth, the economics of justice. In Paul's psalm of love, I Corinthians 13, he defines the ethics of love as internally driven, as the quality that gives value to all of life's activities, as the final ideal of justice. Even acts of goodness "profit nothing" without love, for they are merely external, not driven by moral love. It is love that defines human relations as generous, tolerant, and forgiving. But it is also a remarkably radical understanding of justice: "Love suffereth long, and is kind; love envieth not . . . it is not self-seeking, it is not easily angered, it keeps no record of wrongs" (I Cor 13:4-5). The record of wrongs is well-kept in Shakespeare's Venice, none are forgotten, none are forgiven. And one wrong only issues in another. The justice of love is one that Shakespeare's play can long for, as an alternative, one that the music of the spheres enjoy in the distant skies, but not one that obtains on our sad planet:

> Such harmony is in immortal souls,
> But whilst this muddy vesture of decay
> Doth grossly close it in, we cannot hear it.

V.i. 63

Notes

1. Richmond Noble, *Shakespeare's Biblical Knowledge* (London: The Society for Promoting Christian Knowledge, 1935), 97.

2. *Ibid.*, 66.

3. Daniel J. Kornstein, *Kill All the Lawyers? Shakespeare's Legal Appeal* (Princeton University Press: 1994), 81.

4. *Ibid.*

5. *Ibid.*

6. *Ibid.*, 76.

7. William Hazlitt. *Characters of Shakespear's Plays*. (London: C. H. Reynell, 1817).

8. Edith Z. Friedler, "Shakespeare's Contribution to the Teaching of Comparative Law—Some Reflections on The Merchant of Venice." *Louisiana Law Review* 60 (1999–2000), 1087–1102, 1091.

9. *Ibid.*, 1093.

10. John S. Coolidge, "Law and Love in *The Merchant of Venice*." *Shakespeare Quarterly*, 27, no. 3 (1976): 243–263, 254.

11. *Ibid.*, 243.

12. All references to the *Merchant of Venice* are to the Penguin edition, ed. W. Moelwyn Merchant (London: Penguin Books, 1967).

13. Mark Edwin Andrews, *Law Versus Equity in* The Merchant of Venice (Boulder: Uni-

versity of Colorado Press, 1965); Maxine McKay, "*The Merchant of Venice*: A Reflection of the Early Conflict between Courts of Law and Courts of Equity," *Shakespeare Quarterly* 14, no. 4 (1964): 371–375; W. Nicholas Knight, "Shakespeare's Court Case," *Law and Critique* 2, no. 2 no. (1991): 103–112.

14. Stephen A. Cohen, "'The Quality of Mercy': Law, Equity and Ideology in the Merchant of Venice," *Mosaic*, 27, no. 4 (1994): 35–54, 38.

15. *Ibid.*, 40.

16. Roger Strittmater, "By Providence Divine": *Notes and Queries*, 200, 245: no. 1, p. 71.

17. Miles Coverdale. *The Coverdale Bible*. (1535). (Kent: Dawson, 1975).

18. A genus of spider receives Portia's name: "Portia uses deception and mimicry. It is a cryptic spider and an aggressive mimic, meaning that it imitates something its intended victim finds attractive. Resembling a bunch of torn dead leaves. Portia enters a spider's web and creep up on its victim almost imperceptibly, though it moves quickly when the wind blows. It also plucks the web to imitate a captured insect. Then, when the resident spider approaches, Portia lunges in for the kill." "Portia (spider)." http//encyclopedia. thefreedictionary.com/Portia+(spider).

19. The Möbius strip insight is indebted to an unpublished paper on the *Merchant of Venice* by Mladan Dolar.

20. John M. Buchanan, "Good Economics, Bad Law," *Virginia Law Review* 60, no. 3 (1974), 483–492; John T. Noonan, Jr., "Posner's Problematics," *Harvard Law Review* 111, no. 7 (1998), 1768–1775; Thomas Sharpe, "Review of the Economics of Justice," *The Economic Journal* 93, no. 369 (1983), 248–249, among others.

21. Richard Posner, *The Economics of Justice*. (Cambridge: Harvard University Press, 1981), 67–68.

22. *Ibid.*

23. Barbara Lewalski, "Biblical Allusion and Allegory in *The Merchant of Venice*," *Shakespeare Quarterly* 13, no. 3 (1962), 327–343, 332.

24. *Ethics: An Essay on the Understanding of Evil*, trans. Michael B. Smith and Barbara Harshav (New York: Columbia University Press, 1998), 127, originally published in Paris, 1991. For Badiou, ontology is mathematics: "Pure presentation as such, abstracting all reference to that which—which is to say, then, being-as-being, being as pure multiplicity—can be thought only through mathematics."

25. *Entre Nous: On thinking-of the-other*, trans. Michael B. Smith and Barbara Harshaw (New York: Columbia University Press, 1998), 108.

26. *Difficult Freedom: Essays on Judaism*, trans. Sean Hand (Baltimore: Johns Hopkins University Press, 1990), 172, originally published in France, 1963.

David M. Thompson

The Transcendent Dimensions of Private Places: Personhood and the Law in *Lawrence v. Texas* and *Angels in America*

On June 26, 2003, in the case of *Lawrence v. Texas*,[1] the United States Supreme Court held that laws criminalizing the sexual activity of same-sex couples violate the Constitution. As the *New York Times* put it in a large front-page headline the next day, "Justices, 6-3, Legalize Gay Sexual Conduct." By deciding to strike down laws that prohibit sex between gay people, the Court reversed its controversial ruling in the 1986 case of *Bowers v. Hardwick*.[2] In that decision, the Court had held that same-sex couples did *not* have a constitutionally guaranteed right to engage in "sodomy" as defined by the Georgia statute at issue in the case.

Six months after the decision in *Lawrence*, on two weekends in December 2003, a two-part film version of Tony Kushner's prizewinning play *Angels in America* was shown on television. *Angels in America* is set in New York in 1986, the same year in which *Bowers* was decided and just a few years into the AIDS epidemic. One of the primary characters in *Angels in America* is based on the historical figure of Roy Cohn, the notorious lawyer who, while on the staff of the U.S. Justice Department in the 1940s and as counsel to Senator Joseph McCarthy in the 1950s, devoted his energies as a public official to pursuing alleged Communists and spies. Cohn was also a gay man who, on an almost-daily basis, paid to have sex with an ongoing series of men procured for him by one of his business associates.[3]

As a consequence of this lifestyle, our introduction to the character Cohn in *Angels in America* occurs in the office of his doctor, where Cohn has gone in search of treatment for a variety of ailments that turn out, both in actuality and in the play, to be AIDS-related. When Cohn's doctor tries to discuss the ramifications of having AIDS, however, Cohn rebukes him. "Your problem," Cohn says to his doctor,

> is that you are hung up on words, on labels, that you believe they mean what they seem to mean. "AIDS," "homosexual," "gay," "lesbian," you think these are names that tell you who someone sleeps with. They don't tell you that. Like all labels, they tell you one thing. Where does an individual so identified fit in the food chain, in the pecking order? . . . Homosexuals are not men who sleep with other men. Homosexuals are men . . . who know nobody, who have zero clout. Does this sound like me? No, I have clout.

What is striking about Cohn's denial is its reliance on a factual claim about homosexuals as a category of persons—a claim that they have no clout—even as Cohn, if he consented to being counted as belonging to this category of persons, would himself provide evidence disproving that claim. Rather than be a homosexual who has clout, Cohn chooses to be someone with clout who, for that very reason, cannot possibly be a homosexual. His decision to handle his sexuality in this way could derive partly from shame, but it also derives from a belief in the power of the "pecking order," an organization of reality tied to the ability of its constituents to use language as a form of control. As Cohn says later in the play, when he is lying on his deathbed in the hospital and lamenting the proceedings that are stripping him of his license to practice law, "Lawyers are the high priests of America. We alone hold the words that made America out of thin air, and we alone know how to use the words."

We can take this belief in the importance of how words are used as a point of connection with *Lawrence v. Texas*, because the most dramatic aspect of the decision is the particular set of words in the Constitution that the Supreme Court chose to rely on in invalidating the Texas anti-sodomy law. We speak frequently in contemporary discussions of an "originalist" or "textualist" approach to constitutional interpretation, an approach that aims to respond to requirements established by the words of the Constitution when these words are understood as the drafters of the Constitution originally intended. This is opposed to an "activist" approach to constitutional interpretation, an approach that bends the words of the Constitution to suit a particular ideological or policy imperative of the present day. This flexibility is possible because, in the words of Associate Supreme Court Justice Antonin Scalia, "it is known and understood that if [the logic of existing Supreme Court case law] fails to produce what in the view of the current Supreme Court is the *desirable* result for the case at hand, then, like good common-law judges, the Court will distinguish its precedents, or narrow them, or if all else fails overrule them, in order that the Constitution might mean what it *ought* to mean."[4]

What is not emphasized enough in accounts of this battle between "originalism" and "living constitutionalism" (a term used by some originalists to characterize their opponents' approach) is the extent to which the argument ultimately depends on engagement—or, more precisely, an ongoing sequence of engagements—with words at a very particular level. The decision in *Lawrence v. Texas* offers an excellent opportunity to observe this engagement. Laurence Tribe goes so far as to suggest that *Lawrence*, "more than any other decision in the Supreme Court's history, both presuppose[s] and advance[s] an explicitly equality-based and relationally situated theory of substantive liberty."[5] Implicit in the shift in the view of gay rights represented by *Lawrence v. Texas* is a shift in how the Court relies on the language of the Constitution in resolving the constitutional issues that come before it. Because of this close connection, the particularities of interpretation on which the *Lawrence* opinion stakes itself say a great deal about the process by which law shapes the person even as the person learns to see him or herself in part through the lens of the law. By examining in detail the conception of identity underlying the characterization of gay people offered by the Supreme Court in *Lawrence*, and by comparing this to the modes by which gay people and their relationships are represented in *Angels in America*, I hope to arrive at some general conclusions about the place of sexuality in our notion of the person and, more broadly, about the place of the person in our notion of the law.

The extent to which the *Lawrence* decision says something important about how law affects the person will become more clear if we recall just how the Supreme Court decides the constitutionality of state laws that are challenged as discriminatory. When the Court is confronted with such a challenge, it bases its analysis on the Fourteenth Amendment to and sixty-hours-per-week limits on the number of hours someone could work in a facility that produced baked goods. Although the New York law at issue in *Lochner* was based on known health risks associated with spending long hours breathing flour dust, the Supreme Court held that the law violated the Due Process Clause because it violated one right of due process considered to be workers' "due," namely, their "freedom of contract," that is, their freedom to agree to any work schedule of their choice, even if it meant breathing too much flour dust.[8] The social ills that government was called upon to cure during the Depression made such fetishization of freedom seem dangerous, and hence the "death of substantive due process" was declared by the Supreme Court during the 1930s in order to make way for state governments to enact laws that imposed various burdens on the citizenry in the name of social justice.[9]

Due process analysis reared its ugly head again later in the century, perhaps most notably in 1965 with *Griswold v. Connecticut*.[10] In this case, the Supreme Court invalidated a state law prohibiting the use of contraceptives. The Court based its decision on a right of privacy, although in invalidating a law regulating use of contraceptives, the Court confined this right to the "sacred precincts of marital bedrooms."[11] It is this notion of "sacred precincts" that brings us back to *Lawrence v. Texas*, and to *Angels in America*. In *Angels*, the character of Joe Pitt uses this private space as a place to hide from the task of fully inhabiting his identity. Like Roy Cohn, Joe is a lawyer—indeed, he is chief clerk of the U.S. Court of Appeals for the Second Circuit. But Joe is also a young, married Mormon who is tormented by the growing knowledge that his sexuality prevents him from being the kind of Mormon and husband that he knows he should be. He fights this torment by insisting upon an externalizing interpretation of identity, one that focuses on behavior and social rules. When his wife, Harper, finally asks him the question, "Are you a homo?" he asks angrily, "Does it make any difference that I might be one thing deep within no matter how wrong or ugly that thing is, so long as I've fought with everything I have to kill it? What do you want from me? More than that?" Indeed, he seems to believe that he has succeeded in eliminating what is deep within. "For God's sake, there's nothing left," he tells Harper, "I'm a shell. There's nothing left to kill."

And just in case he has not successfully killed his homosexual identity, Joe Pitt does what any good lawyer would do: he reformulates the categories underlying the question in order to locate himself in the category that he prefers. "All I will say is that I am a good man who has worked very hard to become good," he tells her. Harper understands that her husband's decision to live as a shell of a human being will not suffice if they are to experience what marriage should be, namely, a *substantive* engagement between two individuals at all levels of the person, including what is "deep within." Having a marriage of this kind is even more important when there are children, who will learn from their parents a manner of being in the world that is likely to prove determinative (at least until the children grow older, hire therapists, and become stronger agents in their own development as human beings). Harper warns Joe of what will befall their child if they continue as they are. She tells him, "We're gonna have a baby . . . a baby . . . who does not dream but who hallucinates, who looks up at us with big mirror eyes and does not know who we are." Their child will not know who they are because they (or at least Joe) refuse to live *as* who they are. As a result, the child will not dream—that is, assemble narratives out of the detritus of daily life—but will rather hallucinate, wander in the grip of falsehood.

The Supreme Court undertakes a similar grasping after the realities of personhood in *Lawrence v. Texas*, which opens with the Court focusing its attention not on how the law treats its subjects, but on the "protected spaces" where the law cannot go. The majority opinion by Justice Anthony Kennedy begins,

> Liberty protects the person from unwarranted government intrusions into a dwelling or other private places. In our tradition, the State is not omnipresent in the home. And there are other spheres of our lives and existence, outside the home, where the State should not be a dominant presence. Freedom extends beyond spatial bounds. Liberty presumes an autonomy of self that includes freedom of thought, belief, expression, and certain intimate conduct. The instant case involves liberty of the person both in its spatial and more transcendent dimensions.[12]

Juxtaposed with this announcement of a liberty that is both spatial and transcendent is an ugly scene, a narrative of two adults whose privacy was violated on false pretenses and whose decisions about what content to give to this privacy were then held up for scrutiny and declared unacceptable. *Lawrence v. Texas* arose out of a sexual encounter between John Geddes Lawrence and Tyron Garner. The police received a call from someone suspecting that their neighbor, Mr. Lawrence, had an illegal weapon in his home. The police went to the home, entered, and found Mr. Lawrence having sex with Mr. Garner. Both Lawrence and Garner were arrested, held in custody over night, charged, and later convicted of violating a Texas statute prohibiting "deviate sexual inter-course" between members of the same sex.[13]

The *Lawrence* Court acknowledges that it could have taken the cus-tomary approach and invalidated the Texas law based on the Equal Pro-tection Clause. It could, in other words, have concluded that the law's principal flaw was that it gave unequal treatment to two different groups of people, namely, people who have "deviate" sex with members of the opposite sex and people who have "deviate" sex with members of the same sex. Taking an equal protection approach would have required the Court simply to point out that the law treated two groups differently without sufficient reason for doing so. This approach would have al-lowed the Court to invalidate the law while leaving aside the more basic question of whether it is acceptable at all for a legislature to decide the legal status of any intimate behavior engaged in by consenting adults in a private place.

The *Lawrence* Court underscores its intention to engage with this more basic question. The Court defines its task as much more than en-suring equal treatment by the law, as if simply reorganizing or increasing the number of categories of people subject to the law could address the problem. "Were we to hold the statute invalid under the Equal Protec-tion Clause," the Court says, "some might question whether a prohibi-tion would be valid if drawn differently, say, to prohibit the conduct both between same-sex and different-sex participants."[14] In rejecting an argument under the Equal Protection Clause as valid but inadequate, the *Lawrence* Court mentions discrimination—not discrimination im-posed by a particular law, however, but discrimination as an expression of an attitude that is undergirded by the legal regime in which it is ex-pressed. "When homosexual conduct is made criminal by the law of the State," the Court states, "that declaration in and of itself is an invitation to subject homosexual persons to discrimination both in the public and the private sphere."[15]

Angels in America illustrates the various far-reaching effects of living in a social space structured by such invitations. Whereas Joe Pitt hol-lows himself out trying to behave one way while being another, Roy Cohn directs his energies outward, inflicting violence on individuals who pretend to be Americans but are really, in his view, enemies of America. The achievement for which the historical Cohn is best known is his prosecution of Ethel and Julius Rosenberg on charges that they had passed classified information to the Soviet Union. More than any-one else, Cohn pushed the claim that the Rosenbergs were enemies out to damage the American government, the very system of power and relationships on which Cohn's enormous clout depended. "Rosenbergs Executed as Atom Spies" reads the June 19, 1953 headline on the front page from the *New York Times* that hangs framed in the background of one scene in the film version of *Angels in America*. The frequent visitations made to Cohn by Ethel Rosenberg's ghost in the play raise in a more general sense the issue of how avoiding the implications of one's own identity can lead to an obsession with detecting discrepancies in the identities of others, of how a dependence on the endurability of secrets can require enforcing this endurability by punishing those who divulge them.

The character whose presence in *Angels in America* testifies most powerfully to the importance of moving beyond mere categories and acknowledging law's power to affect who we are is Joe's wife, Harper, who spends her days wandering around a sparsely furnished apartment or in a drug-induced imaginary wintry wasteland accompanied by a character named Mr. Lies. Harper feels betrayed not just by her husband, but also by her religion. After Joe has left her and ends up having a life-changing liaison with a clerical worker from his office named Louis, Harper finds herself sitting in New York's Mormon Visitor's Center with Joe's mother, Hannah Pitt. In an empty museum auditorium, the two women sit and stare at a diorama depicting the journey to Utah undertaken by Mormon followers of Joseph Smith in the nineteenth century.

After noting the strong resemblance that the mannequin representing the father figure in the diorama bears to Joe, Harper relates her own marital delusion to Mormonism's aspirations as a religion, as if to say that both depend on people's capacity to place their trust, sometimes erroneously, in others. She says to her mother-in-law, "He's got a tale to tell, the dummy. The Exodus, the Great Salt Lake, that's the joke, of course. They drag you on your knees through hell, and then when you get there, the water is undrinkable. Salt. The Promised Land, all right. What a disappointing promise." Harper looks at the dummy representing the mother in the group and says, "His wife. His mute wife. I'm waiting for her to speak. I bet her story's not so jolly." What is Harper suggesting? That the woman in the museum diorama has, like her, been duped by a husband whose lies to himself end up being lies to her? That, as a woman, she is likely to have had an un-jolly life, one constrained by her gender and the subordinate social role that it was seen to imply? Harper's loss of faith seems to extend to history itself, as if we can never know when our companion and interpreter is none other than Mr. Lies,

as if we are always at risk of finding out that even our own past is some-
thing quite different from what we have always thought.

This brings us to the question of how the Supreme Court has gone
about answering, while fending off Mr. Lies, the questions that are raised
by the Due Process Clause. As we have noted, the Due Process Clause
is fraught with ambiguity, because it is difficult to decide what
"processes" we are talking about and what, with regard to these
processes, constitutes our "due." The Supreme Court has responded to
this ambiguity by deciding that, in general, the Due Process Clause is vi-
olated only when a "fundamental liberty" is at stake. In order to qualify
as "fundamental," it has been determined through case law that a liberty
has to meet a very high standard. It must be "implicit in the concept of
ordered liberty," such that "neither liberty nor justice would exist if [it]
were sacrificed."[16] History provides some assistance, because another
means of determining what qualifies as a "fundamental liberty" is to ask
whether the liberty in question is "deeply rooted in this nation's history
and tradition."[17] This is why, as Cass Sunstein puts it in his valuable
discussion of several gay rights decisions that preceded *Lawrence v.
Texas,*

> The Due Process Clause often looks backward; it is highly relevant
> to the Due Process issue whether an existing or time-honored con-
> vention, described at the appropriate level of generality, is violated
> by the practice under attack. By contrast, the Equal Protection
> Clause looks forward, serving to invalidate practices that were
> widespread at the time of its ratification and that were expected to
> endure. The two clauses therefore operate along different tracks.[18]

I do not quite agree with Sunstein's charactization of the two tracks. Or
rather, I believe that the due process inquiry leads inexorably to an in-
quiry into personhood—and into the relationship between personhood
and the law—that is no less forward-looking than an equal protection
analysis. This connection between treatment by the law and person-
hood under the law is what Tribe refers to as a "legal double helix."[19]

In addition to highlighting the "forward-looking" aspect of the Due
Process Clause, the Supreme Court's opinion in *Lawrence v. Texas* also
complicates the "deeply rooted in this nation's history and tradition"
standard for evaluating liberties. The Court accomplishes this by chal-
lenging the dominant historical account of the particular manifestation
of "the liberty of the person both in its spatial and more transcendent
dimensions" that is at issue in the case. As the *Lawrence* Court puts it,

"[T]here is no longstanding history in this country of laws directed at homosexual conduct as a distinct matter."[20]

Among the pieces of evidence relied on by the Court in making this claim is the fact that those laws regulating sexual activity that did exist prior to the late twentieth century prohibited sodomy *regardless* of whether it was committed by same-sex couples or opposite-sex couples. In other words, these laws prohibited a *practice* rather than a practice as carried out by homosexuals. As Tribe puts it, "The outlawed acts—visualized in ways that obscure their similarity to what most sexually active adults themselves routinely do—come to represent human identities."[21] When such laws were enforced, moreover, they tended to be enforced when some element *in addition* to mere sexual activity was present, when, for instance, one of the parties involved did not consent because they were assaulted and therefore under duress, or because they were under the age of consent. In other words, these laws prohibited not a sexual activity in itself but a sexual activity as an element of a crime that extended beyond sexual activity to include things that most people would consider wrong regardless of whether the person in question was homosexual or not. Finally, at the level of enforcement, it is important to note that, to whatever extent we might think our society has sought to proscribe homosexual conduct or identity by means of the law, most of the laws actually on the books in the nineteenth century were enforced just as frequently against opposite-sex couples as against same-sex couples. From this, the *Lawrence* Court concludes, "Laws prohibiting sodomy do not seem to have been enforced against consenting adults acting in private."[22] More pointedly, one might say that "sodomy"—referring to a specific, discrete, and reprehensible act performed only by gay men—does not exist.

Rather than try to change anyone's view of gay people, then, the Supreme Court in *Lawrence v. Texas* asks our society to look at how it understands itself, at how it relies on a particular version of history in supporting that understanding, and at how this understanding depends on interpretations of the important words that structure our society. By demonstrating that our laws do not say what we think they might say and that they have not been enforced in the manner in which we think they have been enforced, the Court chips away at our ability to claim the authority of history when we disparage gay people. The Court acknowledges the fact that "for centuries there have been powerful voices to condemn homosexual conduct as immoral," and it acknowledges that, even at this point in our history, the majority of people may find such condemnation justified. In a strong statement, however, the Court points out that "[t]hese considerations do not answer the question before us. . . . The issue is whether the majority may use the power of the State to enforce these views on the whole of society through the criminal law."[23]

After reciting some of the very real ramifications of the Texas anti-sodomy statute, such as the registration requirements to which someone becomes subject once they have been convicted of violating it, the majority opinion in *Lawrence* concludes that the case

> involve[s] two adults who, with full and mutual consent from each other, engaged in sexual practices common to a homosexual lifestyle. The petitioners are entitled to respect for their private lives. The State cannot demean their existence or control their destiny by making their private sexual conduct a crime. Their right to liberty under the Due Process Clause gives them the full right to engage in their conduct without intervention of the government.[24]

With these words, the Supreme Court acknowledges that the law, by its mere presence and the force this presence exerts, affects persons in ways that can potentially "demean their existence" or "control their destiny." These are not small impacts that can be attributed to particular acts of overreaching; they are the consequence of accepting certain beliefs about *who we are* under the law. In *Lawrence v. Texas*, the Supreme Court nudges us toward a more subtle, more expansive, more transcendent understanding of what it means to have the acts of love that one engages in branded as "deviate" and criminal, and of the violence that is done to the persons whose identities take shape within a system of laws that brand people and their activities in this way.

Angels in America illustrates this understanding by insistently leading us through the narratives of its characters' lives, relying on the slenderest of connections to accomplish this. Roy Cohn's nurse during his hospitalization is Belize, who is friends with Louis, who has an affair with Joe, who is a protégé of Cohn. (This is not even to dwell on the device of having actors play multiple parts in the same production, for instance, having the actress who plays Joe's mother also play Ethel Rosenberg. This repetition on the level of representation underscores the connections being established on the level of narrative content.) At the center of this web of connections is Pryor Walter, Louis's partner of four years. What sets the narrative of *Angels in America* in motion is the hiatus that Louis takes from his relationship with Pryor after Pryor is diagnosed with Kaposi's Sarcoma, one of the primary conditions indicating full-blown AIDS. Louis, who is full of words and feelings and fills the play with them, leaves his partner because he cannot abide the physical reality of illness. When a rabbi asks him how anyone could abandon someone they love at such a vulnerable moment, Louis responds, "Because he has to. Maybe this person can't incorporate sickness into his sense of how things are supposed to go. Maybe vomit and sores and disease really frighten him."

The sores and disease that fill the play, a good part of which is set in hospital rooms, become talismans of gay people's uneasy place in the body politic. As Roy Cohn lies in a hospital in 1986 dying of AIDS, he laments that the America he has spent his whole life protecting has left him alone in his time of need. His only interlocutor other than his nurse, Belize, is the ghost of Ethel Rosenberg, the woman he branded as a traitor and helped put to death over three decades earlier. From his hospital bed, Cohn says to Rosenberg,

> Worst thing about being sick in America, Ethel, is that you're booted out of the parade. Americans have no use for the sick. I mean, look at Reagan. He's so healthy, he's hardly human. He's a hundred if he's a day, he takes a slug in the chest, and two days later, he's out west riding ponies in his P.J.s. I mean, who does that? That's America. It's just no country for the infirm.

One suggestion pointedly made by the play as it is structured is that the purpose of the infirmities imposed by AIDS is to provide homosexuals with a way out of the world. An angel, the most obvious of the "angels" in the play's title, visits Pryor in his apartment as he descends into illness without Louis or anyone to care for him. She tries to convince Pryor that his life, and the life of humankind more generally, is really just a rupture in the fabric of the universe, a pocket of turbulence in an otherwise still, undifferentiated sky.

The Angel implies that the division of humanity into man and woman, gay and straight, was itself a decline from a prelapsarian past in which sexuality suffered no division. As the Angel puts it, "Seeking something new, God split the world in two and made you. Human beings. Newly genitaled, female, male. In creating you, our father-lover unleashed sleeping creation's potential for change. In you, the virus of time began." In a story that centers around a virus, time itself becomes a virus, worming its way through us and creating changes that our body, the body politic, may not easily accept. The Angel suggests to Pryor that his death will bring time to an end, that it will stop the cycles of change by which difference and conflict and sickness and loss are produced. As an escape from this endless dialectic, the Angel offers Pryor the role of martyr in a tragedy that will be frozen in time. "You know me, prophet," she says to him, "You are a battered heart bleeding life in the universe of wounds . . . In your blood we write, have written, stasis, the end." Pryor rejects the Angel, however, rejects the idea that he should prefer a static, if secure, moment of loss to the messiness and risk of being in the world. "This disease will be the end of many of us," he says near the end of the play, "but not nearly all, and the dead will be commemorated, and we'll struggle on with the living, and we are not going away. We won't die secret deaths anymore. The world only spins forward. We will be citizens. The time has come."

I would like to suggest that a similar willingness to "spin forward" underlies the Court's decision to embrace a due process analysis in *Lawrence v. Texas*. In *Lawrence*, the Court took a step beyond the externality and formalism of conclusions reached via the Equal Protection Clause, which operates at the level of category rather than of individual experience or, more precisely, the experience of being an individual in a culture the traditions of which are expressed in part through its laws. Just as Roy Cohn is met near the end of his life by the ghost of prosecutions past, so in *Lawrence v. Texas* does the Supreme Court quote the assessment by the *Bowers* Court of the case that came before it seventeen years earlier, that "[t]he issue presented is whether the Federal Constitution confers a fundamental right to engage in sodomy."[23] The *Lawrence* Court firmly rejects this interpretation: "That statement, we now conclude, discloses the Court's own failure to appreciate the extent of the liberty at stake."[25] Statutes prohibiting sex among gay people are "statutes [that] do seek to control a personal relationship that . . . it is within the liberty of persons to choose without being punished as criminals."

This is not a matter of whether a law should be accepted simply because it represents a rational means of protecting a legitimate government interest—that is a conclusion on which an equal protection analysis could be based. A due process analysis, by contrast, asks what a person is entitled to *at all*, what a person needs in order to develop in whatever directions human potential suggests and reality accepts. There are of course constraints upon this development, but they are constraints developed in the best interests of the person, which should also be the best interests of the Constitution. As Roy Cohn's nurse, Belize, says to Louis when asking him to say Kaddish over Cohn's dead body despite Louis's vehement opposition to Cohn's politics, "Maybe a queen can forgive a vanquished foe. It isn't easy. It doesn't count if it's easy. It's the hardest thing, forgiveness. Maybe that's where love and justice meet."

Notes

1. *Lawrence v. Texas*, 123 S. Ct. 2472 (2003).

2. *Bowers v. Hardwick*, 106 S. Ct. 2841 (1986).

3. *See* Nicholas von Hoffman, *Citizen Cohn* (New York: Doubleday, 1988) 360–78.

4. Antonin Scalia, *A Matter of Interpretation: Federal Courts and the Law* (Princeton, N. J.: Princeton University Press, 1997) 39.

5. Laurence H. Tribe, "*Lawrence v. Texas:* The 'Fundamental Right' That Dare Not Speak its Name," 117 *Harv. L. Rev.* 1893, 1898 (2004).

6. Andrew Koppelman, *The Gay Rights Question in Contemporary American Law* (Chicago: University of Chicago Press, 2002) 9.

7. *Romer v. Evans*, 517 U.S. 620 (1995). In this case, the Supreme Court held that an amendment to the state's constitution prohibiting all legislative, executive or judicial action at any level of state of local government designed to protect homosexuals was unconstitutional. Although the amendment had been passed by state referendum, the Court invalidated it on the grounds that it violated the Equal Protection Clause because it disqualified a particular group from seeking protections that might otherwise be available under the Constitution.

8. The literature on freedom of contract is voluminous. For a valuable recent survey, see F. H. Buckley, editor, *The Fall and Rise of Freedom of Contract* (Durham and London: Duke University Press, 1999).

9. For an outstanding account of the constitutional revolution wrought during the 1930s under President Franklin Roosevelt, see Bruce Ackerman, *We the People: Volume 1— Foundations* (Cambridge, Mass.: Harvard University Press, 1991). See also William Novak, *The People's Welfare: Law and Regulation in Nineteenth-Century America* (Chapel Hill, N.C.: University of North Carolina Press, 1996).

10. *Griswold v. Connecticut*, 381 U.S. 479 (1965). See David J. Garrow, *Liberty and Sexuality: The Right of Privacy and the Making of* Roe v. Wade (Berkeley: University of California Press, 1994).

11. *Griswold*, 381 U.S. at 485.

12. *Lawrence*, 123 S. Ct. at 2475.

13. The Texas statute provides that "[a] person commits an offense if he engages in deviate sexual intercourse with another individual of the same sex," and it defines "deviate sexual intercouse" as either "any contact between any part of the genitals of one person and the mouth or anus of another person" or "the penetration of the genitals or the anus of another person with an object." For an illuminating discussion of the indeterminacies embedded in the concept of sodomy, see Mark D. Jordan, *The Invention of Sodomy in Christian Theology* (Chicago: University of Chicago Press, 1997).

14. *Lawrence*, 123 S. Ct. at 2482.

15. *Lawrence*, 123 S. Ct. at 2482.

16. *Palko v. Connecticut*, 302 U.S. 319, 325, 326 (1937).

17. *Moore v. East Cleveland*, 431 U.S. 494, 503 (1977).

18. Cass Sunstein, "Sexual Orientation and the Constitution: A Note on the Relationship Between Due Process and Equal Protection," 55 *U. Chi. L. Rev.* 1161, 1163 (Fall 1988).

19. Tribe at 1898.

20. *Lawrence*, 123 S. Ct. at 2478.

21. Tribe at 1896.

22. For a discussion of the evolution of the term "sodomy," which originated as a theological concept referring to "disordered desire," see Jordan 29–44.

23. *Lawrence*, 123 S. Ct. at 2480.

24. *Lawrence*, 123 S. Ct. at 2484.

25. *Lawrence*, 123 S. Ct. at 2478 (quoting *Hardwick*, 106 S. Ct. at 2841).

26. Id.

Stephen Gillers

In the Pink Room

Trial lawyers have been compared to actors, performance artists, play-wrights, and directors. All comparisons are valid, to a point. Unlike playwrights, lawyers cannot make up information, but short of lying or suborning perjury, trial lawyers can do a great deal to influence their audience—the jury. Whatever adverse testimony a trial lawyer cannot explain away or counter with competing testimony, she will seek to contextualize in a way that benefits the client or, failing that, harms him as little as possible. The trial lawyer will do that in cross-examination and in the two speeches to the jury—the opening statement and sum-mation—that bracket a trial. She will use all the tools of play making, to the extent of her ability, including gesture, facial expression, sarcasm, rhetorical questions, word choice, simile and metaphor, silence, tone, and volume. Her opponent will do the same, managing to find a differ-ent narrative in the same body of evidence. A trial can, in fact, be seen as a contest between dueling narratives. Duelists are not ordinarily in-clined to aid each other. Yet litigation, like traditional duels, does have rules and a few of them do require a lawyer to assist an opponent's case even if it means harming her own. Given the adversarial nature of tri-als, and the natural desire of lawyers to win, these rules are not always honored. In the following story, they were not.

257

I

The Grand Concourse runs four and a half miles north-south in the borough of the Bronx, City of New York. Designed in the 1890s, one hundred and eighty feet wide, it was meant to allow horse drawn carriages quick access to parks in the borough's north. Today, there is nothing about the Concourse that can be called grand. Tourists are unlikely to visit it unless they have a keen interest in urban planning or Art Deco apartment buildings. Unless they are students of neo-classical architecture, tourists are also unlikely to visit the nine-story Bronx County Courthouse. Built in 1934 and designated a city landmark in 1996, the building occupies a full city block toward the southern end of the Concourse. But tourists may have read about the courthouse. This is where Sherman McCoy, the "Master of the Universe" in Tom Wolfe's novel *Bonfire of the Vanities*, faced trial for homicide. It is also where, in 1978, David "Son of Sam" Berkowitz pled guilty to murder.[1] Of less prominence, but not without drama, this is where, on September 6, 1984, Alberto Ramos was indicted for raping a five-year-old girl at a Bronx day care center and where he went on trial the following May.

In January 1984, Alberto Ramos was a twenty-one-year-old student at Hostos Community College, and an aspiring teacher, when a friend told him about a part-time job as an aide at the Concourse Day Care Center. The center operated under the authority of the Human Resources Administration (HRA), a city agency. On Friday, February 17, Ramos was assisting Fernie Skerrit in a class of five year olds. He was alone with the children during nap time. Some of the children talked and Ramos put masking tape vertically over their mouths as a reminder to be quiet. O. was one of those children. When Mrs. Skerrit returned to the classroom, she removed the tape and admonished Ramos. The taping, which Ramos admitted, showed bad judgment, but that seemed to be the end of it. But it was not the end of it. Suspicions, and then accusations, from O.'s family led to two investigations—one by HRA and one by the police. These in turn led to the allegation that Alberto Ramos raped O. in the bathroom adjoining the classroom during Mrs. Skerrit's absence, and then to his indictment and his trial in May 1985.

The jury learned that Fernie Skerrit's classroom was called the Pink Room. Skerrit testified that at 1 P.M. on February 17, 1984, she took her forty-five-minute lunch break during nap time. An aide, Margaret Alieu, left work ten minutes later. Ramos was then alone with the children in the Pink Room for fifteen minutes, possibly longer. O., six years old at trial, testified that in this interval Ramos put tape on her mouth and took her into the adjacent bathroom, closing the door. In the bathroom, O. said, Ramos put his "thing" in "my kitty cat," using anatomically correct dolls to illustrate what she meant. Initially, O. said that both she and Ramos were standing when this happened, a physical impossibility, but on further questioning O. testified that Ramos was kneeling. O. then returned to her cot. Patricia Wilson, another student in the class, also testified. She said Ramos took O. into the bathroom and closed the door and that when O. came back to her cot she was crying. When Skerrit returned to the classroom at 1:45, she said she saw the tape on O.'s mouth. She asked O. why it was there and O. replied that "Alberto put it there" because she was talking. She did not seem upset.

Redell Willis, O.'s grandmother, told the jury that she picked O. up at the daycare center that Friday afternoon. O. had tears in her eyes but did not say why. At home, O. said her "kitty cat" hurt. Esterlita Harvin, O.'s mother, testified that she returned from her night job at one or two A.M. Saturday. O. was still awake and Harvin gave her a bath. She noticed that O.'s panties had stains and detected a foul odor from her genital area. Harvin told the jury that she noticed redness and bruises in the vaginal area and consulted her mother, who noticed the same. Harvin worked two jobs. She had to report to one of them that Saturday morning and to her second job thereafter. When she came home on Sunday at two A.M., the redness was still there. She took O. to Bronx Lebanon Hospital. O. told a nurse that Efrain, a boy in her class, caused the bruises. At trial, O. testified that she had named Efrain because she didn't want the doctor to know about Alberto.

At the hospital, O. was examined by Dr. Paraclet Louissaint, who did not testify but whose record of the examination became a trial exhibit. Louissaint recorded that he found O.'s hymen slightly opened and some redness in the genital area. He concluded "that the irritation could have been caused by 'almost anything, including bathroom play with another child or . . . masturbation.'"[2] Louissaint referred O. to the pediatric clinic, where she was seen by Dr. Annette Vasquez the following Tuesday. Vasquez testified that O. had been "sexually abused." She based her opinion on her examination of O., the medical records, and conversation with O. "Basically," she told the jury, "because she [O.] gave such an accurate description of everything that happened." Two days later, O.'s mother and grandmother informed the director of the Concourse Day Care Center of Vasquez's conclusion and Ramos was fired the next day for taping the mouths of children. Informed as well of Vasquez's opinion, Ramos denied that he had abused O.

The defense called two witnesses. Christina Gonzalez, the assistant director at the day care center, testified that she had encountered Alberto in the hall outside the Pink Room at about 1:25. He was arranging a bulletin board. Gonzalez asked Oscar Rojas, another aide, to look in on the Pink Room while Ramos came to her office. Ramos was in Gonzalez's office for ten to fifteen minutes. She offered him a permanent job. Gonzalez said Ramos left her office at 1:45 or 1:50. Oscar Rojas also testified. He was the friend who told Ramos about the job at Concourse. He told the jury that he saw Ramos in the hall outside the Pink Room at 1:25. He looked in on the Pink Room between 1:30 and 1:55 as Gonzalez instructed. Rojas admonished Ramos for taping the mouths of children. Ramos did not testify. He had no criminal record.

In summation, Diana Farrell, the prosecutor, argued that this evidence proved Ramos's guilt beyond a reasonable doubt. After summarizing O.'s testimony and Vasquez's opinion, Farrell asked some powerful rhetorical questions:

> She [O.] sat in that chair and she told you that it was Alberto. It was difficult for her because she came over here and she showed you with these dolls and she pulled down their pants and showed you where the kitty-cat was and showed you where his thing was and then told you he put his thing in her kitty-cat and then she went on to tell you that the way he did it was he was kneeling and pulled her onto him and that he put it in a little bit and went in and then he pulled it out and is this the type of thing a child makes up? She wasn't telling you that Santa Claus had come to her house with fairies or about—about any nursery rhymes. She was telling you that a man, Alberto, had put his penis into her, into her kitty-cat, into her vagina. A five year old describing it for you, showing you how it was done. That's the type of thing that a five year old child makes up?

The jury deliberated less than a day. It asked to rehear the Vasquez testimony. On May 20, 1985, it convicted Alberto Ramos of raping O. His reaction was immediate. "I want to die," he screamed. "Kill me. Kill me." Ramos was remanded to custody. On June 12, he was given the maximum sentence, eight to twenty-five years in prison. The judge expressed regret that the law did not permit him to impose a life sentence. "It is difficult to comprehend the enormity" of the crime, the judge said.

"One must be completely puzzled in trying to understand how he could have been so cruel, so insensitive, so inhumane as to put a child through that degradation."[3] Ramos lost his appeals to higher state courts.[4]

Prison is especially hard on inmates convicted of abusing children. Ramos's case, and other child sex abuse prosecutions in the Bronx around the same time, received headline treatment in the tabloids. Word naturally reached the prisons and jails of New York State. So when Ramos was incarcerated, he was already known as a "baby raper." He was verbally abused by court officers, guards, administrators, nurses, doctors, and inmates and beaten by inmates. He was threatened with death. As he would later testify, in the prison hierarchy, "I was the lowest of the lowest piece of garbage that walked the jailhouse. I was viewed as a piece of—I was viewed as garbage." On several occasions he was sexually abused by other inmates in exchange for protection or on threat of being cut.

In the summer after Alberto Ramos was convicted, O.'s mother sued the Concourse Day Care Center and the City of New York for her daughter's injuries. The center was insured. The insurance company hired a law firm. The firm retained an investigator to collect evidence. His name was Anthony Judge. The civil case dragged on for five years. A settlement agreement, reached in October 1990, gave O., then eleven years old, a series of staggered payments. She was to receive $5000 immediately, $15,000 on each of her eighteenth through twenty-first birthdays, $25,000 on her twenty-fifth birthday, $50,000 on her thirtieth birthday, and a monthly payment of $1100 for life (with annual increases of three percent) starting when she turned twenty-one. An additional $21,618 was to be deposited in a trust account for O. immediately, which she could withdraw with interest when she reached eighteen. The insurance company also paid $100,000 for O.'s legal fees.

II

This might have ended the story except for Anthony Judge. In the course of his investigation, Judge discovered documents in HRA files that were not given to Ramos and that led Judge to believe that Ramos was innocent. "I was astounded to read what I read," Judge would tell the *New York Times* in 2004.[5] But Judge was not free to give the documents to Ramos. He needed the law firm's clients to agree. They did agree and Judge gave the documents to Flor Cupelis, Ramos's mother. Of course, the documents were of no use without a lawyer to interpret them and evaluate whether they might provide a legal basis for challenging Ramos's conviction. By this time, 1991, Ramos had been in prison nearly six years. Cupelis told her son what Judge had given her. He told her whom to call.

About a year after he was sentenced, Alberto Ramos was incarcerated at the Clinton Correctional Facility in Dannemora, New York, a maximum security prison near the Canadian border, about three-hundred miles from New York City. There he met four other men in a special unit that included inmates convicted of child sex abuse: Nathaniel Grady, a Methodist minister, Albert Algarin, Jesus Torres, and Franklin Beauchamp. The five had other things in common. All protested their innocence and all had been convicted in the Bronx within a two-year period, at a time when the country was seeing a rash of child sex abuse prosecutions.[6] The five convictions were big news in New York City and beyond. The Bronx District Attorney who brought these cases was Mario Merola. Formerly a New York City councilman, he was elected to the Bronx post in 1973. In Big City D.A., his autobiography, Merola wrote with pride about the sex crime prosecutions in his office and about the difficulty of proving cases where the victim is a child. "The crime is so horrendous that sometimes jurors—and even we—need overwhelming proof before we can accept that the accused has done what the children say he or she has done. We look for more evidence than even the law requires—and the law, in my opinion, is pretty tough."[7] Merola explained how he sought this proof. It was necessary, he explained, to win the trust of young children who are asked to testify in court:

> I've been accused of giving them candy. I plead guilty. I give them candy, I stroke them, I kiss them. We try everything humanly possible to relax them. . . . But let me tell you, when it comes to situations like this, you can't put words in the kids' mouths. Kids tell the truth. And if it takes hugging and candy to relax them enough to tell the truth, I'm all for it.[8]

Merola's book discusses the prosecutions of each of the men Ramos met at Clinton, but not Ramos.

Grady was forty-seven in 1984 when he was convicted of abusing three-year-olds during nap time at his church day care center. He was sentenced to forty-five years in prison. The three other men Ramos met at Clinton were in their twenties. All had worked at a day care center run by the Puerto Rican Association for Community Action (PRACA).

By 1991, when Anthony Judge gave Ramos's mother the documents he had uncovered, state courts had already freed the three PRACA defendants on the ground that the indictments against them were legally defective under New York law. The indictments did not provide adequate notice of the charges, making it unreasonably difficult to defend against them. Beauchamp's case reached the highest state court in 1989.[9] Algarin and Torres had their convictions overturned in lower courts the following year.[10] Mario Merola did not live to see the loss of these convictions. He died in 1987.[11] His autobiography was published a year later. Robert Johnson, a criminal court judge elected to replace Merola in 1989, chose not to retry the PRACA defendants although he was free to do so.

Grady's case took longer. On appeal, his lawyer had not raised the grounds that freed the PRACA defendants. As far as the state courts were concerned, that meant Grady had lost the right to raise these issues. His only hope was to claim that his lawyer was ineffective, a violation of the Sixth Amendment that would excuse the lawyer's failure. Grady challenged his conviction on ineffectiveness grounds in federal court and won. The federal court ordered the state to hear Grady's appeal or free him.[12] Johnson chose the second option. He conceded the validity of Grady's legal claim.[13] Grady was freed in 1996, after more than a decade in prison.

Torres, Beauchamp, and Grady had one more thing in common. The same lawyer eventually secured their freedom. So it was perhaps predictable that when Ramos's mother told him about the documents that Anthony Judge gave her, he told her to call Joel Rudin.

III

Many law students have some idea of the career they want to pursue. But their goals are often vague and subject to change. As graduates, they may work at law firms or government law offices while their preferences come into sharper focus. Chance plays a role, too, both in the kind of legal work that happens to come their way and in the senior lawyers with whom they are assigned to work. A much smaller group of law students know exactly how they want to spend their professional lives. Among them are the few who want to defend criminal cases. They may go to a public defenders office for experience before joining a small firm or starting a practice with friends or alone. Joel Rudin wasn't a member of this small group when he started New York University School of Law after a year as a reporter in New England, but that soon changed. While in law school, he worked for a prominent New York defense lawyer and took a job with him after his 1978 graduation. He left three years later and in the ensuing decade worked solo or in small partnerships. In 1991, Rudin was on his own when Cupelis asked him to review the documents that Anthony Judge had given her.

Today, Rudin's ninth-floor, corner office is across the street from Carnegie Hall in Manhattan. The view from one window looks up Seventh Avenue to a sliver of Central Park. Rudin is an easygoing man with a quick smile and no suggestion, other than his curly gray hair, that he has crossed fifty. He has a quality common to many successful trial lawyers. He often pauses an extra beat before responding in a conversation, as if analyzing sentences for latent ambiguities that must be clarified to avoid imprecision.

In taking Ramos's case, Rudin faced significant legal hurdles. New information often turns up after a trial, sometimes many years after. That's unremarkable. The question for Rudin was whether the documents from Cupelis provided a legal basis to challenge the conviction. Principles established in two cases from the early 1960s gave Ramos his best chance. Both required a prosecutor, who ordinarily has superior investigative resources, to give a defendant information in his files that could help the defendant at trial. Alberto Ramos would have had no reason to know the cases of Luis Rosario and John Brady. But each played a pivotal role in his life.

More than twenty-five years before Alberto Ramos's trial, Luis Rosario and two other men were accused of murdering a Manhattan restaurant owner in the course of a robbery. Rosario was convicted and on appeal he raised one issue only. Three prosecution witnesses had made pretrial statements about the crime that were either in writing or transcribed. After each witness had testified, Rosario's counsel asked to see that witness's pretrial statement for possible use on cross-examination. The trial judge, in accordance with New York law at the time, reviewed the statements privately and gave defense counsel only those portions of each statement that were, in the judge's view, inconsistent with the witness's testimony. On appeal, Rosario argued that he was entitled to the entirety of each statement on the subject of the witness's testimony so that his lawyers could decide for themselves whether and how the statements might be useful in cross-examining the witness.[14]

The New York Court of Appeals agreed. Variance with trial testimony, it held, was not the only reason a defense lawyer might wish to see a pretrial statement.

> Even statements seemingly in harmony with such testimony may contain matter which will prove helpful on cross-examination. They may reflect a witness's bias, for instance, or otherwise supply the defendant with knowledge essential to the neutralization of the damaging testimony of the witness which might, perhaps, turn the scales in his favor. Shade of meaning, stress, additions or omissions may be found which will place the witness's answers upon direct examination in an entirely different light.[15]

Nor was a trial judge best positioned to identify the value of a pretrial statement:

> Furthermore, omissions, contrasts and even contradictions, vital perhaps, for discrediting a witness, are certainly not as apparent to the impartial presiding judge as to single-minded counsel for the accused; the latter is in a far better position to appraise the value of a witness's pretrial statements for impeachment purposes.[16]

Today in New York criminal defense lawyers routinely ask for "Rosario material" as a shorthand way to describe a prosecution witness's pretrial statements. As the years pass, fewer and fewer lawyers will remember the Rosario case itself. They are especially unlikely to recall that while Rosario won his argument, and gained a certain immortality that way, he lost his appeal. The Court affirmed his murder conviction after concluding that there was no "rational possibility that the jury would have reached a different verdict if the defense had been allowed the use of the witness' prior statements."[17] The variations in the prior statements, the Court said, were "of a most inconsequential character" and the other evidence of guilt was strong, including Rosario's confessions to friends and the authorities.[18]

Two years after the New York Court of Appeals decided Rosario, John Brady's case came before the United States Supreme Court. Brady and a companion, Boblit, were separately tried in Maryland for murder in the course of a robbery. Brady, who was tried first, testified and "admitted his participation in the crime,"[19] but sought to avoid a death sentence by arguing that Boblit committed the murder. Boblit had admitted as much, but the prosecution did not provide this statement to Brady, whose lawyer learned about it only after Brady was convicted and the jury had sentenced him to death. In a challenge to both his conviction and sentence, Brady claimed that he was constitutionally entitled to Boblit's admission to use in his defense.[20] The Supreme Court held, in an opinion by Justice William Douglas, that Brady was not entitled to Boblit's statement for use at trial, where it would not have been admissible, but that he was entitled to use it at the sentencing hearing, where it could affect the jury's decision whether to impose a death sentence.[21]

Justice Douglas quoted from a 1954 speech by Simon Sobeloff, when Sobeloff (later a federal circuit judge) was Solicitor General of the United States:

> The Solicitor General is not a neutral, he is an advocate; but an advocate for a client whose business is not merely to prevail in the instant case. My client's chief business is not to achieve victory but to establish justice. We are constantly reminded of the now classic words penned by one of my illustrious predecessors, Frederick William Lehmann, that the Government wins its point when justice is done in its courts.[22]

And then, in a single sentence, Douglas set down a constitutional principle that dramatically changed the obligations of every prosecutor in the United States:

> We now hold that the suppression by the prosecution of evidence favorable to an accused upon request violates due process where the evidence is material either to guilt or to punishment, irrespective of the good faith or bad faith of the prosecution.[23]

John Brady, like Luis Rosario, has also attained a certain immortality, at least in the legal canon. Today, defense lawyers routinely ask for *Brady* material, or make *Brady* motions, without necessarily knowing the details of Brady's case or that Brady's own victory extended only to a new sentencing hearing, not a new trial. Over the years, the Supreme Court and lower courts have filled in some of the details of a prosecutor's *Brady* obligations. For example, *Brady*'s requirement of a defense "request" may not be needed, depending on the exculpatory nature of the evidence.[24] But the holding remains undisturbed. In fact, it has also been preserved in ethical rules for lawyers. Model Rule 3.8(d) of the professional conduct rules of the American Bar Association, widely adopted in some form, imposes a duty on prosecutors that is broader than the *Brady* rule:

> The prosecutor in a criminal case shall . . . make timely disclosure to the defense of all evidence or information known to the prose-

cutor that tends to negate the guilt of the accused or mitigate the offense, and, in connection with sentencing, disclose to the defense and to the tribunal all unprivileged mitigating information known to the prosecutor, except when the prosecutor is relieved of this responsibility by a protective order of the tribunal.

In New York, site of the Ramos prosecution, Disciplinary Rule 7-103(B) of the Code of Professional Responsibility stated:

A public prosecutor or other government lawyer in criminal litigation shall make timely disclosure to counsel for the defendant, or to a defendant who has no counsel, of the existence of evidence, known to the prosecutor or other government lawyer, that tends to negate the guilt of the accused, mitigate the degree of the offense or reduce the punishment.

IV

To get the benefit of *Brady* and *Rosario*, Rudin had to satisfy two legal burdens. He had to persuade the courts, first, that the prosecutor had the documents that Anthony Judge had discovered in the HRA files; and second, that there was some likelihood that if the defense had been given the documents, the verdict would have been different. This second burden is particularly thorny. It requires the courts to reconstruct a past event (the trial), that was itself an attempt to reconstruct a past event (the alleged crime), in order to determine the effect that the missing information would have had on the jury's view of the prosecutor's proof of that crime. Through witnesses and documents, and subject to the rules of evidence, juries get information about the past. Always, that information is incomplete. Gaps are inevitable. Also, some of the evidence may be contradictory because witnesses honestly perceive or remember differently. Sometimes witnesses lie. It is the jury's job to decide which purported facts are true. Lawyers want juries to view the facts and fill in the evidentiary gaps in a light that is best for their clients. In summations, lawyers offer the jury competing interpretations of the information it heard. They tell different stories about the evidence. In a criminal case, this does not mean that the jury must decide whose story is true. Jurors are asked only to decide whether the interpretation offered by the defense lawyer causes them to have a reasonable doubt about the prosecution's story. So in 1991, Rudin had to persuade a judge in the

Bronx, and eventually higher judges, that the story Ramos could have offered the jury with the withheld information would have created a reasonable doubt of his guilt and changed the verdict.

But how confident should a court be that with the information the verdict would have been different? Courts will not overturn a conviction simply because a different outcome is conceivable. The defendant has a higher burden than that. Luis Rosario established an important legal right, but he did not get the new trial he wanted because the evidence of his guilt was strong. John Brady did not get a new trial either (only a new sentencing hearing) because the withheld information would not have been admissible in evidence at trial. The defendant's burden has been described in various ways. In New York, some cases have said that a defendant challenging his conviction after his appeals are done must show "a reasonable possibility" that he would not have been convicted if the withheld evidence were available to him. Other cases have imposed a higher burden, linguistically at least, by requiring "a reasonable probability" of a different result. But before Rudin would even be allowed to argue the likelihood that the documents would have changed the verdict, he had to meet the first burden. He had to prove that the Bronx District Attorney's Office ("the BDAO") had the HRA documents because under *Rosario* and *Brady* the BDAO, not HRA, had the legal obligation to turn them over. It's an obligation imposed on lawyers. Anthony Judge found the documents in HRA's files.

Rudin learned that in February 1984, within days of O.'s accusation of sexual abuse, HRA investigated the charge, as legally required, and quickly concluded that it was not credible. At this time, HRA still understood that O. was accusing her classmate, Efrain. But in March, O.'s mother approached HRA to say that O. had named a substitute teacher as the person who had sexually abused her. HRA caseworker Irene Jarvis and her supervisor Robert Wilson reopened the investigation and interviewed O. and Ramos among others. In April, Wilson and Jarvis handwrote a draft report concluding that there was no credible evidence of sexual abuse. That conclusion was based in part on various documents in their file. But the conclusion was ultimately revised, apparently at the direction of their superior who had not been part of the investigation, to say that O.'s claim of sexual abuse was "indicated." A final report with the revised conclusion was then sent to the district attorney. A police investigation ensued, ultimately leading to Ramos's arrest, indictment and trial amid extensive publicity. What HRA did not then send the district attorney were the documents that led Wilson and Jarvis to reject

O.'s charge or their handwritten draft report with a contrary conclusion. Except for the handwritten draft, which was never located, these were among the documents Anthony Judge discovered (as a court later described them):

1. Notes dated February 22 of a day care teacher, Mrs. Skeritt, which report that the child masturbated openly and exhibited herself to others [Document A].

2. A memorandum dated February 23, 1984 of the New York City Human Resources Administration (HRA). It reports Mrs. Mendonez, the director of the day care center, called HRA indicating that the teachers and directors were doubtful of the child's accusation against a five-year-old boy; that the child watches late night HBO movies; that the child plays with dolls, placing them in intercourse positions with movement [Document B].

3. An undated HRA investigation report relating that the director and teachers of the day care center were interviewed and it highlights that the child masturbated openly at the school [Document C].

4. A handwritten letter dated February 22, 1994 by Mary Pizarro, an assistant group teacher, indicating that the child was "sexually wiser," "always masturbating" [Document D].

5. An HRA report dated April 25, 1984 relating that members of the day care center staff observed the child masturbating [Document E].

6. A letter by R. Wilson dated May 3, 1985 addressed to the District Attorney stating, "Enclosed please find the case material on the [O.] file. . ." [Document F].[25]

In addition, Anthony Judge discovered a day care center log (called Document G in the court opinion) showing that O.'s aunt, not her grandmother, had picked O. up on the day of the alleged incident. O.'s grandmother had testified that she had picked O. up and that O. had tears in her eyes.

Still, none of these discoveries was likely to help Ramos unless Rudin could prove that the prosecutor had received the documents before or during trial. Ordinarily, a prosecutor cannot be faulted for withholding exculpatory material that she does not have or know about.

Investigation revealed that the prosecutor's file contained Documents C, D, E and F in 1991. The prosecutor's file also contained information from the HRA investigation that Anthony Judge had not uncovered, including this note of an HRA interview with O.:

> [W]hen asked what Mr. Ramos did to her, she said "he taped my mouth." When asked what else he did, she said "nothing—taped my mouth."[26]

But the question remained whether the presence of these documents in the prosecutor's file in 1991 was enough to persuade a court that they were there back in 1985, when Ramos was tried. Day care center witnesses would later testify that they gave the prosecutor Document G, the sign-in log, before trial. That left Documents A and B. The evidence would establish that after Diana Farrell was assigned to the Ramos case in the spring of 1985, she visited HRA's offices and spoke with Robert Wilson, the supervisor in charge of its investigation. She asked him to send her the agency's file. Document F was proof that Wilson mailed the file, including Documents A and B, on May 3, 1985. But Wilson sent it third class. The district attorney's office received it on May 17, just three days before the trial ended.

On October 17, 1991, using the documents from Anthony Judge, and citing *Brady* and *Rosario*, Rudin asked the court to vacate Ramos's conviction. The BDAO resisted. Farrell, the prosecutor, denied having seen the HRA documents or knowing how any of them had ended up in the file in 1991. Ramos was returned to the courthouse, since renamed for Mario Merola,[27] for a hearing in April and May 1992. On June 1, Justice John Collins issued his opinion. He concluded that Documents A through E and G were in the BDAO file during the trial. Further, these documents constituted *Rosario* or *Brady* material or both. Last, he concluded that there was "a reasonable probability" that the failure to provide these documents "contributed to the verdict." Recalling that in summation Diana Farrell had asked "where else the child could have learned such conduct," Justice Collins wrote, "Now after this hearing, we know the answer to that question."

> If the defense had possessed document A, they could have demonstrated that Mrs. Skeritt was untruthful or mistaken at the trial when she testified that the child had never masturbated openly. Through investigation and the use of documents B, C, D and E the defense could have refuted the theory of the People and the testimony of the

doctor that the child could only have described her molestation by reason of experiencing it. Through the use of document G, the defense could have established that the grandmother and mother's testimony was either untruthful or mistaken. Contrary to their testimony, records indicate that the grandmother did not pick up the child on the day of the incident, hence she didn't see the child crying and didn't report any incident to the mother which led to the mother's examining the child and taking it to the hospital.[28]

Alberto Ramos was freed the next day after seven years in prison.

Justice Collins's opinion does not end the story. The BDAO chose to appeal. It argued that Ramos had not in fact proved that the documents were in its files during the trial (as opposed to 1991) and that in any event they were not exculpatory. For example, responding to the evidence that O. had "plac[ed] dolls in intercourse positions with movements," which Justice Collins wrote could have been used to show the child's precocity about sex, the BDAO offered a reason why this information was not exculpatory: "By placing the dolls in close proximity she could have been simulating wrestling or some other activity."

In affirming Justice Collins two years later, the appellate court also explained how the withheld documents could have enabled Ramos to offer the jury a different explanation—to tell a different story—from the one the prosecutor argued in summation:

> [The undisclosed evidence] overwhelmingly demonstrated that the child's ability to accurately describe sexual behavior long pre-dated the date of the alleged incident and that she had extensive knowledge of sexuality derived from obviously inappropriate exposure to sexual information at home. This was particularly crucial in light of the inconclusive nature of the medical evidence and Dr. Vazquez' testimony that her conclusion that the child had been sexually abused was primarily based on this young child's ability to describe what had happened . . .
>
> The undisclosed documents demonstrating the child's prior knowledge of sexual matter and her prior conduct with regard to the use of anatomically correct dolls would have sharply undercut the basis of both the doctor's opinion and the argument made on summation.[29]

Then the appellate court, in an opinion by Justice Betty Ellerin, went further. It held that it was "unlikely," based on all of the evidence, that Ramos could ever have been lawfully prosecuted for sexually as-saulting O. But, "unfortunately," it added, it did not then have the power to dismiss the indictment entirely. So the BDAO was free to retry Ramos.[30] But by now it realized the case was over. Retrial was impossi-ble. On November 10, 1994, the BDAO formally asked Justice Collins to dismiss the indictment on the ground that "no reasonable cause ex-ists to continue this prosecution." The request was granted.

V

Dismissal of the indictment does not end the story. It has one final chap-ter. Before turning to it, though, a side note that appears in no court opinion: Two days after the indictment was dismissed, the press reported that when O. was eight years old, she claimed that she had been snatched and raped by a "tall man" while on her way to the store. As she had initially testified at Ramos's trial, O. said that both she and the man were standing. A medical examination disproved her claim and she re-canted. "She said her mother never believes anything she tells her," a police officer said, adding that O. made up the story because she was afraid her mother would be angry that her clothes were soiled.

Exoneration, while important, left one unanswered question: Who should pay for Alberto Ramos's seven years in prison? To that question Rudin next turned. The answer would take nearly a decade in coming.

Justice Collins did not find that the BDAO intentionally deprived Ramos of his legal rights. He found instead that its "handling of the mat-ter" was "cavalier and haphazard."[31] He did not have to address HRA's conduct because it was not relevant to the issues before him. But the agency was also to blame. When it told the BDAO that sexual abuse was "indicated" and named Ramos, it did not concurrently provide the ex-culpatory information in its file. It did so later, but by then the case was close to or on trial and the BDAO did not stop to revisit the legitimacy of its prosecution. Looked at most charitably, then, a terrible injustice was done because of bureaucratic incompetence, not evil intention. Pro-fessionals in two fields bungled their responsibilities and a man who could not legally have been prosecuted in 1984 if all the facts were known at the time (as the BDAO ultimately admitted) spent most of his twenties in prison as a "child raper."

There is, of course, no way to compensate for seven years unjust im-prisonment, no way for Ramos to recover the twenty-second through twenty-ninth years of his life and relive them outside prison walls. So any compensation, though inadequate, must be monetary. But who would pay? None of the individuals whose conduct contributed to Ramos's conviction were likely to have that kind of money. Only New York City had it. Rudin's challenge was to find a legal theory that would hold the city responsible for the conduct of HRA and the BDAO. Two theories were most promising. The first was to charge the HRA with malicious prosecution under New York tort law when it held back exculpatory documents in its initial referral to the BDAO. The city would then be liable for the misconduct of its agency. The court accepted this theory. The second theory reached the city via the dereliction of the BDAO. This theory relied on a federal civil rights law creating a right to damages when a person acting under color of state law (that is, with official authority) deprives someone of his or her federal rights. Rudin could claim that the BDAO had withheld documents to which Ramos was constitutionally entitled under *Brady*. The courts had already said so when they freed Ramos.

The argument presented one serious problem, however. A municipality is not liable for the constitutional violations of its employees unless they are implementing a policy of the municipality itself. A city can establish policy through its laws or regulations or simply through the decision of a high official. Farrell, the line assistant who prosecuted Ramos, had no authority to make policy.[32] Rudin had to prove that it was the policy of her office to violate the *Brady* rights of defendants. Of course, Rudin was not going to find a smoking gun memo from Mario Merola or other high BDAO officials stating such a policy. But without a policy, the *Brady* violation would simply be the mistake or misconduct of a single trial attorney and the city would have no liability for it.[33] Ramos would get nothing.

Rudin argued that a policy can exist, at least for purposes of establishing municipal liability, by silence or a failure to act no less than through an explicit assertion.[34] To gather such proof, Rudin first identified all cases both during and after Mario Merola's tenure when lawyers in the BDAO were criticized by trial or appellate courts either for *Brady* violations or for using misleading or inflammatory evidence or arguments, whether or not the convictions were overturned. During the Merola era alone, Rudin discovered thirty-two opinions in which trial or appellate courts criticized a Bronx prosecutor on one of these grounds. One prosecutor was criticized in three of these cases within a four-year period. In 1982, the appellate court reversed a manslaughter conviction, citing this prosecutor's "persistent misconduct" during summation. Three years later, it reversed another manslaughter conviction, faulting the same prosecutor's "willful and deliberate" misconduct. A year later, it reversed a third manslaughter conviction, calling the misconduct "pervasive," "egregious," "deliberate," and "reprehensible." Rudin wanted to know whether the BDAO ever punished this prosecutor or any of the other prosecutors whose conduct the courts had criticized. (None had ever been publicly disciplined by the court committee responsible for lawyer discipline.) Absent such punishment, Rudin claimed, Merola would have established a policy of acquiescence in prosecutorial misconduct, including *Brady* violations, through inaction. And Merola's acquiescence, given his stature, would equal a policy of the city. In a brief supporting his theory of municipal liability and arguing for the right to see the disciplinary records of lawyers on Merola's staff whose conduct was the subject of judicial criticism, Rudin wrote: "The BDAO's failure to take adequate remedial action against the prosecutors involved in these cases would be powerful evidence of the existence of an unlawful policy or practice of tolerating and thereby encouraging such misconduct."

In 2001, the same appellate court that had affirmed Justice Collins's 1992 decision acknowledged that a policymaker's "deliberate indifference" to constitutional rights can support municipal liability. Justice Peter Tom wrote:

> Deliberate indifference may be shown by the policymaker's choice from among various alternatives, not to fully train employees when "in light of the duties assigned to specific officers or employees the need for more or different training is so obvious, and the inadequacies so likely to result in the violation of constitutional rights, that the policymakers of the city can reasonably be said to have been deliberately indifferent to the need." Similarly, the standard may be met circumstantially by evidence that the municipality had notice of, but repeatedly failed to make any meaningful investigation into, charges that employees were violating citizens' constitutional rights.[35]

The court held that a jury could infer deliberate indifference at the BDAO from, among other evidence, its failure to discipline prosecutors "for *Brady* or other violations," its failure to discipline Diana Farrell in the Ramos case itself, and most remarkably, the BDAO's "strident opposition" to Ramos's effort to overturn his conviction based on the undisclosed evidence.[36] Central to Rudin's need to prove his case, the court said he was entitled to learn of any "internal discipline or other remedial action taken" against prosecutors whose misconduct was the subject of judicial criticism.[37]

In the following months Rudin learned the breadth of the problem. From 1975 to 1996, spanning both the Merola and Johnson administrations, courts criticized Bronx prosecutors seventy-two times for *Brady* violations or for using inflammatory or misleading evidence or argument. In sixty-two of those cases the misconduct was a factor leading to reversal of the conviction. Convictions in eighteen of the seventy-two cases involved *Brady* violations and all were overturned. Fourteen prosecutors were cited multiple times. Yet each of the cited prosecutors continued to receive promotions and raises. Only once in these twenty-one years, according to Rudin's review of the records, did the BDAO discipline a prosecutor—suspending him without pay for a month, after which he received promotions and raises.[38] Questioned about this pattern by the *New York Times* in 2003, the BDAO said that not all discipline may be reflected in the records Rudin reviewed. The BDAO "takes even unfounded allegations of prosecutorial misconduct very seriously," the district attorney's counsel told the *Times*.[39] Coming from any law office, but especially from a prosecutor's office, that unspecific answer is woefully inadequate. The BDAO's failure is not merely, not even principally, the failure of a single trial lawyer. It is an institutional failure. The BDAO had the duty, as do all law offices, to adopt formal systems to insure that its lawyers behaved ethically and to detect deviance from professional norms early, before damage is done.[40]

The new information Rudin discovered, coupled with the appellate court's endorsement of both of Rudin's key theories of liability, spurred the city to settle. In December 2003, nearly twenty years after the fifteen or so minutes that Alberto Ramos spent alone with his class in the Pink Room, the city offered Ramos $5 million, which it "believed to be the largest false-conviction award in the city's history."[41] Ramos accepted. Ramos wanted something else, too, but he never got it. "I am still very angry," he said after the settlement was announced, "that no one from the district attorney's office, no city official, has come up yet to the plate and stepped up and admitted wrongdoing."[42]

VI

Where incompetence locked Ramos up for seven years, chance and human decency freed him. Technically, of course, Ramos was freed because the indictment was dismissed. But even that came too late. The BDAO earnestly resisted undoing the harm it had caused. It opposed Rudin's initial motion to vacate the sentence when it should have recognized the miscarriage of justice. And then it appealed Justice Collins's decision, delaying closure for two more years, years in which Ramos lived under the threat, however remote, of an appellate reversal and a return to prison.

So it is not entirely accurate to say that the system corrected itself. Rather, vindication for Ramos was the result of a series of fortuities. It was fortunate that O. sued the city and the day care center. It was fortunate that the law firm hired to defend the suit asked Anthony Judge to investigate the facts rather than assume, as it easily could have, that the conviction established the facts. It was fortunate that Anthony Judge found the HRA documents. It was fortunate that Judge sought and got permission to give them to Ramos and that Ramos got a persistent and careful lawyer to represent him. And it was fortunate that Justice Collins took the time to scrupulously evaluate the new evidence and follow where it led.

Of course, the BDAO and HRA are not solely at fault. Ramos's trial lawyer did not discover the HRA files either. Perhaps he can be excused because the BDAO had made an "express promise to obtain and turn over all relevant HRA documents."[43] But even if that promise entitled him to assume integrity from other lawyers, it was a mistake, as we have now learned, to rely on the BDAO's (and HRA's) attention to their professional duties. The police department, which investigated Ramos following the HRA referral, also behaved poorly, though not unlawfully. It failed to discover the HRA files and provide them to the BDAO before the indictment.

In the end, though, the BDAO is most blameworthy. It is run by lawyers, after all, men and women expected to know their legal and ethical obligations. As lawyers and prosecutors, they had primary responsibility to insure accuracy, keep their promises, and exercise great care. Instead, the office behaved irresponsibly, both during the Ramos prosecution and in pressing on for more than two years after the HRA documents were unearthed and even after Justice Collins's harsh opinion. Its justification for taking the appeal is breathtaking. "The judge is attributing to our office knowledge of certain documents that we did not have," a spokesman for District Attorney Johnson said in 1992 to explain the decision.[44] That comment, with its focus on the BDAO's reputation as the motivating concern, shows no awareness that the unearthed documents destroyed the legitimacy of Ramos's conviction whatever BDAO's "knowledge." And that comment, along with Rudin's discovery that failure to punish unprofessional conduct continued after the Merola era ended, means the office may not have learned its lesson. It could happen again.[45]

Notes

1. Mario Merola, *Big City D.A.* (New York: Random House, 1988), 189.

2. Ramos v. City of New York, 729 N.Y.S.2d 678, 682 (1st Dept. 2001).

3. "25 Years for Rape of Girl 5 at Center," *New York Times*, Jan. 13, 1985, at B4.

4. People v. Ramos, 508 N.Y.S.2d 130 (1st Dept. 1986), app. denied, 506.N.E.2d 550 (N.Y. 1987).

5. "Disciplinary Action Is Rare After Misconduct or Mistakes," *New York Times*, Mar. 21, 2004, at A1.

6. Ramos v. City of New York, 729 N.Y.S.2d at 682. *See generally*, Dorothy Rabinowitz, *No Crueler Tyrannies: Accusation, False Witness, and Other Terrors of Our Times* (Free Press 2004).

7. Big City D.A., *supra* n.1 at 205.

8. *Id.* at 216.

9. People v. Beauchamp, 539 N.E.2d 1105 (1989).

10. People v. Algarin, 560 N.Y.S.2d 771 (1st Dept. 1990); People v. Torres, *New York Law Journal*, Dec. 11, 1990, at 24.

11. "Mario Merola, 65, Prosecutor in the Bronx for 15 Years, Dies," *New York Times*, Oct. 28, 1987, at A1.

12. Grady v. Artuz, 931 F. Supp. 1048 (S.D.N.Y. 1996).

13. People v. Grady, 1997 N.Y. App. Div. LEXIS 10026 (1st Dept. 1997).

14. People v. Rosario, 173 N.E.2d 881 (N.Y. 1961).

15. *Id.* at 883.

16. *Id.*

17. *Id.* at 884.

18. *Id.*

19. Brady v. Maryland, 373 U.S. 83, 84 (1963).

20. *Id.* at 89.

21. *Id.* at 87.

22. *Id.* at 88 n.2.

23. *Id.* at 87.

24. *See, generally*, Robert Hochman, *Brady v. Maryland and the Search for Truth in*

Criminal Trials, 63 *U. Chi. L. Rev.* 1673 (1996), which explores post-*Brady* developments.

25. People v. Ramos, *N.Y. Law J.*, June 3, 1992, at 24.

26. People v. Ramos, 614 N.Y.S.2d 977, 981 (1st Dept. 1994).

27. "In Memory of Merola," *Newsday*, Feb. 27, 1988, at 15.

28. People v. Ramos, *N.Y. Law J.*, June 3, 1992 at 24.

29. People v. Ramos, 614 N.Y.S.2d at 982–983.

30. *Id.* at 984.

31. People v. Ramos, *N.Y. Law J.*, June 3, 1992 at 24.

32. Monell v. City of New York, 436 U.S. 658 (1978).

33. Farrell herself had immunity from civil liability. People v. Ramos, 729 N.Y.S.2d at 687.

34. City of Canton, Ohio v. Harris, 489 U.S. 378 (1989).

35. Ramos v. City of New York, 729 N.Y.S.2d at 694 (quoting City of Canton v. Ohio, 489 U.S. at 390).

36. *Id.* at 695.

37. *Id.* at 696.

38. "Prosecutors Not Penalized, Lawyer Says," *New York Times*, Dec. 17, 2003, at B1.

39. *Id.*

40. *See* Model Rule 5.1(a); New York Disciplinary Rule 1–104.

41. "City Gives $5 Million to Man Wrongly Imprisoned in Child's Rape," *New York Times*, Dec. 16, 2003, at B1.

42. All Things Considered, 2003 Westlaw 65514148 (Dec. 16, 2003).

43. People v. Ramos, 614 N.Y.S.2d at 982.

44. "Man Freed After Serving 7 Years for Rape," *New York Times*, Jun. 3, 1992, at B1.

45. And has. In 2005, New York City paid "$1 million to settle a civil rights lawsuit filed by a man who spent five years in prison after being wrongfully convicted" of a 1990 murder. A state appeals court cited the "especially egregious" conduct of Bronx prosecutors. "Wrongfully Convicted Man Wins $1 Million Settlement," *New York Times*, Feb. 5, 2005, at B3.

CONTRIBUTORS

Leigh Buchanan Bienen is a lawyer, a writer, and a Senior Lecturer at Northwestern University School of Law. Her work has previously appeared in *TriQuarterly*. She is currently a member of the Illinois Capital Punishment Reform Study Committee. **Lan Cao** is a professor of law at the William and Mary Law School. She is also a novelist and is the author of *Monkey Bridge* (Viking Penguin, 1998). **Marianne Constable** is professor of rhetoric at the University of California-Berkeley and is the author most recently of *Just Silences: The Limits and Possibilities of Modern Law* (Princeton University Press, 2005). **Deborah W. Denno** is the McGivney Professor of Law at Fordham University School of Law. She has written on a broad range of areas emphasizing interdisciplinary influences on the law, including the death penalty, and has testified in state and federal courts about the constitutionality of lethal injection and electrocution. **Carolyn Frazier** is the DLA Piper Juvenile Justice Fellow at Northwestern University School of Law's Bluhm Legal Clinic. In this role, she assists attorneys from the law firm DLA Piper Rudnick Gray Cary US LLP in representing minors charged with crimes, as well in examining policy issues affecting minors in conflict with the law. **Stephen Gillers**, professor of law at New York University School of Law, teaches legal ethics, evidence and (with Catharine Stimpson) law and literature. He is currently studying the English and American law of obscenity from the mid-nineteenth century to the litigation surrounding James Joyce's *Ulysses* in the 1920s and 1930s. **Jana Harris** has published seven books of poetry, including *Oh How Can I Keep on Singing? Voices of Pioneer Women* (Ontario Review Press, 2003). Her second novel was *The Pearl of Ruby City* (St. Martin's Press, 1998). She teaches creative writing at the University of Washington and is editor and founder of *Switched-on Gutenberg*. **Nasser Hussain** is assistant professor of law, jurisprudence, and social thought at Amherst College and author of *The Jurisprudence of Emergency* (University of Michigan Press, 2003). **ArLynn Leiber Presser** has published twenty-seven romance novels under the names Vivian Leiber and ArLynn Presser. She lives in Winnetka, Illinois. **Annelise Riles** holds a dual appointment with Cornell University's Department of Anthropology, and serves as director of the Clarke Program in East Asian Law and Culture. Her most recent book is an edited collection, *Documents: Artifacts of Modern Knowledge*, forthcoming from the University of Michigan Press. **Dorothy Roberts** is the Kirkland & Ellis Professor at Northwestern University School of Law, with joint appointments in the Departments of African American Studies and Sociology. She is the author of the award-winning *Killing the Black Body: Race, Reproduction, and the Meaning of Liberty* (Pantheon, 1997) and *Shattered Bonds: The Color of Child Welfare* (Basic Books/Civitas, 2002), as well as the coauthor of casebooks on constitutional law and women and the law. **Ilana Diamond Rovner** is a judge of the United States Court of Appeals for the Seventh Circuit, which comprises the states of Illinois, Indiana, and Wisconsin. Prior to her appointment to the Court of Appeals, she served for eight years as a judge of the United States District Court for the Northern District of Illinois. **Austin Sarat** is William Nelson Cromwell Professor of Jurisprudence and Political Science and Five College Fortieth Anniversary Professor at Amherst College and author of *Mercy On Trial: What it Means to Stop an Execution.* **Regina M. Schwartz** is professor of English at Northwestern University. Her publications include *Remembering and Repeating: Biblical Creation in* Paradise Lost (Cambridge University Press, 1988), which won the James Holly Hanford prize for the best book on Milton; *The Book and the Text: The Bible and Literary Theory* (Blackwell Publishers, 1990); *Desire in the Renaissance: Psychoanalysis and Literature* (Princeton University Press, 1994, edited with Valeria Finucci). Her most recent book, *The Curse of Cain: The Violent Legacy of Monotheism* (University of Chicago Press, 1998), a study of monotheism, national identity, and violence in the Hebrew Bible, was nominated for a Pulitzer Prize. **Catharine R. Stimpson** is University Professor and Dean of the Graduate School of Arts and Science at New York University. Her work includes fiction, studies of women and gender, of education, and of contemporary culture. **Mark Swindle** currently serves as Web applications designer for the School of Education and Social Policy at Northwestern University, following careers in art direction, medical, and technical, and as co-founder of "Chicago's most dangerous record store," the Quaker Goes Deaf. **David M. Thompson** is Associate Dean in the Division of the Humanities at the University of Chicago. After completing his master's degree at Oxford University as a Marshall Scholar, he completed his PhD in Comparative Literature at the University of Chicago and his JD at Northwestern University, where he served as Editor in Chief of the *Northwestern University Law Review*.